DECEIT OF THE EMPIRE TRILOGY

BOOK TWO

PROPHETS OF DEATH

KD NEILL

K D Neill

Also written by KD Neill

The first book in the trilogy
Deceit of the Empire

Book One

To Skin a Leopard

The third book in the trilogy
Deceit of the Empire

Book Three

Weep the Righteous Warrior

Available in paperback and eBook
From Amazon.uk and Amazon.com

Prophets of Death

KD Neill, musician, composer, singer, songwriter, arranger, producer, entertainer and author was born and raised in Scotland and started playing and reading music from the age of eight.

Later in life the company he worked for needed two engineers to work in their branch in South Africa, he applied and emigrated on a two year plan, but fell in love with Africa and stayed there for more than half of his life. He now lives in Scotland.

Follow Kenny on facebook… Kenny D Neill

Tweet Kenny… @kd_neill

Instagram: Kennysa01

Website: www.kdneillbooks.com

Email: kdneill@kdneillbooks.com

K D Neill

Reviews for
To Skin a Leopard

'"To Skin a Leopard" (Deceit of the Empire Trilogy, Book One) by KD Neill is hands down one of the most riveting and well-crafted books I've read in a long time!'
Nicola Flood; Goodreads

'I would love to read more from KD Neill in the future as he has a true gift for creating a well-thought out story and bringing memorable characters to life and I feel like I have more understanding of this part of British/African history. (4 stars)'
Layla Messing

Very, very, very good. It's not often that I start reading a book and it consumes me right away and forces me to re-prioritize my life for a little. "To Skin a Leopard" by KD Neill is not a quick read by any stretch…. There are too many important events and experiences here to gloss over so the author takes his time in carefully developing the various storylines from the different perspectives of the main characters, so that we the readers are thoroughly invested the whole way through. This is an edgy, powerful ride through a fascinating time in South African history, one which I had never known about, the 'Xhosa wars', where the natives fought against the invading colonial forces.
A great start to what looks to be a very promising series. (5 stars) *Tabitha Parks*

Prophets of Death

Copyright

2015 Copyright: K.D. Neill.
The right of K.D. Neill to be identified as the author of this work has been asserted by him in accordance with the Copyright, Designs and Patents Act 1988.

All rights reserved.
No part of this book may be reproduced, stored in a retrieval system, or transmitted, in any form or by any means, electronic, mechanical without written permission from the publisher.

Cover design by K.D. Neill
Cover Photograph by K.D. Neill
Map illustrations by K.D. Neill

ISBN-13:
978-1985807792

ISBN-10:
1985807793

K D Neill

Prophets of Death

Foreword

I lived and worked in parts of Africa from 1977 until 2010 mostly in South Africa and wherever I worked I tried to read as much as I could about the local history.

When I was working in the Eastern Cape I took a great interest in the Xhosa wars of the nineteenth century and often visited the museum in East London and the museum and central library of Cape Town.

Reading the history of this period gave me an insight into the trials and tribulations of the settlers, but especially the native tribes fighting to take back their land and freedom seized by the British Empire.

This book was inspired by actual events, which took place in the Eastern Cape, mid-nineteenth-century that caused a devastating loss of life to the Xhosa people. This is a book of fiction and apart from the old ancestral chiefs all the characters are fictional.

It is necessary to explain the use of certain words that appear from time to time in this book.

The word *Kaffir* is an Arabic word meaning 'unbeliever'. Arab slave traders hunted and captured Africans before the Europeans arrived in Africa. They used this word to denote Africans and, over time, Portuguese explorers adopted the word, as did British and Dutch explorers. The idiom continued to be used over generations until eventually, it became an offensive and abusive term as racial hatred grew.

This word, as with *heathen* and *native*, were words commonly used as part of the terminology of the day by colonials and settlers to describe the local people. I do not mean any insult or disrespect to anyone in any way by using these words in this novel.

KD Neill

K D Neill

Eastern Cape frontier: 19th Century

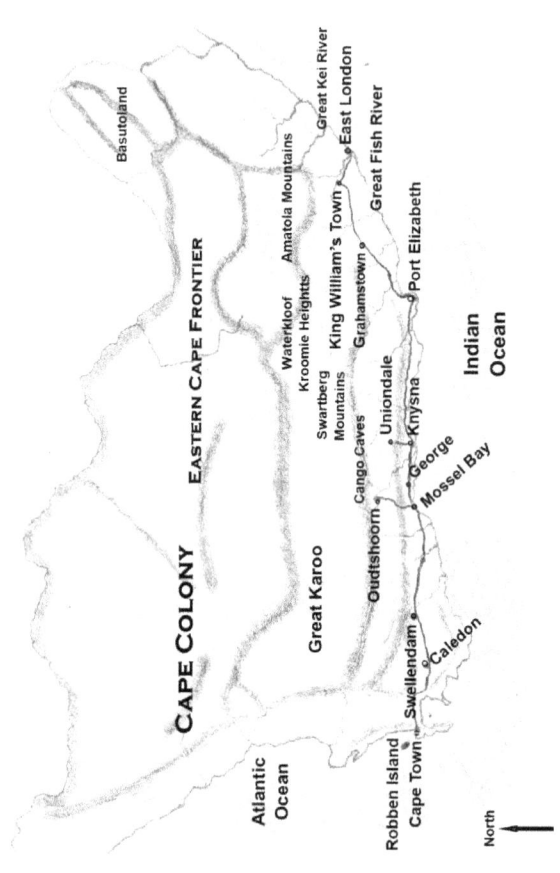

Prophets of Death

Cape Town, South Peninsula: 19th Century

K D Neill

Chapter One

June 1856

The Elephant's Eye, Table Mountain, Cape Town

'Where else would you want to live?' said Jamie.

'Aye… where else indeed.'

Jamie Fyvie and Iain McColl unpacked their picnic and sat down on the rocks at the entrance to the huge cavern known locally as the Elephant's Eye, located just below the cliff-top on the south-east side of Table Mountain. They were taking in the vista in front of them that was part of the Cape Colony, South Peninsula.

The view showed the flat land stretching away to the Hottentot Holland Mountains to the east, Table Bay to the north and the white beaches of Muizenberg on False Bay to the south.

They left their house, in upper Wynberg, by carriage just before sun rise instructing the driver to drop them off at the old Post House in Muizenberg. From there they hiked up the steep, boulder-strewn mountainside and picked their way across the rocky terrain, over a ridge to a large area of grassland, crossed a small stream then a short walk to where they climbed up to the Elephant's Eye.

It was Sunday morning and the sun was shining brightly. They enjoyed cold meat, cheese and bread washed down with Groot Constantia wine from the estate, which could be observed off to left on the lower slopes.

'It seems like years ago when we found the clue in this cave,' said Iain.

'Aye and after we found it we were made redundant,' said Jamie bitterly.

The redundancy was from the Secret Field Police, a cloak-and-dagger, secret service for Queen Victoria's government led by Hugh Armstrong in London until he and the department were suspended.

Armstrong recruited Jamie and Iain and sent them undercover as immigrants to Cape Town with orders to seek out and destroy members, or elders as they were known, of a deadly underground organisation called the **EnL**ightened **O**ne**S** or the ELOS, stop them from taking over the Cape government and prevent them decimating and enslaving the Xhosa tribes of the Eastern Cape Frontier, which the boys achieved just before the suspension of the field police by a new tory government influenced by certain ministers, who were ELOS infiltrators.

The clue found by Jamie and Iain in the Elephant's Eye was the second of a series of clues which, purportedly, would lead to a treasure trove of ancient relics, gem studded trinkets and gold buried by the Knights Templar five hundred years before. The alleged treasure was also sought by the ELOS to fund their campaign to further infiltrate the Cape Government and the first stage of their annexation of Southern Africa.

'In a way I'm glad that we were ordered to stand down,' said Iain. 'It means we can concentrate on our business and spend more time with Clara and Lydia.'

'Aye, there is that but there's just something nagging at the back of my head to get it finalised, you know what I mean?'

'I know what you mean Jamie, and like I've said

Prophets of Death

before, I don't think Armstrong will leave it unfinished.'

'Now that Robert Fairbairn is back from the frontier we'd better be wary. It was no big surprise that he turned up alive after his brother said he'd been killed. Why would he tell us his brother was dead?'

'Probably just to cover his back; sow a bit of confusion, anyway, they were Jonny Fairbairn's last words. Robert also needs to be put down and I would like to be the one to shoot him as well,' said Iain.

'Fairbairn has ambushed us twice and would have killed us and anybody that was with us; I have no doubt that he'll try again to get his hands on the clue, especially after we killed his brother,' said Jamie.

'Why doesn't Fairbairn just follow us and let us do all the work of finding the treasure and then attack us and try to take it. I think he wants it all for himself.'

'Well, one of his masters, James Storer, is dead so let's hope the plans to wipe out the Xhosa natives died with him along with the bleddy treasure hunt,' said Jamie. 'I think Storer's right-hand man, Nicholas Banbury, is pulling Fairbairn's leash now.'

'Aye, you could be right,' said Iain. 'Come on, let's get down the mountain, the carriage will be waiting for us. I've some work to do at home and then I'm going to fetch Clara in the buggy and take her around the peninsula. Are you seeing Lydia?'

'Not today, I'll be having a quiet day.'

The boys had met Lydia and Clara Knowles during the voyage to Cape Town on the clipper ship, The Flying Fish. The ship had been owned by their father, George Knowles and his treacherous new wife Anne.

Anne conspired with James Storer, an elder in the ELOS and the Colonial Secretary for the Cape Government, for her to marry Knowles then kill him and take over his shipping business in order to smuggle guns for Storer to the Xhosa natives in South Africa to start a rebellion against the white men.

Jamie and Iain thwarted this threat whilst at sea by severely injuring and disfiguring Storer and killing his mutineers. It was never proved that Anne murdered George Knowles.

The boys were sitting at the table on the stoep going through some paper work and finishing off a hearty lunch prepared by Mefrou Le Roux, their house-keeper and the owner of the house, when a closed carriage arrived with Bill Hutchison on board.

Hutchison was also an operative for the Secret Field Police and had the dangerous job of being the assistant to the Governor of the Cape, General Sir Gerald Cuthbert, an elder of the ELOS, manoeuvred into the governorship by the elders entrenched in government positions in London.

Hutchison was the liaison between Jamie and Iain and Armstrong, through coded despatches sent with the government couriers unbeknown to Cuthbert.

'Bill! This is a pleasant surprise sit yourself down,' invited Jamie. 'Can I get you some tea or coffee?'

'Yes. I will have some tea please.'

'You're taking a chance being seen with us after all that's happened, are you not?' asked Iain.

'Yes, I am. There have been some developments and we need to talk, let us sit in the house.'

The three men sat around the table in the library and waited for Mefrou le Roux to leave the room after serving tea.

'Come on then Bill, what have you to tell us?' said Jamie impatiently.

'I have received a very complicated encoded message in a despatch from Hugh Armstrong,' said Hutchison.

Prophets of Death

'I knew it. I knew Armstrong wouldn't lie back and let these bastard ELOS get away with this,' said Iain clearly delighted.

Jamie said. 'Are you sure it's from Armstrong and not the ELOS, to lead us into a trap?'

'Yes I am sure, we have more than one confirmation of identity and the code is known only to Armstrong and me.'

'So are we back in business?' asked Iain.

'We are back in business gentlemen,' said Hutchison dramatically. 'But there are conditions.'

'That is good news Bill, tell us everything,' said Jamie.

Hutchison stood up and started pacing the floor. 'Armstrong received an intelligence report from our operative in the local government in Freetown, the capital of our colony in Sierra Leone. Our man was checking the shipping manifests looking for the usual signs of gun-running and slave trafficking and overheard the captain of a ship saying he was unhappy about taking a local black man, a freed slave who is supposed to be a voodoo witchdoctor from the West Indies, to Cape Town with an English businessman by the name of Nigel Renton. The operative checked Renton's name on the passenger list and he was indeed sailing for Cape Town. Now we know that the ELOS have and use two houses in Freetown for their elders who are there on, so-called, legitimate business. Our man had the houses watched and sure enough a senior ELOS elder, Edward Carrington, who is attached to the colonial office in Whitehall with Earl Harold Greyson…'

'The Secretary of State for War and the Colonies and is also a senior ELOS elder,' said Jamie.

'Exactly. Carrington was observed at one of the houses talking to a man who wore a veil over his face;

this man was assumed to be Nigel Renton.'

'Why would he have a veil over his face?' asked Iain.

'We don't know for sure, something to do with a skin condition, but he sailed for the Cape with his servant called Samuel Gubotu. Armstrong is sure Renton must be the replacement for James Storer.'

'Which means they'll carry on with their plans to take control of the government, army and navy in order to decimate the Xhosa natives and sell any survivors into slavery' said Jamie.

'It would appear so.'

'So where did this Nigel Renton come from?' asked Iain.

'Nobody knows. It was rumoured that he came over from America because of his health, more than that I cannot tell you,' said Hutchison. 'Except that he is here in Cape Town. He bought Storer's mansion on the mountain and is there with his servant or bodyguard, Samuel Gubotu.'

'Christ that was quick. He's here already?' said Iain.

'He is and Nicholas Banbury, now elevated to fill Storer's position as Colonial Secretary to the Cape Government and also an ELOS elder, is always with Renton; as he is a supposed, new major investor here,' said Hutchison.

'This can't be coincidence; don't you think?' said Jamie.

'No. I think Renton in Storer's house and being chummy with Banbury has all been carefully planned,' said Hutchison. 'Another thing is, we are not officially sanctioned to start operations again. Armstrong wants us to infiltrate the elite of Cape Town in secrecy to track down and expose the ELOS elders and of course, find the treasure. He will expose and arrest the elders of the ELOS in England, but the timing is crucial to bring them all

Prophets of Death

down at the same time. You have to be aware that the ELOS are moving along rapidly.'

'Then we have to get moving as well,' said Jamie. 'We'll go to Roger Willard and sail for Knysna as soon as possible.'

'Why, what's in Knysna?' asked Hutchison.

'The clue we have points to Knysna to dig up a treasure or find another clue to tell us where to go next.'

'Which means you will both be in the Eastern Cape for the next two to three months; maybe longer?'

'Yes. By the time we get everything and everybody in place it could be longer,' said Jamie. 'Why do you ask?'

'You can't leave right away. You have both been invited to the Governor's Ball at the castle along with the dignitaries of the Cape elite,' said Hutchison handing out two sealed documents. 'The ball will probably be in about two months to allow dignitaries from as far afield as King William's Town to attend.'

'We are planning a day out to the beach in Fish Hoek with Lydia and Clara, the Butlers and Roger Willard in the next four or five weeks we don't want the dates to clash. When is the ball?' asked Iain

'The ball will definitely be after that, so that's fine.'

'Good. But why the hell is the governor hosting a party?' said Jamie.

'He wants to celebrate the defeat of the Xhosa tribes and show everyone that the British Empire is still strong.'

'Well, well,' said Jamie. 'Showing everybody who the boss is.'

'Does this mean we will have to buy some toff clothes with a top hat?

'Well, yes it will be very formal. As new businessmen in the community with obvious wealth and contracts with local government you have now been welcomed into the fold. No-one snubs an invite to the Governor's Ball. Captain Willard will almost certainly be there as well as Lydia and Clara Knowles and their guardians, Godfrey and Sarah Butler.'

'So I take it this is the beginning of infiltrating the upper echelons to find out how the ELOS are going to carry out the enslavement of the Xhosa,' said Jamie suddenly interested.

'Exactly right Jamie. Everybody from the governor down to a certain level in government and society; solicitors such as Godfrey, who, as you know, was the late George Knowles' business partner, businessmen from all over the colony and basically anyone with a prominent position or who is wealthy in the community will be invited with their wives. I, for instance, will not have an invite as I would be deemed far too insignificant to be invited to such an auspicious occasion.'

'But we are just a couple of workers from Scotland that got lucky,' said Iain.

'Ah but you must remember that there are a few businessmen here who, as you call it, *just got lucky*, but made a lot of money and boosted the local economy. The community likes that, aside from the fact you uncovered a plot to start an insurrection and dealt with it. You see, in the eyes of some of the elite, who know what happened to Storer on the ship, you two saved us all by uncovering this dastardly plot and so enabled the army to take steps to put down the natives.'

'So, the thing is, we have to do this. We will go to this ball and get friendly with the non-natives.'

'Yes that's a good way of putting it, but there is something else you need to know. There's a high probability that someone at the ball will be inviting certain people of the upper class of Cape Town to a very private party, I suppose you could call them the elite of

Prophets of Death

the elite, who indulge themselves in closed door secret parties where they act out their sexual desires and fetishes.'

'Fetishes, I must be a bit naïve, what the hell is that?' asked Iain.

'It is mainly sexual perversion, I believe it's rife in London as well as the colonies. Believe it or not people like to have communal sex. It's very fashionable,' said Hutchison clearly trying to be humorous.

'Fashionable? Are people actually in the same room doing these things to each other?' Iain asked dumbfounded.

'They're rich people who don't work and have nothing else to do with their time. They're extremely bored. It's as simple as that.'

'When we were on-board the ship sailing to the Cape, Anne Knowles actually told me that the rich are at it in most of the colonies,' said Jamie. 'She said I would get my eyes opened when I get here.'

'I have led a very sheltered life,' said Iain dismally.

'No Iain, you're just normal; be glad of that,' said Hutchison. 'But I diversify, when you're at the ball you will, obviously, meet and be introduced to many people and you will be expected to dance as well.'

'Dance? I don't dance; I don't know how. I think Jamie should go on his own. I'll be sick with something,' said Iain.

'Make a note to talk to Lydia. I'm sure she and Clara will show us a few steps to get by,' suggested Jamie.

'Have a look at the men and the women closely,' said Hutchison. 'Not so much the younger generation and especially the women; look to whom they are talking to and flirting with and then make your move to be invited to the closed party. There will be a party simply because all the members are together under one roof and it will be finalised on the night of the ball; someone will be organising this, make no mistake. I'll get word to you when I find out if the party is on; or not'

How do you come to have so much information on this party Bill? Asked Iain. 'Have you been to one?'

'This information came from inebriated, boastful men with loose tongues at the club,' said Hutchison.

'Don't worry Bill, we won't let you down,' said Jamie. 'We'll go to Roger and arrange to sail to Knysna the week after the party under the proviso that we want to look at some property there and do some business.'

'Yes do that and I need to know where you two are at any given time. Now. I suggest you, Jamie, infiltrate the party and you, Iain, will be the backup on the outside if there is any need to help Jamie.'

'And we have to find out who's handing out the invites while we're at the ball,' said Jamie.

'Good, we're making headway into finding out how the ELOS will execute their plans. Governor Cuthbert has soundly thrashed the natives, or maybe I should say, massacred them, and received the chief's unconditional surrender.'

'You would think that the Xhosa, now subdued, would be unable to rise and cause any more trouble on the frontier. There's no sign of them being sold into slavery, there aren't any ships that we have heard of taking them away so what the hell is the master plan to get rid of them?' asked Jamie to no one in particular.

'Therein lies the problem Jamie, the Xhosa chiefs have demonstrated this ability to incite the natives to rise again, as you call it. Time and time again they have shown they are capable of starting another costly war and this is what the ELOS want to eliminate in the future. They want to destroy everything that holds up or delays their relentless march to total domination and power; they care

Prophets of Death

not how it is implemented or about public outrage.'

'We'll get to the bottom of this Bill; we want it finished and out of the way,' said Jamie.

'Good luck. I have to get back to town. Oh, by the way, you remember I told you the girls' stepmother, Anne Knowles, will not be tried for treason as Storer and all the witnesses are dead? Well, she was released from custody in London, Armstrong has mentioned that she could be arriving in Cape Town very soon and no, I don't know where she will be staying; very mysterious.'

'We knew she would be arriving sometime or other; Lydia and Clara are aware of her imminent arrival,' said Jamie.

'Enjoy your Sunday gentlemen,' said Hutchison and left.

Chapter Two

June 1856

Cape Town

'We've found out who is following and tried to ambush Fyvie and McColl, Rory, his name is Robert Fairbairn,' said Hamish McFarland. 'He was court marshalled in England for killing a British soldier in Africa, Sierra Leone to be precise, and putting a captain in hospital after picking a fight with him. He was mysteriously cleared of all charges, exonerated and received an honourable discharge, a case of mistaken identity.

'So how did he end up in Cape Town?' asked McGregor?

'He turned up in Cape Town conveniently working for the Attorney General's office. When Governor Cuthbert arrived he commissioned Fairbairn to form a voluntary corps now called Fairbairn's Volunteers. The corps is a nasty piece of work. He is obviously a recruit of the ELOS brought here as the henchman of James Storer and Nicholas Banbury, who probably has replaced Storer, and of course the new Governor, Cuthbert.'

The Grand Lodge of Scottish Freemasonry in Edinburgh was aware of the clues leading to the Knights Templar artefacts and treasure buried somewhere in Southern Africa and sent Rory McGregor to follow Jamie and Iain from Liverpool to Cape Town.

Prophets of Death

He was instructed to use any means necessary to ensure the boy's survival in order for them to follow the clues to either find the ancient relics and treasure or prove that it did not exist.

McGregor had been on these hunts before in places like the Holy Land and honed his own survival techniques over the years in order to locate and retrieve any Knights Templar artefacts and take them back to Scotland for safe keeping. He truly believed that the artefacts and treasure were buried somewhere in the South of Africa. The problem McGregor had to overcome was to convince Jamie and Iain to let him take whatever they found back to Scotland.

Hamish McFarland was Master of a lodge in Cape Town, and along with another brother mason, Arthur Burton, they were helping McGregor to accomplish this.

'So the ELOS are well placed in the Cape Colony. Whatever their business is in this country we, and I am talking about the brethren in Scotland, cannot and will not get involved in this war of theirs,' said McGregor. 'We have one objective here and that is to preserve Fyvie and McColl's lives until they uncover the buried artefacts. They are the only two people who can do this for us, we need to protect them from Fairbairn. We also need to know where Fairbairn is at all times because he is stalking these two laddies and he seems to be hell bent on getting to the treasure before anybody else. I wonder just how much information he has been passing on to his masters. It may be that Fairbairn has got greedy and is looking to retire early in life.'

'Our brother mason in local government informs me that Fairbairn's brother broke into Fyvie and McColl's home with the intent of killing them and stealing the clue; McColl shot him dead. Also, your *laddies,* as you call them, have been to visit the Captain of the clipper, *The*

K D Neill

Flying Fish and hired him to be ready to sail to Knysna a few weeks after the Governor's Ball. The laddies have been invited to the ball' said McFarland.

'So it's safe to assume Fairbairn will want revenge for the killing of his brother.'

'Yes. I would say revenge will be on his mind.'

'I presume there will be a masonic presence at the ball Hamish?'

'But of course Rory,' said McFarland. 'It won't be for another few weeks but you will have an invite.'

'Good man. This is a bit of good luck, I am looking forward to meeting with our two adventurers; it will be interesting to find out first-hand what kind of men they are.'

'I can assure you Rory, Fyvie and McColl may be a bit rough around the edges but my source says they are honest men with integrity and my source is a good brother mason.'

'He must be well placed.'

'He works in the Governor's office and he is, as your laddies are, an operative for the Secret Field Police.'

'How much does he know about the artefacts?'

'He says that initially Fyvie and McColl didn't say anything about looking for any buried treasure, obviously acting under orders to keep it to themselves but when they got to know him they opened up. He did say they were working on another very sensitive operation, the details of which, he could not divulge to me,' said McFarland.

'I will introduce myself to Fyvie and McColl at the ball and make an assessment on whether to reveal myself to them. Meanwhile you could approach the shipping company taking Fyvie and McColl to Knysna and persuade them to give me a berth to go with them as I would like to look at buying some property with the view of starting a business. I have a feeling they are looking for

Prophets of Death

the next clue and I would like to be on hand.'

'Why don't I come as your business partner on the ship? Once we know the date they are sailing we can send Arthur Butler and some men ahead to watch for our arrival and keep an eye out for Fairbairn.'

'Yes, that's not a bad idea. Fairbairn obviously has spies everywhere and is bound to find out where and when the laddies will be going.'

'At the ball you will also be able to see the enemy at close quarters; I will point out who they are, discreetly of course. Cuthbert and especially Banbury will have their informants as well no doubt,' said McFarland.

'I have a feeling that matters will come to a head after we find out what is in Knysna. We must tread carefully Hamish, we don't want to attract any attention to ourselves; especially if we find the artefacts and start to move them out of the country. It's not so much the wealth in the treasure but the ancient relics we have to protect; they could have a profound effect on Christendom as we know it.'

'It might be wise, as you say, to tell the laddies they are not alone; god knows they will need all the help they can get.'

Chapter Three

June 1856

King William's Town

When Robert Fairbairn learned of his brother's death he almost killed the messenger.

'You were supposed to follow Fyvie and McColl and report back to me,' said Fairbairn holding the man by the neck and a knife to his throat.

'Jonny said he would follow them for a while and then hand over to me but he didn't come back sir,' said the messenger. 'He was like a man possessed when he left. I heard he broke into their house and waited for them so he could kill them and take the clue, but he was shot by McColl.'

'You're sure it was McColl who killed Jonny?

'Yes sir.'

Fairbairn released his grip on the messenger and shouted, 'Get out!' and stuck the knife into the table.

He had to get his wits about him and recruit some other ne'er-do-wells and cutthroats to replace the men he lost to Fyvie and McColl in his previous disastrous attempt to ambush them. He now realised that his greed for the treasure and his impatience to be rich had seriously clouded his judgement and cost his brother's life.

Captain Robert Fairbairn, an ex-British soldier, was a member of the ELOS, a psychopath, recruited as their

Prophets of Death

executioner along with his equally psychotic brother, Jonny.

Robert was sent to follow Jamie and Iain in order to lead the ELOS to the treasure. Instead he tried to ambush and kill them on more than one occasion in order to take the second clue, steal the treasure for himself and his brother and flee the country as well as the ELOS, but failed miserably.

Jonny wanted to prove himself worthy to his brother and so broke into Jamie and Iain's home to kill them and steal the second clue but was shot dead by Iain McColl in the subsequent shoot out.

I will have my revenge on McColl and Fyvie, he thought. Stabbing the table over and over.

But now it was imperative that he go back to Cape Town and report to the elder, Nicolas Banbury, and convince him that he was doing his upmost to follow the Scotsmen but he could not keep on their trail because he was under the orders of Governor Cuthbert to police the unruly natives and make sure they were under control.

He did indeed keep the natives under control. He exacted his hatred and vengeance for his failed attack on the boys and Jonny's death by killing any hapless Xhosa man, woman or child he and his men happened upon, taking their trophies of war in the shape of severed ears as decoration, scrotums as pouches and the odd boiled skull.

He spent his last few days in King William's Town getting drunk and abusing some Hottentot whores to vent the last of his anger before sobering up and leading his volunteers back to Cape Town, paying them off with the funds made available to him by discreet delivery to his rooms, knowing that it was an elder's messenger that delivered the money.

Volunteers my arse, he thought.

K D Neill

He had become hard and lean in the weeks spent in the saddle riding through the bush. Although weary from his campaign, he felt strong and confident to chase his prize and thwart the ELOS, to kill the two men who were looking for the treasure; take it and leave Africa to disappear for a new life back in old England or maybe Ireland. With the treasure he could go anywhere.

After a good night's sleep he bathed and dressed in fresh clothes he had not enjoyed for weeks and went to find his informants on the waterfront to find out who and what was coming and going, but most of all if the two Scotsmen were making any arrangements to leave any time soon.

He soon found one of his men in one of the less salubrious taverns of the dockside.

'Fyvie and McColl are sailing on the Flying Fish to Knysna port with two other businessmen. I'm told they're looking for a suitable harbour with warehouses close by,' said the informant.

'So when does she sail?' asked Fairbairn.

'She does not sail sir,' said the informant looking at his empty tankard. 'Not yet anyhow.'

Fairbairn bought two more beers and pushed both to his spy with a payment in his hand under the table.

'How so?'

'The governor's ball sir. Nobody is sailing anywhere because the governor is celebrating the defeat of the Kaffirs by having a ball.'

'Keep looking and listening,' hissed Fairbairn. 'If you fail to find out when they leave you'll be in a shark's gullet.'

The terrified man knew Fairbairn's reputation and promised faithfully he would not let his master down.

As Fairbairn walked away from the tavern, he cursed Cuthbert for having the power to stop everybody's life

Prophets of Death

because… because… '*Because he can*,' he shouted in frustration.

Fairbairn was confused. He was convinced the treasure was in the mountains of the Amatolas; he knew it was there and that is why he ambushed Fyvie and his party.

I am obsessed with killing those two… I want that gold… I will have that gold… Stop it! Stop it! You are doing it again, he said to himself. *Patience, I must have patience, then, all will unfold.*

Fairbairn was still weary from his exertions in the minor military campaign he had undertaken at the request of Cuthbert. His previous army life was physically acceptable but Africa was physically and mentally draining in terms of the terrain, the weather and the fighting spirit of the indigenous people who were naturally adapted to these conditions.

It was only the British technical advancement in armaments and military strategy that conquered them, along with a substantial dose of dirty tricks, deception and lies.

Fairbairn had been recruited by the ELOS because he would carry out their bidding whilst they sat and watched and stayed safe. Yes he was being well rewarded financially but his life was always in danger of being taken by one of their assassins if he was a bad boy, or by some fool he did not know and who did not know one end of a weapon from the other.

He was in a situation of continuous subservience to the ELOS which would lead to certain death because he was not aristocratic or rich enough to progress in their ranks. So he would take this one opportunity, take what he could and run as far away as possible.

He went to the government offices at the parliament buildings and sent a message to Banbury.

Chapter Four

July 1856

Cape Town

Sergeant Brian O'Donnell and Officer Ahmed Jalala from Cape Town Police were in the fishing village of Kalk Bay. They were at the home of Annatje Makasar and her parents, sitting around the table in the front room. O'Donnell decided that he and Ahmed would wear ordinary clothes so as not to attract any undue attention.

Some months before, O'Donnell and Jalala were called to a house in the district called the Bo Kaap, in Cape Town, by the family who had found Annatje unconscious at the foot of an incline on Table Mountain.

The family looked after her after realising she had lost her memory and did not know where she came from or who she was.

Then one day whilst working at the family's flower stall with Aunty Fatima, part of her adopted family, a man driving a cart passed by the stall. He looked in her direction and she recognised his face, this jolted her memory into remembering that this man had done something bad to her as well as starting the process of recovering her recent history bit by bit.

Meanwhile the officers, having found her family in the fishing village of Kalk Bay, had brought her home.

'I know this is hard for you Annatje,' said

Prophets of Death

O'Donnell. But the man whose face shocked you into remembering who you are will probably ride his cart past your flower stall again. Aunty Fatima says she has seen that cart many times before. What I have planned all depends on whether you agree to help us to catch this evil man; you will not be in any danger.'

'What if he recognises my daughter?' asked Annatje's father.

'He will not recognise her. Annatje will be behind the flower stall display sorting the flowers and Ahmed here will be right beside her; he'll be helping her and he'll be armed. Auntie Fatima knows his face and will be watching from outside the display.'

'Maybe I'll learn about flowers and make more money than I do with the police,' said Ahmed, everybody laughing nervously.

O'Donnell said. 'I'll make sure there will be officers patrolling the area as well. Now, when you see the man you recognised passing by the stall, you will tell Ahmed and he will follow him. You and Fatima just need to identify him, that's all there is to do. We'll do the rest.'

'I don't know if this is a good idea,' said Annatje's mother.

'Saldanha Bay and Stellenbosch,' said O'Donnell pausing for effect. 'We visited these two towns recently to speak to the families of the latest two victims who have recently disappeared. They are still missing, we need to catch this man before he strikes again.'

Annatje said. 'Mamma. Papa; I'm not afraid; I have to do this. The police will be there and all I have to do is point to him.'

Annatje's folks nodded their approval and the officers sighed with relief.

'Thank you, Thank you so very much,' said O'Donnell.

K D Neill

The next day everybody was in place at the flower display on Adderley Street; now they waited for the suspect to show.

Annetje was trying to show Ahmed how to arrange the flowers all the time looking nervously between the flowers or trying to look down the road.

Ahmed took some flowers from her and he held her hand as though making a hand shake and said. 'Annatje, you do not have to make it obvious that you are looking for someone, just relax and do your work. When you see him coming along just touch my arm and say softly, *there he is*. Try not to look alarmed or scared, I am here to look after you.'

She squeezed his hand and said. 'I'm sorry, I just want this to be over, I'm quite nervous but I do feel safe with you Ahmed. I'm glad you are here.'

'I'm also glad to be here,' said Ahmed.

'You have to be here, you are on duty,' she said, laughing.

'Yes, this is true, but I'm very happy that my duty is to look after you while you show me how to work with the flowers.'

They worked with each other all day keeping a watch on the street, Aunty Fatima organising tea and food for lunch and noticing the two young people really getting to know each other.

Does this young policeman know what Annatje has gone through; what has been done to her; and what she was made to do to another man? She thought. *Would he understand if they had a relationship? He will need a big heart to deal with these things. Only time will tell how this will work out.*

Ahmed and Annatje talked and laughed away the days with no sign of the suspect but they were quite happy as it meant they could spend more time with each other.

Prophets of Death

One day Aunty Fatima came around to the back of the stall and sat beside Annatje and Ahmed.

'I want you to stay calm Annatje; I know you have prepared yourself,' she looked at Ahmed and said. 'I think the man we are waiting for has stopped his cart at the side of the road up the street just before the corner at Wale Street.'

'Stay here for a moment, I will have a look first,' said Ahmed.

He walked to the front of the stand and could see a two wheeled cart at the side of the road. The driver was sitting on the seat having a conversation with two other men standing next to the cart.

He came back to the two anxious women.

'Annatje, I will move some of the flowers at the edge of the stall to make a space for you to look at the man on the two wheeled cart, facing this way about thirty feet from the corner.'

Ahmed looked like he was rearranging his flowers and made a space for her. She peered through the flower heads seeing the cart immediately. She saw the man talking down to someone and then he looked up and urged his horse forward.

She could see his face clearly now, the memories rushing back; *his face only inches away from hers with his hand over her mouth and then forcing her to drink some vile liquid and then waking up in the cellar.*

But this time, instead of cowering away, the look on her face hardened and she said to Ahmed. 'That is the man who kidnapped me, Ahmed.'

'You are very sure?'

'On my life. He's the one, but he's not the murderer. He kidnapped me and forced me to drink some terrible tasting liquid which made me feel like I could not move. The men murdering the girls are white men.'

K D Neill

Ahmed re-arranged the flowers back and sat down beside Annatje and, keeping an eye on the suspect, he said. 'I want you two to carry on as normal. I'll follow the cart all day if necessary and find out where the suspect works and where he lives. Aunty Fatima, when I leave could you go and get Yusuf and ask him to find O'Donnell for me and tell him what's going on. I don't want you two looking for the sergeant, it'll only attract attention that we don't want. Aunty Fatima, Annatje, you have to understand that you cannot run and tell your family or anybody else that this is the man who has been kidnapping these girls. Firstly; although you have identified him Annatje, we still need to make sure he is the one because if he is not then we could scare off the real suspect and we are left with nothing to go on. Secondly; if he is the suspect then we need to follow him to where he works and try to find his accomplices, especially the men who are doing the killing. It is really important that you do not identify this man to anyone no matter how much you trust them because if the community finds out who he is they'll find him and lynch him; again, we will be left with nothing to go on. Do you both understand the importance of what I have just told you?'

Both women nodded.

'Do not worry Ahmed, I want all of them to face justice,' said Annatje.

'Good. I'll talk to you soon. I must go,' said Ahmed walking casually away from the stall following the cart on the other side of the street.

The suspect drove the cart out to the docks area but not to Rogge Bay, he drove further on to Alfred docks below Signal Hill, it was all Ahmed could do to keep up as he was still on foot.

The kidnapper stopped outside a building just back

Prophets of Death

from the docks and went inside. This suited Ahmed as it gave him a chance to rest. He sat on the corner stoep of a trading store not far from the building where the kidnapper was and waited.

I hope O'Donnell can find me soon, he thought. *If he drives the cart back and out of the town I will never keep up.*

'You must have sore feet by now, Ahmed? Keep looking forward, do not try to see me,' said O'Donnell talking from behind a stack of wooden crates at the side of the store.

'Sergeant! How did you find me so quickly?'

'It wasn't easy to find you. I rode around in a cart looking for you and then decided that maybe our kidnapper may want to go out to the dock for some fresh snoek as the fishing boats have just come in. So I waited on the road; along you came and I followed you here.'

'That was good thinking sergeant, I'm glad you are here.'

'You're doing a good job so far but I think if we both use the cart to follow him from here it would be too conspicuous. When he leaves you follow him on foot again then I'll pick you up along the road a bit and we'll follow him to his destination.'

They talked for a while longer until the suspect emerged and mounted his cart and headed back in the direction of Cape Town.

O'Donnell followed for a while then decided to pick up Ahmed. They followed at a good distance, going through the town continuing south, then driving up to the high road that wound around the slopes of the mountain above the main road.

The suspect cart then turned off onto a well maintained wagon track angling up the slope.

'There are only two houses on large pieces of land up

there,' said O'Donnell. 'One is owned by a rich trader and the other was owned by non-other than our disgraced Secretary of the Colonies, James Storer, but I believe the property has been sold to a new owner. We'll go further along here, then double back and follow the road up. We should find a good position to watch whatever house he goes to.'

They drove their cart to a point in the road where they dismounted and walked up to see over a rise. O'Donnell used a spy glass and could see the suspect driving towards the house Storer used to own.

'He's going to Storer's house. There's a clump of bushes on a hillock about a hundred feet off the road that will give us a good view into the grounds of the house.'

'What! We're going to sit in the bushes all afternoon and night?' asked Ahmed.

'Not quite, leave me at the lookout spot and I'll stay there and watch the house. You take the cart back to Cape Town and fetch a horse from the police stables and bring it back here then you will leave the horse with me, take the cart home and get some sleep. Come back and relieve me just after midnight, because if they are kidnapping or dumping bodies they'll be doing it at night and that is when we'll catch them.'

It was about three o'clock in the morning, the star polluted sky was clear with hardly any light shining from a sickle moon. Williams was driving the two wheeled buggy he kept under lock and key in an old barn on the master's property, only using it for his nightly covert incursions, which tonight was to set fire to the wood store in the yard of Fyvie and McColl Tools in Salt River.

Williams was under a lot of pressure to carry out his instructions from Banbury and Renton, the two white men who were paying him lots of money.

Prophets of Death

There is so much to do, they will have to pay me more for all the dangerous work I am doing for them, he thought. *The master in the veiled hat is strangely scary, he says his name is Nigel Renton but I know he is the master, James Storer; they can't fool me.*

James Storer had been imprisoned in the hospital at the military headquarters in Cape Town and charged with gun-running and treason. When the injuries inflicted by Jamie Fyvie healed he was put on a ship bound for England to stand trial but en-route had jumped overboard and committed suicide, or so the authorities in England were told. His suicide, was, in fact, a carefully executed escape.

After his escape he was taken to Freetown, Sierra Leone by the ELOS where he was given a new identity as Nigel Renton; he was unrecognisable because of the disfigurement to his face and the injuries to his body inflicted by Jamie.

He then returned to Cape Town as Renton, along with the giant servant, Samuel Gubotu, under the guise of a businessman wishing to invest in the colony but was covertly carrying out his previous plans to take over the government in order to control the army and the navy and put down the threat of the Xhosa natives for the ELOS.

Gubotu made the voodoo muti, the potion used to good effect by Renton and Banbury on the young girls they abducted or any unsuspecting adversary unlucky enough to cross their path.

Jamie was unaware that his nemesis, James Storer, had returned as Nigel Renton.

Williams was of the coloured community and had been "Boss Boy" at Storer's, now Renton's, mansion for a long time.

Renton and Banbury paid him to find young local girls and drug them with a potion given to him by

Banbury, which he now knew was made by the giant black servant, Samuel. He would then bring the girls to the cellar under the mansion where Renton and Banbury would abuse, rape and then kill them.

When Storer was still here one of the girls, called Annetje, escaped by jumping through the trap door down into the ravine. *She would never survive a fall like that,* thought Williams. *Besides, Banbury and I took horses and rode into the ravine to search for her or her body; they did not find her; she must have been taken by a leopard; she was so small.*

Since Renton arrived at Arend se Kop, Williams had taken the second of two girls only two nights ago. He had had to hit her hard to subdue her whereas normally they would be so paralysed with fear he would just force the potion down their throats and they would fall into a trance-like state. Then, hidden in the buggy, he took them behind the high walls of Arend se Kop and into the cellar through the outside door at the back of the house. The cellar was specially built with a trap-door, which opened close to the edge of a deep ravine.

Both of the girls were now locked in their separate rooms in that awful cellar below the house where they would be fed the potion with the food they ate and kept in a trance for a while.

Then one day they would be gone, tipped into the hole under the trap door, falling to the bottom of the ravine, there the body to be ripped apart and devoured by leopards or wild dogs and anything else that wanders in the night. *There must be many demented souls searching for peace on that mountain,* he thought as a shiver went through him.

The night air was still: all was quiet except for the horse's hooves and the wheels of the buggy crunching over the dirt road sounding very loud at this time of the

Prophets of Death

morning; a dog would bark somewhere far off every now and again.

The buggy's canopy covered the driver as well as any passengers or bodies. The only passenger on board this early morning was Samuel Gubotu whose enormous size was well hidden and who was waiting patiently.

Williams drove the buggy across Black River Bridge into Salt River and came to a halt at the back end of the wood yard at Fyvie and McColl's premises just east of the river.

The huge bulk of Samuel emerged from under the canopy.

A couple of hours before Williams drove away from the mansion, Ahmed returned to relieve Sergeant O'Donnell; gave him food and water and kept some for himself.

'I've been keeping a close watch; no-one has left the property. The suspect has been in and out of what looks like a barn, maybe he has a place to sleep there and does not have a home elsewhere,' said O'Donnell munching at some bread and cheese.

'It may be that he has some work to do tonight sir,' said Ahmed.

'He may indeed. Another thing, I saw a huge black man wandering around dressed in a long flowing garment and on his head he wears a tall, round flat topped kind of hat with no trim on it but a tassel attached to the centre on top.'

'That would be a fez, sir, it is worn mostly by the Arabic people I have read about; they come from the north of Africa, usually slave traders,' said Ahmed.

'You're very well read young Ahmed. Anyway, when I say he is huge I mean he towers over the suspect, he has a large wide scabbard hanging from his belt with some kind of sword in it. It looks like he has living quarters, but on the other side of the property away from the barn. Then it got too dark and I couldn't see anything else. Stay alert Ahmed, I'll go and get some sleep and get a couple of men for reinforcements and come back, I'll leave the horse for you.'

O'Donnell quietly left Ahmed settling in for a long night, every now and then he would look through the spy glass and could just make out the faint outline of the gates in the walls as well as the main house and other buildings.

A while later he heard the faintest of sounds floating on the quiet night air. He looked through the spy glass at the property and immediately could see the slightest flicker of a lamp.

After a few minutes the light went out and he could see the dark shadow of the gate changing.

Someone is opening the gate, he thought.

He listened intently at the other sounds coming to him. *That is a cart or a buggy with only one horse leaving the house.*

From his concealment he could barely make out the silhouette of the conveyance as it went by; it was a small buggy with a canopy.

Ahmed scurried down the small hill and mounted his horse. He kept to the grass verge along the side of the road to muffle his horse's hooves but further along the road the verge ran out so he had to use the wagon track. He came to a bend in the road and instinctively pulled up the horse and listened. He could not hear the sound of a horse or wheels on the road so he sat and waited.

His instincts were correct as he heard the buggy continue on its journey, *the driver must have heard my horse and did as I did and stopped to listen,* thought Ahmed knowing he would at some point have to leave the horse and follow on foot.

When he saw the buggy heading for the bridge over

Prophets of Death

to Salt River he dismounted and left the horse behind a deserted shack, continuing on foot.

Ahmed waited for the suspect to cross the bridge and go further along the road before following; then ran bent over across the bridge, keeping to the side of the guard rail running from building to building to keep out of sight. He could still see the shape of the buggy and could still hear it, he needed to be on higher ground but this area was flat.

Looking around in the dark he saw a building with a first floor and a stairway going up on the outside. He went up the to the top landing and brought up the spy glass in time to see the buggy turn left and be partially obscured by a high fence. The canopy was barely visible above the fence and a third of the way along the buggy stopped.

What's he up to? That's the yard of Fyvie and McColl, thought Ahmed. *What does he want there?*

'Are you sure this is the correct yard?' Samuel quietly asked Williams in a rich baritone voice.

'Yes of course I am sure. This is the place,' he replied, thinking, *Kaffir! Who does he think he is.*

They looked over the high fence at the silhouettes of neatly stacked logs and cut planking looming in the yard.

'Then let us do our business,' said Samuel leaping over the fence.

Williams jumped down and hobbled the horse then climbed back up to retrieve a bottle full of lamp oil and clambered over the fence.

He could not see Samuel. He whispered, 'Samuel, waar is jy, (where are you)?' *How can anybody see a man that black in the night?* He thought.

'I am right here beside you.'

'Jesus!' Williams jumped a foot to the side with heart stopping fright. He did not see him because of his

size. Samuel then proceeded to smear white markings on his body and face, which seemed to glow in the dark; then donned a head dress of chicken feathers. He looked like a demon from hell.

'Are you trying to kill me from heart failure you bloody heathen?'

Samuel just looked at him and said. 'There is a watchman and he has another man with him. I will deal with them; you spread the oil on the wood and take some wood shavings to make a fuse.'

Samuel then disappeared without a sound.

That thing was sent from hell; I hope he never comes after me, thought Williams.

Samuel moved silently through the yard and stopped at a stacked pile of logs between him and a wooden shack. Outside the door was an old night watchman with a younger man who was his grandson, there to keep him company.

They were sitting in front of a fire chatting quietly in a language Samuel did not understand.

He opened a pouch hanging on his belt and took out a handful of black dust with his left hand. In his right hand he held a scimitar sword taken from an Arab he had killed many years ago.

Samuel cared for his sword, honing the double edges until it could slice through parchment with hardly a ripple. His sword liked the taste of blood.

He climbed cat-like up on to the top of the logs and then leaped into the air bellowing like a wounded water buffalo, at the same time throwing the dust into the fire making the flames flare six feet in the air.

He landed on the opposite side of the fire to where the men were sitting and raised his sword, immediately slicing it down on the old watchman.

The young man fell backwards at the sight of this

Prophets of Death

hideous monster and watched as the huge blade cleaved through his grandfather's body as though it was butter, the cut starting between his shoulder and his neck and down to his sternum.

The old man was still sitting upright as the monster, still bellowing, withdrew his blade and turning it sideways swung it in an arc slicing cleanly through the old man's neck; his head seemed to jump as though to avoid the blade then fell backwards. As the body started to crumple the monster swung the awful blade in reverse and cleaved the old man's small body through the torso halving it into two pieces such was the power of the blow.

In the short space of time all this happened, the younger man was scrabbling backwards in the dirt watching the slaughter unfolding in front of him. As the monster raised his bloody sword and bellowed again the young man jumped to his feet and ran, wailing in panic not knowing where to get away in the dark. He made out a pile of discarded wood beside the fence; clambering up and over it he ran off up the road screaming his head off.

Samuel watched the man run; he would tell everybody about the monster demon in the cursed yard. Lifting a burning piece of wood from the fire he made his way back to Williams without so much as a backward glance.

Williams poured the lamp oil over the thinnest planking he could find in the dark and made a two foot fuse of small bits of wood shavings pouring lamp oil along the length of the fuse as well. He then piled some planking by the fence to climb back over.

Samuel walked towards him and threw the torch on the fuse, igniting it immediately.

Then without a word and three hacks of his sword, Samuel destroyed part of the fence and climbed into the buggy.

K D Neill

Williams looked at the pile of wood for climbing over the fence and shrugged. He went through the ragged gap and up into the driver's seat, driving off at speed as the fire took hold and spread across the yard of Fyvie and McColl.

Ahmed shifted the spy glass to see a small fire in front of the watchman's shack. Shifting the glass back to the fence he could make out the shape of a huge man climbing over, followed by another much smaller man.

What he saw and heard next gave him a spine chilling shiver. The demented roar that emanated from the yard could only be from a monster not of this earth.

At the same time a pillar of flame shot up into the air and he could see streaks of white light, no, it was the flashing of steel, a sword and a man screaming mixed with the roar of the demon.

Ahmed ran down the stairs and on to the road, his horse was too far away to be any help to him so he ran towards the yard. There was someone running up the road towards him, he drew one of the two pistols he was carrying, ready to fire if it was necessary.

It was a young boy screaming at the top of his lungs his face contorted with fear as he ran headlong into Ahmed.

Ahmed grabbed him by the shoulders and shook him.

'Calm yourself; stop screaming. I am a policeman, I will help you,' he shouted at the boy.

'You cannot help me from a monster such as the one I have seen,' he screamed. 'It has chopped my grandfather to death; I saw it with my own eyes.'

The boy was clearly terrified out of his wits, his eyes wild with fear so Ahmed slapped him hard to calm him down. The boy came to some realisation and with rasping breath said. 'I have never seen a demon before; there is a

Prophets of Death

demon.' He said pointing down the road.

Then Ahmed saw the flames sprouting from the yard.

'The yard has been set alight,' said Ahmed. 'If a fire takes hold here this whole area cold burn down. Come with me, there's no demon; it's a man, a big man, not a demon. I need your help.' He said pulling the boy back the way he had come.

'I'm not going back there,' said the boy trying to get out of Ahmed's grip.

'Do you see that fire? It will destroy all the businesses around here if it spreads, there will be a lot of people with no work to feed their families. I know this is hard for you but I need your help,' said Ahmed pulling the teenager along with him. 'What is your name?'

'Isaac, Isaac Jacobs,' he said now running alongside the policeman of his own free will.

They reached the yard to find the gate was locked so they climbed over the fence and ran down the inside of it until they were at the fire.

'Is there any water in the yard?' shouted Ahmed.

'Yes, three barrels by the workshop.'

'Go and get buckets, fill them and come back quickly.'

'But there are sand bunkers all around,' said Isaac pointing to large wooden crates evenly spaced around the fence.

'Sand bunkers!'

'Throw the sand on a fire it will smother the flames,' said Isaac.

They grabbed the shovels lying next to the bunker and started scooping the sand onto the flames.

Two other watchmen appeared through the hole in the fence made by Gubotu, one of them helped with the sand and the other found the water. One or two others appeared from nowhere and helped to stop the fire from spreading.

Then O'Donnell appeared with two other officers. He sent one to alert Jamie and Iain then immediately set about moving some of the wood away from the fire and helping with the water.

They had to save the yard.

Chapter Five

July 1856

Cape Town

It was Jamie who heard the horse galloping up to the front of the house in the early hours of the morning. He looked out of the open window and knew something was seriously wrong.

'What's all the hurry?' he shouted at the rider.

'I'm Officer Ryan, Mr Fyvie. Sergeant O'Donnell sent me, there's a fire at your yard; come quickly.'

By this time Iain heard the commotion and shouted, 'what's up Jamie?'

'Get dressed; the yard's on fire.'

They hastily dressed, saddled up the horses and went tearing down the road. The glow from the fire could be seen lighting up the night sky.

'Jesus Christ! How could this happen?' shouted Iain.

'We'll find out soon enough.'

They galloped across the Salt River bridge and down to the yard where they could see a few people already there fighting the fire.

Dismounting and running into the yard they could see there was a semblance of control by Sergeant O'Donnell of all people. 'Sergeant, what can we do?' asked Jamie.

'Keep bringing the sand and water and maybe try and

move the wood closest to the fire away from the flames,' shouted O'Donnell.

Meanwhile Iain went to the building where the water was stored and ran to the watchman's shack; he stopped at the gruesome scene that confronted him.

The old watchman, what's his bleddy name, he thought. *Jacobs*!

He had been hacked into pieces by god knows what; there was blood everywhere; the old man's grandson was hunkered down beside the dismembered body parts in tears and in shock.

Iain helped the youngster up to his feet and got him to help him drag a tarpaulin over and cover up the remains.

'I'm sorry son, we'll find out who did this, I promise you we will,' said Iain earnestly.

The men fought the fire side by side until the faint light of dawn emerged. More people arriving for work ran in to help.

When dawn broke the fire was all but put out. There were some smouldering embers here and there being dampened down; they were lucky that this part of the yard was mostly heavy logs and still fairly moist. A lot of the fence had been burnt down but the majority of the wood was spared. It was extremely fortunate that the whole yard, or indeed the whole area had not been razed to the ground. 'You saved the whole area Sergeant, never mind the yard, we all owe you a great debt,' said Jamie.

'We were just doing our job sir, and the others are just good people of the community,' said O'Donnell.

'How did the fire start sergeant?' asked Jamie.

'Ahmed!' shouted O'Donnell waving him over.

Ahmed told Jamie and Iain what happened the previous day and that night; O'Donnell related to them why they were following the black carriage.

Prophets of Death

Ahmed went to find young Isaac: leaving O'Donnell with Jamie and Iain sitting in the company's office drinking hot tea.

'So many young girls have gone missing Mr Fyvie, so when we heard about the young girl, Annatje, we asked her to try and identify the suspect who triggered her memory, which she did do and we followed him. Now that we know where he's working we'll find out who he is, but why he came to be coming down here with the giant black man I do not know,' said O'Donnell.

Jamie looked at Iain and they made a silent decision, Iain got up and closed the door to O'Donnell's surprise.

'What's your first name sergeant?' asked Jamie.

'It's Brian,' he said, looking a bit uncomfortable.

'I'm Jamie and he's Iain, we work for the government.'

'I know you work for the government, it is well known you supply equipment…'

'Yes, that's quite correct but we work for the government in Whitehall, London and what I am about to tell you is highly confidential; you will not tell anyone, is that clear?'

O'Donnell looked from one to the other and said. 'Well, I suppose that will depend on what you are going to tell me now, wouldn't it?'

'Iain and I are, like you, also police, we're what you would call field police, we work under secrecy to identify traitors and the like who try to sabotage or commit crimes against the government.'

'So it is true. There have been rumours of the field police but I didn't know whether to believe them.'

'We would like to help you with the missing girls but we have a delicate investigation going on which involves certain individuals who have been visiting the house you were watching last night. We are trying to infiltrate a body of people who are dealing in gun running and trying to incite rebellion and war.'

'Oh, I see a bit of the picture now. That fella Storer that you captured on the ship? Was he part of this, because he used to own that house?'

'He was indeed Brian, but we need to find his accomplices,' said Iain pouring more tea. 'Without hindering your investigation we would like to work with you to see if the same people we are after are perpetrating these awful crimes against these young girls, then we can kill two birds with one stone by exposing them or disposing of them; you would be identified as making the arrest of course.'

'So what you're saying is that my investigation will have to slow down to accommodate yours,' said O'Donnell.

'Look, you don't know how many are involved with the kidnapping and murder of the girls. If I can get into that house with the inner circle of the elite in the Cape, I would be in a position to identify all involved,' said Jamie. 'I'll keep you appraised of whom and what and where.'

'So you would keep me informed of all that is going on?'

'Yes, but no-one, not even your immediate boss can know about us; this is very important Brian.'

'You have my word I'll not disclose anything. There is no-one to trust in the police force. The only person I trust is the man who's with me; Officer Ahmed Jalala, he has a genuine concern for the community, besides I wouldn't like to cross you two.'

'Did the girl, Annatje, tell you anything about this suspect of yours, any parts of her story or memory that has you confused or you don't believe?' asked Iain.

'Her memory started to come back in bits and pieces.

Prophets of Death

She remembers the suspect grabbing her and forcing her to drink something she said was vile tasting. After she swallowed it she could do nothing but do what he told or forced her to do. She said he was not the killer, two white men are doing the abuse and the killing.'

Jamie and Iain exchanged glances and Iain asked, 'This stuff she was made to drink, did she perhaps know what it was?'

'No, she just said it tasted foul and it she was not in control of herself after she took it,' said O'Donnell.

'We promised to keep you up to date so here is what we know. We have encountered this liquid before, on the Flying Fish. It's some kind of potion made from herbs and plants that the doctors here have never come across before and it was used to confuse a very sick man and caused him to die; we think he was murdered.'

'That's the mysterious death of Mr George Knowles, is that right?'

'Yes, that's right; mysterious my arse, he was murdered,' said Iain.

'The fact is, we think Storer supplied the potion on the ship. He also owned that house on the mountain where your suspect works and he also has the potion, if it's the same stuff of course. I don't believe this is a coincidence, everything connected to the potion leads to that house.' said Jamie.

'This is getting very involved and it sounds like it's seriously dangerous,' said O'Donnell.

'That's why we'll tell you only what you need to know. There are some evil men at the centre of this and I'm sorry to involve you but your case could hinder something much bigger and I say again, I'm not trying to belittle your case, but we need to work together and put these people down. Can you show us where the people who took in Annatje found her?'

'Yes I can as soon as I have finished here I'll give you directions and meet you there tomorrow morning,' said O'Donnell.

Iain said. 'I'll come here in the morning and get the clean-up and repairs moving along. You go and meet with Brian.'

'Thanks for sharing this information with us Brian, we'll leave you and your colleague to discover who's working up at that house, meanwhile we'll try to find a way to infiltrate the place,' said Jamie.

'I'll inform you as soon as I learn anything Jamie.'

'Don't forget, we three must trust each other, nobody else,' said Jamie.

'You can put your trust in me and Ahmed, he is a good man,' said O'Donnell.

'If you say so then that is good enough for us. Also if you need any help or information from inside government then let us know and we can see what we can do. Let's go and see if the doctor has arrived to look at the body.'

The three men shook hands and went out to the yard.

The doctor was squatting beside the remains of the old watchman.

'When I heard it was a death at your yard I came out myself,' said Doctor Morgan.

'It's good to see you doctor and I'm glad it's you to see these horrific injuries,' said Iain.

'I have seen some horrendous injuries in my time on and off the battlefield but these are bizarre to say the least. The cut from the shoulder to the sternum would require a powerful force but the decapitation and cutting the torso in two, no man would have the strength to do such damage,' said Morgan.

'I told you,' wailed Isaac Jacobs from behind them. 'It was a monster, a demon; I saw it with a big, big sword.

Prophets of Death

Three times it flashed and that is what it did to my grandfather.' He was losing control again and people from around the area, especially the workers, were listening to him.

'Isaac, you must be calm,' said Ahmed. 'It was a big black fellow not a monster or a demon, we have already talked about this.'

'The doctor, he said no man could have the strength to do that, I heard him say it,' cried Isaac.

'Ahmed, take him inside and get a statement,' said O'Donnell. 'I will get the body back to Cape Town for you doctor. The rest of you go home, the only monsters here were bad men. Go home.'

The body was taken away and everybody left, the workers were given the day off but the story of a curse with a demon monster had taken root.

O'Donnell met with Jamie at the top of Buitengracht Street early the next morning and went to the land slip where Yusuf and his son had found Annatje.

They picked their way up from the land slip and found a path which ran north to south along the side of the mountain.

'If Annatje did escape from Storer's house then it's quite conceivable that she could have made her way along to this point before she fell down the slope,' said Jamie. 'If it was Storer's house, we'll have to make sure. When you were watching the property did you see anywhere, apart from the front gate, where she could have escaped from?'

'The front gate is the only way in and out of that place, unless there's a hidden entrance somewhere.'

'What you need to do is find out where they are burying or dumping the bodies.'

'Well first of all, I have information that the suspect identified by Annatje, is a man called Williams. That's all

I know about him, he is not from around here. But I've got a watch on the house day and night. If they have the recently kidnapped girls in there then we'll wait to see if any of their conveyances leave the premises and follow them to see where they're dumping the bodies.'

'Let's get back,' said Jamie. 'We need to get planning and get to work.'

Chapter Six

July 1856

Cape Town

Nicholas Banbury followed the usher through the Cape Government buildings to the Governor, Sir Gerald Cuthbert's office. Banbury had been James Storer's loyal assistant in government and loyal elder in the ELOS.

He was disappointed when Storer had been declared dead but later relieved when he returned as Nigel Renton. Now they could carry out their plans of purging the Cape of the Xhosa clans, but more importantly, starting the ELOS's thrust into Africa.

He arranged to meet with the Governor to discuss matters of state but more, he wanted to discuss Storer's reincarnation and what was to happen next.

Cuthbert detested these bloated, lying, colonial politicians but was obliged to meet with them especially when it was an elder.

He was pouring two brandies for himself and his guest when Banbury was shown into his office.

Cuthbert had taken a sizable army into Xhosaland and set a bush fire, burning out the Xhosa villages, the army was waiting for the fleeing men, women and children with muskets and cannons; it was a massacre. Cuthbert then ordered his soldiers to confiscate all the cattle and destroy all the food. He ordered the capture of all women and children and the killing of any warriors that could be found. He also ordered Fairbairn to sign up volunteers to roam the frontier and slaughter every man woman and child he encountered, a no prisoner policy.

The Xhosa tribes were now destitute, banished to living on a flat, overcrowded patch of ground south east of the Amatola Mountains; forbidden by Cuthbert to ever go back to their traditional, fertile homelands.

'Good afternoon Mr Banbury, please, have a chair and make yourself comfortable,' said Cuthbert placing the brandy on the desk.

'Thank you Governor Cuthbert, it is a pleasure to meet you at last. You have been rather busy on the frontier of late,' said Banbury.

'Rather busy? Yes, I was rather busy. Busy cleaning up the previous governor's and the Cape Government's bloody mess,' said Cuthbert grinning facetiously.

Banbury was beginning to feel a bit uncomfortable.

'You politicians have this wonderful gift of advising the natives on what is good for them, what they should do and how to do it properly in a civilised manner. If they do not do as they are told your local militia force, who are usually made up of the worst villains and scallywags around, shoot a few and get the tribal chiefs' backs up and start a war you cannot finish. Then you write snivelling letters to the government in Whitehall to bail you out and they send people like me to clean up the mess. Would you agree that that is an accurate assumption Mr Banbury?'

'Well, with all due respect, sir, I would not put it quite as harshly as the way you portray the situation. It is sometimes quite difficult to keep the natives under any kind of control; they have a different way of thinking you see,' said Banbury feeling a bit angry at the Governor's assessment of the situation.

'Yes, I think you are correct, they do have a different

Prophets of Death

way of thinking. It is different because it is not your way of thinking. Their thinking is honest and forthright and with the best intentions for their people and their land, under good but harsh governance and it seems to work for them, does it not?'

'Yes it works if you are a heathen. They must be civilised and be taught Christianity to become a part of our society,' said Banbury indignantly.

'Why on earth would they want to?' said Cuthbert disgustedly. 'Do not answer that, suffice to say that the natives have been defeated, humiliated and resettled in their new homeland. What other business do we have?'

'Well!' said Banbury lowering his voice. 'There is the question of the return of James Storer returning as someone else for the next…'

'Stop right there Mr Banbury. I have heard part of the situation about Storer. I believe you have been elevated to senior elder, which means any decision making pertaining to the Cape falls on your shoulders. It has nothing to do with me and I do not want to know what plans you have, present or future for the elders' expansion plans into Africa. I am but the architect of the foundation required to build the road out of Southern Africa. I do not know your part of the equation and you do not know mine. That's the way the ELOS work.

'The white man will conquer the black man as he did the native Indians of the Americas, the Aborigines, the Maoris, in the colonies of Australia and New Zealand and as he is in India and anywhere else in the name of the Empire. Who knows, maybe we will have them all playing cricket in the future.'

'We do this to take civilisation to the heathen and make them a better race of people,' said Banbury forcefully.

'Do not hope to convince me that you are doing these

natives any favours or showing them a better way of life. You all just want to ease your conscience as you kill them, plunder their land and take what you want. You make up laws to benefit yourself and if the natives object to you taking their lands and lives, you bring in people like me to sweep them away so that you can carry on your merry way leaving the bones and wrecked souls in your wake,' said Cuthbert looking straight into Banbury's eyes wanting to punch him to the floor such was his contempt for this man. 'I have fulfilled my obligation to the elders; I will be replaced by another of the ELOS; do you know anything of this?'

'I do Governor, you are to be replaced by Sir George Whyte in due course,' said Banbury.

'Yes, I will; in due course. I will no doubt see you at the victory ball; we will be courteous and friendly to each other and keep up the charade of good governance but that is where our liaisons end. If you have any correspondence for official work then work with my secretary. I do not want to see you or Storer until I am gone from here unless there is an emergency. So if that is all be sure to close the door on the way out,' said Cuthbert turning his back on Banbury and looking out of the window sipping on his brandy.

Banbury was flabbergasted at the way he was being spoken to. 'I will not be spoken to in su…'

Cuthbert wheeled around, placed his glass on the desk and shouted, *'I can be a very nasty man when I take the notion Mr Banbury; leave my office and never come back as long as I am here; get out before I run you through,'* he said drawing his sword and slapping the flat blade on his desk with a resounding crack.

Banbury got such a fright he jumped up and left Cuthbert's office taking care to close the door behind him.

Prophets of Death

Bill Hutcheson was sitting at a desk in the outer office and said, 'Good morning Mr Banbury, the Governor does not seem to be in a good mood today.'

'He is an awful man and have a care as to whom you are talking to young man.'

'No, Mr Banbury, you have a care as to whom you are talking to sir; you are not my superior. I am answerable to the Governor and only to him, so if there is nothing else I bid you goodbye,' said Hutcheson.

'You have not heard the last of this sir,' Banbury said as he turned on his heel and left.

He was seething as his coach left for Renton's mansion on the slopes of the mountain. *When we have the reins of power I will make these small men pay with their lives,* he thought.

Chapter Seven

July 1856

Fish Hoek

The open carriage left Cape Town a little after sunrise heading south on the Simonstown road. It was a new design built at Fyvie and McColl Tools in Salt River. What made this vehicle special was the concertina type hoods behind each seat that could be pulled up over the seats if the weather turned foul. A wagon followed with the servants and all the food and kit for a picnic.

In the carriage were Captain Willard, with Godfrey and Sarah Butler and the slightly upset Lydia and Clara Knowles. They had wanted to ride horses with Jamie and Iain but Sarah said it was not ladylike for young ladies to ride a horse through the town.

'Whatever would people say,' said Sarah.

They passed through the fishing village of Kalk Bay and continued around the mountain, eventually stopping at the sea side of the road on the approach to the small village of Fish Hoek whereupon the servants set up the bush-like camp on the other side of a sand dune facing the sea.

A large tent was erected with roll-up sides and woven reed mats on the sand; tables and chairs were set up, the food was laid out and covered with a linen cloth and a fire started in a wrought iron fire basket to make some tea.

Prophets of Death

Two small closed tents were erected a few feet away for anyone wishing to change into swim wear.

'I say, this is a novel idea making a bush camp on the beach,' said Godfrey.

'We came up with this when we were coming back from King William's Town. Why not be just as comfortable at a picnic as you are when camping, if you are prepared to put the work in to set it up of course,' said Iain.

'Maybe you could come up with an idea for the deck of a ship,' said the Captain laughing at his own joke.

'Your saloon is much too comfortable captain,' said Jamie.

After lunch Jamie, Lydia, Iain and Clara changed into their swimming attire and were cavorting about in the shallow water going in as far as to lie floating until someone would come from beneath and pull them down into the water spluttering.

Later, the older members in the party strolled along the beach whilst the boys took the girls off to inspect the rock pools where the beach ended and the rocks started curving around towards Kalk Bay.

'Look at those two,' said Jamie pointing at Iain and Clara.

They were splashing each other from the small pools of sea water, Clara pretending to punch Iain on the shoulder.

'It looks like they really enjoy each other's company,' said Lydia.

'Yes it does. Just like I'm enjoying your company,' he said taking her hand.

'So! Have you been invited to the governor's ball?'

'Yes, Iain and I will both be there,' said Jamie with a little guilt. 'I'm looking forward to having some fun; a bit of dancing, if you and Clara could teach us a few steps…

that is.'

'We would love to teach you some dances.'

'Well, hopefully no sore toes,' said Jamie. 'I'm glad we all came out here today and spend some time together.'

'It's so wonderful here, I wish my father was here to share this.'

They stopped, letting the other two wander further along the rocks, wanting a bit of privacy.

'Yes, I can understand you thinking like that, and it is the most wonderful place,' said Jamie lifting his voice to lighten the mood.

'I wanted to come out today on horseback but Aunt Sarah nearly had a cadenza when I said I wanted to ride like a man and not side saddle.'

They were both laughing, enjoying being with each other. 'Iain and I will be going up the coast soon with the Captain…'

'I know, I discussed it with Uncle Godfrey and Captain Willard that he should take you up to Belvidere and Knysna Port, yes? As long as we get your business,' she said laughing.

'You're starting to be the business woman aren't you? Anyway, when I come back what we should do is go for a ride around the peninsula, you could wear riding breeches and boots a wide brimmed hat to tuck your hair into and a loose shirt to cover your eh… upper body,' said Jamie glancing at Lydia's expanding bosom.

Lydia noticed his brief stare at her chest, giving her a most unexpected thrill. 'I will keep you to your word on that. We could find a nice quiet, out of the way beach and go swimming without these cumbersome costumes and maybe get to know each other better.'

'You're not being lady-like again, like that night in the garden. It was so spontaneous, I must say, it was

Prophets of Death

unbelievable,' then he realised what she said. 'What! You mean… swim naked? I must confess, I eh… I never thought about it,' said Jamie caught unawares. *Why do I get so flustered when I'm around Lydia?* He thought.

Lydia slowly leaned over and kissed him on the lips.

Jamie looked to see where the other two were; they were engrossed with something in a rock pool and then he looked across to where the others were walking at the other end of the long beach at Fish Hoek. He lifted his hand and gently put it on the side of Lydia's neck and slowly pulled her into a long passionate kiss his tongue just exploring hers where their lips touched.

When they stopped her eyes were still closed, she brought her hand to her throat and sighed deeply. '*Oh my…*' Opening her eyes she lifted her other hand and touched his lips as if to ensure they were really there.

Jamie took her hand in his and kissed her fingers and palm and held it to his chest over his heart, he had never in his life felt such passion from a kiss such as that from Lydia.

She gazed at him and said. 'I've never felt anything like that… I don't know how to respond… no that is wrong, I do know how to respond,' she whispered. 'I just… Oh; I don't know what I am saying.'

'Just don't say anything. Both of us feel whatever it is; let's take the moment and keep it forever,' said Jamie.

Somewhere far away a voice was invading the moment.

'Lydia! Jamie! Come and see this,' it was Clara, shouting and waving to them.

Jamie and Lydia smiled at each other and then made their way across the flat slippery rocks to see a fair sized crab trapped in the rock pool.

'Look there,' said Clara pointing to a pair of seals basking in the bay, sticking their flippers out of the water to catch the heat of the sun, looking like they were just relaxing in their element. Suddenly a huge fish burst out the water with one of the seals in its mouth.

'It's a shark!' shouted Lydia.

'It's a what?' asked Iain?

The shark bit the seal in half and disappeared into the sea. There was a pool of blood forming in the water where the other half of the seal hit the water. Then a few moments later the shark's head came out of the water and almost casually gathered the remains of the seal in its huge maw and slid back into the sea.

'That was a shark, Uncle Godfrey told us about them; they feed on the seals that colonise an island in the bay,' said Lydia.

'We were swimming about just off the beach there,' said Iain incredulously. 'They could be chewing on us for god's sake.'

'Well thank god the seals are there to attract their attention,' said Jamie.

All four were giggling at Iain's remarks and maybe a bit nervously at the sudden violent death of the seal.

Later, as the sun was setting behind the mountain they arrived back at the picnic site. Jamie and Lydia were now so aware of each other, wanting to touch or hold hands, stealing a glance without anybody noticing and just thinking what an exhilarating feeling this was.

The picnic was packed up and loaded on to the wagon and Jamie said, 'We are all packed up, let's go home.'

Home, he thought. *That feels right, this is home.*

Chapter Eight

July 1856

Cape Town

Renton, was sitting in the library with Nicholas Banbury staring at Samuel and Williams.

'The yard is still intact, they are still working, how can this be? How is it you cannot burn down a yard full of wood?' Renton was shouting and waving his hands.

'Everything was set, the fuse was lit and we were in the carriage watching to make sure the fire took hold,' said Williams excitedly. 'But we saw two men climbing over the fence at the far side of the yard and running towards us; we had to leave lest we were seen.'

'*I wanted that place burned to the ground,*' shouted Renton standing up and almost falling over. '*Get out of here,*' he screamed.

Williams and Samuel left the room and Banbury looked at Renton, who was shaking with rage.

'Bloody buffoons, all that wood and they cannot burn it, how stupid are they?'

'I think you need to calm yourself down and have a drink. We need to focus on the task for the elders and not revenge for past defeats,' said Banbury seeing Renton was losing his mind with his obsession with Fyvie and McColl.

'I will decide when I need to calm myself sir, not you

or anybody else,' said Renton still shouting.

'No sir, I will now decide for you,' Banbury now shouting, surprised at his own audacity. 'You're now in a different situation, in as much as you are not in a position of power as you were before. I am now to report to the elders that you are directing our objective forward properly or they will want to know why. They have put their faith in me to keep up the façade around your new identity and to ensure that the decisions we make do not compromise the ELOS in any way. You need to understand the position you are in, my life is also on the line James, so be aware that we are being watched and that we are replaceable. *Do you understand what I am telling you?'* shouted Banbury even louder to make his point.

Renton gazed through his veil at Banbury then shuffled off towards the door where he stopped and then turned back to sit down with a weary sigh.

'My dear Nicholas, you are right of course. You have saved me from death that is no lie; the plans we have made would all have been for naught had you not helped with the arrangements to facilitate my escape to Freetown. But bear in mind Nicholas, Fyvie and McColl are the enemy, they're trying to find out who else is involved in the gun running and who is behind the incitement of the natives to start a war.'

'I realise all this James… Nigel, and they will be dealt with when the time comes. The point I am trying to make is that you are making their downfall a personal vendetta, and your judgement is seriously flawed as a result, making you do things that could come back to us. If that fire had taken hold at Fyvie and McColl's yard it could well have burnt down half of Salt River with it, then there would have been an investigation that we could not have stopped and an investigation would certainly have

Prophets of Death

uncovered us.'

'Yes, as I say, you are correct. From now on we'll concentrate all our efforts on our task for the elders of the ELOS,' said Renton.

'Good, I'm glad to hear you have come to your senses. Any business from now on will be discussed by both of us and if we agree then we will implement it and do whatever we have to do,' said Banbury sternly.

'I suppose we will then have to meet with Cuthbert to get his permission.'

'No, we are still making the decisions, well you are basically. I just have to make sure any decisions are good ones, besides, Cuthbert wants nothing to do with us. He is a vain, conceited, arrogant man if ever there was one,' said Banbury.

Banbury retold the events of the meeting he attended with Cuthbert to Renton who listened intently to every word.

'I was furious to say the least; I have never been talked to like that by anyone in office, no professional courtesy whatsoever.'

'My dear Nicholas, Cuthbert will have his comeuppance in due course, I can at least promise you that,' said Renton.

'Indeed! And how may I ask will that happen?'

'Cuthbert is to be the fuse which will ignite the firestorm that will decimate the Xhosa natives; he is one of the pivotal pieces on our chess board to take the ELOS into Africa when he is replaced. We cannot afford to have the spectre of the Xhosa natives rising to war every time they feel aggrieved about something. They need to be out of the equation… they need to be put down for good. '

'The replacement for the governor has already been notified and prepares to set sail for South Africa from New Zealand within days. Cuthbert has already told me he cannot wait to be shot of us,' said Banbury. 'But what is to become of Cuthbert, Nigel?'

'I can't tell you that for I am not sure when and where his part will be played, but it will happen Nicholas. We'll just have to wait patiently for that happening.'

'Then we'll continue to consolidate our position and take care of other business such as this so called hidden treasure.'

'Oh, I had forgotten all about that little exercise; what of this treasure hunt that no-one seems to believe in?'

'I've sent one of our order, one: Robert Fairbairn, to follow Fyvie and McColl who will hopefully lead us to the Templar's treasure.

'So why has Fairbairn not discovered the path to this treasure?'

'The truth is I haven't received any reports from him for some time because Governor Cuthbert has seconded him to form a militia which is operating out-with the normal laws of the land, in other words, they don't take any prisoners whether it be man, woman or child. But now that the governor is back and the natives subdued, Fairbairn should have been back from the frontier.'

'It's likely that the governor has kept him there to make sure the chiefs behave themselves and stay in their new townships,' said Renton.

'It is a possibility. I won't be asking Governor Cuthbert to enlighten me on Fairbairn, no pun intended, so I'll send a dispatch to King William's Town and find out where he is.'

'I would like to sit in the next meeting with Fairbairn and get his measure, he seems to be a bit of a blood thirsty sort of chap but not very disciplined; he should be here to tell us what the hell is going on,' said Renton, clearly irritated.

'You being in the next meeting would be a good idea,

Prophets of Death

you certainly have more insight on people than I do, but I would recommend that we keep Fairbairn at arm's length. He's a dangerous man who has, in the past, taken it upon himself to make decisions and carry them out without reporting to me first. I do not trust him.'

'Nicholas, it's very important to recover the timing of our plans to the point where we will be ready to implement our final push to secure the process of the eventual domination of this part of Africa.'

'I have sent dispatches by private messenger to the Boers in the north and to the Elder in London for the Confederate American, Chester Primeaux in Liverpool. They have been assured that the cargo of slaves they were expecting will be delivered soon,' said Banbury.

'As you know payment from these two sources have already changed hands; there will be serious repercussions from these people if we disappoint them. They'll have no fear in killing anyone no matter who they are or where they come from. As soon as the new governor is in place and Cuthbert has left here for his new post, wherever that may be, we must be ready to move quickly and decisively. Our couriers and messengers must be ready to take their notifications to the buyers at their destinations timeously.'

'All arrangements will be put in place and everything will be ready Nigel. We are on the brink of the biggest turning point in British colonial history,' said Banbury, in awe of what was to come.

'What of the ball? Do we just introduce ourselves to the governor and move along?' asked Renton.

'Yes, as I say, he doesn't wish to be involved in our plans so we'll just go along and be good citizens. I will of course accompany you to the ball and see that you are properly looked after.'

'That will not be necessary, I'll have Samuel there

and my new personal assistant who will look after me. So we shall meet inside the fort,' said Renton. Decisively trying to reclaim some control from Banbury.

They were interrupted by a servant knocking on the door and entering the room.

'What is it?' said Renton annoyed at the interruption.

'There is an urgent message from a messenger for Mr Banbury.'

'I left instructions for any urgent despatches or messages to be sent to me here,' said Banbury taking the sealed letter.

He broke the seal and read the letter. 'It looks as though you will get your meeting with Fairbairn sooner rather than later, he is back in Cape Town. Maybe now I can get some answers as to the location of the fabled treasure. I'll convene a meeting for tomorrow for you and me to meet with him.'

'Good, our plans are falling into place.'

'Well let's hope Fairbairn brings good news about a buried treasure; we could use some extra revenue.'

'Indeed,' said Renton looking deep in thought. 'I would like to resurrect our private, naughty parties again Nicholas, they are always so entertaining and I wondered who might recruit some participants for us. Any ideas who could make up a guest list to invite to the house?'

This got Banbury's attention. 'It has been a while since we let our hair down, Nigel, I must remember to call you Nigel. What a good idea. There's a young aristocratic woman who would only be too eager to make up a guest list. The daughter of Sir Robert Wycliffe, the Chief Justice, her name is Felicity; she was at the last orgy here and it is rumoured she was trying to talk someone into having another but no one has volunteered a venue.'

'What if Nigel Renton let it be known to her that he was aware of these parties and being a bachelor was

Prophets of Death

willing to carry on where James Storer left off,' said Renton.

'She frequents her father's suite of offices at the government buildings from time to time and she knows that I have been one of the privileged guests in the past. I will let it be known to her that we can have another party after the Governor's Ball. After all, the majority of the party people will be under one roof and she can finalise the invitation list there and then.'

'I'll leave it to you to inform young Felicity of my offer of a venue,' said Renton.

Banbury made to leave and said to Renton, 'Nigel, remember: no more personal vendettas against Fyvie and McColl, you will only put us at risk. Good day, I'll see you tomorrow.'

Banbury left and Renton thought, *Idiot Nicholas will believe anything I tell him. I will have my revenge on Fyvie, at least. I'll find a way, or find someone to invite him to our private party, then, I will make him the pariah of the Cape.*

Banbury let it be known in the offices of the government that Nigel Renton, the businessman recently resettled in the Cape, would be arriving today and given a short tour.

When Renton arrived, Banbury sent for Fairbairn, who recounted where he had been, detailing his duties carried out on orders from Cuthbert at the eastern frontier but leaving out the failed attack on Fyvie and McColl. All the time he was speaking he tried not to keep his attention on Renton too long lest he would be thought of staring at this strange man dressed in black with a veil hanging from his hat and black leather gloves stretched over his thin fingers.

He was surprised at the guttural voice when Renton spoke, thinking to himself. *He must have been sent by the*

K D Neill

ELOS to replace Storer. But something about this strange crippled man is stirring a deep buried memory… I do not know what it is, but it will come to me eventually.

'Forget about Governor Cuthbert, he'll be leaving us soon,' said Renton in his gruff voice. 'Do you think the Xhosa are beaten? Could there be any probability of them rising up in the future and start warring again?'

Historically, every few years after being subdued, the Xhosa clans would rise up and fight another long drawn out bush war with the British army and the white settlers. The ELOS believed these costly wars were preventing their long term plans to march north; to annex and hold the power over the whole of Southern Africa and take its mineral wealth. The Xhosa clans had to be exterminated in order for this domination to succeed.

'There's every probability they'll start warring again sir,' said Fairbairn without hesitation. 'In my humble opinion, as soon as Cuthbert leaves Africa, the Xhosa chiefs will, once they're full of sorghum beer, start their rhetoric, telling stirring stories of past chiefs and their ancestors' achievements in wars of old. Then the young warriors will want to go looking for a fight, which will be kept under control by the chiefs for now. There will be territorial disputes with white farmers and other neighbours then the cattle rustling will start. The pattern is always the same; as soon as they get weapons they will fight us again for taking away their ancestral lands in the Kroomie Heights and the Amatolas. The Xhosa hate us sir, they'll never stop trying to take back their country unless they are wiped out completely, which is not going to happen.'

'That's a very positive opinion you have of the natives Mr Fairbairn. Why do you think they'll never be wiped out, as you put it?' asked Renton.

'There are too many of them scattered all over

Prophets of Death

country. Cuthbert deployed thousands of men with superior firepower to subdue them in this war but there are still thousands of natives left wandering the frontier.'

I'll keep them thinking I'm still a loyal ELOS until I get the hell out of here, thought Fairbairn.

Renton was watching Fairbairn's face and eyes through his veil and asked. 'What of this treasure, do you think Fyvie and McColl have a clue to it? Do you think it is hidden somewhere up the coast or is it a myth?'

'They may have found a clue to the treasure if there is one; I don't think there could be anything to find after all these years,' said Fairbairn.

And there is the lie, thought Renton, seeing it and hearing it.

'I'll continue to follow them. I have just learned through my network of informants that they are to leave for Knysna Port to look for property but they make no haste to get there, probably wanting to go to the governor's ball instead. Which makes one wonder if they really have a clue or whether they believe there is something to find,' said Fairbairn endorsing the lie.

Fairbairn watched as Renton turned his head at Banbury, 'Is there anything you want to add or ask Fairbairn, Mr Banbury?'

'No, I don't think so,' said Banbury. 'Although you did say they found something at the cave above Tokai village, did you not?'

'They may have found something sir, which is why I need to follow them a little longer,' said Fairbairn feeling his anger rise and getting uncomfortable.

'Are you sure you know what your obligations are pertaining to this task Fairbairn?' asked Renton. 'Are your loyalties still strong with the ELOS?'

I could kill the two of these snivelling excuses for men right now, thought Fairbairn. *But I wouldn't get far, the*

K D Neill

ELOS will track me down eventually; I would be dead before long. Be the devoted subject… for now.

'My allegiance is unwavering sir. I'll do what I have to for the furtherance of the ELOS.'

'Yes I believe you like what you do,' Renton said slowly. 'Please wait outside Fairbairn. We will have new orders for you.'

When Fairbairn left the room Banbury looked thoughtfully at Renton.

'What do think?'

'He's lying about something. I don't think he's telling us everything about the clues to the treasure.'

'So do we need someone to follow the follower?'

'No, if we have to we'll send someone to Knysna when we receive word Fyvie and McColl are leaving. We have other pressing matters to take care of,' said Renton.

'Such as?'

'It's time to lay down the first hint of the plan to subdue the heathens,' said Renton quietly.'

Banbury looked surprised and said, 'How do we hatch this hint of the plan?'

'Fairbairn, with some of his henchmen, will accompany Samuel and Williams in a small mounted party, which will ride out to the eastern frontier traveling at night and staying out of sight by day. Once there, Samuel and Williams will go to a pre-arranged location to meet with the Xhosa turncoat, Misumzi and his niece. Fairbairn will keep watch whilst Samuel uses his muti and voodoo charms on the girl. They will ride back to Cape Town immediately, again travelling at night to avoid any patrols. Then we wait for the seed to be sown. I think you can tell Fairbairn to come back in now,' said Renton.

Renton outlined the plan to Fairbairn and said. 'You will leave Samuel and Williams at the meeting place with the Xhosa, then withdraw only far enough to ensure their

Prophets of Death

safety.' When they're finished you will find a camp somewhere out of the way and then travel back under cover of darkness.'

'What do I do once I'm back from the frontier elder?'

'After the governor's ball there will be a private function here at the house; I am sure Fyvie and McColl will attend after which they will probably leave for Knysna. You, however will have found out when the ship they are sailing on is leaving…'

'The ship is the Flying Fish sir,' said Fairbairn interrupting.

'Is that so,' said Renton, bad memories flooding back to him. 'You will have found out when they are leaving and be in Knysna before them and have your men placed to watch them wherever they go. I want answers on this Fairbairn, do you understand?'

'Yes sir. I'll make all the arrangements and do everything as ordered.'

'See that you do Fairbairn, for I will not tolerate any mistakes. You will report to me without fail, am I clear on all these instructions?'

'You are clear elder,' said Fairbairn suddenly a bit subdued by the force of this man's persona.

'You cannot be seen or recognised on this venture. If you're compromised you will eliminate the person or persons or face the consequences when you return. You can leave now and keep in touch,' said Renton dismissively.

Fairbairn left, fuming. *The pompous fool,* he thought. *When I find the treasure I should come back and kill those two FUCKING ELDERS,* he shouted in his head. *No. I must not. I will head for Durban and sail away. But oh how I would like to kill those two… Patience… Patience.*

Chapter Nine

August 1856

Eastern Cape Frontier

Fairbairn and his men acquired the provisions they needed for the long, hurried journey to the eastern frontier and rendezvoused with Samuel and Williams in a grove of trees off the main road to Bellville. The party had only one pack horse as Fairbairn wanted to get to their destination and get out as quickly as possible.

Renton arrived in his black carriage a while later to make sure everyone understood the importance of this secret expedition to the Eastern Frontier.

Fairbairn looked at the size of Samuel and took note of the scimitar sword on his hip.

'You cannot wear that sword; all blacks are banned from having any weapons that may be a threat to whites,' said Fairbairn.

'I do not think you or anyone else will be taking it away from me,' growled Samuel.

As Fairbairn instinctively moved his hand towards his pistol, Samuel drew his sword and was on him with such speed that he could scarcely believe a man of such a size could move so fast.

'*Samuel!*' Came a rasped voice from the carriage.

Samuel stopped the swing of his sword above Fairbairn's head as he watched in horror.

Prophets of Death

'Fairbairn!' the same voice said.

They both looked at Renton's head sticking out like a spectre through the door window.

'The two of you; come over here.'

Samuel lowered and sheathed his sword and they went to the carriage.

'I'll make this very clear and very simple. You, Fairbairn, will guard Samuel and Williams as though your life depended on it; because it does. Samuel is not from here, he is a free man from Sierra Leone and you will treat him as such.'

Fairbairn was livid at being spoken to in front of these natives in such a way but said, 'I will sir.'

Samuel was smiling as Renton focused on him.

'You will not wear that sword when you're travelling Samuel, it will attract too much attention if you are seen.'

The smile disappeared at this. 'I will not…'

'Yes, you will. You will hide your sword in the pack horse which you will lead and you will do whatever Fairbairn tells you to do if there is any trouble, he is leading this expedition. Is that clear?' said Renton with malice.

'Yes sir, it is clear,' said Samuel reluctantly.

'You will look after each other and get this journey done successfully. Now go,' said Renton tapping the handle of his walking stick on the roof for the driver to move off.

'Samuel,' said Fairbairn taking the initiative. 'Let's all watch each other's backs until this is over and we are back in Cape Town. That goes for you lot as well,' he said pointing at his men. 'And you too Williams.'

They all muttered their agreement, Samuel and Fairbairn shaking hands.

The small party of six mounted up and left at a trot to make as much distance as possible before they stopped for the daylight hours when they would eat and sleep, then carry on at dusk.

They ate before it was light, then put the fire out lest the smoke was spotted by a passing patrol. They bedded down under the shade of some trees in the small copse where they were hidden and tried to sleep.

This was how they camped and travelled until they reached their journey's end. They did not encounter any interruptions mainly because of Fairbairn's knowledge of the country and the fact that the army patrols kept to the main roads.

They arrived at their destination just before dawn; entering the country just north of where the Paramount Chief Samkelo's kraal was located, making camp not far from the Xhara River where they were to meet Misumzi.

As Misumzi was a prominent councillor in the pakati advising the chief, he had freedom of movement and was highly respected in the community. After all, had he not supplied guns and powder as well as good council to his chief?

He was being well paid by the white conspirators and they wanted more from him; what it was he was not quite sure but he was given instructions to meet with the coloured, Williams, and a great sangoma from a faraway land at the great pool of the Xhara River with his niece, whereupon there would be more reward.

His eyes lit up at the thought of wealth and many fat cattle to roam his land; he would be a high member of the Xhosa. But if the chief or indeed any of the pakati found out he was a traitor, he would die a traitor's death at the hands of his people.

He made his way to his sister's dwelling to find his niece who was being taught to become a sangoma, which the white men called a witch doctor.

What is a witch doctor, he thought. *The white men*

Prophets of Death

believe a sangoma conjures up devils and talks with evil spirits, maybe they do. But they do find herbs and roots to cure ills using certain animal and sometimes human body parts to ward off evil spirits. Every tribe has at least one sangoma.

Like Misumzi, his niece was a gifted seer. She had seen visions at an early age, some of which had come to pass, some not, but she would now rise to a higher plane when she meets with a great sangoma and seer from another land.

He found his niece at the hut of the tribe's sangoma where he asked after her health and her family, secretly harbouring fears of incurring any evil spells from her for disrespect. He respectfully asked her if he could take his niece away for a family meeting, not daring to tell her about the foreign sangoma he was to meet, and received her blessing to do so. Misumzi left with his niece and a basket of provisions for the Xhara pool.

When they reached the river at sundown Misumzi lit a fire and his niece prepared some food whilst he went off into the bush.

Williams was waiting for him by a huge lump of rock under a thorn bush. He stepped out from the shadow in front of Misumzi who stopped in fright.

'Williams! Why do you sneak around in the dark like that? Can you not make yourself known to me?'

'Just making sure you were not followed; do not worry my friend.'

'I am not your friend. Let us talk about our business and get it done so I can go back to the township your masters have forced upon us.'

They went behind the large boulder and hunkered down to talk.

'Your niece is known for her visions, is that not so?'

'Yes, she has had many visions.'

Williams produced a small glass bottle from his satchel and gave it to Misumzi.

'When you get back to your camp and eat some food you will put this potion into your niece's water and make sure she drinks it. Then you will tell her to sit by the great pool and wait for her to see a vision; then the appearance of the great sangoma from a faraway land will follow as planned. You will then go away from her to your village and fetch some of your people to come back and listen to her telling of the vision she has seen tonight.'

'What is this?' said Misumzi looking into the bottle.

'It is a potion made by the great sangoma to help give your niece great visions. It will not harm her, but it will make you known to all people, all over the country. As her uncle you would be held in high standing in your village when she tells of her visions.'

'Where is my payment?'

'Your payment is safe and it will be paid to you once you have completed this very simple task. By sunrise tomorrow you will be a very rich man.'

Misumzi's greed made him forget any allegiance he ever had with his people as he thought once again about green plains full of fat cattle.

'I will go now and my niece will have great visions for our people.'

'I will not be far away. What is your niece's name?'

'My niece's name is Nonkululeko.'

The sun had set as Misumzi returned to the small camp beside the river.

'I thought you would be bringing the sangoma with you Uncle?'

'No my niece, he will be along presently, we will eat and then wait for his arrival.'

They ate the food Nonkululeko prepared as they settled down by the fire. Misumzi drank some water from

Prophets of Death

a small balalaika, refilling it and then, unseen by Nonkululeko, he poured the contents of the small bottle into it offering it to Nonkululeko, which she finished and went to river to rinse the wooden implements they had used.

When she came back to the camp fire she felt a strange sensation come over her.

Misumzi said. 'Nonkululeko, you must go and sit by the great pool in the river; that is where you will see any visions and also where the great sangoma from the north will meet with you.'

She went off without a word and followed the river to the great pool and sat on the large flat rock she always used.

The moonlight danced on the water, creating flashes of faces and features, then, as the effects of the potion took hold, a vision appeared in the form of a great chief from the past.

Samuel had concealed himself below the bank of the river at the edge of the pool, a small fire burning beside him. He knew that the young girl would be under the effects of the potion, she would be highly susceptible to anything she would see and hear.

Williams was also concealed, but off to the left of Nonkululeko hidden behind some rocks and, speaking Xhosa, fluently as he did, he half spoke, half whispered to her.

'Nonkululeko! Nonkululeko!'

As he said this Samuel threw a small amount of his black dust on the fire, just enough to create a white cloud of smoke. As it rose into the air he climbed the bank and dramatically walked through the smoke and stood on the edge of the bank.

Hearing her name coming out of the darkness and seeing this apparition appearing through the white mist coming from the enchanted pool, Nonkululeko was transfixed. Staring through the haze created by the potion, she said. 'Who comes here; who speaks to the Xhosa people?'

Then she saw what could only be a vision of the ancestors.

Samuel walked closer to her and stood to his full height dressed in the attire of a Xhosa chief. His skin gleaming from the animal fat rubbed all over his body. He had three lion and leopard tooth necklaces hanging down his great chest with copper arm bands, ivory bangles and leather thongs on his huge muscular arms. Covering the tight black curls on his cranium was a head dress of long feathers of the blue crane sweeping back over his head with coloured beads around the leather. The long penis sheath hung between his legs signifying his great manhood. In his hands were a battle shield and assegais and hanging from his huge body was the sign of a Xhosa chief, a magnificent leopard skin.

He recited the Xhosa words taught to him by Williams in a rumbling whispered voice.

'I am Tshawe; the time is coming when I will lead the great chiefs to free our people. We will return to lead the Xhosa in a fight to victory over the English.'

With that, Samuel walked backwards through the dissipating smoke stepping down the bank he kept moving backwards into the pool. He plucked a feather from the head dress and dropped it onto the narrow beach.

He then lowered himself under the water, disappearing from sight using his arms and legs to crawl along the bottom and out of the water upstream.

Williams quietly left and walked back to their camp. He heard Nonkululeko's voice permeating the quiet night air calling to her uncle.

'My uncle! My uncle!'

Prophets of Death

Misumzi went to his niece and looked at her agitated state and said. 'Nonkululeko! What have you seen?'

'You must go to the chiefs and the pakati and bring them here so I may tell them of my vision,' she said, her voice trembling.

Meanwhile Fairbairn and his men were guarding their camp site, watching from a perimeter around the camp. Fairbairn watched Samuel return from the river with water dripping off him, wipe himself down and change into his kaftan. Then Williams appeared and they spoke in hushed tones before leaving to go back the way Williams had come.

What are those devils up to, he thought. He made to follow them and checked himself. *No. Patience; let them go about their ungodly business. I will take my gold and leave this stinking country.* He went back to guarding the camp.

Nonkululeko was still sitting on the rock when Samuel and Williams slowly approached her in the dark.

'Who is there?' she asked.

'I bring you the great sangoma from the far north to sit with you, to talk of your visions,' said Williams. 'I am to interpret as he does not speak your language.'

They squatted in front of her but she seemed afraid to look at them.

Samuel spoke to Williams in his low soft, rich voice. 'Tell her my greetings and that we are blessed by the ancestors of our own worlds and not to be afraid.'

Williams did as requested and Nonkululeko seemed to relax, the potion making her hear that all was well.

'What do I call you?'

Williams relayed the question, she heard his deep voice speak back and it reminded her of the low rumble of the elephants signalling each other.

'He is Samuel. He asks what you have seen in your

vision as he can help you understand what the vision is telling you.'

She related the vision; what she saw; what she was told and was overcome by emotion. 'What does this mean for us?'

Williams again related what Nonkululeko said and Samuel rumbled his reply.

'This chief, do you know this name?' asked Samuel through Williams.

'Yes, he is the father of the Xhosa nation, the great warrior chief Tshawe.'

The night air was still and a real mist was lifting from the river as Nonkululeko was allowed to think upon the gravity of what she had seen.

Samuel spoke again.

'This means that you will see the great chief in another vision with a sign from the ancestors to tell your people not to despair; that they will return to bring you the freedom from the white man that you desire.'

'How will I know the sign, great sangoma?'

'You will know; be vigilant. The desires of the Xhosa will be foretold in a prophecy when the great chief, Tshawe, next appears in your visions. You will then have to tell your people of this prophecy.'

A dense mist from the river moved across the ground, watched by Williams, who was beginning to feel slightly afraid of the ghosts from the past. He looked at Samuel who flicked his head towards the bush. They both quietly retreated from the mesmerised Nonkululeko, watching for another vision in the mist.

After a time Misumzi returned with three of the pakati, the council to the paramount chief, who were sceptical of these so called visions.

They sat in front of the seer Nonkululeko with respect as they did not want her to put a curse on their

Prophets of Death

kraal.

When she finished the telling of the vision she pointed to the pool in the river and said. 'The old chiefs will give us a sign to return here; they will tell us in a prophecy when they will return to lead us and be rid of the great white queen's armies.'

One of the old pakati stood and wandered over to the bank of the pool and in the moonlight could see a plume from the blue crane lying on the sandy beach. He fetched it up and held it high above his head and said, 'It is as she has spoken, this is the feather of the blue crane.'

Another pakati said. 'Let us wait. We will not speak of this; not yet.'

They all stared at the perfect plumage and felt a stirring in their blood.

Williams and Samuel returned to the camp and signalled for Fairbairn to come in.

'If you are agreeable we can break camp and head back to Cape Town,' Williams suggested to Fairbairn.

'The sun will be up in a couple of hours, I do not think it would be wise to break camp now, we could be seen by a patrol. This is a good spot and we are well hidden; we should wait out the day tomorrow and leave in the evening.'

'I bow to your knowledge of the land; god knows I need some sleep,' said Williams.

'We should leave this place,' said Samuel suddenly. 'There are bad spirits here,' he said looking around. 'The young sangoma has the ear of the ancients.'

Williams had never seen him so troubled.

Fairbairn wanted to tell this kaffir to shut up and do as he was told but maybe he could reason with him. 'We don't want to be found here Samuel. If you feel that you want to move the camp to another location then we can do that but I know this place. We must wait until nightfall tomorrow to make a safe journey away from here.'

Samuel thought about this insufferable fool's words and decided to heed his advice.

He looked down into Fairbairn's eyes; they held each other's stare for what seemed an eternity, each wanting to kill the other.

'Then we can stay here until then,' said Samuel turning away and bedding down.

Williams bedded down next to Samuel and whispered. 'Why do you prod the Englishman to lose his control? If you start something there are four of them and only one of you.'

'You will not stand beside me then?' asked Samuel with contempt.

'No, I will not. You are good with that sword but you cannot withstand four bullets coming at you at the same time,' said Williams pulling his blanket over his shoulder.

'Use dry wood on the fire to lessen the smoke and keep it small, we do not want a patrol to see the smoke and come sniffing around,' said Fairbairn the following morning. 'The branches in the trees should disperse some of the smoke.' He said wanting to be away from here and back to the safety of Cape Town.

It was late afternoon when one of Fairbairn's men came in from watch. 'Riders coming from the north, looks like a patrol.'

'How far away are they?' asked Fairbairn.

'They are not far off sir. They came around a hill very slowly, that's why I never spotted them sooner. The only reason I did see them was because I heard a horse whinny.'

Fairbairn knew his man was telling the truth, he had ridden with him often. 'Samuel, Williams, get out of sight behind those rocks,' he said pointing to a huge pile of boulders. 'Why would they be so quiet? Unless they

Prophets of Death

know we're here.'

It was then he saw four soldiers, one a lieutenant, coming around from the very boulders he had been pointing at. One of the guards was their prisoner, which still left one, Fairbairn knew he would be concealed and watching. The troopers all had muskets at the ready with bayonets fixed.

'Well, well, what do we have here? Everybody stay still please,' said the lieutenant.

He looked at Fairbairn, recognising him from somewhere.

Fairbairn saw this and spoke up as another two troopers rode up with the horses. 'Good tactics lieutenant, I couldn't have done better myself.'

The lieutenant was slightly put off but recovered quickly. 'Search them; all of them,' he said sweeping his hand around the camp.

'There's no need for that sir. I am Captain Robert Fairbairn, you may have heard of my volunteers that fought in the last uprising.'

'I thought I had seen you before; you led that murdering band of cutthroats, no prisoners, is that right?'

One of the troopers had flicked his bayonet at Samuel to stand up and away so he could search his pack. Samuel stood to his full height and looked down at the soldier who was taken aback at the size of him. 'Move back kaffir,' he said to him.

Samuel stood back and the soldier poked his pack and blanket, uncovering his scimitar sword.

'Sir, the black is armed with a huge sword.'

'What are you doing out here Fairbairn?' asked the lieutenant.

'I am escorting that black man to Cape Town; he is in the service of a government minister. The coloured works for me and we are on a sensitive mission to fetch and return that valuable sword for the minister.'

'The trooper made to pick up Samuel's sword. 'Do not touch my sword,' said Samuel in his booming voice.

'Shut up black boy, I'll take what I like.'

Fairbairn glanced at his other man; he was ready to take on the soldiers.

'The black just said it was his sword; I am taking you all in to Fort Beaufort where you will be detained until I can confirm your story. Because that is what I think this is, just a story. There is something going on here and I will get to the bottom of it.'

The musket shot hit the lieutenant in the neck under his right ear. Fairbairn drew his pistols and fired at two of the troopers hitting one and missing the other completely but his companions shot two others. The trooper searching Samuel looked over at the commotion and in that split second Samuel had his sword up in his hand and decapitated him. Keeping the momentum turning, Samuel rounded on the last trooper who was trying to get a shot off but realised his arm was laying on the ground, cleaved off at shoulder, the hand still clutching the musket. Samuel skewered him with the tip of his sword through the chest. He looked back at the troopers head on the ground and said. 'You will not take what you like, white boy.'

It was all over in seconds. One of Fairbairn's men had a bullet wound to his arm but it was not serious and could be patched up.

'Secure the troopers horses we will let them go far from here. Take the bodies into the rocks and leave them for the animals.'

'We could sell the horses,' said one of the men.

Fairbairn looked at him and said. 'They have the army brand on them so you cannot sell them without suspicions being raised. The authorities would know

Prophets of Death

where they were deployed and the men to whom they were given to and we would be hanged for murder you idiot.'

He heard a moan from the lieutenant and went over to him.

'Help me,' he rasped, the blood pumping freely from his wound.

'Why could you not just leave it well alone?' said Fairbairn picking up the lieutenant's pistol and shot him between the eyes.

Williams had not moved during the shootout and was stunned at callousness of Fairbairn and the way he and his men had dealt with the situation. He knew Samuel had no concerns at all when it came to using his sword. *How did I get involved with these people*? He thought. *How do I escape*? *There is no escape.*

By the time they had hidden the bodies and scavenged what they could, the sun had gone down and they prepared to mount up and leave.

'We will not be stopping until dawn, so make sure you have food to eat in the saddle. I have had enough of this expedition,' said Fairbairn

During the days it took for the small band of horsemen to get back to Cape Town, the rumours of the visions seen by the young seer were beginning to pass from mouth to mouth throughout the land. The dead chiefs would be resurrected and return to lead them to freedom.

Chapter Ten

August 1856

Cape Town

As Fairbairn set out on his incursion in the Eastern Cape, the boys upgraded one of their carriages to take them to the Governors' Ball. It now swept over the moat; under the portcullis; around the courtyard and stopped at the grand entrance of the main building in the fort where past Governors used to reside.

They were resplendent in their tails, top-hats and long, black velvet capes as they walked up the steps and into the grand hall, a doorman relieved them of their capes and hats.

'This is what I could get used to,' said Iain as they received a glass of champagne and entered the banqueting room.

'What! Are you going to be a toff?'

'Oh aye, I like this and when we get all our present obligations fulfilled you and I are going to be famous,' joked Iain.

'Just don't lose sight of what we have to do tonight Iain I want these evil bastards dead and buried and then, as you say, we can become famous for being good citizens.'

They wandered through the crowded rooms and introduced themselves to some people then bumped into

Prophets of Death

Doctor Morgan.

'Good evening doctor; looks like it's going to be a night to remember,' said Jamie.

'Good evening Jamie: Iain. Yes, I'm sure it will be,' said Doctor Morgan. He leaned closer to the boys and said quietly. 'Bill Hutchison came to see me today and asked me to tell you that the private party is on.'

'Thanks doctor; now we have work to do,' said Jamie.

'I'll leave you to it then. I'll go and re-charge my glass,' said Morgan and walked away.

'Let's find the girls,' said Iain.

They found Lydia and Clara with Godfrey and Sarah Butler sitting together talking and laughing, sipping their drinks and having the time of their life.

Iain was mesmerised by Clara. 'You are looking beautiful tonight, Clara… I mean you are… what I mean to say is… you always have been beautiful, but more so tonight… if you know what I mean.'

Clara laughed. 'Thank you kind sir, I think I know what you mean,' taking his arm and walking with him across the room. 'Isn't this the most wonderful party you have ever been to?'

'Yes, I must confess it is,' said Iain. 'So you like this kind of luxury do you?'

'Oh yes, I could live the good life like this, Iain,' said Clara happily.

'That's my girl,' muttered Iain.

'I beg your pardon?'

'Nothing, let's take a walk in the grounds before dinner,' suggested Iain.

Jamie said good evening to Godfrey and Sarah then turned his attention to Lydia and gave her his arm to walk beside him. 'You know that you are the most beautiful woman in the room.

'Well; thank you; such flattery from a handsome suitor.'

'Miss Knowles, would you care to walk with me in the cool night air?' said Jamie.

'I would sir, thank you.'

Ten minutes after Jamie and Iain arrived, Rory McGregor and Hamish McFarland alighted from their coach to the sounds of voices and hilarity mixed with music floating through the doorway to the governor's ball.

'Well it sounds like a great party going on Hamish,' said Rory.

'It does too. We'll have to find Arthur Burton inside so he can guide us around,' said Hamish leading the way in.

They found Arthur talking with a colonel from the 81st Regiment

'Your laddies are over there with the lawyer, Godfrey Butler, his wife and the two daughters of the late George Knowles,' said Arthur pointing to the boys.

'Have you seen any other interesting characters, Arthur?' asked Rory.

'There is a strangely dressed man just arrived at the Cape, his name is Nigel Renton and he has a very interesting personal assistant in the shape of Mrs Anne Knowles.'

'So, she has returned from England as the charges were withdrawn for murdering her husband,' said Hamish.

He explained to Rory where Anne Knowles fitted in the equation and the suspicion that she was in league with Storer aboard The Flying Fish and that he was an ELOS elder.

'It is interesting that Renton has purchased Storer's house and that the Knowles woman was supposedly

Prophets of Death

making her bed with Storer when he was alive,' said Arthur.

'Have you noticed if Fairbairn is here tonight?' asked Rory.

'No, he would not be invited to the Governor's Ball. If you wander around the room to where Renton and the Knowles woman are sitting you will see a gentleman there by the name of Nicholas Banbury, he is ELOS and Fairbairn's controller and so, I would presume is Renton.'

'The enemy seems to be gathering their dark forces,' said Rory. 'When we find what I came here to find will we have the resources to repel them?'

'We will have the men to take them on Rory, have no fear of that,' said Hamish.

Jamie and Lydia strolled around the grounds looking for a quiet corner or shadowed alcove but the whole of the castle grounds were lit up with burning torches and lamps, not only that, there were couples and little groups of people enjoying the evening outside of the hot stuffy rooms of the Governor's old residence.

'Oh well, I suppose we should go back inside and eat and dance,' said Lydia.

'Not yet, let's go up on the battlements and look at the view,' said Jamie.

They found their way up and on to the battlements of the fort, stopping to admire the lights across Table Bay. They kissed passionately until they heard some voices and so sauntered around to the view out over the grand parade and saw Iain and Clara ahead of them with the same idea, Iain was waving them over.

'Jamie, take a look down there,' said Iain.

Jamie went up on tip toe and looked over the wide wall of the battlements and saw a very fancy black carriage with four very fine black horses and a very large black man with a fez and large scimitar sword in a fine black leather scabbard.

Jamie and Iain exchanged looks.

'That is one big black bastard. No offense,' said Iain.

'Who is he?' asked Clara leaning over to look with Lydia.

'He works for the new owner of the house that was owned by James Storer,' said Jamie.

'Oh goodness, I'm so glad that he's gone,' said Lydia shaking her shoulders.

'Come on, let's go back to the ball and not talk about the past,' said Clara taking Iain's arm.

They went back to the ball and after dinner the dancing started, the wine, the brandy and indeed the whisky was flowing as the non-drinkers faded away and the revellers took over.

The girls were meeting more friends of Godfrey and Sarah whilst Jamie and Iain were once again walking around socialising and keeping the drinking to a minimum as they were watching for any sign of someone getting around the elite of Cape Town as a conspirator to something else entirely.

Rory spotted Jamie and Iain and said to his companions, 'I see the laddies over there. I am going over to introduce myself.'

'Is that wise at this stage, Rory,' said Hamish.

'Aye, I think it's time to get closer to them,' he looked at his brethren. 'We have to take them into our confidence and let them know they have some friends.'

'What… tonight?' exclaimed Arthur.

'No, not tonight. Hamish and I will talk to them when we sail for the port of Knysna. Arthur, you will, of course, be en-route to Knysna, overland to watch for our arrival. I'll merely introduce myself to make sure they know my

Prophets of Death

face. Excuse me for a moment.'

Rory made his way across the floor and faced the boys. 'Good evening lads, I couldn't help but hear your accent, it's nice to hear a friendly voice.'

Jamie and Iain looked at the stranger who suddenly appeared before them.

'Aye, eh… hello,' said Jamie.

'I hope you don't mind the intrusion but I've just arrived in the Cape. My name is Rory McGregor,' he said proffering his hand.

'Jamie Fyvie and Iain McColl,' said Iain and they all shook hands. 'What business brings you to the Cape Rory?'

'Oh! Fyvie and McColl that is a coincidence. You are my co-passengers on the ship to a place called Belvidere Knysna or Knysna something.'

'On the Flying Fish, sailing to Knysna Port with Captain Willard?'

'The very same Iain, my business will hopefully be sheep farming. Captain Willard mentioned your names when I and my brother booked our berths.'

'It will be good to have some company in the saloon when we get out to sea,' said Jamie. 'We can maybe talk about some business with you as we have a company that manufactures agricultural tools and implements.'

'I look forward to the voyage and to talk about some business, who knows maybe we will become partners at some stage.'

'Well, you never can tell, sheep farming here is about to change for the better so I hear,' said Iain suddenly interested in this new potential source of income.

'I will see you on board then, I came here with my brother so I will go and find him. I will be watching out for you boys,' said McGregor and disappeared into the crowd.

'What does that mean?' said Jamie.

'What?' said Iain looking around the room.

'He said he'll be watching out for us.'

'I don't know, but do ye see the woman over by the big bay window surrounded by some frisky young men; across the room to the right?' Iain said nodding his head in that direction.

'Yes, she is a beauty. Is she not the Lord Chief Justice's daughter, what's his name?'

'Sir Robert Wycliffe if memory serves,' said Iain. 'But look, every now and then she goes off with someone to dance or for a drink, usually men but women as well and then takes something from them and puts it in her purse.'

'I think she's taking names or some kind of mark for a private party Iain, what do you think?'

'I think you could be right big man; time for you to go over to her and turn on the charm.'

'I will, but I don't want it to look too obvious to everybody, she does attract a lot of attention.'

'Well, let's wait a bit and you'll get a chance to move in on her; I think she's a wild one,' said Iain.

'Yes, I think so; definitely part of the private elite that Armstrong spoke of. Where's Lydia?' asked Jamie looking around the room.

'She went with Clara into the ballroom with the Butlers. Don't worry, I'll keep an eye on them when you make your move. You are sweet on Lydia, I know and you don't want to upset her by appearing to be lusting after other women.'

'I will not be lusting after anyone,' said Jamie irritably. 'I just want this business to be over. I just can't see that becoming a reality any time soon.'

'There's so much ground still to cover and villains to vanquish Jamie, I don't think we should take any

Prophets of Death

prisoners otherwise we'll always be looking over our shoulders.'

'There won't be any prisoners, we will be the last men standing when this is done,' said Jamie with finality.

They moved around the room and saw a slight commotion as they entered another room. There was a woman with her back to the boys stooped and fussing over a frail gentleman dressed in black wearing a black hat with a veil covering his face and black leather gloves on his hands.

As they walked through the room the woman stood upright and turned around.

It was Anne Knowles.

'Don't look so surprised, you did not think I would stay in England did you?'

'Well you can't blame us for hoping you might,' said Jamie smiling with no feeling.

'I'm surprised they gave you back your broomstick,' said Iain leaning over and keeping his voice low.

'Mrs Knowles,' said a rasping voice behind her.

They all turned and looked to the man with the veil.

'Introduce me to your friends,' rasped the man.

'Oh we are not her friends Mr........?'

'This is Nigel Renton,' said Anne Knowles. Then turning to Renton. 'These gentlemen are Jamie Fyvie and Iain McColl, local businessmen,' she said acting out the pretence.

'Forgive me if I do not get up and shake your hand, I am a bit frail,' said Renton staring through the veil with hatred in his eyes. 'So not your friends Anne, what have you done to annoy them?' he said with sarcasm missed by the others.

Anne turned to the boys and said. 'I am Mr Renton's personal assistant, not that it's any of your business, so if you will excuse us I must get Mr Renton to his carriage and off home.'

'Well we hope we will see *more* of you in the near future Mr Renton,' said Jamie.

'We knew she was coming back to Cape Town but when did she arrive and how did she get involved with Renton?' asked Iain.

But Jamie was watching Renton and Anne Knowles leaving the room.

Iain looked at Jamie looking at the couple, he looked at them and then back at Jamie. 'What?'

'There's something about him that bothers me, Iain.'

'You mean, apart from the veil, the gloves and that his helper is Anne Knowles; how could he possibly bother you?' said Iain. 'Of course he will bother you, he bothers me but we need to get back to what we are doing tonight before the moment is gone.'

'Aye, let's find the party organiser and I'll make my case,' said Jamie.

Arthur led his brethren to a vantage point where they could see the boys talking briefly with Anne Knowles and Nigel Renton after which they moved off. Then they saw Banbury go over to Renton as he left and converse with him as they turned to watch the boys walk away.

'I hope Jamie is looking over his shoulder when he gets involved with these people,' said Arthur.

'His partner, Iain, is also an agent with the field police; he will be watching out for him, of that you can be sure,' said Rory.

'And we will have people watching them, they will not be alone,' said Hamish.

Jamie spotted her in the ballroom dancing and whispering in her dance partner's ear. They were pointing at some people in the room and then they would both stop and

Prophets of Death

have a brief chat; then move onto other couples on the dance floor; she took something from each person and dropped it in her purse.

'Everyone has to go and relieve themselves sometime during the evening,' commented Iain.

'So you want me to hide in the female lavvy?'

'Very funny, no. I was thinking more like positioning yourself somewhere to bump into her when she goes for, or comes back from a pee.'

'Aye, I'll do that. I'll find you after I talk to her and then we can have a decent drink,' said Jamie.

Jamie positioned himself so that he could see anyone walking towards the passageway for the ladies rooms and just in time as he saw his target fobbing off a young gentleman with a wave of her hand and made a determined direction to where Jamie was waiting.

He decided to wait for her to come back in case her need was desperate and also for anyone lingering to lust after her to go away.

Jamie anticipated she might take a different way back in to the party and when she did he was ready and timed his abrupt blockage of her passage face to face with precision.

'Excuse me!' said Jamie acting a little surprised. 'If you wanted to get my attention all you had to do was introduce yourself instead of ambushing me with such a lovely presence.'

'I beg your pardon?' said the young lady, shocked.

She looked up at Jamie's handsome smiling face, saw the mischief in his alluring eyes and new immediately he was having fun with her.

'And if you wanted to get my attention sir, you could have picked a more suitable place other than the way to the water closet.'

Jamie laughed and she laughed with him.

'In that case let me lead you away from here and find a more fitting place to introduce myself,' said Jamie proffering his arm.

Outside in the cool early morning air and after rescuing two glasses of wine from a wandering waiter he said. 'I am Jamie Fyvie recently, well, quite a while ago recently, a new resident of Cape Town.'

'Your fame precedes you sir, I know of you and your partner Iain McColl and of your business here and, I may add, your exploits. This is a small community, nothing goes un-noticed here. But I am being rude, I am Felicity Wycliffe, daughter of the Chief Justice, I tell you that before someone else does, and bored resident of Cape Town for more time than I care to think of.'

'Bored? But there is so much to do here, how can you be bored?'

'If one is a man then then one would never be bored but being an aristocratic daughter is very boring,' said Felicity sadly.

'I have heard that there are ways to relieve some of that boredom if you are invited into the right circles,' said Jamie.

Felicity looked at Jamie as though to judge whether he was trust worthy or not.

Jamie pressed on. 'I have an appetite, shall we say, for extreme nocturnal sport,' he said knowing that she would either slap him or recognise what he meant. One way or the other he would know if he was on the right track.

'Why don't we take a walk in the grounds and find out how extreme you can be Jamie Fyvie,' she said taking his arm.

'Felicity… Felicity, there you are,' said a voice from the balcony above.

'Oh God, it's my Aunt Beatrice,' moaned Felicity

Prophets of Death

looking up and waving.

'I need you in here with your father,' called Aunt Beatrice.

'Where can I leave a message for you?' she asked Jamie.

'We have a business in Salt River, Fyvie and McColl, leave a message there.'

'Maybe I shall see you later but I fear daddy wants to go home and I shall have to go with him. I will leave a message for you at your premises and keep next week Saturday free,' she said and kissed Jamie's cheek. She squeezed his hand and left.

Rory was still observing discreetly as Jamie manoeuvred himself to intercept a beautiful young lady and guide her outside where they talked in very low tones as though they were co-conspirators. After a while the young lady returned to join an older woman. He wondered what this scheming was about and what Jamie was up to.

He went to find Arthur and Hamish and related what he had seen and pointed out the young lady in question.

'That young lady is Felicity Wycliffe, the daughter of the Lord Chief Justice Sir Robert and we know she is a bit of a wild child,' said Arthur.

'Wild? Exactly… how?' asked Rory.

'She and her upper class clique of friends like to indulge in private parties which involve lots to drink and lots of unsavoury sex.'

'If only the people at home knew what was going on in the colonies,' said Rory. 'The thing is, Jamie does not seem to be the type to be involved in something as sordid as sex parties. No, he is doing something for the…' He moved his head closer to his two masonic brethren and whispered, 'The Secret Field Police of Whitehall.'

It looks as though Jamie is trying to get inside this

secret clique, thought Rory. *But why.*

Jamie walked back inside and went to look for Iain and found him with Lydia and Clara.

'Jamie my boy,' said Godfrey. 'We are about to take our leave and go home to bed. It has been rather a late night for us.'

'Yes, it's getting late Godfrey I think we should be going as well.'

They collected coats and capes and wandered to the carriages in the castle courtyard.

'How is Felicity?' asked Lydia icily as she walked next to Jamie.

'Who?'

'Oh for goodness sake Jamie, I saw how she was falling all over you outside.'

'Aye, Felicity. I just met her and we started chatting. How do you know her?'

'You mean, apart from every Sunday at church and when she accompanies her father and sometimes her awful aunt to high tea or dinner parties at our house?'

'Oh, right, I suppose it is a small community. She seems very nice,' said Jamie thinking. *Why wouldn't they know each other you idiot?*

'I think you should be careful there Jamie I hear she seems to be a favourite with some of the young men in the community.'

'Are you saying she likes to lie down with more than one partner Lydia?' asked Jamie.

'No. Never, although she has hinted at one or two men's performances; horse riding I mean,' said Lydia.

'Horse riding you say,' said Jamie as they approached the carriages.

Lydia stopped abruptly and in a loud whisper said. 'Are you going to see her again?' she was clearly a bit

Prophets of Death

jealous.

'I will in all probability see her in or around Cape Town from time to time but I have not invited her to tea, if that's what you mean,' said Jamie.

'Do not forget you are taking me riding… and soon. Goodnight,' she said turning and climbed into the carriage.

Rory and his brethren watched un-noticed as Jamie and Iain boarded their carriage, presumably on their way home.

'We need to keep following these two laddies very closely until they get on board the Flying Fish; that is where we will make them aware of our presence,' said Rory.

'I agree,' said Arthur. 'The main players are coming together in this game; those two lads are the fulcrum under a see-saw with heavy weights on both sides.'

'Aye but which way will the see-saw finally settle is the question,' said Rory.

When the boys got home it was the early hours of the morning, so they changed into more comfortable attire and were planning on getting nicely drunk on the stoep with a bottle of whisky.

'We are going to knock the arse out of this bottle,' said Iain tossing the cork over his shoulder. It bounced off of the window and landed on the table in front of him. He looked at it stupidly and said. 'Or maybe not!'

Jamie leaned over and picked up the cork. He studied it for a moment then threw it in anger into the night.

'Jamie, things will work themselves out,' said Iain pouring the drinks.

'Very easy for you to say; Lydia and Felicity Wycliffe are friends and share stories so if I shag Felicity to get into this clique I will be well and truly…'

'Fucked?' said Iain and they both burst out laughing.

The tears were running down their faces, they were laughing so hard at the absurdity of the situation they were in.

'Oh stop; my jaws are aching,' said Iain after a while.

'I don't know why I'm laughing, what the hell do I do Iain?'

'Only you can come to that conclusion Jamie. The situation we are in, neither one of us should even think about having a relationship with a woman simply because of the life expectancy of the job, bearing in mind the lunatics we are trying to eliminate.'

'Aye, you are right I have to step back before she or indeed myself gets any more deeply involved. I don't want to give her up Iain, I really want to have a good relationship with Lydia; she makes me feel so good.'

'I know, I feel the same about Clara. I think we have to make a pact that we don't get involved with the girls any further until we finish this bleddy business and if we don't come out alive then at least we will not break their hearts. Besides, we do not want our enemies to find out how much they mean to us, because these bastards would use them against us.'

'Aye. You're right,' said Jamie and put his hand out.

Iain took his hand and shook it knowing that in the coming months the final chapter would come to a bloody end.

Chapter Eleven

August 1856

Cape Town

Mefrou le Roux was going through the house calling 'Goeie môre, goeie môre.' *Good morning, good morning.*

Iain was dousing his head with cold water and shouting back. 'Good morning Mefrou. Please keep the noise down: I have a hangover.'

'Jy het 'n lekker babelas?' she said laughing.

'What was that you said?' said Jamie sitting at the breakfast table.

'You have a nice hangover,' translated Mefrou le Roux.

'Aye, a nice, big hangover. Big enough tae go tae school.'

'I have a good breakfast for you and some very black coffee.'

'No, no, just tea with breakfast please.'

Iain arrived and sat down as breakfast was laid in front of them. He looked through the window and saw the empty whisky bottle on the table.

Jamie looked as well and said, 'Aye, we did knock the arse out of the bottle.'

'No wonder I feel like I do, I need this breakfast to sort me out.'

Mefrou le Roux walked past and gave Jamie a letter.

'This came by messenger this morning, it is for you Jamie.'

Jamie looked at it. It was very good quality paper and very well written.

'Did the messenger say who it was from?'

'No, he just said to make sure I gave it to you in person,' she said.

Jamie looked at Iain and shovelled another forkful of eggs and bacon into his mouth.

'Well… what does it say?' said Iain also shovelling more breakfast into his mouth.

Jamie tore open the letter and started reading.

Go on the road to Camps Bay just after the noon gun tomorrow, when you get up to Kloof Nek take the road to Lion's Rump.

The carriage will be waiting for you.

Come alone. Part of being a member of our little clique is that you burn this note. Leave no trace.

FW

'That's all it says,' said Jamie handing the letter to Iain. 'How did she know where to deliver the letter? I told her where our business premises were.'

Iain perused the writing. 'It wouldn't have been difficult to find out where you live, Jamie. It looks like you've got yourself an invitation to a party.'

'Christ, Iain, I don't want to do this anymore.'

Iain did not say anything and they sat in silence whilst they finished their breakfast. He looked at his friend and knew he was hurting.

'Look, why don't we tell them that I want to be at the party as well, then at least you will have some moral support and both of us will be in the shite.'

'No, that's not going to work, Iain,' said Jamie rubbing the palms of his hands up and down his face. I need you to be on the outside in case I have to make a quick escape.'

'I will be watching your back big man, you know that.'

'I know you will, Iain. Come on let's go and find Bill Hutcheson and tell him I have made contact.'

Jamie was riding along the road below Devil's Peak, the top of the mountain barely visible through the cloud. He was looking down at Main Road just past Rosebank, walking his horse as he was in no hurry; comfortable in the saddle but not comfortable about his destination.

The suburbs below, like the road, were dripping wet because of overnight rain, which had poured down until the early hours. The road was pitted with mud holes and giant puddles, unfortunately the run offs dug down the side of the road were inadequate for the amount of rain that had fallen. He looked up to see the new waterfalls that had suddenly sprouted on the mountain, all the time thinking about Lydia and what he was about to commit to.

He rode around the mountain, passing the suburbs of Woodstock and Oranjezicht, the city further down the slope. He guided the horse up toward Kloof Nek when he heard the boom of the noon cannon, telling everyone in the city within earshot the time.

He pulled up the horse and almost turned back he was so loath to do this thing.

'Fuck!' he said. The horse turning his ears back in miscomprehension. He sat there for a while looking up at the mountain. 'How did we get into this so… so… so deeply; how much deeper does it get?' he said to the horses ears as though he would understand.

The horse turned his ears forward and started bobbing his head up and down with impatience; eager to be moving on.

Jamie lightly touched his heels to the horse's flanks to urge him on up the hill to the Nek. 'Ah… fuck it!' he said in defiance and defeat.

He gripped the animal with his legs at the same time digging his heels a little harder and shouted. 'Hup.'

The horse felt the change in his rider's body language, flicked his ears back and in response, eagerly jumped into a gallop, Jamie leaning slightly forward to compensate for the surge in pace.

The horse stretched his neck out as he galloped up to Kloof Nek, Jamie guiding him right, off the road to Camps Bay, up towards Lion's Head, the road curving right to Lion's Rump. He slowed his horse to a trot, seeing the carriage was waiting at the side of the road before the bend to Signal Hill and the noon gun.

He dismounted and tethered the horse to the back of the carriage, the door was open when he came around the side, inviting him in to the arms of Felicity Wycliffe.

'Hello, Jamie Fyvie,' she said.

She was half sitting half lying on the front seat below the driver with a silver goblet of wine in her hand looking very hungry and very beautiful.

Jamie looked up at the driver who was staring straight ahead.

'He will not look at you and he is trusted to stay quiet; he has known me from birth and would die for me. Come in and have some wine,' said Felicity.

Jamie boarded the carriage discarding his jacket before he sat on the back bench seat and took the wine from Felicity.

She reached up and rapped a door knocker fixed above the window signalling the driver to move on.

'That's a clever idea; I must include knockers in my carriages,' he said smiling.

'You will have to pay me an annual stipend for my

Prophets of Death

idea; maybe pay in kind.' she said seductively. 'I want to watch you take your shirt off.' She said putting her wine on the small fold out table on the door.

She watched Jamie take his shirt tails out of his waistband and pull the shirt over his head; she admired the square lean body and muscles, noting the scars.

Leaning forward she ran her hands over his body, squeezing and scratching, nipping his nipples. She leaned back and undid the hooks hidden in the top of her dress which was separate from the lower piece and took it off to reveal her bared breasts, which hung out the top of a lacy corset.

Jamie stared at them appreciatively; he was always fascinated by the different size and shape of female's breasts.

Felicity's breasts were not large but smaller around, yet were elongated and full, pointing straight out. The large areola covered the front of her breasts back about an inch with wide, thick nipples.

'You are a breast man then?' she asked.

'I am a breast man, a bottom man, a leg man, I am a woman man,' he said, all reason gone.

She reached up and gripped a pair of leather straps fixed to the ceiling; lifting herself off of the seat she presented her breasts in front of his face.

'Bite my nipples, suck them and bite them Jamie.'

He took a breast in each hand and started to lick one then the other, the nipples stiffening immediately. He then started to tease them with his teeth and tongue, chewing and sucking them into his mouth and then pushing her breasts together, taking both nipples into his mouth at the same time.

'Oh yes keep doing that, I have never had that done to me before this,' the lust starting to take her away.

As the carriage went along at a steady speed, Felicity

suddenly sat back and swallowed a mouthful of wine and then pushed Jamie back on the seat to unbutton his breeches, pulling them and his under garment down to the tops of his boots.

She kneeled on the floor taking his hard penis in one hand whilst the other hand massaged his ball bag and stared at his erection, admiring its ability to be flaccid, small and limp to then gradually grow into this hard piece of flesh which she so desired.

She was fascinated by the fact he had not been circumcised and looked closer as she pulled the foreskin back to reveal the throbbing bulbous head.

She started to move her hand slowly up and down, licking the head to keep it moist and slippery; his body fluids mixing in. She leaned over and placed his hardness between her breasts, her hands manipulating them up and down, keeping him in her cleavage.

Jamie reached down to reach under her dress finding, as he expected, nothing underneath. He found her soft wet place and began to massage her clitoris, feeling her react to the tender touch of his feel.

Felicity took him in her mouth, clearly enjoying the act which she was performing on him, taking her mouth off and then masturbating him, then taking him in her mouth again, masturbating him, watching the foreskin gliding up and over, easily back down and back in her mouth.

Jamie was in heaven the way she worked his penis, she was certainly no slouch when it came to giving pleasure as well as receiving it. It seemed to heighten the pleasure for her which Jamie understood, for that was the way he felt it as well.

Felicity noisily slurped her mouth off of Jamie's hardness, though she was loath to do so, she turned around and loosened her frock, throwing it in the corner

Prophets of Death

she bent over and presented Jamie with her gorgeous buttocks, pink anus and a very wet, blonde haired pink slit between the thick lips of her vulva.

'Do you like what you see there,' she asked as though needing confirmation that it was desirable.

'Not as much as my need for you to sit what I see on my cock,' replied Jamie gripping her hips.

She resisted his desire to pull her down and then lowered herself slowly onto his erection, letting it fill her up until her vagina had taken him up to the hilt. She let out a gasp and pushed down as far as she could, wanting more but could not take any more. Pushing her legs on the floor of the carriage she slid up and straight back down again, feeling the sensation of him filling her.

'Oh my god, I am lusting so much I could scream,' she said as she pumped faster and faster on the engorged erection.

Jamie was thrusting up to meet her pushing down trying to get as deep as possible and going harder and harder until she stiffened and contracted her vagina as though trying to hang on. She let out a long sigh as she gave up her orgasm all over him, her body fluids flowing warmly down over his testicles which made him thrust into her as he came. She felt his balls retract and jumped off him and took his orgasm in her mouth, spilling down her chin she kept at him as his spasms slowed and they both fell onto their seats totally spent with the burst of energy they had unleashed.

'That is the best sex I have ever experienced.' she said taking a box from a small cupboard in the panel behind her and took two cheroots from it. Lighting them she gave one to Jamie who was now thinking about what he had just done.

'Why did you come here Jamie?' she asked taking a long pull at the cigar.

K D Neill

Jamie sucked a long draw at his smoke and said. 'You know why, to join the elite club, to be invited to the private parties,' replied Jamie.

Felicity studied his face for a few moments and came to a conclusion. 'I believe you want to the join the private club but you are lying as to why you want to join,' said Felicity taking linen towels from a drawer beneath the seat and tossing one to Jamie.

As they wiped away the sweat and body fluids Jamie said. 'I'm not sure what you mean Felicity; I want to be in with the private... elite party people in Cape Town.'

'I believe you Jamie, but not for the reasons you are telling me; do not take me for a fool. This is not you. You do not belong in this sordid debauchery we indulge in every now and then, no... you are after something else Jamie Fyvie, your heart is not in for this,' she said with finality.

Jamie knew there was no fooling this woman, but was not sure how to proceed. He thought her heart was in the right place, going to her aunt when she called her at the ball and accompanying her father home was a sign of responsibility, so he decided to tell her about the missing girls as he could not divulge he was working for the government to thwart a rebellious plot.

'Let's have some more wine Felicity,' said Jamie, suddenly feeling a kind of bond with this woman, who was in reality a very smart, worldly woman.

The carriage rolled on to where? Jamie did not know.

Felicity poured and handed the wine to Jamie. 'Tell me what ails you Jamie?'

'I have to get into the mansion where you are to have this... special party.'

'Why?'

'Did you know that at least six young girls, the ones that we know of, have gone missing from the Cape region

Prophets of Death

in a very short time?'

'I have heard the servants talking of it but are they not just runaways?'

'No, they're not. They're being kidnapped, tortured and raped before being murdered and the people who are perpetrating these horrific deeds could also be selling locals as slaves up north,' Jamie lied easily. *Most of it is true*. He thought.

'I can't believe what you are telling me,' said Felicity suddenly sitting upright and began to put her clothes on. 'We would have known about murders in the community. I have not even heard of any murmurings of such deeds and believe me my servant girls and I are quite chatty; I would have known of this. Have the police found any bodies?'

'No bodies have been found so far,' said Jamie wondering how much he should tell her.

'Then how can you know the girls are being murdered if there is no evidence of a body? My father is the chief justice, I'm not without knowledge of the law,' she said.

'Yes, I'm sure a clever brain such as yours would know the laws of the land,' said Jamie.

'And another thing, how are you involved in obvious police work?'

Jamie had dressed and was pulling on his boots, leaning back; he enjoyed a pull at the cheroot and refilled his goblet. 'I have to trust you to keep what I am about to tell you to yourself,' he paused.

'Tell me what's going on,' she said now agitated. 'If this is true it's monstrous and the perpetrators must be uncovered and hanged. Tell me.' She said impatiently.

'Not all the girls were killed, one of them escaped but when she was found she was almost at deaths door. When she was nursed back to good health by the good community of the Bo Kaap she couldn't remember a thing about her past.'

'Oh my God; the poor girl. She is Malay? A coloured girl?'

'Yes she is. For months she has been trying to remember what happened to her and then one day a man's face triggered her memory and she has started remember bit by bit of her past life.'

'Does she know her own name or where she comes from?'

'Felicity, I'm not at liberty to divulge too much because the policeman that came to me for help didn't trust his superiors or colleagues; he has only one officer helping him who he can trust. The reason I'm involved is a long story, suffice to say something happened at my business premises and a man who worked for me was killed by men working at the house where the party is to be held; they were followed to the house and then to my yard.'

'Why did they kill your man, did he know about them and the girls that were being kidnapped?'

'I have no idea, that's what I'm trying to find out,' said Jamie truthfully not understanding why.

'It doesn't make any sense,' said Felicity. 'If these unfortunate girls were being murdered over so long a time at this house and the previous owner is dead, then has the new owner taken over his mantle of party host and killer?'

'I really don't know,' Jamie said almost exasperated. 'That's why I need your help. I have to get into that house and search for the answers. I really… really need your help.'

'And you shall have it. I may be a slave to outrageous sex, or be what is called I believe, a nymphomaniac, but the senseless killing of these young women abhors me. You tell me what you need and where you need to see in

Prophets of Death

that house and I will make it happen.'

Jamie leaned forward and took Felicity's hands in his and said. 'Thank you, you are a good woman, Felicity, with your help I will get the people responsible for these atrocities. I trust what happened here today stays between me and you?'

'Of course it does, Jamie. As I mentioned in my note to you everything is kept secret. Also the young lady who has a keen interest in you will never know anything from me that I promise you on my life.'

'What! You know who…'

'Shush, Jamie, its fine, you do not have to worry. I'm now your best friend. You are a good man and I respect that.'

Jamie fell back on the plush leather, feeling much more relaxed.

He lifted his goblet and said. 'I'd like another wine.'

As the carriage kept its comfortable pace around the Cape Peninsula Felicity recharged his drink and he relit his cheroot.

They were now very comfortable with each other having found some common ground in trust and to do something that might alleviate their hidden secrets and desires.

'Felicity Wycliffe, you're an amazing woman and I'm so grateful that we've become friends, you're wise beyond your years.'

'I could say the same about you. I suspect there is more to this saga than you are telling me.'

He let the insinuation hang.

'Felicity, you can't make it known that you are even a remote friend of mine or even that the young lady you mentioned is interested in me or I in her.'

'But why, we are among the aristocracy of the Cape what could anybody possibly do to us?'

'Yes you are the *elite* and you're correct when you say there's more to this saga than I am telling you, simply because these people are ruthless. They care not of creed, nationality, position or what power you have or wield. Believe me when I tell you they will have no compunction in killing you and your whole family; they've done this in the past. You have to be discreet. I'll reveal the truth to you when this is over.'

Felicity extended her right hand and said. ''We will overcome these evil people; we will prevail.'

Jamie held her hand and said. 'I need to get back. What of the arrangements for Saturday?'

Felicity produced a wax sealed letter. 'Come up to Renton's house in an unknown carriage, which all the locals will know,' she laughed. 'Hand this invitation to the person at the gate; you'll be given entrance. You mustn't break the seal otherwise you'll be turned away.'

'You'll be there when I arrive?'

'Yes I'll make sure of it and I'll show you the way around and keep you away from the faggots who would devour you.'

'The faggots?'

'Oh you're so naïve; faggots are men who like sex with other men.'

'Jesus Christ, what am I getting into here?'

'Jamie, I'll guide you through this party at the house and hopefully you'll bring the villains to justice. You will see, at the end of this you will be with your adorable young admirer and I will be betrothed to a lord or a viscount who has the same nocturnal deviances as I have, without my father's knowledge of course, and we will happily live sexually ever after.'

The carriage stopped and Jamie stepped out to see he was back where he started.

He looked into the open carriage door and said

Prophets of Death

sincerely, 'You have to believe me when I tell you to be careful; these people will stop at nothing to get their prize. Promise me faithfully.'

'I promise you faithfully, Jamie and thank you,' said Felicity whole heartedly.

Jamie closed the door, mounted his horse and headed for home; feeling the end was in sight.

Chapter Twelve

August 1856

Eastern Cape Frontier

Rumours of the sighting of the old chiefs began to circulate around the country; a young seer had seen the great chief Tshawe in a vision. The great chief would return with a prophecy that would set the Xhosa people free.

Samkelo, the Paramount Chief, was in his grand hut with his great wife when he first heard the murmurings about the prophecy of Nonkululeko and was about to summon Misumzi when he was informed that Misumzi was asking for an audience with him.

'I see you, Inkosi Enkhulu,' said Misumzi, using the title of the paramount chief.

'What of these disturbing stories and rumours of the sighting of the old chiefs? When were these visions? Why was I not told of them?' asked Samkelo.

'It is not a rumour, Inkos. My niece the sangoma and seer has seen the great chief Tshawe in one of her visions. Some pakati did go to hear her; they did not think it worthy of your attention.'

'What did she see? What was the vision?'

'She saw the father of the Xhosa, Tshawe. In the vision he tells her to carry the message to the Xhosa people that our ancestors, the great chiefs, will assemble

Prophets of Death

and come to help us against the English and drive them away from our land,' said Misumzi.

Samkelo looked at him in disbelief and said. 'You are pakati, you are a leader of the Gcaleka, you are council to me, Paramount chief of the Xhosa nation, whatever comes from us will be believed by all who follow me.'

'It is true what she saw in her vision, Inkos.'

'You will take me to her,' ordered Samkelo.

At the flat rock where Nonkululeko had come to sit every day since her vision of the great chief, still under the influence of the potion, Misumzi left his chief and niece to sit alone and she told him of her vision and what was to be done, after which the chief returned to sit with his pakati by the fire in the small camp they had made close by.

'We must wait for the old chiefs to return,' he said to Misumzi as the others listened in silence. 'In her vision she saw Tshawe, one of the old chiefs, who said to await a sign when they will all return with a prophecy, only then will they tell us what we must do.' Samkelo said, looking very troubled.

Misumzi signalled to the women with them to bring beer and food to the men.

'This could be a divine prophecy, Inkos. We should talk with the other chiefs to be ready for the prophecy,' said Misumzi.

The other members of the pakati murmured their agreement in this wise council.

'When we return to the kraal you will arrange a meeting with the tribal chiefs and we will discuss these visions of Nonkululeko.'

Misumzi arranged for the chiefs to meet at a secret location as they did not want the attention of the white soldiers to give them an excuse to accuse them of some fictional transgressions and throw them in jail, as had been inflicted on some unfortunate natives in months gone by.

'How can we believe these so called visions,' said Kanelo of the Gqunukhwebe tribe, who was usually quiet and never got his people involved in any trouble with the English and certainly shied away from war. 'Why should we listen to the rantings of a young woman who has not even proved herself a seer or a sangoma?'

'Her visions and predictions have come to pass in previous occasions,' said Samkelo.

'She has said that she has seen the great Tshawe, the father of the nation, she has described his form and the way he looks, there was a blue crane feather found at the pool, these are all true of the legends,' said Misumzi, realising he had spoken out of turn, but had made the others think on this truth.

'Beware my brothers, of building a kraal on low lying land,' said Kanelo. 'For the sudden rush of water in the rainy season will wash away all before its deadly wave of destruction.'

'We will wait for the prophetess to tell us of her next vision if the ancestors return to lead us to our freedom or our destruction,' said Samkelo. 'Our land has been taken from us and we are surely lost. Let us pay homage to the old chiefs. Let us pray they return to free us.'

Everyone in the meeting wanted this with all their hearts and souls, but there were some who knew this was all a dream.

Prophets of Death

Chapter Thirteen

August 1856

Cape Town

Jamie, Iain and Bill Hutcheson were in a rented room at the back of the Thatch Inn with Sergeant O'Donnell and Officer Jalala; Doctor Morgan had been invited along as well.

Jamie gave them a detailed retelling of what had transpired in the last few days.

'I made contact with a lady called Felicity at the governor's ball,' said Jamie. 'I then met the contact to receive the invite and instructions on where the private party is to take place.'

'So, there is a substantial number of the aristocracy, who were at the ball, invited to that party?' asked Doctor Morgan.

'Yes there is doctor, aristocracy and prominent members of society. Felicity's name must be kept secret.' said Jamie.

'You do realise what's to be expected of you when you walk into the party.' It was a statement not a question from the doctor.

'You seem to know quite a lot about these parties doctor, have you been to one?' said Iain mischievously.

The doctor's face reddened and he squirmed in his chair. 'You can be very humorous Iain, I've never been to one but I've had first-hand accounts of what goes on at them from listening to loose tongues at the club.'

Iain looked at Bill Hutcheson and then back at Doctor Morgan. 'I think we need to get a membership for this club Jamie. It seems anything sordid that happens in the Cape is discussed at the club.'

'I believe there's a waiting list Iain. Can we get back to the point of this meeting?' said Bill.

'Yes, quite. Do you really think that people of high office are actually kidnapping, torturing and murdering young girls? It just seems so preposterous,' said the doctor.

'That's not the only reason we need to get into that house doctor, there's something else much more disturbing going to happen and we need to try and stop it,' said Jamie.

The doctor, O'Donnell and Ahmed were given all the information on the ELOS and the Knights treasure trail. They listened to the whole story with disbelief.

The doctor said. 'I didn't think there could be anything more disturbing than multiple murders of young girls, but if what you say is true, then this would be a calamity on an unprecedented scale.'

'That's why I need to get into the house to search for any clues as to how they use this potion to subdue, not only the kidnap victims, but hundreds of natives and get them into ships to slavery in America,' said Iain.

'Doctor, the potion we discovered on the ship has now been mentioned by the girl, Annatje, do you think it could be used to subdue whole tribes of Xhosa natives?' asked Jamie.

'Impossible,' said the doctor without hesitation. 'How would you get them to drink it, it stinks to the high heavens and the taste is disgusting. It would be an impossible task to pollute the drinking water or indeed the

Prophets of Death

rivers; I cannot see how they could do that.'

'The people will always follow their leaders, would you agree?' Asked Iain as an open question.

Everyone said yes.

'Most people would,' said Doctor Morgan.

'Then all the ELOS have to do is use the potion on the chiefs and their councillors or pakati or whatever you call them, they will then make the decisions for the people…'

'And the people will follow,' said O'Donnell.

'Then I must try and find out if there is an answer in that house otherwise we are staring at a blank wall,' said Jamie.

'And the only reason we're going into that house is the connection of the potion, which is linked to Annatje and the man, Williams, Ahmed and Brian followed to the house,' said Iain. 'Without these two policemen doing their detection work we would not even have this slender lead.'

'The party is on this Saturday coming,' said Jamie. 'Ahmed, will you drive my carriage to the mansion, you are, with all due respect, the right colour to be a driver?'

'I will, gladly Mr Fyvie,' said Ahmed.

'Jamie, please, call me Jamie.'

Ahmed nodded and sipped his tea.

Iain and Bill will be hiding in the coach, just in case. Once I'm in the house I'll be with the woman I made contact with and she'll cover for me when I start my search of the house. I'm presuming the party will be over by sunrise; only then will I summon the coach to take me home. Otherwise, if there's any commotion or shooting or general screaming and fighting, I expect you lot to be fighting each other to storm the wall to come and get me out,' said Jamie smiling.

'You smile now but you are taking a hell of a risk

going into the lair of the monster, as it were,' said the doctor.

'Don't worry doc, I like my body just the way it is, with no pieces missing.'

Jamie was in a pensive mood as the carriage rolled up the road to the mansion. Iain and Bill were sitting with him in the closed interior.

'Don't forget,' said Iain for the umpteenth time, 'don't take any chances just get what you need and get out.'

'Will you shut up for Christ's sake, I won't be able to get out until the carriages and coaches are allowed back in the morning. Ye're worse than an auld sweetie wife the way ye nag.'

'Aw shut up yourself,' said Iain nervously not liking his friend going in without him watching his back.

'Take this with you Jamie,' said Bill holding out the palm of his hand with a small pistol on it. 'It's called a Derringer, one shot only, but it might be enough.'

'I can't risk being caught with a gun at a party for goodness sake, if I have to take my clothes off, where will I hide it? Up my arse? Thanks; but no thanks, if there's any trouble I'll lift the nearest heavy object and belt somebody with it.'

Ahmed drove up to the mansion and as per Felicity's instructions, Jamie handed over his sealed invite to the masked person at the gate. He was handed a mask and told to put it on, then the carriage was waved through the gates and into the courtyard.

'Here we go lads,' said Jamie quietly.

Jamie stepped out of the coach, which was then directed around the courtyard and back out of the gates; He went through the front door of the house and into the reception hall, dimly lit by candles flickering on the walls.

Prophets of Death

A woman wearing what looked like a white nightdress exposing one of her breasts, gave him a flannel sheet, then pointing she said, 'Go through that door and disrobe, then wrap this around your naked body as the Greeks once did; keep the mask on at all times.'

He did as he was asked and then entered a large darkened room full of people. He could see them vaguely in the darkness with their sheets hanging in different ways showing off skin and flesh. Some with the sheet draped over their shoulders not caring what was showing whether skinny, fat, firm or saggy they just lay or sat around drinking and fondling each other.

Through the gloom he could see a woman was making her way toward him, her breasts protruding from the sheet tied around her waist.

He recognised those breasts. 'Hello,' he said.

'I'm flattered that you recognised my bosom,' said Felicity, putting her hand under his sheet and groping his private parts. 'We don't say much here until later when everybody starts to get drunk. Do not remove your mask until you're in a private room with someone you want to be with.'

She felt his arousal and started to masturbate him. She turned around and shamelessly used her free hand to put his hands on her breasts, which he did without much encouragement.

Using his penis as a lead she pulled him through the room to an alcove containing a couch with soft cushions.

They sat down and she kissed him deeply still massaging his raging erection. The mask was shaped to keep the mouth free to kiss or lick, drink, eat or suck anything one fancied.

'When do I get to start my search,' he whispered into her ear.

'We need to make this look right,' she whispered

back. 'So you might as well make the best of it, you have plenty of time as we'll be here all night. I have been looking forward to seeing you, I must confess.'

She pulled his sheet back and looked at his erection as she slowly moved her hand up and down.

He was looking around the room in the dim light and could see a man standing at a table thrusting in and out of a female who was lying on her back on the table, her ankles resting on his shoulders, her head was turned to the side to accommodate another man in her mouth.

Another couple were on the floor giving each other oral sex at the same time, her on top facing the opposite way from him.

In another part of the room he could see an older woman, her huge, pendulous breasts hanging almost to her waist, sucking greedily on a much younger man's penis.

Jamie felt a warmth on his and looked down to see Felicity's head moving up and down on him. He reached around and slid his hand between her legs and felt her wet sex and started to massage her.

Felicity lifted her head up and straddled her legs over Jamie's and lowered herself down on him, she sighed as he filled her passion right up to the hilt once again.

'Lift me up and carry me down the corridor to the right of the bookcase… with me still impaled on you,' she whispered in his ear.

He slid his arms under her thighs holding her buttocks with his hands, her legs gripping around the waist as he stood up, taking her weight easily as he proceeded down the corridor she had indicated.

'Where do we go?' he asked her.

'Anywhere you like as long as I'm still where I am,' she smiled back cheekily.

'Felicity, this is serious, I can't lose focus of why I

Prophets of Death

am here tonight.'

'I am hurt, you're not here for my body, Jamie Fyvie? You're not here for the wonderful sex with me?'

He stopped and she tightened her legs around him.

'In there,' she said nodding at a doorway off to his right.

He entered the room and immediately went to a wall at the side of a window, lifting Felicity up slightly he put her back against the wall and, wanting to finish this, started to pump her slowly against the wall, gradually getting faster and harder. Every now and then he would thrust deep inside her grinding his pelvic bone up and down on her clitoris, until at last he felt her start her orgasm and really pounded her until she let out her guttural moan. 'Harder… harder… fuck me harder,' she said with difficulty.

And he did, until she shuddered and came over him, releasing her warm fluid which triggered his orgasm and they both came together.

He carried her over to a divan to lay her down. 'Don't you dare come out of me yet, it feels so good,' she said dreamily.

He sat until his erection receded, their bellies, groin and thighs wet and the smell of sex all around them; it was intoxicating.

Their breathing came back to normal; eventually Felicity went to fetch drinks whilst Jamie lit two cheroots. They lay beside each other, she said. 'The reason I came in this room, and I did, did I not? Is because there's a door over there.'

She sat up and pointed to the corner of the room where the outside wall was. 'That door leads to the kitchens and to the corridor that leads to the cellars.'

'Cellars, you mean there is more than one?' asked Jamie.

'From what I remember from a conversation I had with someone in the past, there's a huge cellar with more than one room; that's all I know.'

'What about other buildings and outhouses?'

'There's another much smaller house and servant's quarters, stables and a barn of some sorts. The whole property is walled in, the only way in or out is the main gate.'

'I'm going to have a quick look around; I promise I won't be long.'

Jamie went through the door into a short corridor leading to a stairway, going down to another door to the kitchen.

Someone was moving around so he waited until they left. He went through the kitchen to the outside door leading to the court yard behind the house. Going across the yard to the guest house he looked in the window, but could see nothing, he tried the door and to his surprise it was unlocked.

Chapter Fourteen

August 1856

Cape Town

Renton had used Felicity Wycliffe to lure Jamie into his trap to sow the seed of his revenge against the man he blamed for his near death, the disfigurement of his face and the contortion of his body; but what really rankled him was the fact that Jamie Fyvie had outwitted him and out manoeuvred him.

That all changed when he instructed Samuel to watch for Fyvie arriving at the house and wait for him to meet with Felicity.

Samuel was covered with a sheet and full head mask and watched them from the dark shadows of the house while they fornicated and then followed them to see them enter one of the other rooms at the back of the house.

That was when he poured the potion into the wine decanter and retreated to the shadows to watch Felicity eventually come out to re-fill their glasses.

When she returned to the room, Samuel replaced the tainted wine and then went to the kitchen through the dining room to return to his quarters, but when he went to the kitchen door he saw Fyvie disappearing through the guest house door and so dashed silently into an outbuilding.

This white man is too nosey by far, thought Samuel.

When Jamie went into the guest house he could smell something he had smelled before. Moving through the house very quietly he came upon the kitchen and could see bowls of dark liquid sitting on tables and what looked like roots, leaves and powdered herbs laying around.

This is where they make that awful concoction, he thought. *That's what the smell is.*

He decided he had seen enough and left, going back the way he came, but first he went to the side of the house and could see a pathway going down a gradient to a huge door in the base of the building. *And there is the way into the cellar,* he thought.

He made his way back to where he had left Felicity; she was sitting waiting for him to return. He took the proffered cheroot from Felicity and sucked deeply on it and drank deeply from his wine glass and told her what he had found at the back of the house.

'Do you really think those young girls were murdered here, Jamie.'

'I'm really not sure yet, I must wait for a while longer before I search for the way into the cellar from inside the house.'

He thought about the cellar and went to get up for another drink and found it difficult to stand up, his eyes started to lose focus when he looked from one point to another. He managed to look at Felicity; she wasn't moving, her cheroot had fallen on the floor and the wine glass had fallen out of her hand.

He tried to say her name but his mouth would not work in conjunction with the commands from his brain. *The wine, Felicity, where did you get the wine,* he was screaming inside his head. *They have poisoned the wine with that fucking potion. You idiot Jamie.* He thought as he tried to get up but slid to the floor, helpless and at the

Prophets of Death

mercy of whom?

Remarkably his brain was still aware; he could hear a door opening. The world went black as something was pulled over his head, he felt himself fall away for a long time, his body seemed to tingle with a sickening sensation and then everything went away.

Samuel watched as Jamie quietly closed the door to his quarters and go back to the house, he waited for fifteen minutes then went to the room where Jamie and Felicity were by now lying unconscious; he had made a special potion to render them both unconscious.

He locked the door leading into the house then pulled a loose satin bag over Jamie's head. Using his great strength he wrestled Jamie's limp body through the back door and down to the cellar where he locked him in one of the rooms. He then went back up to the house and laid Felicity on the couch still unconscious and replaced the wine glasses, unlocked the door to the house and went back to the cellar.

The other people upstairs were none the wiser of what had just happened but then they did not care as they were totally engrossed in their own sordid sexual fantasies.

Samuel stood looking at the table with the straps wondering to himself what kind of sick games Renton played down here.

'You are wondering what the table is used for?' said a rasping voice from behind him.

Samuel turned to see Renton standing in the doorway that led from the wine cellar.

'I did not here you come in sir.'

'You were not supposed to,' said Renton.

'Do you wish me to kill this man now?' asked Samuel.

'No, you will not kill him you will keep him in this state until I tell you otherwise.'

Renton hobbled over to where Jamie was imprisoned and said, 'open it.'

Renton looked in on the inert body on the floor, feeling the desire to torture his nemeses and then kill him slowly, but he fought it down knowing what he had in mind would destroy him in the eyes of his peers; then he would kill him when he was at his lowest ebb.

'Leave him for tonight, we will come back tomorrow and seal his demise. Make sure no-one gets into the grounds to try and find him when the sun rises.'

Jamie was kept sedated all through the next day, Samuel explaining to the carriage driver who came to fetch him that Jamie was *still busy and did not want to be disturbed.* Ahmed drove away and reported this to Iain.

When night came, Samuel dragged Jamie out of the cellar and put him in one of the carriages then transported him to a rented house in Wynberg. There he was stripped of his clothes and put into a large, brass framed bed. His clothes were folded neatly and placed on a chair behind a dressing screen in the bedroom, taking care to leave his boots in plain sight. Samuel went back to the coach and left.

When he opened his eyes the following morning, Jamie immediately remembered what had happened when he was with Felicity and he knew he was, at this moment in time, somewhere he was not supposed to be.

He sat up in a bed in a bedroom he did not recognise. He could hear voices outside, people talking animatedly, horses and wagons or carts moving on a roadway nearby. He went to stand up but immediately felt dizzy so sat back down again and closed his eyes.

He tried to gather his thoughts about what happened

Prophets of Death

after Felicity and he were at the party.

The drinks Felicity brought back to the room they were in must have been laced with that fucking potion, he thought. *Felicity has led me into a trap; no! She was unconscious when I started to feel the effects of the drug.*

He rubbed his face with his hands and tried to remember what had happened after that but could not remember anything.

Where is Felicity now? I must get up and look for her, he thought looking around for his clothes.

He saw his boots in front of a dressing screen, found his clothes behind it and hurriedly dressed. Looking around the room he could see it was definitely a woman's bedroom. He looked through the window into a well laid out garden but couldn't see anyone. In front of the window there was a dressing table with a small stool in the centre space underneath, the top surface covered with an assortment of brushes, combs and scents. The big centre mirror was slightly tilted downwards on its swivels on either side and the wing mirrors on the left and right were angled in to give an all-round reflection to the person sitting directly in front.

There was a large wardrobe against the back wall crammed with all kinds of dresses, hat boxes stacked on top, this woman liked to look good.

He opened the bedroom door and looked into a small hallway and listened for any movement, but nothing and nobody stirred, it sounded as though he was alone.

He looked into the other rooms and sitting room... no-one. He went through the kitchen and looked out of the door to the back yard, seeing nobody around he went out and looked up at Table Mountain above Wynberg.

Christ, I'm not far from home, whose bleddy house is this? He said to himself.

He crossed the yard to the stable and saddled up one

of the horses, deciding to get the hell out of there. He would send the horse back later.

The week before the party, Renton, had met with Godfrey Butler on the pretext that he needed a good solicitor for his business dealings and that Godfrey's reputation in the colony as a diligent, fair and honest man was beyond reproach.

Godfrey was a bit reluctant to have dealings with Anne Knowles' employer but after receiving assurances from Renton that this was strictly a business deal between them and had nothing to do with Anne Knowles and after discussing the matter with his wife, Godfrey agreed to represent Renton.

After they had concluded their business Renton had invited Godfrey and Sarah Butler along with Lydia and Clara to take them to lunch with Banbury and another colleague and his wife on the following Monday to one of his favourite restaurants in the city and their carriages were now, conveniently, passing by a rented house in Wynberg.

Jamie mounted and walked the horse along the narrow track at the side of the house towards the main road. As he was about to spur the horse on, a woman's voice spoke out from the garden.

'Goodbye, see you in the week Jamie,' she shouted.

Jamie reined in the horse and turned to see Anne Knowles standing there smiling and waving.

'Remember me in future when I destroy your life as you have destroyed my life,' she spat with venom still smiling and waving.

'What the hell are you doing you witch?' shouted Jamie as he trotted the horse down to the road.

It was then he heard the carriages coming along the

Prophets of Death

road, he turned to see three of them passing by the front of Knowles' house.

The first carriage was Renton's closed-in black coach, the huge black servant driving the horses. In the second carriage Godfrey and Sarah Butler, along with Lydia and Clara, looked at Jamie with a mixture of utter dismay and disgust on their faces. Bringing up the rear in the third carriage was Nicholas Banbury and another couple he did not recognise, all, apart from Renton, were glaring at him.

'That's Jamie,' cried Lydia. She could not believe her eyes as she saw him with his clothes in disarray sitting on the horse looking at her; she almost fainted with the shock of seeing him outside her stepmother's house.

'What on earth is he doing there?' Sarah Butler asked.

'I don't want to know and neither do I care,' said Godfrey.

'It's very obvious what he is doing there Aunt Sarah,' said Lydia trying to hold back the tears but could not and she broke down with a heart wrenching sob. She drew her legs up and curled into a ball on the seat with Clara's arms around her trying to comfort her.

'Oh Lydia I'm so sorry,' said Clara. 'How could he do such a thing to you,' she said cuddling her sister.

'Driver!' shouted Godfrey. 'Take us home.'

The driver turned the carriage and stopped at Banbury's halted coach.

'Please give Nigel my apologies, Lydia has taken ill so we must return home,' said Godfrey and told the driver to carry on.

Jamie went after them but then pulled up his horse knowing that it would be a futile exercise to explain his being there. He couldn't explain anything without giving away the whole plan and who he was working for.

He watched the carriages disappear from sight then turned to confront Anne Knowles, but she had gone; there were people looking at him and there was other traffic on the road so he decided to head for home.

Banbury had seen Jamie as well and had his driver pull up next to Renton's coach which he boarded.

'Did you see what happened back there?' he said to Renton.

'See what Nicholas? I can see nothing whilst sitting in this thing.'

'Fyvie just left Anne Knowles' house; do you know anything about it?'

'How would I know anything about it?'

'Butler sends his apologies, he and his family have turned and gone back home.'

'Oh, nothing serious I hope?'

'One of the girls has fallen ill,' said Banbury, 'but let's carry on for lunch, I'm starved.' Banbury went back to his coach and they set off to the city.

It wasn't Nigel Renton, but James Storer who was sitting grinning as best he could with his deformed mouth feeling very pleased with himself.

When Jamie rode up to his house, Iain came running out to meet him closely followed by Hutchison. Dr Morgan, Brian and Ahmed were standing on the stoop.

'Where the fuck have you been? I've been worried sick about you,' shouted Iain.

Jamie dismounted and said. 'Get some food and some whisky; there's lot's to tell you.'

Jamie told them everything that had happened from the time he went into Renton's house and passed out and when he awakened in Anne Knowles house.

Iain said, 'The only good thing that may have come out of this may be the fact that the girls are out of the

Prophets of Death

picture now in case our enemies use them against us.'

'So we know this bloody potion is being made at the house which means Renton and Banbury are up to their ears in this conspiracy,' said Hutchison.

'And that there is a cellar to be searched,' said O'Donnell.

'We didn't know what to do when you didn't come out in the morning,' said Iain. 'You've been missing for a day Jamie.'

'What? What do you mean? What day is it?'

'It's Monday, you have been missing for a whole day. We were sitting here making plans to get Brian and the police force to storm the house.'

'Thank god you didn't, but what has been going on for a whole day, I don't understand and I do not remember anything until this morning.'

'Are you sure you cannot remember how you got to Anne Knowles house?' asked O'Donnell.

'I swear Brian, if I did I would tell you; everything else is so clear yet I have no recollection of the past twenty four hours. Felicity! My contact in the house,' exclaimed Jamie. 'Have you seen or heard from Felicity Wycliffe?'

'No, we were waiting to see if you were going to turn up first, dead or alive,' said Iain.

'Bill. You must use your position of authority to, discreetly, find out if Felicity is at home or is missing,' Jamie said almost pleading. 'She took a huge risk helping us so we must ensure her and her family's safety. Sergeant, you and Ahmed will need to keep surveillance on Renton's house at all times to watch who is going in and out.'

'You do not think they would go after the Chief Justice of the colony do you?' said Doctor Morgan.

'Doctor, these people are capable of anything; when

are you going to get this into your head,' said Jamie exasperated. 'Find Felicity and let us see where we go from there. What a fucking mess.'

Chapter Fifteen

September 1856

Cape Town

In the days after arriving back in Cape Town, Fairbairn reflected on the actions of Samuel and Williams at the Xhara pool with the young seer and had decided that although there was something substantial about to happen on the frontier he would keep his distance, do what was asked of him, then when the opportunity arose, he would take a buggy full of gold, precious gems or money and run. He would bide his time.

He received reports from his informants that the Flying Fish was due for departure to Knysna port with four passengers as well as cargo. Two of the passengers were listed as Jamie Fyvie and Iain McColl; the other two were business men so they were of no concern to Fairbairn.

He reported to his office at the government buildings, part of his duties being, to liaise with Nicholas Banbury on matters of official government business. In truth he was reporting on the expedition to the Eastern Cape to meet Misumzi and the unfortunate run-in with the British troops.

'You'll come up to Arend se Kop at midnight two nights from now, I'll send a coach for you and we will go through the whole venture with elder Renton. Our plans are moving up a pace, it is important that our communication is more frequent,' said Banbury.

'I'll see you then elder.'

Fairbairn went back to his lodgings and started drinking brandy. He was full of confidence that he had the elders where he wanted them and he knew when the next clue was to be found in Knysna. He would be in control and he would sail away from here with a fortune in gold to live in the luxury he deserved.

But now he needed a woman to satisfy his lust and his hunger for brutality. He would take it out on the whores he was about to encounter. He bathed and dressed then went in search of a victim.

The victim was brutalised, sodomised and beaten to death by the drunken Fairbairn.

He could not control his anger towards the people he hated; Fyvie and McColl who had killed his brother: but it was mostly his loathing towards himself and his inadequacy to achieve anything worthwhile in his life. He was just a pawn in the game of the ELOS from which he would never be free unless he had the means to get out, get away and disappear.

When he eventually woke up from his drunken stupor he saw the body of the young Hottentot whore was where he left it, bent over the arm of the easy chair in front of him, her battered head in the seat, her anus and vagina in plain view. Through the haze of the alcohol and his hangover he realised he had a very painful and hard erection which he decided to get rid of in the dead body.

'I think I am going mad,' he said and started laughing. 'I am going mad.'

When he finished he passed out on his bed and slept until it was dark, he had to get rid of the body tonight. He washed and dressed once more and went out to find a couple of his men whom he paid handsomely to bring a

Prophets of Death

wagon with a large wooden box to his lodgings to put the body in, take it out of town and dump it in the veldt.

That night he boarded the coach Banbury had sent for him and he was now on his way to the meeting at Arend se Kop.

It was clear when he sat down in front of Renton and Banbury that he was not in good favour with them. He told them what had happened with Misumzi and Nonkululeko and the shoot-out with the British patrol. Banbury and Renton had been badgering him with questions for half an hour now and he was monumentally fed up with it.

'Are you sure you cannot be linked to the deaths of the soldiers? Did you leave the area under cover of darkness?' asked Renton in his raspy voice.

Fairbairn could contain himself no longer and he lost his temper.

'I am not a fucking idiot,' he shouted as he stood up; he wanted to kill these two fools.

Just then Samuel appeared from nowhere, the huge scimitar in his hand.

'I think you forget to whom you speak, Fairbairn.' It was Renton's turn to shout.

'Sit down Fairbairn,' shouted Banbury, just as loud.

Fairbairn looked at Banbury and Renton and then at Samuel who looked like he wanted the tiniest of excuses to slice his head off. Fairbairn knew he had crossed the boundary; no-one talked to an elder the way had just done.

He gathered his composure and slowly sitting down, said. 'I do apologise elder, I don't know what came over me. The last few days have been rather… um… strenuous to say the least.'

'Strenuous you say? Are you saying that you are not up to the task?' said Banbury.

'Yes sir, I am, that is to say I'm most definitely up to the task elder.'

'What of Fyvie and McColl?' asked Renton.

'They'll be sailing within the next three to four weeks; I'll be riding for the Eastern Cape with my men tomorrow to take up position in order to follow them to the so called hidden treasure.'

'You don't seem to be convinced there is a treasure to be found when it's clear that there must be something of value buried; otherwise why would they go to all the trouble to chase down these clues?'

'I'll believe it when I see it elder.'

'You had better bring back whatever is there, we need the wealth of that treasure to fund our operations here. I am about to execute the biggest upheaval in British history Fairbairn, and you'll be part of it. You'll be rewarded very handsomely when you come through for us.'

'Elder, I have already made clear my devotion and my commitment to the ELOS and that will never waiver,' said Fairbairn lying easily.

'See that your commitment stays strong. Send a report from Knysna as soon as possible. That will be all.'

Dismissed, Fairbairn boarded the coach and went back to his lodgings; it was all he could do to keep his anger in check. *Patience… patience… patience, you nearly ruined everything because of your temper,* he chided himself. *I'm losing my mind.*

The next day he hand-picked ten of the best men he could find from the usual psychopathic cut-throats he had the choice of and made sure they were kitted out for a long expedition as he did not know how long they would be gone. They had five pack horses, loaded with extra ammunition.

He sent out word to find a man who had been brought

Prophets of Death

to his attention by a couple of enlisted soldiers he had tried to recruit. His name was Davie Flint and he had been the best marksman in his regiment before being court-marshalled for insubordination and striking an officer.

Flint had been seen in a tavern close to the docks where Fairbairn found him. He bought two ales and sat down at Flint's table, pushing the ale across the table to him.

Flint looked up with surprisingly clear brown eyes; his face was unshaven, his fair hair short and neat. His skin was tanned and healthy looking, a smallish man with a controlled look about himself.

'And why would you be buying me beer; I've never met you before,' he said in a very good English accent.

'My name is Robert Fairbairn. I hear you have special skills and that you're for hire.'

'Fairbairn!' repeated Flint. 'Fairbairn's Volunteers I presume?'

'That would be me and you would be Davie Flint the best shot in the British army before your court-marshal.'

'The army was my life. I made one stupid mistake and now I shoot rogue lions and hyenas for a living and the odd elephant hunt. Your volunteers are a blood thirsty lot from what I read and hear; no prisoners eh? Well I'm not for hire to shoot people no matter what colour they are. I shot at the enemy for the army, I don't shoot human beings outside of that discipline.'

'That's very noble of you Davie but would you like to have enough money to buy yourself a new wardrobe of clothes and book a first class berth in a ship back to Blighty?'

'As I just said, I don't shoot people for money; I presume that's why you're here and I don't want to go back to England, I want to sail for the Americas where a man with my talent can make a good living as a sharpshooter.'

'All I ask you to do is listen to my proposition and then make your decision, is that fair enough?' asked Fairbairn ordering two more drinks.

'Fair enough, let me hear your proposal.'

'I'm about to embark on a secret mission to thwart a potential rebellion against the government by certain well known businessmen intent on taking over the Cape Government by making an accord with the Xhosa chiefs,' the lies coming easily. 'All I want you to do is cover us from enemy fire when we encounter these rebels, you do not need to be in the thick of it, just make sure you pick off the sharpshooters of the opposition and I will pay you in gold; enough to set you up in America with your own business.'

'So this mission will not be recognised by the authorities and if it goes wrong it'll be the hangman's noose?' said Flint. 'Besides I don't have a rifle for a job like this.'

'Believe me that will not happen. We'll be looked after if anything should go wrong and I have managed to acquire a specially adapted Enfield marksman's rifle with a modified flip-up blade sight.'

Flint looked up from his ale and said. 'You have the latest Enfield for a marksman?'

'Yes I do, and in a few weeks after the job is finished you can keep the rifle as well as the gold. Davie, this will be easy for you and you can be away to a new life in America.'

Flint knew in his heart he did not want any part of Fairbairn but it was too good a chance to pass up and a brand new Enfield rifle, he really wanted to hold that.

'Where do I meet up with you and when do we leave,' said Flint.

Chapter Sixteen

September 1856

Cape Town

Jamie was beside himself about Lydia. He wanted to go to her and tell her he had not slept with her step mother, well, not in Cape Town at least, but knew he could not and it was better this way, having her out of the picture. He tried to speak in private with Godfrey Butler but he would not see him.

Eventually the four under cover field policemen met again at the Thatch Inn.

'Felicity, it seems was at home and she's fine but is away with her father to Durban in Port Natal to visit old friends,' said Hutcheson.

'That's very convenient,' said Iain. 'Do you think she's been warned off?'

'It would be very likely the ELOS have threatened Sir Robert and he's gone to protect his only child.'

'Gentlemen,' said Jamie. 'Is it just me or was I deliberately made to be seen leaving Anne Knowles' house?'

'Who would want to show you up as a philanderer with a woman who has a bad name?' asked Iain.

'I wish I knew; it does not make any sense.'

The doctor said. 'Maybe Felicity wanted you all to herself and decided to let Lydia see you with another woman.'

'No. Felicity is not a possessive or jealous woman; she just likes to have her fun and carry on with life. It makes me wonder who tried to burn down our business premises and now this; someone is trying to turn people against me or in fact both Iain and me. It seems as though someone's out to destroy our character or at the least besmirch our name.'

'Anne Knowles would have reason to have her revenge on you both. Considering what happened on the Flying Fish and then her arrest for murder,' said Hutcheson.

'She has neither the influence nor the resources to carry out a vendetta against anyone,' said Jamie.

'It must be the ELOS, they have taken a bit of a blow in their plans and are keeping a low profile until they get some more people in place. But then again; why would they, they have bigger things to accomplish than petty vengefulness,' said Iain.

'We'll find out soon enough who's behind this vendetta,' said Jamie looking at the doctor. 'Doctor, what I'm about to ask you to do for me I will say in front of all of us. I have thought long and hard about Lydia, Clara and the Butlers.' Jamie got up and paced the room. 'I would ask you, doctor, to make an appointment to meet with Godfrey in your rooms where you have your surgery, so that Iain and I can corner him and tell him what's going on. I want to take him into our confidence and give him some background as to who we are really working for and what is at stake. Yes, it's also to tell him that I am not the man he thinks I am. Once I tell him, I will swear him to silence until this sorry business is all over.'

'Do you think it is wise to involve him Jamie,' said Hutcheson.

Prophets of Death

'Yes I do, we can trust him. I need to tell him for my own peace of mind or I'll go mad. Will you help me doctor? He would believe your word if you confirm everything I would tell him.'

'Of course I will, Jamie. I will have a message sent to him tonight for an emergency meeting tomorrow.'

'Thank you doctor, it means a lot to me.'

'I know it does my boy, I know it does.'

Godfrey arrived at Doctor Morgan's surgery at the appointed time and was shown into his consulting room whereupon the Doctor came through from an adjoining room.

'Hello, Godfrey, thank you for coming at such short notice.'

'Well I must say I am a bit bewildered as to why you would want to see me in such a hurry. Is there a legal matter you need help with?'

'No, not really, I just need you to talk with two very decent and brave fellows.'

The Doctor went over and opened the door and let in Jamie and Iain.

Godfrey jumped from his chair and said. 'What is the meaning of this sir, I do not want to be in the same building never mind the same room as this blackguard,' he said pointing at Jamie.

'Godfrey, if you will just let me…' Jamie started to say.

'I do not want hear anything from you after what you have done to that poor girl, after all that she has been through. I am leaving.'

He turned to leave but found his way barred by Doctor Morgan standing with his hands clasped behind his back.

'Godfrey Butler, I am a doctor and a surgeon, I am

also an officer of her Majesty's Secret Field Police as are these two,' said the doctor in a stern voice indicating Jamie and Iain with his chin. 'There is something that you need to know about these lads and why they are putting their necks on the block for this colony. Now let us all sit down and you will be told all.'

Godfrey looked at the three men and nodded, he said. 'Since you feel so strongly about this Derek, I will listen.'

They all sat down and he was told the whole story of why Jamie was caught in the position he was seen in.

'So you see Godfrey,' said Iain. 'Jamie had been drugged by the same potion as was used to drug George Knowles and then transported somehow to Anne's house so that you and the girls were meant to see him leaving there; it was all timed to the second.'

'I find all of this hard to believe, if it were not for the fact the good doctor here has confirmed this story of sedition and murder, I would have called the both of you liars,' said Godfrey.

'I know it's a lot to take in Godfrey but I swear I did not sleep with that woman in that house; I was duped,' Jamie said. 'I needed to tell you so that you would not think badly of me but you cannot tell anyone what we have just told you.'

'But Sarah and the girls need to know that you are innocent Jamie.'

'No. I know you share everything with Sarah but you would only put their lives in danger if the ELOS found out that you know about this plot against the colony they would use the girls against you, against us. You have to stay quiet until it is all over.'

'Well, of course I will not breathe a word of this, after all it is client confidentiality, is it not?'

'It is indeed Godfrey,' said the Doctor.

'So you are all in the Secret Field Police; I have never

Prophets of Death

heard of that. Who is the head of this department?' asked Godfrey.

The others sat and looked at him.

'That was a stupid question,' said Godfrey.'

'Thank you for coming here Godfrey, I want to tell Lydia what happened but I can't say anything to her for now as you must not, but try and quell the flames a bit as far as I am concerned, without giving anything away,' said Jamie.

'Lads, I'm sorry for doubting the both of you but it did look very convincing. Leave it with me and we will just have to see what the future unfolds for us. I'll also have a word with Captain Willard, he's a good fellow and he hasn't forgotten the fact that you saved his life and his ship, leave it with me.'

'We must leave without being seen,' said Jamie. 'I look forward to the day I can knock on your front door again Godfrey.'

The boys said their goodbyes and left through the rear entrance.

'May God watch over them,' said Godfrey sadly.

Chapter Seventeen

September 1856

Knysna

The Flying Fish was looking very ship-shape. The captain had had the ship taken out of the water and given her annual inspection after which a lot of work was done to restore her to the sea worthiness expected by Roger Willard.

Jamie and Iain had been given separate cabins on the starboard side nearest to the saloon then went up on deck to talk with Captain Willard.

'Godfrey has had a word with me about some hush-hush business that you lads are involved in but he could not divulge any details, would you care to enlighten me?' asked Willard.

'Sorry Roger, the less you know the better,' said Iain. 'I promise you, you don't want to get involved.'

'Fair enough, I respect your word and I'll ask no more questions. The whole town is talking under their breath about you being seen with the Knowles woman Jamie; gossip is rife here and I would pay it no heed.'

Jamie said. 'That incident will also be cleared up in due course and I promise you one thing Roger, you will be told the whole story once it's all over, and we may call on you for assistance.'

'I'll do anything I can to assist you; my ship is yours,

Prophets of Death

that goes without question.'

'Thanks, I knew we could count on you.'

As they chatted the crew were bringing on some last minute provisions and the boys' trunks in which their weapons were stored.

They watched as the Captain went about his business and welcomed two other passengers on-board.

'Is that not the Scots lad we were speaking to at the Ball?' asked Iain.

'It certainly is,' said Jamie. 'He's the one that said *I'll be watching out for you boys.*'

'Aye, that's right, I remember you thinking it was a bit odd.'

They saw Captain Willard pointing towards them and the two new passengers made their way across the deck to them whilst their luggage was stowed below.

Jamie took a step forward and extended his hand and said, 'We meet again gentlemen. You did say you were to be our traveling companions.'

'Indeed I did Mr Fyvie, Mr McColl.'

'It's Jamie and Iain but I'm afraid I don't recall your name.'

'I am Rory McGregor and this is Hamish McFarland. Hamish lives here at the Cape, I am visiting from Scotland and as I said, hunting around to see if there is any business to be made here.'

A North West wind was blowing in some drizzly rain as the crew started the process of casting off and unfurling some sail to get them underway.

Iain said. 'Well I'm in the mood for a sail up the coast, why don't we talk after you two get settled; we'll meet you in the saloon for a wee dram.'

'That sounds grand,' said Rory. 'We'll see you there.'

The Flying Fish left Table Bay and headed south,

sailing around Cape Point then east past False Bay and Cape Agulhas where the Atlantic Ocean becomes the Indian Ocean.

'It feels like home from home,' said Jamie as he poured drinks for himself and Iain and settled in a chair in the familiar saloon.

Rory and Hamish joined them and Jamie poured whisky for them as well.

'Well this is a sight more comfortable than that bucket I sailed in coming over from Scotland,' said Rory.

'Roger is a stickler for running things in a professional manner and making sure the passengers are comfortable,' said Jamie.

The four men drank good whisky and talked about Scotland and what had changed in all the time that Jamie and Iain had been in South Africa. They then dressed and dined with the Captain after which they retired to the passengers' saloon for a nightcap.

'So are you going to be investing in sheep farming Rory? I hear there is money to be made up in Port Natal in sugar cane, near a place called Durban,' said Iain.

Rory stood up and poured himself another stiff whisky, unhooked the saloon door and closed it, turning to the boys he said, 'This man here is my brother,' pointing at Hamish.

'A brother with a different surname?' said Jamie.

'Yes Jamie, my brother in the brotherhood of the Freemasons,' said Rory. 'I'm afraid I have deceived you, but for good reason. It's time to tell you why I'm really here and it's not to invest any money. I'm here to take home some things that have been lost for a long time; some things that you and Iain are looking for.'

Jamie and Iain looked at Rory and Hamish for a long time.

'I've heard of the Masons. How would you know

Prophets of Death

what we're looking for?' said Jamie the tension in the saloon suddenly rising.

Iain reached his hand into his jacket and put his hand around the handle of his knife. 'What the fuck is going on here?'

Rory put his hand up, palm out and said. 'Easy lads we are not your enemy; we are and have been your friends for quite a long while.'

'Our friends? We don't even know you,' said Jamie.

'I realise that but we have been watching you since you were in Liverpool. Remember the two thugs shot in the street in the rain and the shots fired on the mountain when you retrieved the clue from the Elephant's Eye?'

'What! You killed those thugs and scared off Fairbairn's men on the mountain?' said Iain in disbelief. 'I think you had better start explaining yourself Mr McGregor.'

'Boys, I promise you we're here to help you. Let's refill our glasses and I will fill you in on what my mission is.'

They charged the drinks and Iain said, 'Right Rory, let's be having your story.'

'Like you, I am with a secret organisation, but I am at the head of an investigative section of the Freemasons created by the Grand Master and past masters of the Scottish constitution of Freemasons, masters who have the Knights Templar degree. What we do is try to track down the ancient artefacts of the Knights Templar and take them to a safe haven to be preserved. We were aware of the clues to the lost treasure of the Knights Templar, the forerunners of the masons, but the old man who had made us aware of the clue died unexpectedly before we could retrieve the information from him. Before we could search the house the Secret Field Police had moved in and removed all the paperwork. So we had a team of brethren follow the only lead we had, which was the Secret Field Police and then we discovered you two had been given the task of recovering the treasure and I think it does exist.'

'How do we know you're not the ELOS, here to take the clue to the treasure after Fairbairn's stupid attempt?'

'Why would we expose ourselves to you if we were the ELOS?' Fairbairn is a greedy idiot, in fact he'll be in Knysna when we get there, closely followed and watched by some brother masons. I don't think he is reporting to his masters truthfully, but he will be eliminated if he poses a problem.'

'You say he's greedy; what about you masons being greedy; wanting the treasure for yourself?' said Jamie.

'Please don't misunderstand our intentions. Yes we want the treasure back but it's mainly because there are ancient artefacts and scrolls, which could destroy the Christian Faith or even start religious wars. The treasure's worth is immeasurable and you have got a job to do keeping the ELOS from getting their hands on it. We would stop them as well but our mission is to stop them discovering the artefacts and using them to start world changing wars that would enhance their goal of the domination of sovereign countries. Our main task is recovering the artefacts and of course the treasure and take them to a place of safe keeping; we don't do this for any reward, we do it for the benefit of mankind.'

'That's all very admirable, but if or when we find the treasure we have to hand it over to the British government. We are bound by our contract to the field police,' said Jamie.

Rory leaned forward and said earnestly, 'We have brethren in the government at Whitehall as well as here in the Cape; we know that all levels of government have been infiltrated by the ELOS. By giving the treasure to

Prophets of Death

the government you will be handing it to the enemy on a silver platter.'

'I must confess, I hadn't considered that view,' said Jamie.

'If we do find it how will you get it out?' asked Iain.

'We have the resources to arrange for transport to the coast; it won't be easy but we will do it. Ships from the coast will not be a problem; one large ship should do it.'

Jamie looked at Iain and said. 'You know, since we started this mission there have been a few twists and turns. Your story is so correct in detail that I have to believe you and if my partner is agreeable I would be grateful for any reliable help at this stage. What do you think Iain, do we really need to take a chance on handing that kind of wealth over to corrupt government officials?'

'It doesn't bare thinking about. If we could have the help of the masons to find this hoard of relics...' Iain turned to Rory, 'Are there only two or three of you or are there more?'

Hamish said. 'As we speak, Arthur Burton is heading for Knysna with a substantial amount of men and equipment to take on Fairbairn and his crew and much more.'

'So, with your help we find the treasure and let the masons spirit the lot away to safety?' said Iain. 'It's not our problem anymore and we can concentrate on the task of stopping the ELOS from carrying out their plans?

'Exactly right,' said Rory.

'Rory, if I find out you are not what you say are, you had better pray to your God that you never meet me again, am I clear?'

'You are loud and clear, Iain. I give you my word we are just and upright men.'

'You are right, Iain, we need to get this treasure hunt finished and get on with stopping the ELOS. The powers that be will just have to accept that the treasure does not exist; we'll tell them it must have been looted decades ago,' said Jamie turning to the two masons. 'We'll help you get your relics.'

'Thank you; thank you gentlemen you have made the correct decision,' said Rory happily.

'I know we have and the decision might be a bit selfish. It's so good to share the burden of this task; it takes a weight off our shoulders and you probably saved our skin on more than one occasion,' said Jamie.

'We're delighted to share the burden. Now, I have a great desire to see the clues,' said Rory.

'Oh… the clues, it feels a wee bit strange to give them up. Not give them up so much as share them with someone else; we've had the secret between the two of us for so long,' Jamie said.

'I've got the clues hidden in my cabin Jamie,' said Iain getting up to retrieve them.

'Are you feeling alright Jamie?' asked Hamish looking a bit concerned.

'I am fine Hamish. I just feel this sudden relief as though a hundredweight has been lifted out from inside my head; it feels like I could float away on a breath of wind.'

'A big lump like you wouldn't float away, but I share your feelings,' said Iain returning with the clues.

Iain put the copy of the first clue and the gold box with the second on the table and they all stared at it.

'Would you like to open it Rory?' asked Iain.

Rory looked up at Iain and then to Jamie, who raised his eyebrows, pulled his lips in tight and nodded.

He quickly perused the copy of the first clue then lifted the gold box as though it would dissolve in his hands and laid it down in front him opening the lid carefully and removing the leather pouch with the

Prophets of Death

remnants of the wax seal still evident. He undid the flap, took out the parchment, unfolded it on the table and read the historical words.

'Below the waves the rocks bare their teeth,
Two sentinels watch o'er the dark place beneath.
The eagles' seal is there to show you the way,
Past the heads, through the narrows to the calm in the bay.
The way that you seek is there on the shore,
To the west of the stones that rise from below.
Walk fifty paces from the waters' edge,
Find the path to the south and fulfil your pledge.
The dark place beckons for those to aspire,
Eager in pursuit of an object much desired.

'This is a moment in my life I will always treasure gentlemen. To see the writings of a Knights Templar who gave his life to his order, and to humanity,' said Rory truly overcome with emotion.

He moved over to let Hamish look upon the parchment and read the ancient scripture.

'It is truly a revelation Rory. I recognize the seal of the double headed eagle which is the highest rank earned by a Scottish Rite Mason. It also signifies "one eager or hot in the pursuit of an object much desired" as written in the scripture,' said Hamish.

Rory looked up at the boys and said. 'I don't think you two are aware of the enormity of what you've uncovered here. It will truly be a moment in time that when we uncover the hidden treasure, of which I am now convinced does exist. I'm afraid only a few of us can share in the discovery; but it will be written into the folklore that will be the history of Masonry.'

'Hamish, you say you recognise the seal?' said

Jamie.

'Yes it is unquestionably an old seal of the Knights Templar. I have seen this on more than one occasion in books stored in the library at the Goede Hoop Lodge.'

'Is there anything else in the clue that you recognise?'

'The sentinels are obviously the heads at the entrance to the lagoon and estuary into Knysna which is well known to all and sundry but there is nothing more I can tell you,' said Hamish.

'Aye, we were hoping this clue would have been as easy as the first one as far as recognition of landmarks is concerned,' said Iain unravelling the clue which led them to the Elephant's Eye and showing it to Hamish.

'Aye, the whales in the bay and the table cloth on the mountain are well known not to mention the Elephant's Eye itself; easy to find as long as you have the clue to follow.'

Hamish looked at the Knysna clue again and said, 'The clue says walk fifty paces to the west from the shore and then find a path running south which, if I remember correctly, would take you back towards the heads and the entrance to the lagoon.'

'Are there any caves in the cliffs around that area?' asked Jamie.

'I don't know, the best man to ask would be Arthur Burton but he's ashore waiting for us. Why do you ask, do you think the next clue will be in another cave?'

'We think so. There's a high probability the writer of the clues is using caves to hide the clues simply to protect them from the elements,' said Jamie.

'That's good thinking,' said Rory. 'So we all need to be watching from the port side of the ship as it passes through heads towards the lagoon and see if there are any caves on the cliffs.'

Prophets of Death

'Aye, the Knight who wrote the clues could not have known how his landmarks would become so identifiable,' Jamie said draining his whisky.

'We'll find out soon enough gentlemen,' said Iain pouring fresh drinks. 'Let's toast the brave Knight.'

It was overcast and windy but no rain; the sea was a bit choppy as the Flying Fish neared its destination. Willard was looking through his spy glass at the heads of Knysna.

'We could have been here a lot earlier but I needed to be here at high tide to go through the heads. There are some dangerous reefs and rocks under the water at the entrance and more than a few ships have paid the price of not going through when the tide and the weather is right,' he said to Jamie offering him the telescope.

Jamie looked at the close up image through the spyglass and witnessed the waves crashing onto the rocks around the entrance under the looming heads but with the narrow waterway flowing easily through to the estuary beyond.

'That looks like a bit of maneuvering to get through there Roger,' said Jamie.

'That is why I say you need to watch the conditions, the wind and the swells before making your run through the narrows. Had the conditions been calm then it would be a simple matter of just sailing on through but it's a bit rough today so I have my best man at the helm.'

'That would be Mr Reynolds.'

'Yes it is Mr Reynolds, he's still with me and he's a good hand. We'll be going through shortly Jamie so tell anyone who wants to be on deck to get up here.'

Jamie went below and called the others up on deck where they congregated around the port side of the middle cargo hatch. They watched with fascination as the helmsman expertly maneuvered the ship to ride the swells and line it up to sail neatly through the middle of the narrow waterway into Knysna lagoon.

The four men looked up at the heads as they sailed through, Jamie and Iain looking for any sign of a cave up on the cliffs but could see nothing. Rory and Hamish were also searching with the spyglasses they had brought with them.

The cliffs gave way to high steep slopes with thick vegetation running down to the top of a rock face which was at eye level to the passengers. As the ship moved in towards the lagoon the waterway was getting wider but still no sign of a cave.

Rory came over to the boys and said, 'After all these years the terrain must have changed or if there was a cave it would have to be overgrown by now.'

The ship moved on with the momentum of the incoming tide. Below the steep slopes, the narrow rock face on the shore suddenly curved away making the channel grow wider. As the swells moved along the channel the water covered and then uncovered two dark spaces in the rock face.

'*There!*' They all chorused together.

They could see what looked like the tops of two very small caves, the waves covering the openings as they passed by; they were nowhere near the dimensions of the Elephant's Eye. One opening was set a bit further back from the other and slightly higher up.

The problem was they were almost under water.

'We could row a boat up here; maybe there's a small beach at low tide,' suggested Jamie.

'I've done a bit of sailing,' said Iain, 'and I'm no expert but I'm pretty sure there's not a hope in hell of rowing a boat back out here without killing yourself, even at low tide. The conditions would have to be very calm to attempt something like that.'

Prophets of Death

'Iain's right,' said Hamish. 'Besides that we don't even know if the clue is in any of those caves.'

'The clue says the sentinels are watching over the dark place beneath. I didn't see any other openings, although there could be a cave hidden by the overgrown vegetation, but there is a good chance that those caves below the waterline is where the clue is hidden,' said Jamie. 'The clue tells us to find a path, so we'll have to find a way overland back here and find a way down to the caves.'

'And there had to be two caves just to make it easier for us,' said Iain cheerfully.

The ship sailed on into Knysna lagoon and the crew went scurrying up to the rigging hauling in the sails to slow the ship's headway.

'Roger,' shouted Jamie. 'Can we drop anchor somewhere around here, we don't want to go too far into the lagoon at this stage?'

The captain came over to Jamie and said. 'We can anchor closer to the beach on the west side that will leave a clear way for any other ship coming through the heads.'

'You know best Roger,' said Jamie.

'My, this is such a beautiful place,' said Rory. 'Wouldn't you want to live here?'

'Knysna would be a wonderful place to live but the narrow entrance from the sea through to the estuary does not lend itself to doing any good business; any coastal town needs a good accessible port,' said the captain.

Jamie was not listening he was peering through the spyglass in search of the stones from below.

'The stones from below might well be under water,' said Iain looking over Jamie's shoulder.

'I think you could be right. They are under water as long as they haven't shifted or fallen down or dissolved or… bloody anything could have happened to them after all this time.'

'Come on, let's go and have a bite to eat and wee dram and wait for low tide, then we'll see where we are,' said Iain.

'Aye, you're right let's have a drink. It's just so frustrating.'

'I know big man, I know. All things will come to those who have the patience to wait.'

In the early afternoon the tide turned and ebbed. The Captain had a crewman plumb the depth of the water just in case the ship would bottom but the draught of the ship was still safe.

Jamie, Iain, Rory and Hamish each had a spyglass and were searching up and down the water off the western shore of the lagoon in an effort to locate the stones from below but there was no sign of any stone or rock protruding from the water.

Jamie was standing beside Willard smoking a cheroot; Iain was sitting on the edge of the cargo hatch with a cigarette when Jamie said. 'Captain, we'll need to drop two dinghies into the water so we can take a closer look up and down this shore line.'

'We can do that but the tide will be coming in again in a couple of hours so I suggest you do it at low tide tomorrow.'

'Yes, you're right of course.'

'The crew have been doing a spot of fishing the result of which means that the cook is serving up a fine fare this evening, so let's retire to eat. We'll take up your mission again tomorrow.'

Low tide the next day was just before midday and the conditions could not be better. There was virtually no wind at all so the water in the lagoon was flat. Rory and Hamish would inspect the north side of the shoreline with Jamie and Iain covering the south end. They had put the

Prophets of Death

boats in the water before the tide ebbed to give them the longest time possible to search for the stones as high tide would be in about six hours.

They rowed the boats up and down the shoreline but could not see anything; they changed the pattern of their sweeps to no avail. The water was not clear, one could see through so far then it became murky.

They heard the bell on the ship and looked over to see Captain Willard waving them in. They rowed alongside the ship and climbed aboard, followed a bit later by Rory and Hamish.

'It's time to call it a day lads,' said Roger. 'The tide is in and there's nothing to see. We'll leave the dinghies in the water and try again tomorrow.'

'Thank god for that,' said Iain. 'That rowing is bleddy murder, my arms are killing me.'

'Aw stop moanin' ye big baby, you would think it was hard work when in fact it's a nice afternoon on the water,' said Jamie cheerfully.

It was a little gloomy in the saloon that night as they discussed what else could be done to find the stones mentioned in the clue.

Tobacco and whisky were being abused as they tried to come up with an idea.

'We can't swim up and down the water diving down every now and then to feel around for a pile of rocks,' said Iain.

'What about a boat hook tied to the end of a rope; we could then drop it in the water dragging it along to see if it snags on something,' said Hamish.

'That could work,' said Jamie. 'But the hook would snag on any piece of rock or old tree that's down there; but maybe worth a try.'

Rory drained his glass and stood. 'Let's sleep on it my friends I'm heading for my bunk. Pray we find something tomorrow. Goodnight.'

The weather turned for the worse overnight as a North-West wind picked up and strengthened. It brought rain and although they were sheltered in the lagoon, out beyond the heads the sea was rough and the channel through the heads was fast flowing with the waves crashing down on the entrance.

The weather did not let up for three days. When finally the wind quietened and the sun shone on peaceful waters in the lagoon, despondency reigned as the dinghies, which had been brought back on board, were lowered once more onto the water.

Chapter Eighteen

September 1856

Knysna Lagoon

The ride to Knysna was, as usual, long and dreary the only shots Fairbairn heard on the whole journey were from the Enfield marksman's rifle when Davie Flint was practising his aiming with the strange feeling rifle.

When the troop arrived outside Knysna they made camp on top of a hill north west of the river estuary, which gave him a view of the channel and any ship that sailed into the lagoon.

Neither Fairbairn nor his men were aware they had been observed from the moment they arrived in the area and were being surveyed on a daily basis.

Arthur Burton and his men rode out of Cape Town well ahead of Fairbairn and had made good time getting to Knysna Port.

He had recruited a dozen good men, there were a dozen more on standby. They were all masons and most of them knew the bush and had been involved in bush warfare at some point in their life.

He also had a couple of Hottentot trackers with him; one in particular called Hendrik, who had been in Arthur's employ for years and was not interested in the native wars. He was happy with his house and his family on a small piece of land *The Boss* had given him and was happy to travel and track with him and fight when necessary.

Arthur and Hendrik had travelled these hills often and knew the old well-trodden game trails as well as the old native tracks. Two days earlier they had traversed the east side of the lagoon looking for any strangers setting up camp; finding nothing out of place they made their way to the west side to make camp in the bush well back from the heads and within easy reach of vantage points to watch the entrance to the heads from the sea and the lagoon.

Arthur had sent Hendrik out to watch for any other riders making camp around the lagoon and sure enough he came back with news of riders camping further back above the south bank of the Knysna River where it flowed into the estuary.

They were now watching the camp; hidden in the bush they were all but invisible to even the trained eye.

Arthur whispered. 'It's Fairbairn and his volunteers, eleven of them including Fairbairn, you'd better hang on to your ears and your balls Hendrik.'

'They will not get my ball sack for a money pouch. Those motherless devils are not of this earth boss, we must wait until they sleep and cut their throats.'

'All in good time my friend, they are good bushmen as well. We will keep watching them for now and wait for the ship to arrive, then we will see what they do.'

Fairbairn noticed the men were starting to get irritable waiting around for the ship to appear. Then one morning one of the lookouts came to the camp with news.

'Sir, a ship has just come through the channel, it looks like the Flying Fish.'

Fairbairn jumped up and went to the lookout position and looked through his spyglass; it was indeed the ship

Prophets of Death

they had been waiting for.

The ship's crew furled the sails and the anchor was dropped. *Why drop anchor there, unless of course they are looking for something,* thought Fairbairn.

He kept a watch on the ship until nightfall and decided whatever they are going to do, it will not be tonight. As he walked back to his camp he thought about how comfortable the passengers would be on the ship, sitting down to a fine meal prepared by a ship's cook while he was sitting down in the dirt in front of a small fire to eat cold pork and chicken with some dry bread.

The next morning Fairbairn watched two dinghies with two men in each move up and down the line of the beach looking like they were just enjoying a day out in a boat.

Fairbairn, watching with Davie Flint, said. 'What the hell are they doing?'

'They keep looking in the water and then at the shore,' said Flint.

'Looking for markers, or something to point the way to where the prize is,' said Fairbairn. 'Tell the men to stay alert for another force onshore that may be helping them. Send two men to scout along the west side of the shoreline but not to be seen and do nothing but watch or I'll have their heads. We'll only attack once we know they have found our treasure.' *I'll not fall into that trap again*, he thought.

At high tide the two small boats went back to the ship and at sundown the two scouts came back to report they had seen nothing other than what was observed from here.

Arthur and Hendrik had watched two men leave Fairbairn's camp and followed them down to where they spied on Rory and Hamish rowing up and down the shoreline until the sun started to go down;

'Boss, I know you white men have some strange

habits but why are they rowing up and down looking in the water?'

'They must be looking for something in the water or on the shore, it's hard to tell. We must make sure Fairbairn and his devils do not interrupt them.'

They followed the two spies back to their camp then Arthur followed Hendrik back to theirs.

That night the weather turned windy with heavy rain and lasted for the next three days with no movement off or on the ship.

When at last the weather cleared the dinghies were back to the routine of rowing up and down the coastline with Arthur and Hendrik once again following the two spies sent to scout along the shoreline.

The time aboard the ship during the bad weather was not wasted. A boat hook was attached to the end of a rope and one of the crew found an old net which was weighted down with some small pieces of iron found in the chain locker; now they were about to see if their ideas would work.

It was tedious work as they trawled up and down the shoreline to no avail. The tide was rising and the light was failing so they rowed back to the ship.

The next day they were out again and Jamie said. 'Maybe we're too far into the lagoon, Iain. We can't see through the water because the river flows into the estuary and carries the silt down with it and into this lagoon, so you can see bugger all.'

Iain said. 'So you think we should go further back towards the entrance from the sea?'

'Aye, I do. Do you see there, where the shoreline starts to widen after the rocks in the channel and where we saw the two wee caves,' said Jamie pointing at the place.

Prophets of Death

'Where that small stretch of beach is?'

'Aye, let's take the boat there up onto the sand. I want to climb up that steep hill behind the beach and take a look down.'

'There you are,' said Iain handing the oars to Jamie. 'Your turn, I'm buggered.'

Once they had hauled the dinghy up on to the beach they took the machetes they had brought from the ship and chopped their way through the dense foliage up the steep slope until they found a tree where they could climb up to get a clear view of the lagoon below.

Getting as comfortable as possible on a branch they took turns with the spyglass to look at the water just offshore. Jamie saw something moving in the water making a small wave-like ripple.

'I just saw a fish in the water.'

'Mark the spot and we'll catch it for supper,' said Iain.

Jamie continued to scan the water up to a point and then bring the spyglass back again but slightly left or right. He saw the ripple of water again, looking up to get his bearing he saw that it was the same spot he had seen the ripple before.

He kept watching the same spot; something was definitely moving in the water, then he realised that it was not something moving in the water but the water moving around something that was standing still in the water.

He lowered the spyglass and sat and looked down at the lagoon.

Iain looked up at him sensing a change in his friend's demeanour. 'What! What did you see? Do you see something?' he said excitedly.

'You know the fish I saw?'

'Aye, what about it? Did it leap into the boat; save us catching it?'

'No, there's something in the water that is not moving but is disturbing the water, take a look.'

He handed Iain the spyglass and showed him the bearing to guide him to the disturbance in the water. Iain saw it almost immediately.

'You're right Jamie, there's something in the water and you would only see it at low tide.'

They climbed out of the tree and made their way back to the boat, shoving off they rowed to the spot where the landmarks guided them too.

The ripple in the water was still visible now they knew what to look for. They slowly guided the dinghy to the spot and Jamie put both hands into the water and shouted out excitedly, 'Rocks, there are fucking rocks here Iain.'

Iain stood up and let out a whoop and nearly toppled over into the water. Jamie pulled off his clothes down to his long johns and slid over the side.

He went under the water for longer than Iain expected but soon surfaced and wiped the water from his face.

'This is it Iain. As far as I can tell there's a pile of flat stones piled on top of each other; it must be quite wide at the bottom I suppose because I cannot see that far down, but I think the top stones have been washed off or been knocked off by a passing ship; but there is definitely a man-made structure under there.'

'It's a cairn Jamie,' said Iain.

'A what? A cairn… yes, you're right, it's a bleddy cairn. I've seen them in Scotland, they're used as landmarks.'

By this time Rory and Hamish had rowed to their position to join them in the discovery. Rory produced a whisky flask and passed it round saying, 'Well done lads, this is a great moment.'

Prophets of Death

'What the hell are they searching for,' Fairbairn said to Davie Flint who had come to watch out of pure boredom as he could not fire his amazing new Enfield gun because it would attract attention.

'Whatever it is they're looking for I wish they would hurry and find it. I'm growing weary of waiting for my pay,' said Flint.

'Have some patience my friend your pay will come soon enough; wait… something is happening,' said Fairbairn lifting the spyglass to take a closer look.

He could see Fyvie and McColl going onto the beach and disappearing, then re-emerging to row the dinghy to a particular spot in the lagoon and the dark haired one, who must be Fyvie, stripping off his clothes and going into the water.

After a while the swimmer climbed back into the boat and the other boat joined them. He could barely hear raised voices as the boatmen looked to be congratulating each other. They rowed back to the ship.

When the two spies returned Fairbairn questioned them at length.

'What did you see in the water,' asked Fairbairn.

'Boss, we tried to see what was making them so excited but we could see nothing, we were too far away. It had to be something they could see under the surface.'

'How could you not see anything you blind idiots; you must have been able to see something,' said Fairbairn losing his patience once again.

'I'm telling you, Boss, there was nothing to see,' said the spy exasperated.

Fairbairn was desperate to find out what they had found but knew he had to wait for them to make their next move, what he didn't know was, Arthur and Hendrik would never let Fairbairn's volunteers out of their sight.

Chapter Nineteen

September 1856

Cape Town

Sir George Whyte arrived in Cape Town to the full pomp and ceremony afforded the new Governor of the Cape. He was made welcome at the quayside by Nicholas Banbury who headed a guard of honour from the 73rd Regiment and then they were on their way to the government buildings.

Banbury was sitting opposite Whyte, behind the driver in the open carriage, which was part of a parade of mounted cavalry and regimental splendour coming from the dock at Rogge Bay.

The people of Cape Town, who had of course been warned of his arrival, turned out to greet him and waved to him as he was driven through the streets. He did not disappoint the residents of this fair town; dressed in his uniform of high office he made sure he was seen in his best finery such was his vanity.

Whyte had been corresponding with Cuthbert over the last few months and was aware of the problems faced in this land of powerful native tribes. He was also aware of his obligations to meet the demands of his elders in the ELOS and their hunger for the domination of British authority in Southern Africa.

First he would confer with Cuthbert. It was well

Prophets of Death

known within their own circle that Cuthbert did his business for the elders and went on his way; he was a soldier first and foremost. Then he would meet with Banbury and the new man, Renton, sent by the elders in London, whom he did not know, but he had to work with them to implement the destruction of the Xhosa just as he had overseen the Aborigines' decline in New Zealand.

The crowds were waving and cheering as the dazzling parade clip-clopped up Adderley Street towards the Company Gardens leading to the government buildings when Banbury happened to look down to his right and glimpsed a girl's face in the crowd.

He almost fainted with terror and had to grab the hand rail on the side of the carriage to steady himself.

She's dead, he thought. *After all this time she must be dead, perhaps it's a sister, no it wasn't a sister, he saw the look on her face, she recognised him, it was her.* Panic was starting to overcome him when Whyte looked at him.

'Nicholas you have turned a deathly pale colour, are you ill?' he said raising his voice slightly above the din.

This brought Banbury back to reality, he said. 'I'm feeling a bit queasy sir, I'll be fine.'

As the cavalcade went through the gardens Banbury leaned across to Whyte and said. 'I will take my leave of you when we meet with Governor Cuthbert; you will have much to discuss, and we can convene again at your leisure sir.'

'As you wish Nicholas. All this for power, riches and subservience for life,' said Whyte sweeping his arm at the magnificent backdrop that was Table Mountain under clear blue skies.

When the carriage stopped outside the government buildings two footmen stepped down from their small platforms at the rear and came around to open the door and lower the steps from which Banbury climbed down to stand aside followed by Sir George who was greeted by the outgoing governor.

'Sir George,' said Cuthbert who had come out to meet the new governor.

'Governor,' said Whyte. 'It's good to meet with you again after all this time.

They shook hands firmly as Banbury made a discreet exit and they walked into the cool interior of the government buildings to Cuthbert's suite of offices.

'Thank god you're here George,' said Cuthbert quietly. 'I tire of the heat of Africa I am re-called to the north where war stirs.'

'You've been given new orders?' asked Whyte.

They went through Bill Hutchison's office, who was afforded a short introduction, and into Whyte's new office.

'Crimea. The Russians are at war with the Ottoman Empire, the British are allied with the French and Austrians to keep the Russians out of the Middle East; please, sit; I'll pour us a drink.'

'I'm sure you will be eager to get off to your regiment Gerald.'

'Indeed, once I have handed over to you I'll be sailing for England and then on to the Crimea. You were an army man George, why did you leave?' said Cuthbert pouring brandy.

Whyte accepted his drink and sipped at it with relish. He was a man of medium height with dark thick hair parted on one side. He had sharp features, a slight stoop in the shoulders on a wiry frame.

'I discovered that I am more the politician rather than the soldier.'

'That's why you are here, to keep these natives down with hidden cruel diplomacy, which will look like good governance; yes, you are good at that George,' said

Prophets of Death

Cuthbert.

'Yes, I seem to be,' said Whyte thoughtfully.

'I presume you'll be meeting with Nicholas Banbury and the other chap to finalise the plans of the elders.'

'Yes but I won't make it too obvious. I will have a clandestine meeting with both of them and after that Banbury can meet with me here in his official capacity so as not to arouse any suspicion.'

'I have to warn you George, that Banbury and Renton may be compromised,' said Cuthbert.

'How so?'

'I commissioned a chap by the name of Fairbairn, who put together a motley crew of volunteers to fight in the war with the Xhosa. Under orders from Banbury, he has been following two young fellows who, apparently, are looking for clues to lead them to a fortune in gold and artefacts; a treasure hidden by the Knights Templar. The two men being followed are Jamie Fyvie and Iain McColl who have already confronted Fairbairn, the idiot, so we must assume that they will suspect Banbury, merely through association with Fairbairn.'

'Yes, I have been briefed on this so called treasure. If the treasure is there we are going to need that wealth to fund our operations in Africa. Why don't we eliminate Fyvie and McColl and take the clues, surely we could find this treasure?' said Whyte.

'You'll have to be careful, we think they are government men with the Secret Field Police. If they are and we kill them we would bring a lot of unwanted scrutiny down on us I think. I would let the government men continue to follow the clues and Fairbairn to follow them, if anything is discovered then we can take it.'

'The Secret Field Police; then we have to assume they are working with colleagues placed in Cape Town.'

'They have to be working with someone. Fairbairn

seems to think that there is nothing to find after all these years; if there is a treasure it would have been plundered or buried in the sands of time. Do not trust anyone outside these walls, especially Fairbairn, I don't trust him at all,' said Cuthbert.

'I'll have my own network of informants in place soon enough Gerald. Now, moving onto matters of state. Have the natives been suitably put down?'

'They have, as I reported in my despatches to you, all of the Xhosa clans have been resettled west of the Kei River and told they will never return the strongholds in the mountains of the Amatolas; especially the Ngqika in the valleys of the Kroomie Heights.'

'What of the lands they were driven out of, are they to be re-settled by the colonists?'

'No, never sell that beautiful land to those greedy land grabbing hypocritical settlers, which would only incite the Xhosa natives, especially the Ngqika, to eventually take up arms against the whites once more. That is what we are trying to avoid. Also, I have allowed the chiefs to maintain governance of their own people with the commissioners appointed by the Cape Government keeping an eye on them and to report the slightest hint of sedition among the chiefs.'

'Why not strip the chiefs of power and bring the natives under English law through the commissioners?' said Whyte.

'Again, that would only incite them to stir up the natives and start another war, George. They're not ready for our civilised way and they do have their own way of control and punishment. Better to keep them in one area and rule themselves with the Cape authorities watching over them, keep the forts well garrisoned and always have a show of force; it's all they understand.'

'Well, I'll take your advice on the locals for now, one

Prophets of Death

never knows what the future will bring.'

'Indeed,' said Cuthbert.

The hand-over to the new governor lasted a further two weeks when finally Gerald Cuthbert left the Cape Colony feeling very pleased with himself that he had handed over a peaceful well governed part of the empire.

He was the only person who was pleased with the peace in this part of the empire.

When Banbury left Whyte with Cuthbert, he made his way to Arend se Kop as quickly as possible. Renton was not happy that he had arrived without prior notice and that he had arrived as though the end of the world was nigh.

'Are you positive it was the same girl Nicholas? Think carefully.'

'Of course it was; I'm not an idiot. It was Annatje, she looked right at me and recognised me but she knows that I recognised her as well, that's how I know it was her. How did she survive that fall into the ravine for god's sake?'

'That's irrelevant at this stage. Get a message to Williams to come here. He has to find this girl and get rid of her, no trace to be left. She must be taken out to the middle of the bay and dumped into the sea for the sharks,' said Renton.

'If Williams had done his job properly we wouldn't be in a position such as this,' said Banbury.

Renton raised his voice and said. 'If you hadn't let her go in the first place and killed her when I told you to, we wouldn't be in this position. When Whyte gets here you better have your wits about you. He mustn't know about our nocturnal activities otherwise the ELOS will throw us to the sharks for compromising the plans… now go and find Williams and get back here before Whyte arrives.'

A late dinner had been arranged for the secret meeting with the new governor and elder, George Whyte, which would last well into the early hours of the morning. Cold cuts and bread with fine wine were laid out on the table in the dining room where Renton sat as Banbury ushered Whyte into the warm room.

'It was years ago when I last spoke with you Nicholas,' said Whyte as he walked into the room and stopped when he saw Renton sitting at the table. 'You must be Nigel Renton.' He said extending his hand to this strange man hidden behind the veil.

Renton shook the proffered hand and in his rasping voice said. 'It has been a long time since you have had any communication with me as well George.'

Whyte looked quizzically at this stranger. 'You have me at a disadvantage sir; I don't remember ever meeting you.'

'Oh it's been years since we met but I did send you a communique just before I left for England and then died.'

'I beg your pardon?' said Whyte totally confused.

'I sent you a report about using more missionaries to set up missions for the education of the natives.'

'But that was James St…'

Whyte sat down and tried to take in what he had just heard this man say, and then it dawned on him.

'James, is it really you?'

Renton rasped a laugh and said. 'Yes my friend, it's really me. Come, sit and eat, I'll tell you all that has happened and we will discuss all that we have to accomplish.'

Renton told the story of his demise and his re-incarnation with Banbury pitching in every now and then with his end of the story.

'It seems incredulous that you're here James, after all you've been through it's a miracle you are alive.'

Prophets of Death

'It was, I must say, vengeance in my heart toward the two men who did this to me, but more, it was the determination to carry out our plan for the domination of Africa that gave me the strength to come back from the dead, as it were.'

They talked into the night until Renton decided it was time to outline their plans for the demise of the Xhosa.

Renton was speaking. 'Ideally, when we implement our plans, we would want the chiefs and therefore the different tribes to fight with each other; we need to sow the seeds of mistrust into their midst.

'Now that Cuthbert has gone to fight other battles we can concentrate on the final phase with the assurance that the Xhosa nation will never rise to fight again and that the annexation of all territories around and north east of the Orange River, will take place' said Renton.

'The powers that be in Whitehall have instructed me not to talk to the Boers in the Orange Free State, they don't want to annex it as part of the Cape Colony. The same goes for the Transvaal or South African Republic, but I believe they want to join us to create a Federation of Southern Africa as they will need help to fight the Zulus.'

Banbury said. 'Don't worry about the colonial office they will be put in their place by the elders in London. It's imperative that you contact the Boers in the Free State and the Transvaal and talk with them. What will you start with, in terms of reforms and new policies for the Xhosa?'

'I'll begin by unravelling Cuthbert's policies for the natives. We must divest the chiefs of all responsibilities of governance of their people and have the commissioners take over that roll. After that I think we should take a look at the land left vacant by the Xhosa natives and see what is to be done with it. This will take time as I have just started my term as governor. We must crush the natives' spirit and make them so despondent that they will never find the resolve to rise and fight again,' said Whyte.

'When that time comes I will execute the final part of my plan as all the Xhosa people will be in a weakened state. We must be ready to have Fairbairn and his men move large numbers of surviving natives to the beaches for transfer to the waiting slave ships and be rid of them for good,' said Renton.

'But given the time we have to move the slaves to the beaches, will we have enough men to round them up and get them offshore?' said Whyte.

'The Americans will land a substantial amount of men onshore, as will the Boers, but at different beaches over a few days between the Great Kei River and the Buffalo River near East London to the South West. They'll be met by our men and co-ordinate the extraction of the slaves. They can only take a few hundred each, but the once the word goes out that the slavers are taking people, the ensuing panic will be to our advantage then you, as the governor, will call in the troops to show no mercy in putting them down.'

'What is the final part of your plan James?' asked Whyte.

'You'll be told soon enough, there are two acts of this drama still to be played out then you will see all hell break loose.'

'Your final act had better be worthy of a standing ovation James, otherwise it will be your final performance.'

'Please keep me informed immediately you hear any news from the Crimea, George, this is very important.'

'As soon as I know of anything you'll be the first to know.'

Chapter Twenty

October 1856

Cape Town

Prior to the arrival of the new governor, Sergeant O'Donnell recruited two local young officers to help Constable Jalala keep watch on Renton's house up on the slopes of Table Mountain.

They watched the coming and going of traffic from the mansion but nothing out of the ordinary. They had even sneaked a search of any cart or carriage Williams was driving when he left them unattended to see if they could find any evidence of bodies having been there but found nothing.

As they had on numerous occasions, O'Donnell and Jalala accompanied Annatje up the mountain to where she had been found to see if she could remember any other details of her captors or where she had been incarcerated.

'Nothing coming to you Annatje?' asked Ahmed.

'No, I'm afraid not, it's locked out of my head and I can't find the key to open the door and let it in.'

'Don't fret,' said the sergeant. 'In time you'll see something that will unlock your memories; we won't give up.'

'Annatje and I are going to watch the arrival and the parade of the new governor, will you join us sergeant?' asked Ahmed.

K D Neill

'No, I think not. I must get back to the station and then go home. You two enjoy yourself and be careful,' said O'Donnell and wandered off.

Ahmed and Annatje walked down Strand Street then turned right into Adderley Street to find a place to see the parade showing off the new governor.

They were thoroughly enjoying each-others company in the hot sunshine, talking as though they had known each other forever.

A crowd had formed at the entrance to the Company Gardens to watch the carriage carrying the new governor, so they pushed their way through to the side of the road to get a better view of the spectacle of mounted cavalry with gleaming swords and breastplates, shiny boots and tall helmets, sitting on big strong horses.

The succeeding governor was sitting on the rear bench of the magnificent carriage waving to the crowds in a regal manner.

'I think he must fancy himself as royalty,' said Annatje into Ahmed's ear.

Ahmed leaned down to her and smelled her fragrance which enthralled him. 'He certainly looks like royalty,' he said looking into her eyes.

As the carriage went past the man sitting opposite the new governor turned his head and looked straight at Annatje.

She caught her breath and let out a guttural sound as she brought her hand up to her mouth.

Ahmed heard her and turned to ask her what was wrong just in time to catch her as she fainted into his arms.

Ahmed easily picked her up and carried her away from the crowds down Adderley Street to Aunty Fatima's flower stall.

Aunty Fatima saw them coming and cleared a space

Prophets of Death

behind her stall.

'What's happened Ahmed?'

'I don't know Aunty, one minute she was looking at the parade and the next she fainted,' said Ahmed as he gently laid Annatje down on a blanket.

Aunty Fatima wiped her face with a cool wet cloth and asked. 'What was she doing? Was she feeling the heat or not feeling well?'

'She was fine Aunty, there was nothing wrong with her, she just made a funny noise and collapsed; I caught her, picked her up and brought her here.'

Aunty Fatima thought about this for a minute then said. 'Did she see or recognise anyone, Ahmed?'

Ahmed stopped and looked at the old woman and said, 'Oh my goodness… do you think she saw one of her attackers?'

'It's very possible. I think we should get her to a doctor.'

Just then Annatje's eyes fluttered as she started to come around. She was helped into a sitting position and Ahmed gave her a cup of water.'

'Annatje, are you feeling alright?' he asked.

'Oh my!' she said as she saw Aunty Fatima, throwing her arms around her hugging her for dear life.

She eventually recovered and let the Aunty go, her arms crossing over her chest.

'What happened girl?'

She was looking at the ground and said. 'I saw him, I saw my master.'

'Your master?' said Ahmed alarmed.

Aunty Fatima looked at him to stay calm.

'That's what I called him when I was his prisoner,' said Annatje bursting into tears.

Ahmed sat down beside her and took her hand. 'Who was it and where was he?' he asked her quietly.

K D Neill

She looked up at Ahmed and then to Aunty Fatima and said. 'He was the man in the carriage.'

They both looked at her in disbelief for what seemed an age.

'You cannot be serious Annatje,' said Ahmed. 'The new governor…'

'No… the other one sitting across from him, I don't know his name.'

'But these are English gentlemen of high office in the government, Annatje, you must surely be mistaken,' said Ahmed.

'I am not mistaken Ahmed; it's him.'

Aunty Fatima turned to Ahmed. 'Annetje isn't stupid Ahmed, she hasn't been wrong so far; you should listen closely to what she has to say.'

Ahmed knew she was right.

'Forgive me Annatje, I believe you and if this is the truth then we have a bigger problem.'

'Who will believe me? No-one will,' said Annatje. 'Who will take the word of a poor coloured girl against a powerful Englishman in the government?' She was gathering her wits about her now and starting to think.

'There are people, white people with a certain amount of power who'll believe you,' said Ahmed. 'I can't say too much at the moment but there are evil men at work not only in the kidnappings but other sinister dealings. I promise you we'll bring these people to justice.'

'Do you know who the other man was in the carriage?'

'I am not sure but the only person that high up in government to keep company with the governor would be Mr Banbury, Nicholas Banbury.'

'Nicholas you say?'

'Yes, that's his name.'

Prophets of Death

'Ahmed, I remember the murderer using that name when I was listening at the door of my cell in… a cellar… I was being held captive in a cellar,' she said, her memory flooding back now. 'There was a trap door where he used to push the bodies into when he had abused and then killed the other girls, that's how I escaped Ahmed, I remember.'

'Come, we must get you away from here to somewhere safe,' said Ahmed.

'No, I must tell you both what happened now lest I forget again.'

'She's right,' said Aunty Fatima. 'Better to tell us all, now.'

Ahmed relented and said. 'Go on with your story.'

'I remember the other one calling my master Nicholas before he opened the door of my cell to make me do things to him for the last time,' she said as she looked at Ahmed not wanting to hurt him because she knew of his feelings for her.

Ahmed sensed this and said. 'Continue, it's fine; how did you know it would be the last time?'

'The other one was going away and they agreed to kill me then. When the other girl was murdered and pushed through the hole in the floor, I… it's all so hazy… I injured my master and… yes… I ran for the trap door, I took the chance to escape. I remember pushing the other one, the killer that is, on to the floor and I jumped through the hole. I slid and toppled through the air into a ravine… it was dark and… I hit some rocks and… oh… I can't remember… wait! Yes: I landed on top of the other girl's body; she saved me Ahmed… she saved me and I made a promise to her.'

'What did you promise?' asked Aunty Fatima.

'That if I survived I would go back for her and bury her properly.'

She started crying again but then continued to tell them how she made her way down and across the mountainside, finding the pathway and falling down the landslip until she passed out and then woke up in Selome's house.

'My god child, you have been through a terrible time of it.'

'I'm sorry to ask you this but could you take us back to where the other body is?' said Ahmed.

'I honestly could not take you there Ahmed. I would if I knew but I don't know where that ravine is or what house I was in.'

'Don't worry we should be able to narrow down a search below each house on the mountain,' said Ahmed.

'There is another problem,' said Annatje.

'What other problem?'

'The man in the carriage… that Nicholas…'

'Yes, Nicholas Banbury, if it is him.'

'He recognised me and he knows that I recognised him.'

'Oh, then we have to move fast. Aunty Fatima can you take Annatje home with you?'

'Yes of course I can.'

'I'll go and get the sergeant and tell him what's happened, I'm sure his next move will be to report to our allies, the other white men I told you about. Annatje, you must stay out of sight and lay low until we get these people. I'll go to your family and tell them you're safe and reassure them that all will be well.'

Fatima closed up the stall and asked a friend to look after the stock she had then took Annatje to safety of the Bo Kaap.

Ahmed trotted off to find Sergeant O'Donnell. *These people will not be allowed to be brought to trial*, he thought. *They will die for their crimes* he decided.

Chapter Twenty One

October 1856

Knysna

In the early morning light Jamie and Iain along with Rory and Hamish were standing on the shore of the lagoon. They watched as Captain Willard and his crew went back to the Flying Fish, pulled the boats from the water and sailed the ship towards the small settlement of Knysna.

'Be aware lads,' said Jamie. 'Fairbairn and his cutthroats will be out there watching us, I hope Arthur and his men are close Rory, we will need them eventually.'

'Don't you worry laddie, Arthur is about.'

Jamie was armed with his familiar guns and knives as was Iain with his blunderbusses and knives.

'The clue says fifty paces from the shore,' said Iain. 'After all the years maybe it's a wee bit shorter than fifty.'

'Well let's find out, shall we.'

Jamie stood on the shore looking directly at where the cairn was built in the water, then turned and looked inland. He started to pace his steps up the beach which got to only seventeen, then the thick vegetation stopped him from going any farther.

'My god Jamie, can I not leave you to do one simple thing like walk inland for fifty paces and not fuck it up?' said Iain feigning exasperation.

'Aw, shut up,' said Jamie, responding in kind.

Rory and Hamish chuckled. 'Let's break out the machetes and get to work.'

Iain said. 'If the four of us try to hack through that lot at the same time somebody'll get their bloody leg chopped off. I suggest we hack in twos with the other two keeping a watch for a murdering arsehole.'

They hacked a corridor into the thick bush for approximately fifty paces going up the slope of the hillside and then chopped an ever widening circular clearing.

'Over here,' shouted Hamish, pointing into the bush at a pile of stones.

'Another cairn,' said Jamie.

'Aye but look at the shape of it,' said Iain, clearing away the branches and leaves. 'It's not round and pointing up, as it should be, it looks like it's been shaped to point south towards the heads.'

'Look, over here,' said Rory hacking some vegetation away from a trail of stones.

Jamie said. 'It looks like the Templars built a small stone dyke wall running south from the cairn, but the roots of the vegetation have toppled the stones, over time.'

'I don't think it's a wall Jamie, it looks like they have laid a stone dyke path, so we just have to follow the stones to the clue,' said Iain.

'Aye, you're right, the stones have not fallen they've been set like that. But to follow it is easier to say than it is to do, look at the thick bush we have to hack through.'

Rory said, 'If the Templars built the path the same way they would have built a wall in Scotland it should last for a very, very long time. We just have to walk along it and hack away the overgrowth.'

'Let's make camp and eat, we'll get some sleep and

Prophets of Death

carry on in the morning,' said Jamie.

A fire was lit and the four men ate and drank tea or coffee, relaxing by the fire smoking pipes and cigarettes.

'So, Rory, I'm intrigued as to how you became a finder of ancient artefacts and treasures,' said Jamie.

'When I became a Master Mason, that is, when I passed my third degree, I started to visit the vast library in the Grand Lodge; in there I found another world. I read about men who had travelled their whole lives in search of answers, men in search of other lands but most of all men in search of knowledge to share with mankind. Eventually, after passing many degrees, I began to read about the Knights Templar and how they were betrayed and persecuted, but they never died out completely; masonry is their legacy. I took it upon myself to find all or as much information as I could about other Knights who had been scattered across the globe. Then I was summoned to a very secret meeting at the Grand Lodge whereupon I was sent out to the holy land with a direct descendant of a Knights Templar to find lost artefacts and treasures that had been hidden away by the Knights and bring them home to a safe haven.'

'So where is your companion now? The descendant of the Knight?' asked Jamie.

'He lies in a grave in Palestine where we fought off a hoard of Arabs trying to rob us of manuscripts and books unearthed at a site by the Dead Sea. I was lucky to escape with my life. You see he sacrificed himself so that I and others could escape.'

They sat sipping whisky while they contemplated what Rory had just told them.

'He must have been some man,' said Iain.

'He was all that and more,' said Rory. 'But now it's time for sleep, there's a lot of work to be done tomorrow.'

K D Neill

Flint joined Fairbairn at the lookout point and watched with interest as the Flying Fish's crew deposited Fyvie, McColl and two others on the shore along with their kit and went back to the ship.

'Only the four men have been left on the shore; so as you suspected, they must have companions on shore,' said Flint.

'That's right Davie, go and tell the two idiot spies to see what the four men are doing and tell them to keep aware of others on the slopes.'

He could not see anyone on the shore which meant they were heading inland. *To find what?* He asked himself. *The treasure? Another clue?* He would have to rely on the reports from his spies until he could find out. He made a decision to get a better view.

When Flint came back Fairbairn said. 'Davie, let's get mounted and go around to the east side of the lagoon.'

Fairbairn addressed the camp. 'I want you lot to stay close to the camp and keep sentries out. Flint and I will go to the other side of the channel where it's narrowest and see if we can find out what the treasure hunters are up to. Remember what's at stake here lads, we come through this we'll be well rewarded.'

'We're all fed up sir, let's all go to the other side of the channel,' said Jones, one of his best killers.

'That will attract too much attention to us; two riders will go un-noticed, we'll be back in a couple of days. Are we having a problem with the plan I have laid out Mr Jones?'

Reynolds knew immediately, he was in deep trouble. He swallowed and said. 'No sir, we'll stay in the camp and keep watch, we'll wait for you to return.'

Fairbairn stared a challenge into Jones eyes for a long time and eventually said. 'Good, Mr Jones, you'll be in command here until I return. Make sure everything goes

Prophets of Death

to plan or I'll want to know the reason why; is that clear enough for you?'

'That is very clear sir,' said Reynolds knowing he had been very close to being killed by this psychopath.

Fairbairn and Flint made camp behind some large boulders just short of the eastern sentinel of the heads. It was the only location close enough to let them survey the west side of the lagoon and channel, taking turns with the spyglass to keep watch on any developments along the slopes and the shoreline on the opposite side of the waterway.

'The bush is too thick to see anything,' said Fairbairn.

He noticed two dark holes at the bottom of the opposite cliff were getting wider as the tide went out.

'There are two small caves over on the other side of the channel,' said Fairbairn handing the spyglass to Flint.

Flint had a look and said. 'Should they have some significance?'

'That may be where those two bastards are trying to get to.'

There is more to this undercover operation than Fairbairn is telling, thought Flint. He said nothing; just kept up the watch until dark.

The next morning was overcast. Jamie and his companions set about hacking a pathway along the line of the stones which actually proved slightly easier than at first thought.

They took spells of rest time because the heat was sapping their strength, especially when the clouds cleared. When the sun reached its zenith they had some lunch and found fresh water bottles and provisions stacked beside their kit.

'Arthur has been to visit us I see,' said Hamish.

'God bless Arthur,' said Iain drinking gratefully from the water bottle.

The clearing of the path went on for the rest of the day until they gratefully sat down to the evening meal in front of the fire.

The stone path had followed the contour of the land, going up steep gradients then along the side of a steep gully and sometimes it would disappear so they had to cast around to find out if this was where the clue was or if there was another sign. Eventually they would find where the ground had moved in a land slip and take up the pace again.

It was tiresome work and they were exhausted.

On the day they eventually discovered the location of the clue, the path veered straight up a steep incline, around the top end of a gully and then straight down towards the channel to the lagoon. The path stopped at the edge of a small overhang.

Jamie went down on his belly and peered over the edge.

'We are right above the two small caves we saw when we sailed through the channel.'

'They didn't intend to make it easy for us, the old bastards,' said Iain. 'No disrespect Rory.'

'I know Iain, I share your impatience. I think we all knew this is where the clue was all along.'

'The caves are flooded so we can take a rest and wait for the tide to go out,' said Jamie.

'How do we get down there?' asked Rory.

'It won't be that difficult; we can slide down the slope on the hillside to the rocks and hopefully there will be a beach in front of the caves.'

It was late afternoon when the tide turned and they talked about waiting until low tide the next morning.

'Iain and I know what to look for now, we could find

Prophets of Death

the clue in a relatively short time and be out before dark,' said Jamie.

'Aye, come on, let's get this bleddy thing and go and find a nice hostelry with a hot bath,' said Iain.

Amen to that,' said Hamish. 'We should tie a rope to a strong root and drop it down next to the caves, just in case we need to haul ourselves up in a hurry.'

'Good idea,' said Rory unravelling a rope and securing it.

They slid down the rope to the small beach in front of the caves with their guns and equipment including four lamps.

'Rory, Hamish, do you two want to take the left cave, whilst Iain and I take the other?'

'Aye, so we're looking for a circle with a two headed eagle inside it,' said Rory.

'That's right but you won't know what size it is or if the wording on the seal is around the eagle. You'll certainly have to clean away moss and dirt from the walls in order for you to see any outline of something etched into the rock,' said Iain.

'Let's get started then,' said Jamie.

They had to bend over slightly to enter the cave walking with a stoop until the ceiling got higher as they progressed inward. The cave wasn't deep as they could see the back wall when the light from the lamp reflected off the moist moss on the wall, but the roof of the cave was much higher at the back.

The floor was rock at the entrance and then became sand as it inclined slightly upwards the deeper inside it went.

'The tide has washed this sand in and out of the cave and kept the depth of the sand at this level,' said Iain.

Holding the lamps above their heads to distribute the light more effectively Jamie noticed some debris trapped in the jagged rocks at the edge of the cave.

'Look, over there Iain.'

Wedged in the rocks were the remnants of what looked like pieces of iron and a small piece of leather.

'Now what the hell could that be?' said Iain.

'If nothing else if proves that someone has been here,' Jamie said pulling at the leather, which crumbled at his touch.

'It could be the bits of a raft of some sorts, smashed against the rocks at the entrance to the channel and washed up in here.'

'It could be. Maybe the Knights tried to paddle a raft to the entrance and it was wrecked and that's why they laid down the pathway.'

They shone the lamp light around the whole cave but could see no discernible markings. The floor of the cave was completely covered with sand save for some stones about four feet from the back wall.

Jamie put his lamp beside the stones and said. 'Iain, come and look at these stones.'

Iain put down his lamp on the opposite side from Jamie's and picked up one of the stones. 'These are not the same kind of rock as the caves are formed from.'

Jamie unsheathed his knife and scraped away the moss and slime and said. 'These are the same type of stones the path is made from.'

'And the cairns as well,' said Iain.

Instinctively they both started to dig away the sand around the stones with their hands and could see immediately there were stones below piled on top of each other.

'Iain, I think it might be a good idea to fetch the other two in here to dig this sand out.'

'Right, I'll get them then I'll go above and get the shovels.'

Prophets of Death

Rory and Hamish bustled into the cave beside Jamie and saw at once the pinnacle of a cairn jutting through the sand where Jamie had scraped away a bit more.

'There's too much water,' said Jamie. 'The sand just keeps sliding back in as soon as I scoop it out.'

Iain returned with the shovels.

Hamish said, 'I've some experience in clearing ground for building. The floor is inclined upwards so what we need to do is start digging from the front here and work our way back to the cairn, that will allow the sand to fall this way and any excess water will run off as well.'

'That's a sound plan Hamish,' said Rory.

They started shovelling the sand to the front of the cave.

'Throw the sand to the cave entrance as far as possible, I'll pile it up there so if the tide comes up it'll keep it at bay at least for a while,' said Hamish.

After what seemed to be an age they had cleared the sand away down to the rock floor, around the cairn to the back wall of the cave.

'The water's drained away, throw me the stones from the cairn and I'll shore up the dyke I've made with the sand; I'm assuming the clue is at the bottom of the cairn,' said Hamish.

Jamie and Iain looked at each other.

'I don't know Hamish and that's the truth,' said Iain.

'There's only one way to find out,' said Jamie as he started throwing the stones to the cave entrance.

'You'll have to work a wee bit quicker, the tide is coming in,' said Hamish.

Finally the last of the stones were cleared from the cave floor and the lamps were moved over to see if there was any a sign of the eagle.

They could see nothing.

Iain scraped the rock with his shovel as did Jamie and Rory but there was no sign of any etching or drawing, nothing to indicate the where the clue was located.

Hamish shouted. 'The water's up to the door step boys and there's a big wave coming down the channel.'

The wave broke over the small dyke Hamish had created but the water did not quite reach the searchers.

'There's no sign of anything here,' said Iain. 'After all that bleddy work.'

'It has to be here somewhere we followed the clue to the letter.'

'Here comes another one,' shouted Hamish.

This time the wave came over and flooded the cave floor.

Jamie said. 'Everybody out before we are washed away.'

Iain was still scraping at the wall and the floor searching for the clue.

Jamie pulled his shoulder to turn him around. 'We'll come back tomorrow morning Iain, we've missed something, but we'll find it. Come on, let's get out of here.'

They were exiting the cave when another wave, larger than the previous ones almost swept them of their feet and back into the cave.

'Grab the rope,' Rory shouted from above the cave.

Jamie looked to the right of the cave entrance and saw the end of the rope swaying around in the water he grabbed a hand full of Iain's shirt and pulled him towards the rope.

They both got two hands on the rope, Iain going up first. Jamie saw another swell looming at the entrance of the channel and the wave rising. 'Move yer arse Iain, there's another big one coming.'

Iain did not stop to look as he clambered up the short

Prophets of Death

climb to the overhang with Jamie right behind him. The wave swamped the caves beneath them as they stood on the path which they had so painstakingly followed to the caves.

'Jesus, this tide rises in a bit of a hurry,' said Iain.

Hamish said. 'The sea is fierce and rough at high tide on this coast. Further up the coast towards Durban there are many ship wrecks because of the wild weather, they call it the Wild Coast.'

'We're going to have to start cleaning out that bleddy cave again until we find the clue,' said Iain sitting on his haunches looking at the rising water passing through the channel.

'Come on, let's go back to camp and relax; tomorrow we start again,' said Jamie.

That night the camp fire was such a comfort for the four men sitting around it; the temperature had dropped quite considerably. Iain and Rory were sitting crossed legged on their woven reed mats with woollen blankets pulled over their shoulders and around knees. Jamie and Hamish had unfurled their mats to full length and were lying on one side stretched out in front of the fire. They had eaten and had tea and now were passing the whisky bottle around.

They were all quietly watching the flames from the wood burning almost smokeless in the circle of rocks containing the fire. Pipes were lit, Iain sucked on a cigarette he had rolled and Jamie inhaled the smoke from the cheroot which was always so satisfying after a fulfilling meal, followed by good whisky.

'Maybe one of us should keep watch,' said Iain.

Hamish said. 'Don't worry Iain, Arthur and his men are watching.'

Jamie exhaled some smoke and said. 'There were no markings or indications or anything to lead us to the clue.

What did we miss, Iain?'

'Jamie, I'm so tired I don't want to think about anything in that bleddy cave. I want to look at the flames in the fire, smoke tobacco and get a wee bit inebriated.'

Rory and Hamish glanced at each other, concern on their faces but said nothing.

Jamie saw the exchange and said. 'Iain's just having a wee tantrum lads, he gets impatient when he doesn't get an early result for his efforts, don't you Iain?'

Iain knew Jamie was having a go at him to get him out of his bad mood and said, 'Aw shut yer face, ye big eejit, I suppose you've figured out where we went wrong in finding the clue?'

Iain had a way of putting a damper on things when he was in a mood but he was finding his sense of humour again.

Jamie sat up and poured some whisky into his tea cup and said. 'Well as long as you're in a better mood let's go over what we did see and what we didn't see.'

'Pass the whisky,' said Iain.

'What do you think about the bits of iron with the bits of leather bound around them?' asked Jamie.

'It could be flotsam washed into the cave, like a barrel that could have been part of a raft,' said Rory.

'Or maybe it's the remnants of a scaffold or ladder that broke up over the years,' said Hamish.

'That's possible, but there was no indication of the clue that we could see. The first clue at the Elephant's Eye was relatively easy to work out so this one should have been simple as well. If the walls and the floor of the cave did not show the clue then there is only one other place it could be.'

'The roof of the cave,' said Iain suddenly coming to life. 'The emblem on the clue we have is an eagle, an eagle flies in the sky above us and the cairn was built with

Prophets of Death

a pointed top, pointing at the roof of the cave.'

'That's what I'm thinking,' said Jamie. 'The bits of iron and leather could have been one of two things, part of a scaffolding of some sort to climb up to the roof, as you said Hamish, or a small raft, not washed into the cave but left in the cave after the Knights used it to float to the roof of the cave when the tide came in so they could work on hiding the clue.'

'A raft would be too unstable for working on the stone to hide the clue; it had to be some kind of primitive scaffolding or a big ladder. Even if the cave flooded the scaffold would just have floated in there as it was too big to be able to float away at low tide.'

'The level of the sea must have changed after all these years,' said Rory. 'The Knights must have used a scaffold in those days and had the time to work on the hiding place.'

Hamish said, 'We will have to chop some branches and rig up a ladder and take a look at low tide tomorrow.'

Iain said. 'I'm going sit here by our cosy wee fire and drink some more whisky and smoke. Then I'll pile some wood on the fire and sleep for as long as I can without anybody wakening me.'

'Aye, Iain's right; let's get some sleep and tackle the problems tomorrow,' said Jamie.

Two days after arriving at the lookout point, Fairbairn watched Fyvie and McColl with two other men appear above the caves.

He waved to Flint to join him. 'Well now, it's about time we had some bloody action from them.' said Fairbairn.

They watched the four men split into pairs and go into the caves then eventually the four concentrated on one cave and toil inside until the tide started in again.

They abandoned whatever it was they were doing and ascended above the cave to their camp.

'You say that these two men have an ancient clue to find another clue which will lead them to… how many more clues before they find this hidden treasure?' said Flint.

'There must be another clue in that cave, it's too small to hide any kind of treasure, besides, getting anything in or out of there would be just about impossible; this cave must be the one that has the clue to uncover the prize.'

Darkness descended once again and they retreated behind the rocks to their camp. The fire was obscured from the enemy across the channel but they could see the glow from theirs quite clearly.

Chapter Twenty Two

October 1856

Knysna Lagoon

Iain opened his eyes as the grey dawn introduced the coming day, the fire had been replenished with wood and water was being boiled. He just lay there enjoying the warmth of his blanket; dreaming; *what's Clara doing; why am I out here risking my life for a possible myth, never mind a psychopathic Englishman and his band of murdering bastards waiting for the chance to kill us all and take the loot for themselves.*

'What the fuck am I doing here?' he said to no-one.

'Good, you're awake,' said Jamie. 'You can help tie these branches together and make a couple of ladders.'

'Aye, after I get my tea and my breakfast.'

The tide had ebbed and flowed back again during the night so they fashioned the ladders then dropped them down to the cave entrance when the tide ebbed once more.

After the ladders were coaxed into place against the back wall, Iain had a hard time getting the long branches in to attach the lamps but persevered until they could shine a light up into the roof of the cave.

'Rory,' said Iain, 'you can have the pleasure of helping Jamie up there whilst I hold the lamps with Hamish.'

'That's very kind of you Iain.'

'No, it's not a kindness; I don't like to be high up on bits of wood tied up with tree vines, I am quite happy to be down here.'

Jamie and Rory went up to the top of the ladders till they were about two feet short of the roof.

'Let's use the shovels to scrape the moss and growth from the roof and see what's underneath,' said Jamie.

After half an hour of stretching and scraping they could not see anything resembling a cut in the rock.

'We are directly above the spot where the cairn was and there's nothing etched on the rock,' said Jamie.

'What is that mark there?' said Rory pointing to a small rough part of the roof.

Jamie strained to see the mark.

'Iain, bring your lamp over to the left of Rory's ladder.'

As Iain moved the lamp across the shadows changed and Jamie could see immediately what the mark was.

'The shape of a cairn has been chipped into the roof, it's pointing to the wall above the ladders,' said Jamie.

Jamie and Rory could easily reach out and scrape away the growth and moss from the wall just below the roof and the circle of the seal revealed itself, then the letters surrounding the seal between the inner and outer circles were exposed; the majestic two headed eagle was there in the middle of the inner circle.

'There it is gentlemen we've found the bleddy bird,' said Jamie.

'Thank fuck for that,' said Iain. 'Is there a shiny pebble Jamie,' he said referring to the discovery of the first clue.

Jamie wiped down the seal and the area around it with a rag of linen and could see the shiny pebble in between the two heads of the eagle one facing left, the other facing right.

Prophets of Death

'It's there Iain.'

'Iain, do you want to come up and help Jamie with the retrieval of the clue?' asked Rory.

'That's very thoughtful of you Rory but you can have that honour today; I'm quite happy down here.'

'Right then,' said Jamie unsheathing his knife. 'If it's the same procedure as the last time I should be able to prize that pebble out of its recess.'

He teased the point of the knife into the tiny space above the pebble and, using a little patience and not too much force he worked the stone free, catching it as it fell.

'Catch!' he said to Iain as he tossed it down.

Jamie could see the dark hole where the pebble had been, he then traced the seam of the larger recess with the point of the knife, clearing away the dirt and roots of the ancient moss. He then inserted the blade into the hole, going in up to the hilt and then pulled down on the handle. The two heads of the eagle popped out slightly from the wall.

'My god; look at that,' said Rory.

'Take the handle Rory, pull it down and out. Don't use too much force, it should slide out with ease,' said Jamie. 'Look out below.' He warned the others.

Rory pulled on the knife handle and the whole form of the two headed eagle came away from the wall. Rory nearly lost his balance and Jamie had to grab his arm to steady him.

Rory held the eagle out and tilted the knife so it could slide off.

Hamish had put his lamp pole against the wall so he could catch it and he looked at it in amazement.

'Well held Hamish,' said Iain.

Jamie held his lamp in front of the gap in the wall and, looking in he could see something at the back of the hole. He gave the lamp to Rory then reached in and carefully pulled it out.

'It's the same as the last time, a leather pouch; there should be a gold box inside. Let's go down and open it up.'

Jamie waited until Rory was down on the floor and then checking there was nothing else in the cavity came down the make-shift ladder and they all went outside on the small beach to the welcome brightness and warmth of the sun.

'Let us see what the next clue has in store for us my lads, maybe we'll have to chop down a forest or shovel away a desert; I am beside myself,' said Iain sarcastically, rubbing his hands together and pretending to be excited.

Rory and Hamish giggled; Jamie shook his head and said. 'What am I going to do with you, ye bleddy idiot?'

Fairbairn and Flint watched with interest as the four men tackled the cave again, but this time they had fashioned two ladders to take into the cave. A while later they emerged, one of them carrying what looked like a satchel.

Then to Fairbairn's absolute astonishment the two spies he had sent to follow Fyvie, appeared on top of the caves and fired shots into the sand in front of the caves.

'What the fuck are they doing?' shouted Fairbairn rising up to walk forward to the cliff edge.

Flint jumped up and grabbed Fairbairn by the shoulder and pulled him back. 'Showing yourself is not going to help.'

They tried to hear what they were shouting at Fyvie but could not because of the wind and the ocean.

'Flint, get your gun and shoot those two rats.'

'You want me to shoot your own men?' said Flint wide eyed.

'Yes, shoot the fucking idiots before they ruin everything.'

Prophets of Death

Arthur had sent two men to follow Fairbairn and another rider who had saddled up and left their camp. One of his men had come back to report that they had camped on the other side of the channel and were using a spyglass to keep watch on Jamie and his friends.

The scout also reported that the other rider with Fairbairn had an extra-long rifle scabbard.

'Do you think it is a marksman's rifle?'

'I do,' said the scout. 'It could not conceivably be anything else.'

'That's not good, you better get back to the other side and keep watch.'

Then the strangest thing happened. The two spies Arthur and Hendrik were watching suddenly vanished.

'Shit, where are they?' said Hendrik.

'Slippery bastards,' said Arthur. 'Hendrik, you go down on the left flank I'll take the right.'

Two shots rang out.

The echo from the rifle shots was so loud the four men reacted as one and dived for the cover of the cave as they heard the musket balls slap into the sand.

'Jesus, that bastard Fairbairn is shooting at us,' said Iain.

'That's impossible,' said Hamish. 'He couldn't get past Arthur.'

'Unless Arthur is dead,' said Jamie.

'*That was a warning shot*,' shouted a voice from above them.

'Who are you? What do you want?' shouted Jamie.

'*It does not matter who I am, I'm going to lower a rope down to the front of the cave. You will take what you have found in the cave and tie it to the end of the rope and then I will pull it up and be on my way and you will continue to live,*' the voice shouted.

'Listen ye fuckin' arsehole,' shouted Iain. 'After the work we put into this, if you want anything from us you're going to have to come and get it.' He looked at the other three for assurance. 'Isn't that right lads?'

'You're not armed I can see your guns from here.'

Sure enough they had left their guns beside a large rock out in the open.

'Make it easy for yourselves and do as I tell you. If we have to come down there, we don't take prisoners.'

Arthur and Hendrik could hear the two spies shouting something as they sneaked up behind them. Arthur laid his rifle on the ground and pulled out his two pistols. He looked over to where Hendrik was concealed and raised the pistols in the air. Hendrik understood and laid his rifle down bringing up his two pistols and nodding at Arthur they stood up in plain sight and casually walked towards the two men. Hearing a noise behind them the two spies turned, Arthur and Hendrik fired two shots each at their chosen targets hitting them square in the chest. Both men disappeared over the cliff.

Down in the cave they heard a volley of shots and two bodies came crashing down. One landed on the rocks to the left of the cave and the other on the sand in front of them.

'That would be Arthur's work,' said Hamish.

'Is everybody all right down there?' asked a different voice from above.

'We are all fine. Is that you Arthur?'
'Of course it's me Hamish, who else would it be?' Said Arthur as though this was an every-day occurrence. 'Sorry I took so long, these slippery buggers nearly got away from me. I'll go back on watch now.'

Hamish went out to the small beach followed by the

Prophets of Death

others and looked up. 'Send someone back in a couple of hours to take us to your camp, we will be leaving here shortly.'

'I'll do that Hamish.'

Jamie and Iain took a leg each of the dead man on the beach and dragged the body to the sea and rolled him in.

'We don't take any prisoners either ye fuckin' arsehole,' Iain said to the body.

'You've really got to stop talking to dead people Iain.'

'They don't answer back,' he said eying the other one on the rocks.

'Let's pack it up and get back to the camp,' said Jamie. 'At least we'll have some cover from any other prying eyes.

Before Flint could respond to shooting the spies, two men suddenly appeared out of the bush and walked calmly towards Fairbairn's men. They fired a volley of pistol shots at the two henchmen as they turned; they died before one hit the beach and the other smacked sickeningly onto to the rocks.

'Jesus, where the hell did they come from?' said Flint.

'The other force I warned my men about. They've been up there watching out for Fyvie and his men since they arrived here.'

They saw McColl talking to the corpse on the beach as he and Fyvie rolled it into the water.

'Was the red headed one talking to the body?'

'Yes I believe he was, he's a mad man that one; from what I have heard, they both are.'

McColl killed my brother, thought Fairbairn. *If I order Flint to shoot him I will be showing my hand and might never see the treasure. Better to wait; I will have my revenge soon.*

They watched Fyvie, McColl and their two companions leave the area above the caves and disappear into the bush.

'I suppose it's safe to assume we are being followed as well,' said Flint.

'You can bet your pay on that,' said Fairbairn.

'So how do you propose to follow them to the prize when they know your every move?'

'I have been giving that problem a lot of thought and I've come up with a plan which I'll discuss back at the main camp,' said Fairbairn.

Fairbairn and Flint packed up and headed back to their main camp which was now minus two men.

Prophets of Death

Chapter Twenty Three

October 1856

Knysna

They sat in a circle while Jamie opened the pouch. He removed the gold box placing it on top of the pouch. Then, opening the box he took out a smaller fat greased pouch, delicately removing the parchment from within and unfolded it on the white linen towel he had laid out for that purpose.

They all four bent over to read the script.

'The best thing to do is for me to read it out and then we can look at the seal and ponder on the clue,' said Jamie. 'It reads as follows.

'Nor west two hundred leagues and eighty,
In the mountains of hell the heat will get ye,
If you read this script you are close to the end,
That which awaits you is not for mere men,
Just and upright they need to be,
To guard the power entrusted to thee,
Light the fires in the deep dark place,
To show the seal in the cavernous space,
The spears will point the way that you seek,
The knights guard the chapel in which they sleep.'

Jamie showed them the crude drawing of the Knight's

seal which consisted of two circular emblems next to one another with Latin words engraved around each of them between the inner and outer circles on the circumference; a horse with two riders and two spears inscribed within the first circle and a domed chapel in the second. Jamie said, 'Well, that's it lads, does anyone have any idea where the clue is describing?'

'If my memory serves me,' said Hamish, 'I think the mountains of hell are the mountain range running east to west, north of a small settlement called Oudtshoorn; yes that's it, but I think we should talk to Arthur, he will know exactly where this clue is going to lead us.'

A bit later Arthur appeared out of the bush like a ghost and said, 'can we pack you lads up and retire to our cosy little camp up on the mountain?'

'Aye Arthur you can indeed,' said Rory.

They packed up the kit and were led up the mountain to the well concealed camp and were given their saddles and tack for the horses.

'We'll rest up here tonight then cross the river to Knysna in the morning,' said Arthur.

'The two who ambushed us, were they Fairbairn's men?' said Jamie.

'Yes they were, my apologies for letting them get past me.'

'No apologies are necessary; is Fairbairn close by?'

'They're camped north west of the Lagoon. I think the two ambushers were sent to watch only but decided to try and be heroes and bring the boss some good news, which would be your clue unearthed in the cave; the brainless idiots,' said Arthur.

'Speaking of clues,' said Jamie, 'Hamish says you might be able to identify an area that is mentioned in the clue.'

'I think the five of us should sit by the fire, drink

Prophets of Death

some whisky and find out where you want to go.'

Jamie showed Arthur the piece of parchment with the writing and the seal.

'The mountains of hell have to be the Swartberg Mountains,' said Arthur. 'Because in the summer, it can get as hot as hell in there. On the other side of the mountains is the semi-desert of the Great Karoo, the heat could kill a man with no water or shelter in no time at all.'

'Do you know of any caves or caverns, maybe holes in the ground like potholes in the area?' asked Iain.

'I personally do not know of anything like that but I seem to remember a story of a farmer, a Boer who talked of a cave on his land… let me ask Hendrik.' Arthur got up and looked around. 'Hendrik, could you come over here?'

Hendrik wandered over and sat beside Arthur. 'Do you remember the story of the Boer who had a big farm north of Oudtshoorn with caves on it?'

'Yes I do know the story although it is not so clear, Boss,' said Hendrik. 'When there was fighting during the Kaffir wars he and some other local farmers would take their families and possessions and hole up in the caves as it was a natural fort and easily defended; but that is the story, whether it is true is another story.'

'How far is it to the Swartberg Mountains, Arthur?' asked Jamie.

'A few days ride over rough and wild country.'

'Hendrik, could you take us to the farm where the caves are reported to be?'

'I could not but there's a friend of mine in Oudtshoorn who is nearly as good a tracker as me and he has been around that area all of his life. If the cave is around there then he'll know of it.'

'Thank you Hendrik we'll need your help to fulfil this quest,' said Arthur.

Hendrik went back to his friends at another part of the camp and Iain asked. 'I don't want to sound… um… look, I'll come right out with it, are all these men to be trusted, Arthur? I have to ask this question.'

'I know you and Jamie have concerns young Iain, and so you should, sharing a burden such as this with complete strangers, but let me tell you that all these men who are around us, except for the coloureds, are on the square an…'

'On the square?' asked Jamie.

'It means they are all Freemasons, they are all just and upright men committed to fight and lay down their lives to ensure the preservation of whatever the Knights have left us to save and protect.'

'Just and upright men, that's what it says in the clue.'

'It does indeed. That's our legacy from the Knights and we won't fail them,' said Rory.

'Hendrik and his trackers can also be trusted, Iain,' said Arthur.

'So let us eat a good supper, smoke some tobacco and taste some whisky for tomorrow we head for Knysna to replenish our provisions and plan our route,' said Rory.

'I have been giving that a bit of thought,' said Jamie. 'If what we are led to believe is actually true…'

'It's true Jamie,' said Iain. 'I can feel it in my water. How could anyone go to all this trouble of laying this trail of clues for it not to be true? The treasure's there.'

'Thanks for that vote of confidence Iain, as I was saying, if the treasure is there we are going to need five, maybe six large, heavy wagons to get whatever we find back to the coast depending of course on what you're going to do with it,' said Jamie looking at Rory.

'Five or six wagons may not be large enough. When I was in Cape Town and realised that you and Iain were going to follow the clues to the end, I knew I had to put a

Prophets of Death

provisional plan of action in place to get the artefacts and whatever else back to Scotland. So I had a discussion with Captain Willard when we signed up for this voyage, that depending on our business in Knysna, we would hire his ship in the near future, of course mentioning that I may do some business with you and Iain. He said if I was in business with you two then there would not be any hesitation on his part. I will of course speak to Captain Willard when we get to Knysna and set about procuring the Flying Fish to transport some delicate cargo to the Northern Hemisphere.'

'Roger will accommodate you Rory, that I can promise you,' said Iain. 'We should go along with you when we arrive in Knysna, you can take Roger into your confidence he is a good man. We should ask him to look at his charts for a suitable loading point further down the coast rather than haul the treasure back here.'

'Yes, Hamish and I have had some discussion on that very point; Captain Willard would be the very man to advise us on that.'

'I've also been giving some thought to our trek,' said Arthur. 'I would suggest that when we acquire the wagons we send them on ahead as they will travel a lot slower than mounted men. We should send each wagon with a two man team on the main roadway west from Knysna and then north to Oudtshoorn where they will make camp and wait for word from us when we secure the cave site. Iain, you may want to furnish the teams with delivery notes from Fyvie and McColl for the transport of farming equipment or wagons to some non-existent farmers so as not to raise any suspicions of where they are actually going.'

'That's a damn good idea,' said Iain.

Arthur continued. 'Meanwhile, we and the bulk of our force, which will be the mounted men, will gather at a designated camp-site north of Knysna. From there we'll take a shorter route north through the Knysna forest, up towards the mountains and then west, which will eventually take us north of Oudtshoorn. Once there we have to find the farmer who owns the land with the caves on it and look to see if that is indeed the place which we seek and secure it. Then we send a couple of men to meet the wagons in Oudtshoorn and guide them to our destination.'

'Gentlemen, it sounds as though we have a plan of action.' said Jamie. 'I can't tell you what a privilege and a relief it is to have you with us on this mission. I don't think Iain and I really knew how much was at stake or how much was involved in this task until now; thank you all.'

Rory said, 'I will be glad when we are sailing away with a fortune denied to the ELOS. It came to a point in time, Jamie, when you and Iain did not have a choice in what was going to happen, but you always had a guardian angel.'

Jamie raised his whisky and said. 'Amen to that. Tomorrow we plan for the Mountains of Hell.'

Chapter Twenty Four

October 1856

Cape Town

Sir George Whyte went at his new governorship with gusto, reading every government paper that Cuthbert had signed or changed or forced through and logged all the dubious decisions that had been opposed by government officials, the clergy and upstanding citizens of the Cape.

'Mr Hutcheson, please come in to my office,' said Whyte through the open door of his office.

'What can I do for you sir?' said Hutchison facing his new superior.

'I want you to arrange an expedition to the Eastern Cape, Bill. We'll travel overland to King William's Town to assess the situation on the route and at the frontier, then return when I am satisfied with my findings; we will return by sea.'

'Sir, I have to point out to you that it would be safer to get there by sea as well as returning.'

'Yes, I realise that, Bill, but I want to get a feeling of the land, stop at one or two hamlets along the way and talk with the settlers,' said Whyte.

'I think you may find many settlers and community leaders with many gripes sir. If I may be so bold and with all due respect, your predecessor was not disposed to talking with or listening to anyone but himself.'

Whyte smiled and said. 'Gerald Cuthbert was never the politician, Bill; he is a soldier through and through. He'll go in, get the job done to the satisfaction of his superiors and move on to the next war. I'm an army man myself but my calling is to ensure that the future generations of the settlers have a foundation on which to build places of education, hospitals and profitable businesses. I was sent to mould the infrastructure of the colonies of the empire and that is exactly what I… what we, are going to do here.

'I appreciate you pointing out the fact that my safety may be at risk but I'm sure you can put together an army escort worthy of the new governor, a show of force for the natives and a show of reassurance for the settlers. What do you say, Bill?'

'I can do that for you sir, we'll give them all a show of force to remember.'

'Good. Now I see we have a Captain John McAllister and one, Charles Blackwell who are both commissioners to the Xhosa natives, is that correct?'

'Yes sir, they live and work in the Eastern Cape. Shall I send word to Charles for them to be available for a meeting in King William's Town?'

'Yes, do that but tell them to make arrangements for me to meet with all the Xhosa Chiefs without their councillors. I want to see McAllister and Blackwell before the meeting with the chiefs as I have to brief them on our plans for the next step of the Xhosa natives' immediate future.'

'That will prove to be very difficult sir.'

'Nonsense, order them both to make the arrangements with the chiefs but meet with me a few days beforehand.'

'What I mean sir, is; I don't think you will get a meeting with the chiefs without their pakati.'

Prophets of Death

'Pakati?'

'Pakati is the Xhosa name for the councillors to the chiefs.'

'Just how powerful or important is… or… are the pakati. Surely the chiefs don't have to say anything to them or just simply order them to stay away,' said Whyte.

'It's not quite as simple as that sir,' said Hutcheson getting very annoyed with the new governor's attitude of indifference. 'Each chief has his own pakati to help advise him on the day to day running of their clan. Shutting them out would be like asking the Prime Minister to leave out his cabinet ministers while he makes a deal with the Tsar of Russia to pay him off so Britain can leave the Crimea and leave it to the Russians.'

Whyte looked at Hutcheson with contempt and said. 'I do not like your tone, Bill, your analogy is hardly appropriate considering you are comparing the civilised world to a bunch of natives in loin cloths.'

'Sir, we are talking about a culture that has endured for centuries and created a structured governance which has been able to control its people for a very long time.'

'Times are changing; people are changing; the world is changing, Bill. Britain's Empire is expanding; civilisation has come to Africa so the inhabitants must change to suit.'

Hutcheson could not debate this subject with Whyte any further without compromising his position as an undercover operative and his job with the governor.

'Yes, I suppose you are correct sir. I'll send a despatch to Charles Blackwell to meet with you in King William's Town.'

'Good, let's get this strategy moving along and bring everlasting civility and peace to Southern Africa,' said Whyte.

'I'll make all the arrangements immediately sir. Will

there be anything else?'

Whyte looked at him wondering if Hutcheson was being facetious and said. 'Yes, there is something else. I am sending a large contingent of soldiers north of the Cape Province to Victoria West. I have reason to believe the local natives are spoiling for a fight with the settlers, so I'm sending the army to dissuade them from taking up arms to fight farmers who are producing food for us. There is one other matter. I have had a signal from London to send any Royal Navy ships anchored in Simon's Town to proceed up the west coast as far Luanda, the main port of the Portuguese colony there. It seems there's some kind of civil war and there could be slavers in the area. The navy has, as you know, orders to blow slave ships out of the water or seize and board any ships suspected of having slaves on board. That's all I think. Thank you.'

Hutcheson retreated to his outer office and looked unconcerned as he appeared to prepare for the coming journey to the Eastern Cape. He could feel Whyte watching him through the open door connecting their offices.

'Could you close my door Bill?' said Whyte.

'Yes sir.'

Hutcheson closed the door and was very concerned. He sat down at his desk and composed his letters and despatches for the governor's expedition to be sent to the various departments and addresses.

He then wrote a lengthy letter to Armstrong describing what Whyte was about to embark upon in the Eastern Cape and the deployment of troops away from the Cape Region; more importantly, the Royal Navy being diverted elsewhere. He then had his coded letter despatched through diplomatic channels to London, finished his work and went to search out Doctor Morgan.

Prophets of Death

He hailed a Hansom cab and went past the doctor's house but did not stop, seeing no lights or any sign of life. He then told the driver to go to the infirmary on the off-chance Morgan was there; he was told by a nurse the doctor had gone to the officers' mess in the fort.

That's just perfect, he thought. *I can't go and talk to him with a bunch of addled officers… unless… I make up a story.*

Bill went to his house and asked the cab driver to wait for him. He rushed into his writing bureaux and wrote a letter to Doctor Morgan, then sealing it, re-boarded the cab and rode for the fort.

When he approached the gatehouse he looked like he was in a great hurry; dismounting the cab with such haste that the guard raised his rifle with bayonet attached.

'Please deliver this letter to Doctor Morgan in the Officer's mess; it's an emergency.'

The sentry took the letter. 'At once sir.'

The sentry then summoned another soldier who took the letter and ran into the castle.

Doctor Morgan was indulging in his favourite pastime of tasting whisky at the bar with a couple of army officers from the 73rd Regiment when an orderly came up to him with a letter in his hand.

'Sir, there is an urgent letter for you.'

'Oh what now.'

He took the letter and opened it focussing his spectacles on the words which said;

Mrs Hutcheson has taken her labour pains; her water has broken and needs your attention immediately.

Yours sincerely, Mr. Bill Hutcheson

The doctor nearly gave out a burst of laughter and then thought through the haze of the whisky. *Something is wrong.*

He turned to the patrons of the mess and said. 'Please

excuse me gentlemen, duty calls, I may or may not return tonight.'

He went out and summoned his carriage, stopping for Hutcheson waiting beyond the gate. Bill paid his cab and jumped in to Morgan's carriage.

'I nearly gave the game away in the officers' mess, Bill,' said the doctor thumping the roof and shouting. 'Head for home driver. A pregnant wife indeed, another couple of whiskies and I would have thought it a hoax and had you put in the stocks. Now what is the real emergency?'

As the carriage bounced along the road Bill retold what the governor was planning and the doctor was greatly alarmed.

'The movement of the armed forces away from the colony is definitely not right,' said the doctor. 'So you think this is the start of the ELOS's plan to incite the Xhosa warriors to take up arms for war?'

'I am convinced that's the case, Doctor. I need to get word to Jamie and Iain, but I don't know where they are exactly. I know they went to Belvedere and Knysna Port but they could be gone from there by now.'

'When do you leave on the Governor's trek to King William's Town?'

'The day after tomorrow.'

'Are you in charge of the route the entourage will take to the frontier?'

'Yes I am organising the whole expedition,' said Bill.

'Good, then you will convince Whyte to stop over in George because he has to impress the people there. That will give you time to ride to Knysna and find Captain Willard, the skipper of the Flying Fish; it will be anchored somewhere at Knysna. He'll know where the boys are.'

'Then that's what I'll do. Thank you doctor.'

'You can't leave this to anyone else, Bill, you have

Prophets of Death

to deliver the message yourself.'

'I know and I will deliver it Doctor.'

Doctor Morgan thumped the roof again. 'Change of address driver, take us to the club,' he shouted. 'You need a drink lad, let us sample the club's whisky.'

K D Neill

Chapter Twenty Five

November 1856

Knysna Forest

Jamie and Iain packed up the camp with the rest of their companions; mounted up and headed around the lagoon to Knysna, the large entourage attracting more attention than Jamie would have liked.

Finding suitable accommodation, which could house the coloured contingent in the group, Iain was first in the door of the hotel and up to his room and then into a steaming hot tub in the communal bathroom.

The bathroom was unique in the sense that it had six tubs separated by curtains. The room was constantly serviced with hot water by servants who kept a boiler fired up for most of the day.

When Jamie climbed into his tub next to Iain he lit a cheroot and ordered some whisky from the waiter who was wandering in and out the room.

Rory came in and said. 'This is as good a place as any to start planning the journey to the resting place of the Knights treasure.

Hamish and Arthur arrived. 'I asked the brethren to give us an hour for a private chat,' said Hamish.

Rory ushered the waiters out; locked the door and immersed himself in a tub.

They started the discussion with what provisions

Prophets of Death

they would need and extra equipment and who would be responsible for what and eventually Jamie said. 'Right lads, I think we're all agreed on what has to be done and how we go about finishing our crusade.'

'Crusade is it?' said Iain. 'Did you become a knight when I wasn't looking?'

Jamie threw a sponge at him and said. 'Well it is a kind of crusade.'

There were murmurs of agreement.

Jamie continued, 'Iain and I have been playing with some ideas about how to transport the artefacts and any other valuable items that we find. We suggest that we have wooden boxes made to fit snuggly to the measurements of the wagons and not only that, make the boxes water tight and give them buoyancy, like a boat. Iain has worked on ship building so he could supervise this.

'Why would they have to be watertight Jamie?' asked Rory.

'To avoid scrutiny at a dockside or a harbour, we could drive the wagons into the sea and float the boxes off, tie them together and tow them to the ship with a dinghy, obviously on a calm night, but it would be quick and easy and you would have everything dry and secure in the ship in no time at all.'

'By god, that is a damn good idea,' said Rory. 'Can you have that organised Iain?'

'Yes I can, very easily.'

'Good, we can leave that in Iain's capable hands,' said Jamie. 'When the wagons leave here we send bales of hay with them for packing and I think we should send a rider with each wagon and tell them where to meet us to avoid being followed.'

'I've been thinking along those lines as well,' said Arthur speaking for the first time. 'But send maybe one or two men with each of the wagons and the rest of the men can leave Knysna one or two at a time to avoid any unwanted attention and I'll give them a rendezvous to meet up.'

'Fairbairn and his thugs will be watching for Jamie and me to leave so he can follow us, so we intend to sneak away one night,' said Iain. 'One of your men will have our horses and kit somewhere out of town, then we'll leave on foot to retrieve the horses and ride to the rendezvous.'

Arthur said. 'Hendrik will take your horses and wait for you. Also, everyone be aware that Fairbairn has a marksman with him, my men have seen his gun, not that there's much you can do if he takes aim at you, but be aware nevertheless.'

They all left the bath-house and met for dinner after donning fresh clothes. Captain Willard was invited to join them in a private room where they confided in him what they were after in the caves and to make arrangements to commandeer the Flying Fish.

'So there you have it Roger,' said Jamie. 'You now know where we are going and what we are trying to find. I have given you the approximate location of the cave, as soon as we find out exact location I'll send a rider to inform you. If we recover anything from the cave I'll send another rider to inform you that we're on our way.'

'Why would I need to know the location of the cave?' asked Willard.

'In case anyone in Cape Town needs to inform us of any developments and remember Roger, not a word to anyone,' said Jamie.

'I understand, no-one will know where you will be.'

'Now all we need is the location of the pick-up point to load the cargo from the cave assuming we find anything, of course,' said Rory.

Prophets of Death

Willard produced a chart from the satchel he was carrying and spread it on the table.

'There's a small town to the west of Knysna called Mossel Bay,' said Willard pointing at the place on the chart. 'That bay is very well sheltered and the water is always calm. Now, before you get to the town there is a wide deserted beach which has easy access from the road; that's where you can float the cargo to the ship. It'll be quick and very easy to load and, maybe Arthur can confirm this, there is a road from Oudtshoorn to that area.'

'There is a road, it'll take us straight to the pick-up point,' said Arthur.

'The problem is we don't know how long we'll take to finish this Roger,' said Rory.

'Take all the time you need. I and my crew will be standing by for the word and we will be there,' said Willard.

Jamie put his hand on Willard's shoulder and said. 'Thanks Roger, I knew we could count on you.'

It took a lot of time to put everything in place but eventually all the plans were finalised and the wagons were ready to leave.

The story was that the wagons, five of them, were going to Cape Town to collect goods and bring them back to Knysna Port. Some of the men started drifting away saying they were going home because there was nothing happening here but were actually heading for the rendezvous with Arthur.

Fairbairn's tracker informed him that Fyvie and McColl and the rest of their sizeable troop had broken camp and crossed the river into Knysna.

He waited a few hours then had his men move camp to the north east of the town to be in a better position of pursuit if they needed to move quickly.

He went into town at dusk and booked a room in a lodging house where he cleaned up and changed, then went to walk the town and find the boss boy of his informants, Jan Greyling, who had been instructed to find out where Fyvie and his men were staying.

He found Greyling in a seedy tavern down by the small dock. *This is where I usually find these cretins,* he thought.

And as usual he bought the beer and sat at a quiet table.

'What of Fyvie and McColl?' asked Fairbairn.

'They have been in their hotel since… not last night… the night before sir… yes, the night before.'

'Two nights ago for god's sake Greyling, can you not say two nights ago,' said Fairbairn impatiently.

'Two nights ago sir. They haven't been seen to come out since the Captain of the big ship came to eat with them, this I found out from one of the waiters. Except the one called McColl, he went to the carpenter's yard and spoke to some men working with wagons.'

'I will be going back to my camp. Keep me informed of any movement of the people with Fyvie and especially those wagons,' said Fairbairn.

Jamie and Iain were sitting in the hotel bar finishing their beers, Jamie said. 'Time to put our escape plan into action.'

'I'll wander ahead of you while you do the talking,' said Iain.

Jamie went to the reception. 'I would like to make sure we have our rooms booked for another week please.' Said Jamie loud enough for all within earshot to hear.

'Yes sir, you have four rooms booked until next week,' said the receptionist.

Prophets of Death

'Thank you. We have a lot of work to do so we don't want to be disturbed.'

'I will see to it sir, have a good night.'

'Good night then,' said Jamie.

In the early hours of the morning they quietly left their rooms and went to a pre-booked room at the back of the hotel, opened the window; threw their light kit down to the alley and jumped down after them.

They strapped on their guns and knives, then, hugging the wall of the hotel, they made their way to the outer fence of the property and climbed over. They kept to the lanes and alleys between buildings when they could until they reached the outskirts of the settlement and then ran for the tree line on the hill overlooking the town.

Hendrik was waiting patiently at the pre-arranged location with their horses. He had left the previous day with the boys' horses, using them as pack horses to throw off any spies watching the stables.

'Come Bassies, let us be gone from here,' said Hendrik.

They rode off to the main rendezvous point where they would probably wait a day or so for the others to find and then they could go on a treasure hunt.

The weather had been good so far and the camp had an air of optimism as the men went about cleaning equipment and looking after the horses. Some of the men sliced raw game meat to hang in the sun to make biltong; the dried meat would sustain the men whilst in the saddle and when there was ban on making a fire.

All the men had arrived and the leaders of the final expedition were gathered around their fire in the camp to discuss the route to the caves.

Arthur Burton started the proceedings. 'We're still waiting on two of my men, they should get here tomorrow morning. We'll be riding through the Knysna Forest to our next camp just before we leave the forest. The forest has a dense growth of trees and vegetation but there's a single track that Hendrik and I know of, only a handful of bush-men know of it so it will be safe to travel and not easy for anyone who wants to follow. We won't be traveling fast as the ghosts of the forest don't like to be disturbed.'

'Oh! Right; here we go; bleddy ghosts,' said Iain. 'What next… devils… demons? We have already fought a couple of them.'

Arthur chuckled along with the others and said. 'No Iain, but these ghosts are real enough. These ghosts are Knysna Elephants which were, supposedly, wiped out years ago by hunters.'

'So you are saying that some might remain?' asked Jamie.

'Hendrik and I came through the forest a couple of years back and we found this hidden trail we are going on now. When we found the trail we went off it and searched through some thick bush and found the spoor of elephant, there was elephant dung as well so there was no doubt. That was the first time we found them; you don't see them or hear them until they are on top of you.'

'Like ghosts,' said Rory.

'Exactly, on further visits we took along mealies to leave on the spoor, they always disappeared, that's why Hendrik has a few bags of mealies with us to feed our friends.'

'Do you think they'll show themselves to us?' asked Jamie.

'It's very possible, just don't start shooting or shouting, just stay still and let them go on their way.'

Everybody murmured their agreement on this.

Arthur continued, 'When we leave the forest we'll head up the mountain side to a pass where there's an old

Prophets of Death

animal path, again virtually unused, that takes us west towards Oudtshoorn.

'I would like to get going as soon as possible. Fairbairn is sure to send out trackers to find out which way we're going,' said Jamie.

'Hendrik will be back tracking to watch for any pursuit.

The next morning they waited patiently until the last two of the team arrived and reported that the wagons were on the way to Oudtshoorn.

With Arthur leading the way the single file of riders snaked through the Knysna forest at a slow gait.

The noises of the forest were pleasant, birds and monkey chatter could be heard above the constant hum of insects, the sun peeping through the canopy here and there.

Every now and then Hendrik would raise his hand and everyone would stop and both Hendrik and Arthur would look for signs and listen for the elephants and then move on again.

Before sundown they stopped and Arthur said. 'This is where we leave the path and go to the campsite, everybody dismount and follow me. Hendrik will backtrack to make sure we have left no sign of our passing.'

They led their mounts and pack horses into what seemed to be an impenetrable wall of foliage but somehow Arthur led them through the huge leaves and small boughs and branches without a single blockage of tree or thick bush.

About an hour later they came to a clearing, which had an enormous mass of rock in it, there was a small stream running past one side of the rock formation and signs of old fires that had been burnt inside stone hearths in a large concave recess on the rock face.

'We light the fire against the rock so there will be no danger of setting the forest alight; we must be careful with ashes from pipes and cigarettes put them in the fire place,' Arthur told everyone.

The bush had encroached on the clearing so everybody unsheathed pangas and chopped it back. The horses were tethered at the opposite end from the stream and two fires were lit as the sun was setting.

Hendrik suddenly appeared and took a sack of mealies and, just as suddenly, disappeared back into the bush, coming back later with an empty sack and taking another.

'The elephants will know it is me, Boss, they always remember who it is,' said Hendrik.

There was a sombre mood in the camp that night, even the sentry looked to be staring at the stars most of the time. The men in the party all wanted to get into the fray and find this fabled treasure, they all wanted it to be over so they could go home safe to their families and loved ones; it would be a long night.

The next morning Jamie opened his eyes and heard a horse snort and a hoof pawing the ground. He moved his eyes to where the horses were tethered and saw Hendrik whispering to them and keeping them calm.

He thought *something is wrong*.

He slowly turned his head to see the camp; he saw Arthur sitting up with his hands in his lap looking straight forward. He turned his head a bit more and there on the edge of the camp was the biggest animal Jamie had ever seen in his life.

The elephant, an old matriarch, was standing there munching on some mealie husks which must have come from Hendrik. She was flapping her ears and using her trunk to lift the food to her mouth obviously enjoying the treat.

Prophets of Death

He caught another movement in his peripheral vision and saw another elephant, then he realised the whole camp was surrounded by the herd. He would never have noticed them had they not made some kind of movement.

Iain had woken and was sitting up looking at this wondrous event in their lives.

'How can something so big be so unnoticed,' whispered Iain.

'I don't know Iain, it's beyond me.'

The whole camp was now awake and still, watching these huge creatures share the space they were in and then the old matriarch elephant rumbled her sign to the others as she turned and walked slowly back into the bush.

When Jamie looked to see the other elephants go, they were nowhere to be seen. He got up and walked to the edge of the camp as did some of his companions but could see nothing; they had melted away so quietly.

'The ghosts of Knysna Forest right enough,' said Jamie.

'That is something to tell your grand kids, eh?' said Iain. 'How do you tell a moment like that to anyone?'

'That is the beauty of Africa lads,' said Arthur. 'And all we humans do is try to destroy it.'

'That would be white humans, Boss,' said Hendrik walking past.

'And you are a cheeky little shit,' Arthur called after him.

There was a different mood in the camp as the men ate breakfast and broke camp to walk back to the path and on through the north edge of the forest and ascend the mountain to the pass.

'Well here we go again Jamie boy,' said Iain.

'Here we go again; what?'

'Here we go to get our balls shot off yet again.'

'Speak for yourself I'm keeping my balls safe and

sound, thank you very much.'

As they were laughing at the banter they heard a rifle shot go off quite far away.

Chapter Twenty Six

November 1856

Knysna Forest

As Jamie and his companions made their way through Knysna forest, Fairbairn was beginning to wonder if, in fact, Fyvie had found any clue to the treasure; he was getting restless.

His informant was giving him daily updates saying Fyvie and McColl weren't doing anything, but two days had passed with no word from his informant so he decided to go and find him and find out why there was no movement.

'What of the wagons?' Asked Fairbairn when he found Greyling in the tavern.

'They have been sent to Cape Town to fetch some tools and then they are returning here sir; looks like they are doing some business here.'

'What about the rest of their men?'

'Some are waiting around and some have gone to look for work because nothing is happening here. A few of the white men went with the wagons back to Cape Town and that Hot 'not tracker went with them as well.'

'What about him?' said Fairbairn suddenly more interested.

'He left with two pack horses.' said Greyling.

'Where did he go?'

'He left the wagons and headed north; disappeared into the bush.'

Fairbairn lunged over the table and grabbed Greyling by the throat and realised his mistake when everybody in the tavern stopped and looked at him, the only white man in the place.

He let the shaking Greyling go and calmed himself. He got up and bought more ale and sat down again.

'So you did not think to tell me all of what has been happening?'

'Because nothing had changed sir.'

'You fucking idiot, the men were leaving. The white men leaving with the wagons, the tracker leaving, Fyvie and McColl have not been seen and you do not think this strange?'

'Sir, you told me to watch Fyvie and McColl and they are in the hotel, my men have been watching all the time, and they are still there in the hotel.'

'No, they are not there, the pack horses were their mounts being taken to meet them later when they sneaked out of the hotel.

'Impossible sir, we would have seen them leaving.'

'Go right now and get one of your informants to find out if they are still in the hotel.'

Greyling left and came back after midnight and, trembling with fear said. 'Sir, the two white men have paid till the end of the week but they have gone and I don't know when they left.'

Fairbairn was so angry he started shaking and Greyling went to leave when he saw the anger in his eyes.

'Sit where you are,' said Fairbairn suddenly changing tack. 'It seems we have all been fooled Greyling, not just you but me as well. Let us finish our drinks and then I will pay you, but not here in front of these villains. Let us go along the road and discuss what

Prophets of Death

is to be done.'

Greyling was relieved that Fairbairn was taking the deception so lightly and that it was not his fault. He followed Fairbairn out and down the alley towards the dock.

Fairbairn stopped and held out a bag of money to Greyling and said. 'Your pay; take it.'

As he moved to take his purse, Fairbairn drew his knife and stabbed him through the neck.

The look on Grayling's face was total shock. He started to convulse. Fairbairn withdrew the knife and watched him stagger and fall down, blood pumping from the artery in his neck. He leaned over him and put the point of his knife to his eye and pushed slightly, the eye popping and dripping down his dying skin.

Greyling tried to scream but the blood in his throat prevented this and he gurgled his way to a very painful death.

Fairbairn went back to his horse and rode to the stables behind the hotel where Fyvie and McColl were staying. There was a shack at the end of the property, it had to be where the stable hand lived.

As he approached the shack someone lit a candle, the light shining in the window, the stable hand probably thinking someone had arrived at the hotel and needed to stable their horse.

He opened the door and the startled man inside said. 'I am coming for your horse sir.'

Fairbairn looked around and could see there was no-one else in the shack. These workers usually stayed in places like this while their families lived at their real home in one of the native locations.

'Never mind the horse. I want you to tell me when the two white men left the hotel?'

'Sir, there are many white men coming here and

leaving, how would I know who you are talking about.'

'They came here quite a while ago, both tall, one with brown hair and the other has red hair and red faced,' said Fairbairn.

There was instant recognition at Iain McColl's description. 'Ah the red haired devil, but they have not taken any horses from here, they must still be in the hotel.'

Fairbairn started to lose patience and grabbed the man by the scruff of his shirt and slammed his face on the table covered with dirty dishes and scraps. He pulled out his knife and stabbed him through his right hand he had used to steady himself.

He started to scream but Fairbairn hit him on the side of the head with the butt of the knife handle, knocking him to the floor. He dragged him up and sat him on a stool and said. 'You will tell me what I want to know and maybe you'll live.'

'I don't know anything sir, please don't hurt me.'

'The two white men I speak of, where are their horses?'

'The horses are gone sir. The Hottentot tracker who was with them, his name is… it is… Hendrik yes, he took the horses sir, he used them as pack horses which I thought was strange. I asked him where he was going but he said it was not my business and if I told anyone he would come back and cut out my tongue.'

'You must have heard something about where they were going,' said Fairbairn.

'I swear sir, I don't know where he or the two white men were going. I thought Hendrik was stealing the horses and I didn't want to get involved.'

Fairbairn lifted the knife again and the man squealed. 'No sir… no… I only heard words here and there of Oudtshoorn and the forest.'

Prophets of Death

'What forest? Where was the forest?'

'Knysna Forest sir, to the north.'

'I know where it is, what else did you hear?'

'Nothing sir I swear to you, on my life.'

'On your life be it then,' said Fairbairn and stabbed him in the heart.

The stable hand fell dead to the earthen floor and started to bleed out.

Fairbairn saw a pair of blacksmith's tongs propped against the brick hearth and fetched them over to the body. He gripped the dead man's tongue with the tongs and pulled it out as far as was possible, took his knife and cut it off at the root.

'Why should Hendrik have the prize when I can have it,' he said, wrapping the piece of flesh in a bit of flannel.

Fairbairn rode out of Knysna to his camp in the hills and thought. *I am definitely losing my mind.*

When he reached the camp he went to the fire and poured himself a cup of coffee.

Flint went to him and said. 'What did you find out about our treasure hunters?'

'They are gone,' said Fairbairn simply.

'Gone? What do you mean gone?'

'Gone, disappeared, they've slipped away without anyone seeing them. The rest of their men left the town in drips and drabs without raising any suspicions with my so-called spy.'

'What did the spy tell you?'

'Not much, but he'll not be spying anymore.'

Flint looked at him and said. 'What? You killed him?'

Fairbairn slowly turned his gaze on Flint but said nothing.

Flint looked away; poured himself some coffee and said. 'So what do we do now Mr Fairbairn? I want my money.'

'You'll get your money. I found out they're going to or somewhere close to Oudtshoorn; travelling through the Knysna Forest to get there. It's safe to surmise that they're looking for another cave as the first two clues were at caves, so in the morning, after I get some sleep, we'll have to find someone who knows the area. Perhaps one of our own men would know but right now I'm too tired to think. Have the men ready to ride at dawn,' he said and bedded down.

The next morning Flint had the men ready to go. Fairbairn gathered them together and asked out loud, 'Does anybody know the country around Oudtshoorn and up to the mountains?'

'I do sir,' said Jonas Barnaby, a villain recently released from jail.

'Come over here Barnaby. Do you know of any caves around that area?'

'Only one cave, sir,' he said without hesitation. 'It's a well-known story that there's a big cave with many offshoots in the foothills of the Swartberg close to a farm owned by a Boer.'

'Can you take us there?'

'Yes sir, I can.'

'Good man. At last some luck for a change. I believe there is a way through the forest, is that correct?'

'It may be possible to find a way sir, but you don't want to go through the Knysna forest, people have gone in there and never been seen again. The spirits of the forest they say, don't like people to disturb them. The best way is by the main road to George and then north to Outdshoorn.'

'The spirits of the forest Barnaby? Do you actually believe that rubbish?'

'I don't know what to believe sir, but people have

Prophets of Death

died in there. Its nigh-on impossible to find a path through it, so dense is the bush.'

'Well, Fyvie and his companions know a way through the forest so that's the way we'll be going and we'll find their path. Flint!'

'Yes sir.'

'Get everyone in the saddle and let's move out. Barnaby, you have just been designated lead on this expedition.'

'Yes Sir,' said Barnaby.

The new tracker led Fairbairn and the other men to the outskirts of the forest and stopped.

'I have to have a look around to find out where they went in sir.'

'Very good, get moving.'

Barnaby tracked up and down the tree and bush line and then shouted. 'Captain Fairbairn, sir.'

Fairbairn rode to where Barnaby had dismounted and was hacking at the foliage.

'Is this the path?'

'Yes sir, they tried to cover their tracks, the vegetation has moved back but this is definitely the way they went.'

'You lead the way Barnaby and we'll follow. Now; we're wasting time,' said Fairbairn, impatience once more taking over.

The troop went into the forest in single file. The forest felt cooler once inside but very slow going because of the thick bush.

'Are you sure this is the best way Barnaby?'

'I'm sure sir. They tried to cover their tracks but I can follow them.'

They plodded on until late into the afternoon when suddenly they came across a small clearing in the path.

'Let's stop here and rest; get some food.'

'Sir, it's not wise to stop, we should keep going and rest when we get out of the forest,' said Barnaby.

'Barnaby, we shall stop here for a while and then move on.'

The men dismounted and looked around for wood to light a fire and brew up some coffee.

The elephant's great head parted the large green leaves and stalks as it emerged from the bush, its tusks curving out and upward, its great trunk waving around smelling the air for corn husks. The huge front legs of the matriarch stood at the edge of the clearing as she took in the sight before her.

The startled men stood transfixed, rooted to the ground with fear.

Barnaby was about to say *stay still, do not move* when the great beast lifted its trunk and trumpeted loud and long.

The men grabbed their rifles and started firing.

'Noooooooooooo…' screamed Barnaby.

But no-one was listening; they were firing blindly in the general direction of where the elephant was.

At least that's what they thought. They were firing at the whole herd as they crashed out of the bush and attacked the humans who were trying to kill them.

The muskets were no threat to the elephants as they gouged the men with tusks, lifted them bodily where they stood, threw them in the air and stamped on their bodies when they hit the ground.

The screams of the men mixed with the bellowing and trumpeting of the elephants was deafening as the rampage carried on. One man was flung to the ground with the sweep of a mighty trunk and before he could get up the elephant skewered him to the ground with a tusk straight through his chest.

Another was lying on the ground, his legs clearly

Prophets of Death

broken screaming for mercy when a mighty foot came down on his head, bursting it like a ripe pumpkin revealing tiny gleaming shards of the skull glinting in the light.

Fairbairn had scrambled to the edge of the clearing to grab his horse when he realised they were all dead men to the ghosts of the forest, Flint and Barnaby were right behind him. The three men fled the slaughter of their comrades leading the horses through the thick bush and by luck came upon the path with their tracks on it.

'Mount up and let's be gone from here,' said Fairbairn.

They urged their mounts as fast as they dared in the dense undergrowth until they reached the edge of the forest as the sun dipped below the mountains. They rode away from the forest and stopped to look back, only three of them had survived.

'I'm sorry I didn't believe in your spirits of the forest Barnaby. I can't believe what just happened.'

'Well, now we know what the ghosts of the Knysna forest are. I didn't realise there were still elephants in there,' said Barnaby.

'We'll ride for Oudtshoorn; once there we'll get fresh supplies. Barnaby, you'll take us to the cave from there,' said Fairbairn.

'What… now… after what has just happened?' said Flint. 'Have you no conscience man?'

'No, I do not, and don't question me again; if you want your money we go on now.'

'I have to point out to you that we are only three against god knows how many men that we pursue, should we not recruit more men from Knysna?' said Flint.

'We don't have time to go back and look for more men. Fyvie could find whatever is in the cave and be gone by the time we could recruit and get back. If we need any help with drivers or men to carry and load wagons, then we'll hire them locally,' said Fairbairn his voice rising. He pulled out one of his pistols and, holding it down by his side he said. 'We three are going to Oudtshoorn right now or it can be only two who will depart.'

Barnaby said. 'I can find men in Oudtshoorn, Flint.'

Flint knew that Fairbairn was a lunatic and would not hesitate to kill him.

'Then we three will ride for Oudtshoorn,' said Flint spurring his horse on.

Chapter Twenty Seven

November 1856

Cango Caves

'Where do you think that shot came from?' said Jamie

'That shot came from the forest,' said Hendrik riding back along the track a bit.

They all pulled up the horses to listen.

Another shot was fired and elephants started trumpeting in alarm.

'Aw Jesus Christ save us, someone is shooting at the elephants,' said Arthur.

There were other sporadic gun shots and the trumpeting changed to anger, then there were screams of men, this lasted for about ten minutes then all was quiet again.

'We should go back and take a look Arthur,' said Jamie.

'No, no we mustn't go near the elephants they'll be rampant now that humans have attacked them. We'll have to move on.'

Hendrik rode up to them and said. 'We cannot return to the forest any time soon, Boss.'

'I know, it will take years to earn the trust of the elephants again, they will attack us if we try to traverse the forest again, even with bags of mealies.'

'Fairbairn must be on our trail again and encountered

the elephants,' said Jamie.

'It does seem that way unfortunately, they'll be lucky to have escaped alive. You see, you'll never have a decent shot to bring down an elephant in the forest; bloody idiots have caused untold damage.' Arthur turned his horse and said. 'There's nothing we can do, let's move on.'

The troop walked on north up to the pass where they turned due west along the escarpment on a narrow animal trail which had been used by the Khoisan clans, the original, indigenous peoples of this harsh country.

It was slow going along the rocky path with few decent places to stop for the night.

Then they turned north at one point and followed a dry river bed up a deep gorge, the mountain cliffs looming above them on both sides trapping the incessant heat and making the riders use up their precious water supply.

At the top of the gorge they once again headed west. Dismounting, they led the horses along a path with the mountain on one side and a steep drop off the other, which was precarious to say the least. Then thankfully Hendrik raised his boney arm once more and they all came to a stop.

'There's a camp site in the rocks there,' said Hendrik pointing to what looked like a wall of mountain rock. 'There's a lot of water as well Boss. The farm we're looking for with the cave is a short distance to the west of here.'

'Then we'll camp here for the night and scout the farm tomorrow,' said Arthur.

Hendrik led them through an opening in the rock face which was naturally concealed until approached and suddenly it was there.

The camp site had been well used and once again the fire place was below the overhang of a hollow in the mountain used by the Khoisan for hundreds of years.

Prophets of Death

The ground was flat and more useable than the previous camp sites. There was a noise of rushing water. Jamie and Iain climbed up and through a crevice, which led down a short path to a pile of fallen rocks, beyond that was a natural hollow in the mountain enclosing a rock pool surrounded with thick grass and bush, the sparkling clear water coming from a waterfall pouring down through a narrow gorge.

Sentries were placed on the path along which they had come and Hendrik had gone back quite a way to obscure the tracks left by the expedition, but he knew a good tracker would figure it out eventually. He was particularly careful to cover the tracks to the camp.

All the men washed and rinsed their clothes and washed off all the grime of the trail. The sun had set when the last of them came back from the pool with lamps to see the way and then the food was cooked.

Away from the fires Jamie and Iain were looking once again at the spectacle of the expanse of stars in the night sky.

'I swear I will never get tired or stop looking at the night sky,' said Iain.

'I would want to be sitting on a mountain looking at this when I die,' said Jamie. 'What a way to go.'

'Aye, that or shagging or drinking fine whisky, doing something worthwhile… ye know?'

'Aye, I don't want to be sitting in a comfy chair or plumped up pillows on a bed with a tartan blanket over my legs, dribbling slavers down my chin waiting to die, especially with people around looking at you, wondering when you're going to fuck off,' said Jamie.

They started laughing at their own humour and then went quiet again.

'I hope all these boys with us get through this alive, Iain.'

'So do I Jamie, but somehow I don't think we'll get through this without some casualties.'

'For the men that don't make it we must ensure their families are well taken care of for the rest of their lives.'

'That is a given, we'll help them all,' said Iain. 'Come on, let's go and have a drink.'

'Aye, that's a good idea.'

They went back to camp and sat at their respective bed rolls, Jamie lit a cheroot and Iain a rolled up cigarette. Then the whisky was introduced.

They were all enjoying the flames in the fire when Iain said. 'So these mountains are called the Swart… berg? Is that the correct way to say it Arthur?' asked Iain.

'Yes, Die Swartberg, it's Afrikaans for The Black Mountain.'

'The Black Mountain?' said Jamie. 'It sounds a bit ominous.'

'Further west there is a narrow pass up to the Great Karoo, in there is the Wall of Fire which, when the sun hits it, looks like it is on fire, believe me the heat in there feels like a blacksmith's forge when heating the metal white hot.'

'How far is the farm we will be going to tomorrow?' asked Rory.

Arthur turned to Hendrik and asked. 'How far are we going tomorrow, Hendrik?'

'A few hours away, no more than that Boss. I don't know exactly where the farm is but when we get closer to the area we want to be in, I'll ride down to Oudtshoorn and find my friend, Oupa, to get directions. There won't be many big farms, there's not enough fertile ground and it's too hot to farm anything worthwhile.'

The next morning Hendrik decided to leave before dawn for Oudtshoorn to find his friend. The rest of the camp stirred at sun-up and Arthur gathered the men to tell

Prophets of Death

them the plans for the day.

'We five, myself, Jamie, Iain, Rory and Hamish will scout the way ahead for you weak kneed women who will stay here for another night,' said Arthur to cheers and guffaws.

'We don't mind staying here but why don't we all go, Arthur?' asked one of the men.

'Firstly we don't want to attract too much attention and secondly we don't know exactly where we're going. I'll send Hendrik back tonight and you will all meet up with us tomorrow so make the best of your night here. We'll take what we need and camp at the cave, if we find it.'

The five men mounted their horses and set off, picking their way down the rocky path toward the pre-arranged meeting place with Hendrik. The heat intensified as the sun climbed up the sky; the rocks on either side of the path were natural heat traps which sapped the life out of everything, even the indigenous flora and scrub were dry and lifeless, waiting for the seasonal rains to re-start their life cycle once again.

When Arthur signaled to stop, they all sat while he looked around at the terrain.

'Do you see that large outcrop of rock up there?' said Arthur pointing at it. No-one said anything. 'That's where we'll meet Hendrik.'

When they arrived they dismounted and led the horses a bit farther along the path until it intersected another path and walked over to the shade of the rock.

As they sat down Iain lifted his water bottle from his saddle, Hendrik walked out from behind a rock and said, 'Howzit?'

'Jesus Christ, Hendrik, my bowels nearly emptied into my breeks,' exclaimed Iain. 'Can you not give us some bleddy warning before you appear like that?'

Jamie had watched the whole thing and was laughing so much he had to lean against the rock. 'That was funny, I can't wait to tell that story in the tavern.'

'Oh... you think it was funny, I nearly had a bleddy cadenza ye eejit,' said Iain.

'Sorry Boss, I didn't mean to startle you,' said Hendrik.

'I'm glad you're sorry, don't do it again.'

'Right then,' said Arthur. 'The fun's over, what do you have to report Hendrik?'

'Oupa says the cave is up in the Cango area. He says you could go to the cave and stay for a while and leave and nobody would know or care.'

'That's all very well but did you get the directions?'

Hendrik looked at Arthur and Arthur knew he had said the wrong thing.

'My Boss, do you think I'm a fool?'

'No Hendrik, I don't think you're a fool. We're going to be at the cave for quite a while so we need to talk to the farmer and make sure he's happy with us being there.'

'Ah, well... in that case we will go to the farm of Stephanus van Wyk and I know the way there as well.'

'Then let's go and talk with him,' said Arthur.

'We'll have to give him some kind of story as to why we want to go there,' said Iain, 'otherwise he'll get suspicious of all these men camping in his cave.'

'I've been thinking about that,' said Rory.

'I was going to leave a couple of men to guard the farmer and his family while we moved what we came for out of the cave but what did you have in mind Rory?' said Arthur.

'We tell him we are an expedition sent by Her Majesty's government to survey the mountains and explore the cave as archaeologists. We give him some gold coins and tell him he will be paid a balance when we

Prophets of Death

are finished.'

'That sounds good to me,' said Arthur. 'Does everybody else agree?'

Everybody agreed and they set off for van Wyk's farm.

Stephanus van Wyk was a big Afrikaaner with a large belly and meaty arms. He wore a wide bush hat on top of lots of hair, his huge beard reaching down to his chest.

He had two teenage sons who sat on the stoep behind him; there was no sign of a wife.

Speaking in Afrikaans with Hendrik translating for all, Van Wyk invited everybody to sit on the stoep where he listened to Arthur's proposition, his eyes lighting up at the mention of gold coin and payment.

'Ya, the entrance used to be on the old Steyn farm but nobody was ever bothered about the boundaries of the land. My Pa explored a little bit of the cave, the main cave is named after him. He was lowered into the big part of it and he looked around but it is huge, it will take forever to find the end of the caves inside. You are welcome to do your business and camp there for a while, nobody ever goes up there.'

Hendrik spoke to van Wyk for a while and got the directions to the caves, then they rode off to find the entrance.

Anyone not looking for the cave would not have noticed the entrance, such was its position in the cliff face. They went in and lit some lanterns to go farther but it was so deep, with numerous offshoots, they decided to leave it. Hendrik would ride back to the men at the camp and bring them to the cave in the morning.

When the other members of the expedition arrived the next day they unloaded the pack horses and set up a camp just inside the entrance to the cave and made their surroundings as comfortable as possible for the coming days or maybe weeks, many of the men preferring to make camp in the bush nearby.

They wasted no time in searching the interior of the cave which was extensive with passageways and recesses everywhere one looked.

Small stalactites and stalagmites were to be seen here and there and then they found the opening to the huge part of the caverns as described by van Wyk.

Hamish made a torch from some cloth dipped in oil and wrapped around the end of a branch. Once lit, he threw it into the black void of the cave and it landed not too far down. The meagre light from the torch could not penetrate the gloom to see anything else.

'Right, Jamie and Iain, let's get some ropes secured and dropped down there before the torch goes out,' commanded Arthur. 'Hamish, you make some more torches and make them to last as long as possible, bind them tight. Rory, take some men and find as much wood as you can find and dump it down there to the right of the mouth of this opening. We're going to need a lot of light.'

Some of the men along with Iain and Arthur went down the ropes to the cavern floor and started tying bundles of brush and branches to be distributed throughout the cavern when they started the search the next day.

They toiled throughout the day only stopping when Rory said, 'The sun has set lads, it's time to eat and sleep.'

'Oh! Already! I had no idea; working in darkness all the time,' said Jamie.

Cooking fires were lit and the weary men ate and settled down to sleep, some in the protection of the cave; some under the stars.

'I'd much rather be back up the mountain in that last camp,' said Iain drawing deeply on his roll-up cigarette.

Prophets of Death

'So would I,' said Jamie. 'Arthur, we're going to have to make some kind of frame with maybe three, wide, strong ladders from the cavern entrance down to the floor.'

'Iain, you're the carpenter, that'll be your task tomorrow,' said Arthur.

'Aye, just give me a broom and I'll stick it in my arse and sweep the floor of the cave at the same time, Arthur.'

They were still giggling as they lay down to sleep.

The next day the work carried on, time was lost in the perpetual darkness of the cave as the men were split into teams to search the floor of the vast cavern and leave piles of brush and wood for fires, thicker logs had been put next to the fires to make them burn as long as possible when the time came to light them. Eventually they had reached every corner of the floor and now it was time to light the fires and find the seal to lead them to the treasure.

The floor of the cavern was treacherous as jagged rocks and deep crevices were everywhere. There had been minor injuries and a couple of broken bones but there were no major accidents that could not be taken care of.

The men were clearly very tired so Jamie and Iain, after consulting with Rory decided that they would take two days off and rest.

'Are you sure this is a wise decision Jamie?' said Arthur. 'The enemy isn't far behind.'

'I know but the men need to rest because when we open this up there'll be a lot of work again.'

Chapter Twenty Eight

November 1856

Cape Town

Bill Hutcheson finalised the arrangements for the Governor's *Journey of the People* as the Governor liked to call it. He liaised with the army at the Castle of Good Hope, otherwise known as the fort, for the Governor's escort and security and now the entourage was leaving Cape Town on the first stage of the Governor reaching the people. *The people being the white people*, thought Hutcheson, who was in his own carriage, which would be his transient office for the weeks to come.

Whyte had already been to places such as Stellenbosch and other towns within striking distance of Cape Town, but now they were packed to travel and Hutcheson had organised accommodation for the Governor and his close aids, including himself, at all the stops whereas the rest of entourage would camp.

They would stop over at prominent settler villages and towns giving priority to George, Port Elizabeth, Grahamstown and the crucial frontier settlement of King William's Town where the governor would meet with the Xhosa chiefs and their commissioners.

Hutchison had made the town of George a priority as it was close to Knysna and communication with Jamie and Iain.

Prophets of Death

The governor's tour eventually reached the quaint town of George, nestled a few miles inland between the beautiful beaches and cliffs of the Eastern Cape coast and the foothills of the Grootswartberg Mountains.

They were at the Town Hall in the offices they had commandeered; Hutcheson was sitting with the Governor sorting out the details of meetings past and still to come.

'Governor, I would request a few of days off to go to Knysna just up the coast.'

'Oh, do you have relatives living there, Bill?'

'No sir, I have very good friends there but I want to look at some land I may invest in and there will be a little bit of work. Captain Roger Willard is in Knysna, I believe, with the Flying Fish. I want to confirm he will have a ship at East London for your return to Cape Town when you are ready to return.'

'Oh, then by all means take a few days off and enjoy yourself, you've earned it, Bill. You have worked hard and the expedition thus far has been a resounding success.'

'Thank you sir, I would like to suggest that if Captain Willard is going to East London with The Flying Fish I should like to go with him and make sure the arrangements with your accommodation and the meetings with the local authority are in place; then I could meet you in King William's Town,' said Hutcheson.

'What about the remainder of the journey between here and King William's Town?' asked Whyte.

'The young man, Boyce, who is being trained in government practice has all the details and is quite capable of handling the rest of the journey, sir.'

'Well you do seem to have everything worked out to the last detail, Bill; I'll see you at our destination,' said Whyte.

'Then I'll leave in the morning sir.'

Hutcheson decided to take a carriage to Knysna and found the hotel where Willard was staying. The Captain was not at the hotel so he deposited his bags in his room and went off to rent a horse and tracked down Willard at the docks supervising some rigging repairs.

'Captain Willard, can I talk with you sir, I'm in a devilish hurry to find out where Jamie and Iain are located.'

'Bill Hutcheson! When did you arrive?'

'Not long ago, I have urgent news for Jamie. Has he sent word where they are?'

'A rider came and gave me the directions. Let's go to the hotel and have some lunch and I'll tell you where to go.'

Hutcheson left the next morning before dawn and rode as fast as was possible for the cave site.

When he thought he was getting close to where the cave was located, a voice boomed out from somewhere in the rocks.

'Halt and identify yourself.'

Hutcheson pulled up his horse and said. 'Who would want to know?'

'We're guarding an archaeological expedition in the name of the Cape Government.'

'I'm Bill Hutcheson from the governor's office; I seek Jamie Fyvie and Iain McColl who are at the dig site.'

Two men emerged from left and right of the road, one said. 'We'll fetch our horses and take you to the site.'

At the same time as Bill Hutcheson's arrival in Knysna, Governor Whyte received a despatch from Cape Town, It had come from Whitehall in London. Basically it said, *Major General Gerald Cuthbert, was killed in action at the Battle of Balaclava in the Crimea. He was a fine and brave officer of the British Army.*

Prophets of Death

Whyte immediately wrote a letter, sealed it and had it sent to Cape Town by a military despatch rider to be delivered urgently to the Colonial Secretary, Nicholas Banbury, at the government buildings.

As soon as Banbury received the official despatch from Governor Whyte about Cuthbert's heroic demise on the battlefield, he immediately cancelled all his appointments for the day and went straight to Arend se Kop.

Renton stared at the letter through his white veil; he wore this when he was alone or only with Banbury as it was more see-through than the black one.

'This is what we have been waiting for Nicholas,' he said excitedly. 'Pour us some brandy to celebrate the passing of that fool Cuthbert.'

Banbury poured the drinks and said. 'I don't know how you managed Cuthbert's demise, but you did say it was imminent and that is very impressive. What's the next part of the plan now James,' asked Banbury.

'We'll savour this drink then I'll go and get changed. We'll reconvene here in three hours' time. Go and alert Samuel and Williams to be here as well. What is the news from Fairbairn? We'll need his services. Confound the man.'

'I'll have a rider sent to Knysna to find out where he is, James, I can do no better than that. When we're finished with this operation I suggest Mr Fairbairn should be relieved of his duties permanently.'

'Agreed. We're on the threshold of greatness Nicholas, there's much to be done,' said Renton sipping his brandy.

Three hours later they were assembled around the dining table in Arend se Kop.

Williams was, once again, feeling uncomfortable at being in such opulence with these psychopathic high born gentlemen, apart from Samuel who was just a rich, free black man.

Renton went through the recent events for everyone's benefit and then gave out his orders.

'Williams, you and Samuel will once again ride for the eastern frontier; you'll go and meet with Misumzi out in the homelands and instruct him to have the seer, Nonkululeko at the Gxara river pool again to see the great chief once more. This will be very delicate as Samuel will give you a stronger potion for Misumzi to give to the girl. Samuel, you will then re-appear as the old chief to tell the girl that the great chiefs have been fighting with the Russians, who were black people and together they killed the demon Cuthbert and defeated the British armies over the seas in foreign lands. They were now coming home to lead the Xhosa people to defeat the English and their armies who invaded this land and take back their freedom. The potion will make her believe that she is seeing what she is being told, she will see the old chiefs and she will believe.'

'I'll do as you say sir,' said Samuel. 'Will Fairbairn be with us with guard support?'

'I don't know where that man is,' Renton passed a piece of paper to Samuel and said to everyone. 'As well as voodoo, Samuel has a gift of performing hypnosis practised by the Hindus in India. This was taught to Samuel by an English Captain stationed in Freetown, who served in India. On that piece of paper, Samuel, are the words you will hypnotise the seer with; the words which she will retell to her chief and thus begin a wave of destruction which will be printed in every newspaper in the empire.'

'I'll make other arrangements to replace Fairbairn,' said Banbury. 'There is another militia leader by the name of Winston Murray who has an inherent hatred of

Prophets of Death

anything native. I'll send him and his men with Samuel and Williams. What else can I do?'

Renton said. 'What else you can do is compose two letters. One for the Governor in King William's Town to use his initiative and make sure the local natives hear that Cuthbert has been killed in a war led by the old chiefs and black men called Russians in a land far away over the sea. The second letter will be to all the newspaper editors to print and strengthen the truth about Cuthbert's death at the hands of the Russians. This will endorse the lie we will inculcate about the ancestral chiefs leading the Russian black men who defeated the British and killed Cuthbert.'

By the end of the week the letters had gone out, Renton and Banbury were standing at the bay window overlooking Table Bay sipping brandy.

Renton said. 'We'll soon be the masters of the whole of the Cape region Nicholas, let the killing begin.'

Chapter Twenty Nine

November 1856

Cango Caves

On the third day after the men had rested, laundered clothes and eaten well, Jamie led them back into the cavern to light the fires. They had their designated areas to watch for the Templar's seal and point it out, all was ready.

The only men allowed in and standing by each pyre with lit torches were master masons except for Jamie and Iain. All had been shown the sign of the seal from the clue so they knew what to look for when the cavern was lit up.

'Light your fires,' shouted Rory from the entrance of the main cavern.

Each man plunged his torch into the kindling of their respective pyres and as the flames took hold a wondrous sight lit up before them.

'My god almighty,' whispered Jamie.

Iain said. 'Oh my god, look at that.'

The colossal space in the cavern was overwhelming in its enormity; the ceiling was barely visible but hundreds of stalactites pointed down from the darkness to the floor.

The walls sparkled and glinted in the firelight from the minerals left by the water that had seeped through here for thousands of years forming the stalactites and

Prophets of Death

stalagmites which seemed to erupt from the floor of the cavern; many had met their counterparts stretching down to form smooth creamy coloured pillars and columns.

There were thin stalactites just forming like long pieces of straw stuck to the ceiling and others resembling lace curtains frozen by extreme cold.

'It's as though a giant candle has melted and been petrified as the wax ran down the walls and dripped from the roof,' said Hamish staring around in awe of the spectacle.

'It emulates the godlike proportions of Europe's great cathedrals,' said Rory.

'How are we ever going to find the clue in this, it'll take us an age to search,' said Iain breaking the spell.

Jamie stood up on a mound of stalagmite and shouted, 'You've all seen the Knights' seal, look carefully in the area you're in. The seal has two parts, the chapel in one circle and the two riders on one horse in another circle with two spears pointing away from them. Look very carefully as they will be well disguised.'

The searchers all renewed their torches a half a dozen times throughout the day as they searched in vain for the elusive seal until Jamie called everybody off for the night.

Rory convened a meeting next to the mouth of the cave when all the men had eaten and rested; they all gathered around the fire to plan the next day's search.

Jamie began. 'Rory and I have talked with all of you and the consensus is that there are too many places to search; offshoots from the main cavern, other caves and passages, leading to god knows where. The cave system in there probably runs deeper and further than we can imagine. In fact there's more than likely miles of tunnels and I'll be honest with you, I don't know where to look any more. We can't possibly take the time to search every foot of this place it's just not feasible.'

'Jamie is right,' said Rory. 'But the good news is if we can't find the Knight's seal then neither can the enemy. The bad news is we didn't recover the historical artefacts and information we came here to find and that's a sad loss. If you're all agreed we'll try for another two days then we'll call it off.'

One man said. 'Brother Rory, we're here for as long as you need us.'

'I thank you for that brethren, now let's pass around some grog and then get some sleep.'

'Grog?' said Iain. 'Grog? Good whisky is not grog, it is the amber nectar,' he said tasting his drink and savouring it.

Rory laughed with the rest of the men and said. 'I do beg your pardon sir, we will pass around the wine and some fine scotch whisky as well.'

'Aye, that's better,' said Iain winking at Rory.

The men dispersed and Rory went over to sit with Jamie and Iain who were lighting up their respective smokes.

'Thanks for keeping the morale up Iain, God knows we need something to lift us,' said Rory.

'Do you have any ideas on what to look for to discover the seal?' said Jamie drawing on his cheroot and blowing the smoke upwards into the night.

'I don't know what to say anymore Jamie. I really thought it would be a fairly easy exercise to find the seal. Just as long as the ELOS don't find it and not because of the untold wealth of the treasure but the historical implications of the information in the artefacts.'

'The scriptures must be very damning to the church whether catholic or protestant, Jewish or otherwise for the consequences to be so devastating,' said Jamie.

'Well, the enormity of a catastrophe such as that is not for the likes of me or you to debate or figure out, I

Prophets of Death

was sent to find and keep the artefacts safe and hidden from the evil powers such as the ELOS. Tomorrow is another day lads, I'll say goodnight.'

'Goodnight Rory,' said the boys together.

'He's really taking it hard that he's not found what he came here for,' said Iain after Rory had walked off.

'So would you, coming all this way not to get a result and the risk of anarchy in Europe resting on your shoulders. I wouldn't like to be in his boots,' said Jamie.

'Aye, I suppose you're right. Maybe we'll find the bleddy seal tomorrow, never give up; we have to find it Jamie. See you in the morning,' said Iain, and rolled over to sleep.

As soon as the sun was up the next day they were back in the gigantic cavern scouring every nook and cranny, every crevice and hole in the walls but to no avail, the elusive seal stayed hidden.

After lunch Jamie went back into the cave; lit up a smoke and sat on a lump of stalagmite. He propped his torch up so he could fetch out the piece of rough paper with the clue on it and stared at the drawing of the seal, going over the clue for the umpteenth time.

He looked across the cavern at the torches moving around and men coming and going, never giving up on their search. He thought about last night's conversation and how big the consequences would be.

Something sparked his brain and he looked at the clue again:

Light the fires in the deep dark place,
To show the seal in the cavernous space,
How big. The consequences be would be huge. The enormity… cavernous… big. Cavernous… big, he thought.

He looked up and slowly moved his gaze around the cavern again.

Then he saw it.

'Jesus Christ, how could we not have seen it?' said Jamie as Iain was walking towards him.

'Seen what?' Iain said looking at the massive wall. 'What? What is it?'

'Iain look at me.'

Iain looked at Jamie.

'Find Rory and a couple of others and make some long poles from branches or bits of wood anything that can get the torches and the lanterns high up.'

'What did you see; tell me?'

'I can't tell you or show you until you get the light high up. Oh and bring the big hammers and crowbars.'

Iain looked at him.

'Iain… please, will you move your arse.'

'Aye right, I'm going.'

A long time later Iain and Rory led some men back into the cavern and started lowering long wooden poles made from tree branches and newly bound torches down to the floor.

'We had to look far and wide to find big enough trees to make the extensions for the torches,' said Iain.

Rory said, 'Jamie! What have you found?'

'I'm about to show you. Get the torches bound to the extension poles and hand them out. Before they light the torches the men must position themselves about twenty feet from the far wall and about ten feet apart,' said Jamie.

The men were all in position and Jamie called Iain, Rory, Hamish and Arthur to where he was standing.

'Right now, I want you all to look at the Knight's seal and keep that picture in your head. *Light the long torches,*' shouted Jamie as the rest looked at the clue.

The torches were lit and hoisted up by the men holding them as they struggled to find their footing on the vast rock strewn floor.

Prophets of Death

Jamie addressed the other four saying. 'The clue says to *light the deep dark place* and the seal will be in *a cavernous space...* the words *cavernous space ... cavernous...* means very big. Look at the wall lads and think of the seal as being bigger than a house.'

'What on... earth... are...'

'You men on the left... lower your torches slightly to your left,' shouted Jamie. 'Now you men on the right... lower your torches down, not left or right but straight down.'

They did as instructed and the shadows moved accordingly on the back wall behind the outcroppings of stalactite and stalagmite growth.

'Do you remember the pillars holding up the chapel roof in the sketch of the seal?' asked Jamie of his four companions.

'Yes,' they all said.

'Then look over there,' Jamie said pointing at what looked like thick, high pillars holding up a large wall like balcony with a large dome in the middle. The circles surrounding the chapel were vague but could be seen to be there. The angle of the light had change the shadows and highlighted the domed chapel shown in the seal.

'Well I'll be damned,' said Rory. 'It must be forty feet high.

'How the hell did they build it so big,' said Arthur. 'Look to the left, there's an indistinct shape of the horse and double riders.'

Sure enough, there was the outline of the horse and the two Knights also with the outline of the circles around it.

Over the years the running water had covered the roughly sculpted outline of the seal with deposits of minerals but there was no mistaking the Knights seal.

'Bring the hammers and the crowbars, you'd better

bring some rope as well,' said Jamie.

The four men were looking at him and Iain said, 'How the hell did you figure that out?'

'I was thinking about last night's conversation about something big and I looked at the clue which said cavernous space and something just clicked in my head that we should be looking for something huge.'

'Well congratulations Jamie that was an inspired bit of thinking,' said Rory.

'That's not necessary Rory let's go and get your treasure.'

'I suppose you think you're a clever bastard now, eh?' said Iain picking his way across the rocky floor next to Jamie.

'Nooo, I just had an idea, that's all.'

'Well it was a brilliant idea my friend, well done,' said Iain smiling.

'You can be a real shite sometimes, you know that?' said Jamie.

'I know,' chuckled Iain.

They all made their way to where the horse's head was and could make out the outline of where the double lances protruded at almost ninety degrees to the head. A couple of the brethren erected a rough scaffold up to it with Jamie and Iain poised ready with hammers and chisels and crowbars to chip away the layer of minerals covering the supposed lances or spears depicted in the clue.

'What if we're chipping at the wrong place?' said Rory.

Jamie said. 'We could well be, but if anything is pointing to the treasure, it would probably be the spears. If it isn't then we'll try somewhere else.'

After an hour of chipping around the protrusion they managed to jam the end of the crowbars into the edges of

Prophets of Death

the rock to lever it off.

'Look out down there,' called Iain.

They pushed on the crowbars and the piece of rock fell away revealing two perfectly preserved spears embedded in a different type of rock in a similar recess to the previous clues, only much, much larger and right between the spears was a bigger oval shaped pebble.

'Rory, this is the right place, come up here, you need to be witness to this,' said Iain.

'This is truly incredible lads, I don't know how to thank you,' said Rory.

'Ye can thank us by taking all the junk out of here when we find it and give us all some peace,' said Iain smiling at Rory.

Jamie wiped down the work area with a piece of cloth and used his knife to remove the pebble.

'It's a hell of a lot bigger than the previous ones Jamie, for god's sake don't break the knife,' said Iain.

'That's fine. I'll be taking it nice and easy.'

Jamie used his knife to worry the pebble around its edge but could not move it. He looked closer at one end and noticed a slight gap. He pushed the point of the knife into the gap and using the heel of his hand struck the handle of the knife pushing it deeper and the other end of the pebble popped out slightly.

'Iain, get ready to catch it.'

Jamie pushed the knife again and the whole pebble fell out and into Iain's hands.

'Got ye, ye wee bugger,' said Iain with satisfaction.

Jamie inserted the knife into the hole until it was in up to the hilt and pulled, nothing happened. He tried to push in the opposite direction but could not move anything.

'I think you had better use the crowbar in case you break the knife in the hole, then we'll be right in the shite,' said Iain.

Jamie picked up the crowbar and inserted it into the hole and it went in quite a way and with all the other men now crowded around the scaffold looking on with interest, he pulled with all his might, but nothing happened.

'Right, Iain, Rory, you both push and I'll pu… wait… look there.'

'What are you looking at?' asked Iain.

'To the left of the spears,' Jamie called to the torch bearers. 'Bring the light over to the left a bit… there… hold that light there. Again you have to look at the bigger view, does that look like a big slab of rock leaning against the wall; I mean it's covered with the stalactite stuff, but what does it look like to you Iain?'

Iain looked long and hard at what Jamie was talking about, as was Rory.

'I don… oh I see it now… it's a big bleddy door,' exclaimed Iain.

'So it is, a huge slab of rock, used as a door to block a passageway I'll bet,' said Rory.

'Right lads, listen to me for a minute,' said Jamie standing at the edge of the scaffold and addressing the entire cavern. 'We need to build another scaffold next to this one with two different levels to chip around that big slab against the wall. We'll need to make a clearing on the floor in front of it as well, so start clearing the rocks and debris from around that area. Bring in the hammers, chisels, picks, shovels and anything else to help get this cleared away. The sooner we get this done the sooner we get out of here.'

They worked until they were again exhausted and Jamie called a halt for food and sleep.

Jamie went to where Arthur and Hendrik were sitting talking.

Prophets of Death

'Make sure the sentries are alert, we are at a crucial part of the recovery in the cave and the men are tired and focused on doing manual labour so keep your men vigilant.'

'Don't worry Jamie,' said Arthur, Hendrik here will kick their arses should he catch them slacking, he'll be making his rounds more often.'

The next day saw the work finished in front of the seal and the area cleared in front of the slab. Jamie, Iain and Rory had returned to the top of the scaffold to pull and push on the crowbar, Hamish decided to join them and they positioned themselves to give the best purchase on the crowbar.

'Right lads, I will count to three and on four we heave... one... two... three... *Heave.*

They pulled and pushed with all their might... but nothing gave way.

'Take a breather lads,' said Jamie and looked down to men on the floor. 'Some of you men pick up the heavy hammers and when we heave on the crowbar again I want you to pound repeatedly on that big slab as hard as you can, get ready... one... two... three... *Heave.*'

The men pounded the slab with all of their might whilst the four on the crowbar pushed and pulled. Suddenly the stone with the two spears seemed to swivel on something as it swung out of the wall catching the four men unawares and almost crashing off the scaffold.

The top of the slab tilted forward an arms-length and stopped.

'Put wedges in the gap at the top of the slab,' shouted Jamie. 'Keep it from going back. Get some ropes and feed them through the gaps.

The men pushed pieces of rock into the gap where the slab had parted from the wall.

Jamie and the other three joined the men on the floor

and helped to wrap ropes around the top piece of the slab and they took up the slack pulling the ropes taught.

'Right lads, on three again… one… two… three… *Pull.*'

It was so easy they all nearly fell down as the huge slab of rock slowly fell over, and with a thunderous crash came to rest in the cleared space.

The men all stopped in their tracks and looked on as the billowing dust eventually started to settle on the floor of the great cavern.

Jamie picked up a lantern and went to where the slab had fallen and walked up it like a drawbridge and held up the lamp to reveal the opening of another cave.

Jamie turned still holding the lantern up and all was quiet.

'Aw… not another fucking cave,' cried Iain.

The tension was immediately released and all the men started to laugh and badger Iain.

'Aw… you poor thing.'

'Not another cave Iain.'

'This should be easy for you now Iain.'

'Ah, shut up the lot of you,' said Iain taking the lambasting.

'Rory! I think you better take over from here, you're the expert who's been in old places like tombs and caves,' said Jamie walking down the ramp.

Rory stood up at once and said. 'Gentlemen, some of you go up to the entrance and arm yourselves, make sure we won't be compromised and secure the approach to the caves outside. As discussed we four, myself, Jamie, Iain and Hamish will go in to the cave and see what's there. The clue says this is the final resting place of the sacred cargo the Knights Templar brought all the way from Europe. Let's all calm down and get on with the business of securing whatever is in there and getting it and us to

Prophets of Death

safety.'

The four friends lit four lanterns rather than naked flame torches in case of any accidents and proceeded to the cave, two armed men at the entrance. Rory led the way single file down the tunnel waving the lanterns back and forth to look for anything untoward.

'Is it my imagination or is the roof of this cave getting closer to the floor?' said Jamie being the tallest among them.

'Aye, it is Jamie, I noticed that as well,' said Iain.

The roof became lower to the point where they were bending over slightly but the deeper they went in the roof went higher again and then they came to a wooden wall with a great door in the middle of it.

'The wood is solid yellowwood and it is still nearly as good as when it was built here,' said Iain dusting down the structure and inspecting it.

'No air for nearly five hundred years so there would hardly be any rot,' said Hamish.

There were deeply etched engravings of ancient seals and emblems of the Knights Templar all over the door of which only a high degreed mason would understand the meaning. There was a brass handle on the right side of the door, Rory used it and the door opened.

'No locks on the door I see,' said Iain.

'If anyone had gotten this far there would be no point in locking a door,' said Rory.

'I suppose.'

The thick wide door swung back towards them.

There was a musty smell as they entered what looked like a hallway with oil lamps placed at measured intervals along the wall until a big black space appeared before them.

'I recommend we light every second lamp as there will be less air to breath if we have to bring in more men,' said Rory.

They lit the lanterns and went into the darkness watching the floor for any surprises like gaping holes. Holding the lanterns a bit higher they could see the shapes of something in the gloom.

'Jesus Christ, look there,' said Iain.

Lowering the lamps they saw the remains of a Knight laid out in his well-preserved uniform and armour. His sword laid on top of his ancient skeleton, each gloved, skeletal hand gripping the handle on his chest, the point between his booted feet.

Rory turned to the opposite side and there lay the remains of another Knight, identical to the other, the famous white tunic with the red-cross now a faded gray with an almost black cross.

'There are always two Knights guarding,' said Rory sadly. 'Please excuse us for a moment lads.'

Rory and Hamish knelt between the corpses and uttered a prayer and made some kind of sign.

'The Knights guard the chapel in which they sleep,' said Jamie. 'The two Knights on one horse.'

Rory said, 'Look around for some kind of apparatus for lighting this cave, there's always something… ah there we are.'

There was a thin gutter chipped into the rock wall going up at an angle into the darkness. The gutter was packed with some sort of hemp rope steeped in lamp oil.

'There will be one on the other side as well,' said Rory. 'Put a torch to it and it will light up.'

Rory and Jamie lit both sides at the same time and they watched the flame travel up the wall to a bigger lamp than the ones in the hall and then the flame travelled to another and another until there were five oil lamps on each side of the cave shining brightly on the contents stored there.

Prophets of Death

The four men gaped with open mouths at the gleaming, glinting treasure before them. Some of the boxes had rotted and burst no doubt because of the salt water and weather conditions they had endured from Europe on the ships.

Gold coins and bars, gold necklaces and trinkets studded with diamonds and rubies, other coloured gem stones that were not known to ordinary men. Goblets and chalices, plates and serving dishes of silver and gold had cascaded all over the floor. There were candlesticks, gold crosses and jewellery, in other words, a king's ransom; a treasure of wealth beyond belief.

They all stared in wonderment at such riches all from payments made in deals with the Knights Templar almost five hundred years ago.

'Right, Jamie, let's shoot everybody, grab as much of this shite as possible and run for it,' said Iain.

'Aye right, you wouldn't get very far on your own with this lot, Iain.'

'Aye I suppose your right,' said Iain feigning disappointment. 'It was a nice thought though.'

'The real wealth is in these here gentlemen,' Rory said kneeling down beside numerous clay jars stacked on one side of the cave. Two of the jars must have been damaged as the clay had crumbled from the side of the jars revealing what looked like parchment scrolls inside.

'Are these the scriptures that you spoke of, Rory?' said Jamie.

'They are, Jamie. I have read everything the Knights have recorded about the discovery of these scrolls and it's not much, as a lot of their history was destroyed during their persecution. The information is kept under lock and key in the great library in the Grand Lodge in Edinburgh and from what I've learned these jars were buried hundreds of years before Christ, in caves to the west of

Jericho, and to the north of the Dead Sea. This was in the time of ancient Palestine, in the lands of Judea, Samaria and Peraea. The scrolls were discovered by accident by Bedouins and some were taken to be sold or traded to the nearest outpost which was built and owned by the Knights. The Bedouins took the Knights back to the caves where they found them and excavated the site and found more scrolls in large clay pots or jars, these jars. The Knights wanted to search for others as they knew there had to be more caves with more of these historical scriptures but they didn't have the trusted resources or the time and money for such an expedition.

'How did they get the jars back to their headquarters?' asked Iain.

'They made rope baskets and loaded them on to camels. They then took them back for safe keeping; just as well because they had scholars start to investigate the ancient writing which was a mixture of Greek, Nabataean, Aramaic and Hebrew written on papyrus, parchment and even bronze. They mention the ancient Jews, called Essenes, and the beginnings of the Hebrew Bible. The Knights then decided the information was too dangerous and closed them all up in the vaults of one of the forts on an island in the Mediterranean; now here they are, brought here by the fleeing Knights Templar. These have to be secured and loaded first and then the riches afterwards.'

Jamie took over and said. 'Iain, could you go out and send a couple of men to get the wagons moving up here, make sure they are well armed and tell them to be bleddy careful and maybe bring us back some whisky, this deserves a toast.'

Iain went off and Jamie turned to Hamish. 'How long would it take to clear a way across the floor of the cavern to the ladders leading up to the entrance Hamish?'

Prophets of Death

'It'll take far too long Jamie; nigh on impossible.'

'Aye, I thought you would say that.'

'But I have a much better idea than that and it'll be quicker as well.'

'Ah Hamish, I knew there was something good about you,' joked Jamie. 'What is your plan?'

'An overhead rope pulley.'

'A what?'

'The Royal Navy built one in Simonstown although theirs is much more elaborate than ours will be. They built an iron frame on top of the mountain above the town, a couple of frames on the slopes down the side of the mountain and a frame in the naval yard. They then rigged a pulley system to pull a cradle up on a rope between the iron frames; not big stuff, but it was better than hauling it up by horse or cart and it's very effective.'

'And we could build one in here?' asked Rory.

'Aye, we build a scaffold here, two slightly higher ones spaced across the floor and then a sturdy frame above the ladders at the entrance. We then rig up a kind of block and tackle and pulley system, splice the ropes so they're long enough to go around, hook the boxes on and pull the rope to convey the box down to this cave and then reverse it to come back up. But mind you, they'll have to be built strong to take the weight of the gold.'

'Iain specifically made the boxes to manageable sizes so it shouldn't be a problem,' said Jamie as Iain returned with a satchel inside which was a bottle of whisky and four mugs.

They all toasted the find and Iain said. 'Did I hear my name being mentioned as I came in?'

'You did,' said Hamish and he outlined his plan to Iain.

'I can build those frames. I'll tell the riders before they go to bring some timber back on the wagons from

Oudtshoorn then we can build them really solidly and they can bring heavy duty pulleys and rope as well.'

Rory and Hamish stayed in the cave and tried to patch up the broken jars with some linen strips and twine whilst Jamie and Iain went up to get some fresh air outside the entrance.

Riders coming up the path, came a shout from one of the sentries.

The boys looked to see who was coming and recognised Bill Hutcheson between two of the sentries who had been placed on watch.

Iain walked down to meet them and signaled the guards to let him through.

'Bill! What on earth are you doing here?'

'Hello Iain, where is Jamie… oh there he is up there. Is that the cave where the treasure is buried?'

'Aye it is Bill and we have found it… why are you here? There must be something going on.'

'There's a lot going on Iain, let's go and get Jamie and find a private place to talk; can I see the treasure? I've never seen a treasure.'

'Not many people have, Bill.'

The three men found a camp fire with no-one around and brewed some tea. Hutcheson told the boys what had happened since they had last spoken.

'I was afraid of this,' said Jamie.

'What? The navy going up the coast or most of our best troops riding north to quell a mythical disturbance?' said Iain.

'Well, yes, that as well but more the fact that we have been away for so long chasing this bleddy cave we've been out of touch with developments. If the governor pays the chiefs in order to dominate the policing of the natives then he has full control of whom to jail and who to send into exile on Robben Island and no doubt he'll lay

Prophets of Death

on the brandy and food for the chiefs to enjoy a bit of colonial luxury.'

'So the ELOS are putting their plan of action into play,' said Iain. 'What of Renton and Banbury?'

'I don't know, I haven't seen Renton for weeks but I have seen Banbury coming and going from government house; come to think of it he did look kind of agitated,' said Hutcheson.

Jamie said. 'Bill, your being here is actually very good timing, I need to ask you to do a bit of leg work, or rather horse leg work. I need you to go back to Captain Willard in Knysna and tell him to stand by to sail in the next few days and that I'll send word when we are ready; you can confide in him, he's with us. Now, from what you've told me you'll have to meet up with the governor at some point, is that correct?'

'Yes, that's correct.'

'Iain has just sent our men to bring the wagons up from Oudtshoorn so once you have seen Capt…'

'Jamie, I think I know what I have to do,' said Hutcheson. 'After I deliver instructions to Captain Willard, I will immediately return to Oudtshoorn and make sure the wagons are safely on their way and then I can catch up with the governor.'

'That's about it, Bill. Have you sent word to Armstrong?'

'Yes I have, that dispatch is on its way marked very urgent.'

'Is there anything else out of the ordinary that you have heard or seen?' asked Iain.

'Nothing I can think of except… there is a rumour, or stupid stories really, that the ancestral Xhosa Chiefs have appeared in a vision of a Xhosa prophet, that they're coming back to help fight the British and drive us all into the sea. All nonsense of course but you know the natives and their myths.'

'Well, if that's all you have heard, just fairy stories, then come and see our treasure and then you can be on your way,' said Iain.

Iain and Hutcheson went off into the cave leaving Jamie deep in thought. He was bothered about the story of the chiefs coming back to free the Xhosa.

When Hutcheson came out of the cave Jamie was waiting for him and asked. 'Where did this rumour about the ancient chiefs come from, Bill?'

Hutcheson mounted his horse and said. 'It came from a young girl who is supposed to be a seer; prophetess. She is the daughter of one of Samkelo's pakati, who are about to be told they are no longer needed to council the chiefs. Apparently she saw one of the old chiefs in a vision, declaring he would return with the other ancient chiefs to free the Xhosa people from the white invaders and stealers of the land and to await a sign.'

'And the chiefs believe this nonsense?' said Iain.

'They are destitute, they are so desperate to get back what has been taken from them they are ready to believe anything, Iain.'

'Thanks, Bill. Have a safe journey, don't forget Fairbairn is out there looking for us, so be aware,' said Jamie.

'I will, I hope to see you in Cape Town very soon,' said Hutcheson and rode off.

'I think I know what's worrying you, Jamie,' said Iain. 'I have given some thought to what Bill said as well, you think someone or some people are being manipulated with that bleddy potion… right?'

'I don't think it, I know that's what's happening. I don't know how they are doing it but Renton and Banbury with that big black bastard and probably Williams are dishing it out somehow. I've had a dose of that stuff and

Prophets of Death

believe me it's not pleasant,' said Jamie. 'We need to finish up and get out of here. We need to get back to Cape Town as quickly as possible; we have work to do.'

Chapter Thirty

December 1856

Xhosa Township

Charles Blackwell, Chalis to the Ngqika, had always sought the best for the Xhosa natives and the Xhosa people all knew this of Blackwell, but the British Government in London six thousand miles away did not.

Governor Whyte had made it quite clear that Whitehall was running out of patience with the Xhosa resistance to change and their unrest. The British Empire needed its resources in India so the Xhosa had to toe the line or face serious consequences. *We would not want a blood bath to persuade the natives, now would we?* Whyte had said.

Blackwell arrived at the Ngqika Township and was speaking with the designated spokesman for the Xhosa nation, the war Chief, Mzingisi.

They had done the formal greetings, asked about family, cried and moaned about the Xhosa clans returning to the Amatolas and the Ngqika to the Kroomie Heights.

'Chalis, do you come to my kraal with good tidings?' asked Mzingisi.

'I do, the new Inkosi Enkulu, Governor Whyte, who speaks for the great white queen in England, wishes to speak with the chiefs at a camp of your choosing,' said Blackwell.

Prophets of Death

'Does the new Inkos have a softer heart than the demon Cuthbert, Chalis?'

'He does Mzingisi. He wishes to ease your burden of dealing with the day to day problems of exacting fines and punishing offenders who break the law. He also invites all of your people who have the mist in their eyes, the blind ones. He has with him a doctor sent by the great white queen who will perform a surgery on the blind and make them see again.'

'Surely this cannot be?'

'It is true I have seen it with my own eyes. Can you imagine how your people would look upon you if you could take the blind ones away and bring them back to see their kinfolk?' said Blackwell.

'This indeed would be a wonderful thing Chalis, if you say it is true then I believe you,' said Mzingisi. 'What does the governor mean to say to the chiefs?'

'I do not know the details, only he can tell you and all the other chiefs together at the same time. There is one thing however.'

'There is always one thing more with the white man Chalis,' said Mzingisi. 'What would it be?'

'The governor will only see the chiefs without the pakati.'

The mistrust immediately passed over Mzingisi's eyes.

'This cannot happen, the pakati are part of our ruling system and they will have to be at the meeting.'

'You are known to all as the mighty war chief of the Xhosa nation, you have the ear of the paramount chief and all the chiefs, you must convince them to tell the pakati that they will not be allowed to attend the meeting with the new governor. You have to listen to me very carefully; if you think the demon Cuthbert was bad, it is nothing to the wrath of the great white queen who will send an army twice as big and take everything that is left to you and leave you with nothing, please heed my words,' said Blackwell passionately.

Mzingisi sat and looked at Blackwell for a long time and then said. 'I will meet with Samkelo the other chiefs and we will make a decision.'

Days went by whilst the chiefs deliberated and argued and eventually they decided to meet with the governor and take the blind ones to see this doctor who makes people see and see if Chalis was true to his word. Then they would simply come back and discuss with the pakati what had been said at the meeting with the inkos governor, anyway.

Chapter Thirty One

December 1856

Amatola Hills

Governor Whyte was sitting in his tent at the camp set up near the foothills of the Amatola Mountains waiting for the Xhosa chiefs to make an appearance.

He had departed from the town of George deciding he had to get to King William's Town as quickly as possible. By-passing all the other towns on his route, except Port Elizabeth and Grahamstown, he had stopped only when it was necessary to camp for the night.

With him was the trainee, Boyce as Bill Hutcheson was supposed to be sailing from Knysna, to East London. Also with him were Charles Blackwell and Captain John McAllister.

Whyte appointed a Medical Superintendent for the Eastern Cape. He had arrived from England only weeks before and had already demonstrated his mastery at removing cataracts. He had operated on some of the tribe's people and the reaction had been tremendous as people could now miraculously see again. The doctor had set up a large tent as a makeshift surgery and waited for his new patients.

'Why is it, these natives are never timeous when coming to a meeting?' said Whyte.

'They don't work to the clock as we do sir,' said

Blackwell. 'When they feel that they should go then that's when they will come and meet us.'

'It is damned infuriating never mind frustrating that they just wander in anytime they feel like it; however, when we finish this meeting the chiefs will go and deliberate our proposals for god knows how long. You two will be around them at all times and you will have agreements from all of them.'

'What if only half agree or one does not agree, do we then come back to the bargaining table?' asked McAllister.

'Gentlemen, let me be clear on this, there will be no disagreement, I will put forward a proposal to them that will have them salivating to sign,' said Whyte. 'You, Blackwell and you, McAllister will talk to them in their own tongue and sell to them the merits of having a stipend every month along with the other proposals.'

'We'll do our best to bring the chiefs to agreement sir,' said McAllister.

Blackwell was not as enamoured to this as his colleague, but he had to go along with it.

The Xhosa chiefs knew from past experience that to arrive late rankled the white men with their dates and time pieces, so they made their camp at sundown two days late and met the next morning to hear what the new inkos of the English had to say.

All the chiefs were there sitting in front of their white conquerors, the Paramount Chief, Samkelo, of the Gcaleka clan; Mzingisi, Sandla, Xolaxola, from the Ngqika; Siyabulela and Mihlali, from the Ndlambe and from the Gqunukhwebe clan; Phumzila and Kanelo. All were untrusting and all were nursing their anger at their vulnerability to the English rulers.

Once they had dispensed with the formal introductions and pleasantries they got down to business.

Prophets of Death

Whyte would speak and Blackwell would translate to the Xhosa who would then look at their own translator and he would nod that it was true or explain it a different way and it worked vice-versa when a chief outlined any points or asked a question.

Whyte had made sure his new assistant had laid on plenty of food, sorghum beer and especially brandy; he knew of Sandla's fondness of the spirit.

After praising the chiefs and recognising their stature Whyte began to explain what would be the usual empty promises, after all they were just savages in loin clothes.

'As I have said, I thank you for coming here to hear what I have to propose to you to ease the burden on you and your people,' said Whyte actually believing what he was saying. 'The burdens I talk about are the tedious duties of serving justice and exacting fines and laying down the law, in other words policing your people. I also want to offer all the chiefs a stipend, a regular payment every week or every month to make sure that you and your families are comfortable and eat well. All we want to do is send magistrates to take over the duties of serving justice; that is all. You will still be the chiefs of your tribes but without the bothersome day to day running of the tribal courts.'

The chiefs' eyes widened when Whyte told them what their generous payments would be.

The deliberations went on for a few days as the chiefs milked the generous food and drink at their disposal but eventually they decided they had to go back to their kraals and deliberate further so they re-convened with Governor Whyte to tell him of their decision.

Samkelo stood up among his other chiefs and said. 'We will need time to think on your offer governor, as the people will expect their chiefs to do the right thing by them; so we will go back to our kraals and send for you when we have made a decision.'

Whyte nearly had an apoplectic fit. *They will send for me*? He thought. *They will go back to their councillors or pakati or whatever they call them and allow them to talk them out of this offer because the pakati will be getting nothing.*

Whyte now stood up and said. 'This decision has to be agreed by all the chiefs before you leave here. If you do leave without making a decision then the offer will be withdrawn and it will not be offered again; ever again. This will be resolved before we part company one way or the other. Mr McAllister, Mr Blackwell, you will accompany the great chiefs and bring me their decision. You have two days, I await your answer.'

The interpreters translated Whyte's demands and the chiefs knew the intent behind the governor's words; they ate and drank and debated until finally Phumzila stood up and said. 'We have nothing. We can barely feed ourselves. Many years ago we had thousands of cattle roaming our grass lands, now we have a few hundred between us on a small piece of land that we all must share.'

'Everything we had has been taken away,' said Kanelo, Phumzila's brother. 'With this stipend offered by the governor at least we can live better without scraping a living.'

'The offer is very generous,' said Phumzila. 'I do not see that we can refuse. I vote that we accept the offer.'

Sandla eyed the food and drink greedily, especially the brandy and could see a comfortable life ahead, he said, 'Mzingisi does not trust the white man's promises but he will stand by my decision to accept the offer. We truly do not have a choice.'

Samkelo then spoke up. 'Siyabulela, do you agree to accept the governor's offer?'

Prophets of Death

'I do inkos. I was pardoned from Robben Island and came back to live in squaller. It is better that we live as chiefs should live.'

'We are all agreed then,' said Samkelo. He sent for Blackwell who responded at once.

'Chalis, tell the governor we accept his generous offer and his terms,' said Samkelo.

All the chiefs put their mark to the worthless piece of paper the offer was written on. Just as worthless as all the empty promises that had been made by the ignoble governors in the ignoble past.

Chapter Thirty Two

December 1856

Gxara River

Williams and Samuel met up with Captain Winston Murray and his men on the outskirts of Cape Town and paid half their money in advance with a promise of the balance when they returned to Cape Town.

Williams then led the small column of men through the night to the Eastern Cape to meet with Misumzi.

Where does Banbury find these psychopathic cutthroats? Williams thought. *The British must breed them and send them to the colonies to kill everybody when ordered.*

'What of the patrols, are we to slay another few troopers on the way back again?' asked Samuel.

'The army is away putting down unrest somewhere else, that is the British way is it not? If it does not obey, kill it,' said Williams.

When they reached the rendezvous to meet up with Misumzi, he was not there so they made camp at the same place as the last time and put out sentries. Then they had to wait for Misumzi to make an appearance.

Two nights later the sentries spotted him coming towards the camp and allowed him to go through where he met with an angry Williams and a disgruntled Samuel.

'Where have you been? We have been here for two

Prophets of Death

days already?' said Williams.

'There is much trouble in the land since the first prophecy. The chiefs' meeting with the new white inkos has not been well received by the people; we are a people without hope. Do you have brandy with you?' said Misumzi suddenly changing tack.

Williams knew Misumzi had developed a taste for the alcohol and produced a flagon of brandy. Samkelo's chief pakati swallowed the drink with relish and said. 'Did you bring my money?'

Samuel suddenly drew his scimitar and moved with such speed that Misumzi fell back but did not drop the brandy.

'You will not make demands of us,' said Williams. 'Where is Nonkululeko?'

'She is at the flat alter stone to await the sign from the old chiefs.' said Misumzi terrified out of his wits at this giant demon.

Williams leaned forward and said. 'Your money will be paid when we are finished and do not forget that you have done too much to turn away from our plans. If your people discover your betrayal I do not even want to think about how they will kill you and your family.'

Misumzi took another slug of brandy. 'I will finish what I have started,' he said finding new courage. 'Give me the potion then get your business done and be gone from me.'

'There is more to talk about. When the prophecy has been spoken you will go to the chief and the pakati and repeat the words from Nonkululeko, you will have them and many people coming to hear her words spoken from her own lips. You will provide food, milk, water and sorghum beer and you will have another dose of the potion to pour into them. Do you understand?'

Misumzi took the bottle containing the vile liquid

and said. 'Yes, I will do as you request.'

When Misumzi left, Samuel said. 'I will take great delight in separating his head from his body.'

'If anyone ever deserved to die it is that treacherous black bastard,' said Williams and sat down to wait.

Misumzi made his preparations then went to Samkelo's kraal, as he was summoned to meet with the chief, who had returned from the disastrous meeting with the governor.

Samkelo held council with his pakati and told them what had transpired; they were infuriated at being left out of the discussions but even more so that they would not receive a stipend.

'I had no choice,' said Samkelo. 'The other chiefs agreed therefore I had to agree otherwise the people would have been punished and sent away from what pitiful little we have here. I do not know where to turn anymore, the white men have taken everything. If only Nonkululeko would see the promised prophecy and bring the old chiefs back to save our people.'

The plight and sorrow of the Xhosa nation was felt by all. They were as lost children without guidance from a mother or father; without hope, without freedom in their own land.

Misumzi saw his chance to raise his stature in the Pakati, he stood up and said. 'My niece, the seer, Nonkululeko, is wandering to the great pool in the night waiting for the vision to give her a sign. She feels something is stirring within the ancestral spirits, perhaps the time will soon come to tell of the prophecy.'

Samkelo said.' Misumzi, go to Nonkululeko and find out if she has seen a vision in the great pool.'

Misumzi excused himself and went off to fetch Nonkululeko. He gave her food and water laced with the potion then returned her to the flat rock beside the river

Prophets of Death

pool where she would see her visions and deliver her prophecy.

She sat and waited for a sign of the old chief to give her the prophecy for the people. The stronger potion started to play with her mind and she imagined people moving in the waters of the pool.

In her mind she wanted to see the chiefs appear before her in all their glory, she desperately wanted to help her people by giving them hope from a lifesaving prophecy.

Samuel rose out of the pool fully dressed as a Xhosa Chief and stepped slowly through the misty smoke he created from the small fire below the bank of the river as he had done before, his mere presence filling the young prophetess with awe and trepidation.

He then spoke to Nonkululeko. He had rehearsed and learned the Xhosa words he needed to tell her, reassuring her and calling her name. When he deemed her ready to be hypnotised he began the process of implanting the poisonous words of the false prophecy into her mind. He said the words with such passion that she became breathless and almost fainted.

When he was sure she had listened and believed his words Samuel retreated slowly, again leaving the crane feather on the bank of the river, disappearing into the water to emerge up stream and join Williams. They watched as Nonkululeko called to her uncle and told him of the prophecy. He listened and then sat in front of his niece stunned into silence.

'He is not moving Samuel I think he's too scared to go to the chief,' said Williams.

Samuel moved around behind Nonkululeko and jumped up on a rock in full Xhosa regalia with his huge sword in his hand.

Misumzi jumped to his feet with fright and scuttled

off to Samkelo's Kraal as fast as his legs would take him.

He sat with Samkelo and told him of the prophecy.

Samkelo called a council of the pakati. They were devastated at what they heard, some refusing to believe such a story. Samkelo then told Misumzi that he wanted to hear the words of the prophecy from the seer's own mouth.

'I will go ahead inkos and have sitting mats, food and beer for you and the pakati,' said Misumzi.

When they arrived, they sat down in their places next to the chief, depending on their status in the group. They had food and beer, some drank water, one or two drank some goat's milk, and all of the refreshments were laced with Samuel's potion.

'Nonkululeko. Tell the Inkosi Enkhulu of the prophecy from the great Chief, Tshawe,' said Misumzi.

Nonkululeko, clearly in a trance, held up her hands, her eyes were looking at something only she could see, her ears listening to something only she could hear.

'I have seen the great chief Tshawe and he has shown to me the long dead chiefs of the Xhosa,' said Nonkululeko her voice quivering and pitching higher. 'Hintsa, Mdushne, Ndlambe, Nqeno and Ngqika, I can hear them crying out to save our people.

They have been fighting with black people called Russians and together they killed the demon Cuthbert and defeated the British over the seas in foreign lands. They are now coming home to lead the Xhosa people into battle and kill the British, who have invaded our land and taken it from us.'

This devastating news set off shouts and widespread murmuring among all who were listening.

Then Nonkululeko's demeanour changed. She pulled her arms to her chest and said. 'I see death all over the land, skeletons of cattle, the grain pits burnt and empty;

Prophets of Death

there is not a living animal to be seen anywhere.'

Samkelo and his pakati grew very disturbed at these words and as word started to travel, more and more people gathered at the pool in the Gxara River to hear for themselves this prophecy of destruction.

'The people must show that they believe,' said Nonkululeko suddenly raising her voice. 'All have to believe and trust in the ancient ones returning by burning all of the crops; planting of any crops must be stopped. All the cattle must be killed, goats and sheep must be killed; all the beasts must be killed; all witchcraft must be renounced and rejected. When all the people have done this the great chiefs will return bringing wagons filled with guns, powder and shot. They will bring tools to till the land and maize to feed the people but above all they will bring fat cattle to graze on the great pastures of our country. The old will be young again and the young will be young forever.

Misumzi made sure all who were within earshot of his niece were drinking the refreshment laced with the potion.

Samkelo and the pakati, themselves now in a trance, succumbing to the intoxicating refreshment, were so taken by these revelations that there was hope of being free of the hated British invaders. They also started to see visions of the faces of the old chiefs in the flowing waters of the pool in the river accompanied by the lowing of cattle. Someone found the plume of the blue crane on the river bank while others wandered to the sea and saw the chiefs riding through the waves rolling up on the beaches, such was the deep rooted yearning for freedom from the English governor.

But there were also a lot of unaffected people watching who could see none of these visions.

Over the following days Samkelo had seen his long

dead father and his old, long dead warhorse. He could not sleep, the pressure from his pakati and the burden of his office began to pull him down.

In desperation he ordered the tribe to start the killing of all the cattle and beasts along with the destruction of the crops and grain pits and the cleaning and tidying of all the kraals in preparation of the return of the old chiefs.

Samkelo had then sent word to the other chiefs ordering them to obey the words of the prophecy otherwise they would not come true. If the people did not have faith in the coming of the old chiefs then all was lost.

Mzingisi and Sandla were not so convinced to slaughter their only wealth and dithered with the decision whilst Mihlali said he would cut the throat of any fool who killed even one cow.

Scepticism was rife as some of Samkelo's own men, loath to kill their beloved cattle, sold them and buried the money in hopes to buy them back.

Misumzi could see the confusion and differences of opinion and declared. 'On the next moon from now the people will gather wearing new coverings, white blankets and new brass wire rings. Two suns will be seen rising on the Ntaba ka Ndoda, the high peak in the mountains, then you will see the old chiefs arrive,' he said with passion, digging the hole he was making for himself ever deeper.

Chapter Thirty Three

December 1856

Oudtshoorn

By the time they reached Oudtshoorn even the robust Fairbairn was exhausted. Barnaby found reasonable lodgings on the outskirts of the town where they bathed ate and slept.

Early the next morning Barnaby was up and out to find the exact location of the cave and if there had been any unusual movements around town or any rumours of a band of horsemen in the area.

He tracked down and found one of his old friends from his raiding and robbing days, before they both were jailed. He gave Barnaby some very interesting news for an exchange of money.

Finding Fairbairn and Flint in a tavern. He sat down to a tankard of ale and said. 'One of my old mates says someone has been buying up a load of supplies for a bunch of government professors and archaeologists doing some kind of survey and digging at the Cango caves up in van Wyk's farm.'

'So the cave is there. Did he say how many there were?' asked Fairbairn.

'No but there must be a few of them from the amount of stores and provisions they bought,' said Barnaby.

'So they're in the cave and they have bought a

substantial amount of stores which means they're going to be there for a short while at least,' said Fairbairn.

'They bought a lot of rope and lighting oil as well as sheets of tarpaulin.'

'I wonder why they need such large quantities of those items; that's very strange. The main problem is planning a way to get into the cave or at least close to it without being seen. Did your old friend have anything else of importance to say?' asked Fairbairn.

'Nothing else... except... he says four or five large wagons came into town destined for delivery to farmers up north but are still sitting at the big yard on the north side of the town,' said Barnaby.

Fairbairn's head came up. 'Wagons you say?'

'Yes sir.'

'Find out how many men are guarding those wagons; maybe hire your friend to keep an eye on them. Can he be trusted to watch the wagons for us for a price?'

'He will do anything for the price of a wine sack but why... aahhh, the wagons are not for the farmers they are for hauling the treasure from the cave.'

'Precisely, and that will be our way into the cave,' said Fairbairn. 'Tell your friend he'll be well paid to buy his wine but he better stay awake and report anything that happens with those wagons.'

'You won't have to worry about that sir he knows what's required. When do we leave?'

'We leave tomorrow morning to scout a vantage point to watch the mouth of the cave then we'll make camp there and wait to see what develops. We must be ready to move when riders are sent for the wagons, then we'll strike. Flint! You will need to bring your Enfield rifle to knock off a few of the enemy.'

It was decided that Barnaby would remain in Oudtshoorn to recruit some men to man the wagons and

Prophets of Death

round up some of his old colleagues and make sure they were armed to fight off the enemy at the cave when called on.

Fairbairn and Flint left before dawn staying off the roads so as not to be spotted by any sentries. They found the perfect position to watch the pathway and the entrance to the cave, which looked to be very busy with Fyvie's men, or enemy soldiers as Fairbairn liked to call them, and within easy range of Flint's Enfield rifle. They knew from experience that this could be a long wait and made sure they had comfortable bedding, food and drink for a long stay. The fire could be hidden in a hollow down from the ridge where they would keep watch.

It was a long wait. Day after day they kept watch knowing they had to keep their heads down lest they should be seen.

Fairbairn was dozing at the small camp when Flint woke him.

'There's some excitement at the camp by the cave, you'd better come and see what you want to do,' said Flint.

They scrambled up to the vantage point and Fairbairn looked down through the spyglass and could see the men running around, in and out the cave entrance with a purpose. Then he saw Iain McColl talking to two riders, gesticulating with his arms as though trying to explain something.

'This is it,' said Fairbairn. 'McColl is sending riders to Oudtshoorn to bring the wagons up and start loading.'

'Shouldn't we follow the riders into Oudtshoorn and take the wagons when they get there?' said Flint.

'No, we'll wait. We know where they are, let them hitch up the horses to the wagons and then we'll strike. I want to wait for a while and see what else happens at the cave,' said Fairbairn.

After about an hour a rider was escorted by sentries off the road and went up the path towards the cave. Fairbairn lifted the spyglass and almost stood up when he saw who it was.

'What's happened?' said Flint seeing the alarm in his boss.

'That snivelling little bastard is one of them,' exclaimed Fairbairn.

'Who's one of them?'

Fairbairn gave Flint the spyglass and said, 'Look at the three men at the entrance to the cave; the two tall ones, one with red hair, and the shorter one.'

Flint took the spyglass and looked. 'I see them. Who are they?'

'The tallest one is Fyvie, the red haired one is McColl; remember them because I don't want you to kill them, they're mine, but the short one works for the Cape Government in the governor's office and he has now shown himself to be one of the enemy. His name is Bill Hutcheson, the treacherous bastard. God I wish you could shoot him now but that would give the game away, but take a good look at him and if you see him again you have my permission to put a bullet in him,' said Fairbairn. 'You stay here and keep watching and I'll go and get Barnaby, he'll have some men recruited; then watch for us arriving on the wagons.'

'I'll be here sir, don't worry, I have your enemies in my sights,' said Flint still believing he was engaged in government work.

Fairbairn saddled up and rode out for Oudtshoorn at a decent gait, *I don't want any accidents when I am so close to being a rich man*, he thought.

He found Barnaby with his motley crew in a disused barn they had *rented* from a watch boy.

'What do you have to report Mr Barnaby?' said

Prophets of Death

Fairbairn pouring some coffee kept warm on a pot-bellied stove.

'Two riders arrived at the wagon driver's camp; they all sat down and had a conversation. Then the two riders went into town, I suppose to get some other equipment and the others they broke camp and started hitching up the wagons. They are still waiting for the other two men to come back. I have a man watching them,' said Barnaby.

'Everybody listen,' said Fairbairn. 'When the other two riders come back we will make our move. Barnaby and I will take care of the two riders sent down from the cave. There are seven of you, five to take over the reins of each wagon, the other two to help each man overpower the drivers and drive the wagons up to the Cango caves. When you dispose of the drivers take their jackets and hats and put them on, we need to keep the element of surprise for as long as possible.'

The man watching the wagons reported that the two riders had eventually come back followed by another wagon.

Fairbairn told his men to get to their positions. They watched the transfer of timber, thick rope and other equipment to the wagons after which the delivery wagon turned around and headed back to town.

Fairbairn watched two of his men silently climb on the last wagon in the train and cut the driver's throat, his man taking the clothes off the dead man and taking his place on the driver seat. This happened again with the fourth wagon in line, still no-one had noticed.

As his men prepared to take the third driver, Fairbairn and Barnaby came out from their hiding place and casually walked towards the two riders and the driver of the lead wagon to keep their attention.

'Hello there,' said Fairbairn. 'I wonder if you could

tell me the best road to take to a cave full of treasure.'

In the split second it took for the men to register what Fairbairn had said, he and Barnaby pulled their pistols and shot the three of them where they stood. During this time the other drivers had been silently disposed of and replaced.

'Drag the bodies into the barn, oh and kill the watchman,' said Fairbairn as he and Barnaby donned the rider's clothes.

'How is it that there are no troopers around, that gunfire should have brought somebody out,' said Barnaby.

'Don't worry about any troopers or patrols, I believe they are elsewhere protecting the bloody empire.'

The men came back and mounted the wagons, Fairbairn held his hand up and waved to go forward and shouted, 'Move along.'

The wagons led by Fairbairn and Barnaby snaked away along the road to riches.

Chapter Thirty Four

December 1856

Cango Caves

Hutcheson made good time since leaving the caves and arriving in Knysna. He went to the jetty and found that Captain Willard had been rowed out to the Flying Fish, so while he waited for his return he went to the hotel to clean up. On his return he was just in time to meet the Captain walking from the jetty.

'Bill, you are back again I see?' said Willard as he shook Hutcheson's hand. 'Is there any news from Jamie and the lads?'

'Yes sir, there is.'

Hutcheson told him about the meeting and the treasure and how he would be notified when the wagons would be on the move.

'Where are the wagons at the moment?' asked Willard.

'They are at a large commercial yard and stables just outside of Oudtshoorn; I am on my way back there when I leave you. There is still a lot of daylight left, I will ride up there tonight by carriage and check in the morning that they are safely on their way. Then I'll attempt to find the governor wherever he may be, as I'll not be going to East London on The Flying Fish.'

Hutchison arrived in Oudtshoorn the next morning to

find the yard where the wagons had been kept was deserted.

They're all safely away, he thought.

He alighted from the carriage and looked at the tracks left by the wagons heading north and then he noticed other marks in the dirt as though some things had been dragged away; there were also dark stains on the grass and stones at the side of the road.

He back tracked and could see more stains.

'These are blood stains,' he whispered to himself.

He looked up quickly to a barn just off the property and saw someone duck back behind a fence. He pulled out a pistol and ran over to the fence, looking over he saw an old native man hobbling away from him.

'You there! Stop where you are,' commanded Hutcheson.

The old man had a lame leg and used a piece of a tree branch as a crutch. He had grey-white curly hair and a sad face, he turned to Hutcheson knowing he could not outrun him.

'I am sorry boss, I am not to blame,' he said.

'Not to blame? Not to blame for what?' asked Hutchison looking around for anyone else hiding.

'The dead men in there, boss; the white man and his men who took the wagons, they killed them.'

'What are you talking about man, who is dead? And what white man took the wagons? Why is there no-one around here, where is everyone?'

'I am the watchman for that barn,' said the old man pointing. 'The wagons were about to leave when the other men hiding in the barn killed all the people in the wagons and dragged them into the barn, boss.' He was not going to tell him he had taken money to let them use the barn.

'Show me,' said Hutchison.

'I had to hide in the bush, they would have killed me

Prophets of Death

as well because I saw them,' said the old man as he opened one half of the large double doors in the middle of the barn.

A cloud of flies flew out as the door opened, the stench of death already overpowering. Hutcheson saw the bodies and had to stop himself from vomiting. Maggots were already appearing in the wounds and the flies were relentless. He noticed the bodies had no hats or jackets.

Fairbairn, he thought. *It can only be him. They will ride straight into the camp at the cave site with the wagons and take them by surprise.*

'My name is Hutcheson,' he said to the old man and he repeated it back to him. 'Go to the police station in the town and find the Captain in charge and bring him here; show him these bodies. Tell him my name and that I work for the governor. Do you understand?'

'Yes boss, you are Hutcheson and I must find the Captain, the police Captain, I know of him boss.'

Hutchison ordered his driver to unhitch one of the horses from the carriage, take his saddle from the baggage boot and saddle up the horse.

'Make sure the old man gets to the police,' he told the driver and then mounting the horse rode for the Cango caves.

I must get there before the wagons and warn my friends.

Chapter Thirty Five

December 1856

Cango Caves

Jamie and Iain watched as the wagons arrived late in the day and stopped as close as they could get to the caves. Everybody was called in to help including all but one sentry. The drivers and their helpers started unloading the wood onto pack horses to take up to the cave to build Iain's wooden frames for the rope conveyer in the cavern.

Next came the wooden boxes, which were stored inside one of the massive caves ready to be carried over the floor of the cavern to be filled with the jars of ancient scrolls and treasure.

Jamie was in the cave directing the storage of the boxes and equipment while Iain was down inside the main cavern organising the wood to be distributed for building the frames.

Jamie looked at some new faces carrying the equipment and thought they must have been hired in Oudtshoorn to help with the carrying otherwise they would have taken twice as long; something didn't feel right.

He went out to the front of the cave and lit a cheroot and drank some water.

Something is not right, he thought.

Everything had been unloaded and all the men

Prophets of Death

moved from the wagons and around to the path which led to the camp, then Jamie realised what was niggling him.

There are no guards; the two riders we sent to fetch the wagons. Where the hell were the guards? He thought.

'Hey you,' he shouted to one of the men from the wagons. 'Where did the guards go to?'

'Ek veet nie bass.' (I don't know boss.)

Just then a horse came bolting up the path from where the wagons had been parked, the rider was Bill Hutcheson.

Jamie ran down the path to meet him; *there's something seriously wrong.*

Hutcheson was shouting as he got closer. 'Jamie it's a trap, its Fairbairn,' pointing behind Jamie.

The bullet hit Hutcheson a split second before Jamie heard the shot. Hutcheson was bowled out of the saddle and landed about twenty feet away. Jamie dived for cover then immediately went to Hutcheson, knowing the shooter had to reload.

Shots were going off at the entrance to the cave as he dragged Hutcheson behind a large rock and turned him over; he was still alive.

'I am sorry Jamie,' he said in a whisper, lifting his hand to Jamie's shoulder. 'I tried to get here ahead… of… them… they killed your men in Oudtshoorn… Jamie… don't let them win… do... not…'

Bill Hutcheson's arm fell away and he died, his sightless eyes still fixed on Jamie.

'Bill… Bill,' but he knew Bill could not hear him and put his fingers on his eye lids to close them.

Jamie came to his senses as the noise of gunfire penetrated his awareness. He looked up as he went to pull his pistol from the holster suddenly remembering the marksman who had shot Bill and ducked back down again as a bullet ricocheted off the rock in front of him.

K D Neill

He scrambled on all fours around the rocks to where he could see some of his men, he shouted. 'There's a marksman up on the ridge behind us, keep your back covered.'

The warning came too late as one of his men keeled over from a shot in the back from the hidden marksman.

'Pass it on, watch your back,' shouted Jamie again.

He looked further up towards the cave entrance and saw Fairbairn glancing out and firing at Arthur who was firing, reloading and firing again back at him. Next to him was Hendrik doing the same at other gunmen, who now had commandeered the entrance to the caves.

Jamie crawled to the side of the path, which had suddenly become very wide now there was a marksman waiting for someone to show his head. He steadied himself on his toes and lunged across the path to the shelter of the rocks as a bullet pinged away off the path. He crawled up to where Arthur was crouching.

'Fairbairn and some of his men must have left the wagon train as it arrived because they came up from the west side and started firing at our men. They caught us with our knickers down Jamie; completely by surprise,' said Arthur.

'I know, they caught us all off guard, the murdering bastards. Arthur, is Iain with you here?'

'No, he's not here. The last time I saw him was in the main cavern.'

'Christ, then he's still in there.'

'That's not the only problem, I've just finished storing all the gunpowder in the cave at the back of the entrance way. If Fairbairn finds the gunpowder he can blow us all to hell and escape.'

'What about Rory and Hamish?' asked Jamie.

'They'll still be in the chapel cave where the treasure is, hopefully hiding by now.'

Prophets of Death

'What can you do about the marksman Arthur?' asked Jamie.

'I've already thought about that. I'll take Hendrik and we'll flush him out. Hendrik will take great delight in cutting his yellow throat,' said Arthur.

Iain had been bursting to go outside for a pee for about two hours but had now decided that he would pee in here. *To hell with it, there's no-one around I'll pish in a dark corner*, he thought.

He had gone down one of the many short tunnels and was in mid-pish when he heard the shots.

He said out loud. 'Oh great, how do you stop in mid-pish.' He tucked his manhood back in his breeches feeling the warm water soaking them as he scampered back to the main cavern. He carefully looked around the wall to see two gunmen shooting the only two men who were with him in the cavern, apart from Rory and Hamish who were in the chapel cave.

Iain picked up his belt with his pistols and knives where he had dropped them. Baby blunderbuss was on his belt but big blunderbuss was over to the left of the chapel cave entrance propped against the wall. He saw Hamish looking out to see what the shooting was about.

Iain waved him to go back inside. Then when Iain saw the intruders looking over his murdered comrades he dashed across the floor, picking his way neatly between the rocks he grabbed the blunderbuss as he ran passed and nipped smartly around a huge lump of stalagmite. He chanced a quick peek back but they had not seen him.

'What the fuck is happening now,' he muttered.

Looking around and then up he decided to climb up on to the stalagmite which was joined here and there by stalactites from the roof forming nice fat pillars; the substance was very smooth and wet in some parts and he had to be careful not slide back down.

He found a niche quite high up between two of the pillars which gave him a good view of the floor and the cavern roof, which was much lower at this point and festooned with long thin stalactites.

He could still hear the battle raging outside as he watched the two gunmen climb down to the cavern floor and pick their way across the floor towards the chapel cave.

Three quarters of the way across a shot rang out and the ricochet bounced away from one of them; the man looked up, the light now on his face.

'Fuck. It's Fairbairn,' said Iain muttering again.

Fairbairn just stood there not even trying to find cover he pulled out a pistol in each hand and said. 'I am prepared to spare your life, but if you fire at me again I promise you I'll kill you slowly and then cut your heart out and feed it to a bird of prey.'

'Don't come any closer,' it was Hamish's voice.

'Don't be a bloody hero you idiot,' said Fairbairn his voice getting angry. 'My men will be here shortly and you'll run out of powder and then I'll kill you,' he said starting to shout walking slightly closer to the chapel cave. 'There's no-one here to help you.'

'Fairbairn!' called Iain from his hiding place. 'I'm here to help them ye fuckin' arsehole.'

Fairbairn heard the voice from above him and loosed off a shot which pinged off the pillar Iain was hiding behind.

Iain showed himself briefly trying to get Fairbairn to fire his other gun but Fairbairn refrained and laughed seeing Iain's gun. 'McColl! Well, well. You murdered my brother. I am going to enjoy putting you out of your misery. Are you seriously thinking of threatening me with that old blunderbuss? I might have to pluck a few pellets

Prophets of Death

out of my skin, but I've had worse.'

'Aye, I killed your murdering arsehole, brother. As for this old blunderbuss it has a slightly modified charge in it,' said Iain wondering if the fire power would be enough at this range.

Fairbairn looked a bit more serious now, 'I've found the gun powder by the way,' he said lifting up a small sack of powder. 'I'll just throw it in the cave and fire a shot at it and kill whoever's in there, now give it up or your friends get blown up,' shouted Fairbairn.

Iain did not hesitate; he pointed the blunderbuss at the low ceiling and fired.

Gravity did the rest as the heavy shot blasted the thick base of the thin stalactites, they broke off and plummeted earthwards.

Fairbairn looked up and tried to get out of the way of the falling projectiles but knew he wouldn't make it. He tripped on a rock and screamed, '*McColl… nnooooo.*' One of the spikes skewered him through the nape of his neck, the point coming out of the rib cage under his right arm.

The other man dived out of the way but landed heavily on the rocks. As he tried to get up another shot came from the chapel cave and he fell down, dead.

Iain looked on as he re-loaded and then seeing Fairbairn was immobilized, turned and almost slid down the slope he was on. He came around to where Fairbairn had fallen and saw him kneeling awkwardly between the rocks, sitting on his heels. The base of the stalactite was protruding from his neck next to his head. He was trying to reach the sack of powder but Rory came out and picked it up.

Fairbairn sat there looking into the cave at the glittering gold wondering where he went wrong and thinking, *could he not just have the gold and leave*.

Rory and Hamish were standing looking in horrified amazement when Iain interrupted them.

'Come on lads; with me, hurry.'

They crossed the floor to the ladders and fetched up the pistols and rifles left there and loaded them.

'When we get up to the top of the ladder you two go left and I'll go right. Do not worry about shooting these fuckers in the back because believe me they've done a lot worse.'

With that they went up the ladder and Iain ran to the right of the entrance tunnel and shouted. '*Hey!*' Barnaby and seven others turned in surprise. Iain fired the blunderbuss at close range killing two of the enemy. Rory and Hamish were firing at the others and another two fell, including Barnaby, the rest threw down their weapons shouting, 'No more, stop shooting we yield.'

'All of you lie down with your nose on the ground; lift your nose off the ground and you're fucking dead. Am I clear?' said Iain.

The attackers lay on the floor too afraid to say anything.

Iain fired a shot from his pistol into the ground and shouted. '*Am I fucking clear?*'

'Yes sir... yes, don't shoot... you are clear.'

'Rory, Hamish, I am going to tell the men out there to stop shooting; my back will be turned to these bastards, do not hesitate to shoot anyone who moves,' said Iain walking to the side of the cave entrance and shouted, 'Jamie... it's Iain... stop shooting we have the area secured up here.'

Iain heard the order being shouted out, '*Cease fire.*'

The guns went silent and Iain peeked out waving his hat and saw Jamie, he waved back but the men remained behind their cover.

'Iain, do not come out of the cave, there's a

Prophets of Death

marksman firing from the ridge behind us; he's killed Bill,' shouted Jamie.

But Iain was pointing down the path and shouted. 'Look there.'

Jamie craned his neck past the rock he was sitting behind and saw Arthur and Hendrik walking up the path, he was about to shout a warning when he noticed the long Enfield rifle being carried over Hendrik's shoulder.

The men came out of hiding and Jamie went to meet them.

'You got the bastard then?' said Jamie.

'We got the marksman, Jamie.'

Hendrik held up his huge knife and said. 'The coward has the taste of steel in his blood,' and he spat on the ground.

'Hendrik has a new rifle,' said Arthur.

'Well done lads, use the rifle well Hendrik.'

Jamie went to where Hutcheson lay dead and knelt beside him checking him again as though to make sure he was really dead.

'You two lads, please help me with this body; take him up to the cave entrance,' Jamie asked of his comrades.

They lifted Hutcheson's body and placed him at a cleared area outside the cave, other survivors were taking care of the injured and collecting the bodies.

'Where is Fairbairn? Is he still alive?' asked Jamie.

Iain said. 'Fuck! I don't know. He has a stalactite sticking out of his chest so he could be dead; let's go and look.'

They went into the cavern and Jamie said. 'A stalactite sticking out of him?'

Iain told him what had happened in the cave as they picked their way across the floor to where Fairbairn was still kneeling looking at the gold. He had not bled out as the stalactite protruding from his chest seemed to have stemmed the blood draining from his body.

Jamie and Iain stood in front of him and Fairbairn looked up with hatred in his eyes. 'You may have won this time but the ELOS will have you killed eventually. Renton and Banbury are snivelling fools but they have the power along with Whyte to do whatever they want to do; Renton's slave, Samuel, he will slice you into pieces. You will never stop them, the ELOS are relentless and ruthless, with resources deeper than most countries wealth.'

So there it was, Fairbairn had confirmed the members of the ELOS.

Iain said. 'You have killed some fine people Fairbairn, family men; your men are dead or captured and your marksman is dead. He killed a very good man, a friend of ours, such a good man.'

'Oh… good, I am happy your friend is dead. I don't fucking care. Why are you telling me this rubbish?' said Fairbairn.

'So you know why you lost your life today,' said Iain reaching for baby blunderbuss, cocking it and pointing it at Fairbairn's face. 'I don't know if you're worth the shot.'

Suddenly, Fairbairn lifted his uninjured arm, in his hand was a derringer pistol, but he fired too soon missing Jamie and narrowly missing Iain.

Fairbairn started crying. 'You bastards… aaahhh...'

Iain pulled the trigger.

Fairbairn's head exploded; disintegrating into a red and grey mess on the floor.

'Fuck's sake Iain,' exclaimed Jamie.

'I feel nothing for this animal. I told you I wanted to put him down.'

'You certainly did that.'

Prophets of Death

Iain looked at Jamie, then turned around and saw the men at the entrance to the cavern beside the scaffold.

Someone said. 'You put him out of his misery Iain, he was definitely suffering.' Then they all turned and went back to what they were doing.

Iain re-loaded baby blunderbuss and Jamie said. 'Remind me never to get on your bad side.'

The injured were made comfortable and the dead buried. The camp and the cavern were cleaned up and everybody sat down in front of fires and ate; they toasted absent friends and drank whisky. It was a quiet camp that night as some fell to sleep through sheer tiredness, others could not sleep and watched the flames in their fires.

The next morning saw the start of the erection of the wooden frames for the overhead conveyer to get the boxes to the chapel cave.

A couple of days later the clay jars were carefully removed from their ancient resting place, wrapped and packed securely in the boxes for travel once again after nearly five hundred years.

The gold and other treasures were then packed until they ran out of boxes.

Only Rory, Hamish, Jamie, Iain and Arthur along with two other trusted high degreed masons were allowed into the chapel cave to fill the boxes and then hitch them to the conveyor to be taken to the wagons for transport to the coast. It had been decided that the risk of temptation to steal the riches in the cave would be cut to a minimum by only allowing certain people in to the cave.

'There's still a fortune in gold and precious gems here gentlemen,' said Rory. 'We can't remove any more simply because we don't have the means to carry it. The wagons are full and the ship will only take so much weight anyway.

'It makes one wonder how on earth the Knights

Templar moved all that weight and cargo from Knysna to here, the work involved must have been back breaking,' said Hamish. 'Still, what do we do with the gold we can't carry?'

Jamie said. 'I have an idea. I think we should reward the men still with us with a split of some of the gold on top of what we are going to pay them. Also, I'm sure Iain can knock up a few small boxes we can fill with gold so when we get back to Cape Town we set up funds with, say, Godfrey Butler in conjunction with a bank, for the families of the men who gave their lives for this expedition. Then we should entomb the remains of the two Knights in crypts of rocks right at the back of the cave with the remaining treasure and set explosives to bring down the front half of the chapel cave and the entrance and seal it up forever.'

'I like that idea Jamie but I think we should take it a step farther and blow up the seal pointing to the entrance so no-one else will find it, which means that we'll have to tell all the men with us that all the gold is gone and we're blowing up the cave as a tomb for the Knights,' said Rory. 'So we seven in here will have to make a pledge not to divulge to anyone what we're about to do here.'

All seven men gave their pledge to keep silent as to the whereabouts of the remaining Knights Templar treasure.

The two Knights, who were now the second last guardians of the trove of historical documents and assets of the Knights Templar, brought thousands of miles to this resting place, were each interred in a crypt of rocks carefully built as a dry stone dyke would be. Jamie and Iain went outside as the five Freemasons performed their burial ritual and said a prayer for whom they considered their brethren.

The charges were set and the cave that was now a

Prophets of Death

tomb, was blown up. The slab that covered the entrance was replaced and the rock above, along with the giant seal were collapsed in a second explosion leaving not a trace of a clue or cave just a pile of rubble that resembled a natural rock fall.

All the equipment was removed and the torches were doused, Jamie, Iain and their companions stood and looked at the dark cavern once more then everybody gratefully left the caves and moved camp beside the wagons and had a final night of eating and moderate drinking; the sentries keeping a sharp eye for any trouble.

The morning saw them up before dawn and eating breakfast to get an early start to the coast for the rendezvous with the Flying Fish. Jamie and the other lads were drinking coffee when one on the sentries came into camp.

'Arthur, Hendrik is bringing in a couple of locals, I think you should come and see.'

As they stood up to follow, Hendrik appeared with four painfully thin Xhosa natives, their clothes were rags hanging on what looked like skeletons wrapped in skin.

'Hendrik, where did you find them?' asked Jamie.

'Walking along the road towards the path that leads up here,' said Hendrik.

'Why are they so skinny?' asked Iain.

'They said all their cattle have been killed and all the grain in the pits have been burned; there is no food. They say they are waiting for the old chiefs to be resurrected and return to lead the Xhosa people to war and victory against the British. They are going to kill all the white men.

Chapter Thirty Six

December 1856

King Williams Town

Governor Whyte wrote his letters and despatches outlining his successful meeting with the Xhosa chiefs, *paying them off* and stripping them of their right to administer justice to their own people, and sent them to the Secretary of State for the Colonies in London and copies to the elders of the ELOS.

He was sitting at his desk in his temporary office in King William's town thinking of the emaciated and starving black people he had seen on the road. *Renton's plans must now be at work*, he thought.

But he had his duties to perform, he had urgent despatches waiting for him, breaking the wax seal on the first one, the letter informed him that the natives were on a killing spree, slaughtering their cattle and beasts, burning the crops and leaving no food to feed themselves. It was happening all over the country.

He called for Boyce and said. 'When did these letters arrive?'

'According to the sergeant on duty, they arrived from Cape Town a few days ago sir,' said Boyce. 'The word from the locals is that the kaffirs have heard a prophecy telling them to destroy all of their food, kill all the cattle.'

'But the cattle are the prized possession of the natives

Prophets of Death

what on earth would compel them to do this?'

'I don't know sir,' said Boyce.

Whyte put the letter to the side and opened the second despatch from the local authority in Knysna and Belvidere Port, which informed him of the death of one, William Hutcheson, a government employee and assistant to the governor, killed by a rogue officer by the name of Robert Fairbairn, who was also killed.

Whyte looked up to the ceiling and then back to the letter, he had to sit down.

Boyce saw his face. 'Sir, are you all right?' he asked pouring him a glass of water.

'I am fine Boyce; pour me a large brandy and leave me please,' said Whyte.

He took a swallow of the spirit and hastily wrote a letter to be taken to Cape Town by military despatch for Nicholas Banbury, who would take it to Renton.

He then called Boyce back in and told him of Hutcheson's demise. He had feigned shock at Hutcheson's death, his big shock of course was of reading that Fairbairn had been killed and his volunteers killed or taken prisoner; Fairbairn had been blamed for the death of Hutcheson.

The report said that after interrogation of the prisoners, they said that Fairbairn had attacked an archaeological dig at some caves north of Oudtshoorn, which was sanctioned by the Cape Government.

They attacked the cave in the belief the archaeologists were in fact insurgents plundering a hidden treasure to fund a rebellion which, of course, was laughed off as utter rubbish.

Hutcheson had found out that the dig was going to be attacked and tried to warn them but was shot by an ex-army marksman hired by Fairbairn.

The men guarding the caves had, apparently, been

ex-militia, recruited for the protection of the archaeologists and their assistants while the dig was in progress. Two other men also in the party were Jamie Fyvie and Iain McColl who had provided wagons and excavation implements for the dig and had been instrumental in Fairbairn's and his men's defeat.

Fairbairn was supposed to recover that treasure from those two Scotsmen how could this have happened, thought Whyte. *The ELOS wanted that treasure and whatever ancient secrets were buried there. This is a serious setback for the campaign in Africa; I must warn Renton what has happened. The whole operation is now compromised.*

Whyte decided to sail back to Cape Town and continue with his official duties until he heard back from Renton.

Renton could deal with the elders in England, he thought, *and explain why his man Fairbairn, had botched his role so badly.*

Chapter Thirty Seven

January 1857

Cape Town

Renton had Whyte's letter in his hand and he was livid. He was also wondering how scared he should be when the elders in London were told of Fairbairn's demise and the loss of the treasure to fund the continuing operation after the Xhosa were finished.

Fairbairn was Banbury's choice but Renton himself had not done anything to change that decision when he was the senior elder. Both Banbury and Renton now had to make the excuses.

'What are we going to do without the funding from the treasure, we'll have to ask the elders in London for more money,' said Banbury.

'I was right about Fairbairn; we should never have trusted him. He was your choice Nicholas.'

'You were quite happy to let him go and do our killing for us, you never said not to use him, did you?'

'No, I did not and that is my burden to carry. We will both have to face the elders when the time comes. I wonder what happened to him. Whyte mentions Fyvie and McColl, they must have killed Fairbairn and his men.'

'Then they must have the gold, if we can find them then we will have the gold,' said Banbury.

'We don't even know if they found it or if it was ever there in the first place. It is painfully clear that if it was there Fairbairn was going to take all the wealth for himself, but you may be right and there may yet be a way out of this mess created by that fool Fairbairn,' said Renton suddenly changing his mood. 'We'll go to the Eastern Cape and take charge of this final phase ourselves.'

'What! I can't leave Cape Town. What would people say? What would they think?' said Banbury, panic setting in.

'For god's sake Nicholas it won't matter what people think. When this is over we'll either be in control of the government, hanged for treason or dead, so keep your wits together, and start thinking clearly. Go and bring Samuel and Williams here, we need to make plans.'

When all four were assembled Renton gave his orders.

'We'll need to pack and equip for a long stay in the Eastern Cape, we'll eventually set up a headquarters in King William's Town. Williams, you'll go on ahead and find Misumzi. Tell him find another prophetess to re-enforce the lie which is already decimating the Xhosa natives, then, when the rest of us arrive at Eastern Frontier, Samuel can use his skills to induce her into proclaiming another prophecy and his job will be done.'

'Then I can go home a wealthy man,' said Samuel unaware the treasure was lost.

'Yes indeed,' said Renton. 'Nicholas, you'll book berths for you, me and Samuel to sail to East London where we embark to King William's Town. Notify Murray, have him ready to escort us to the frontier from East London, he and his men can ride along with Williams and be in place when we arrive. Murray will also need to be briefed on the arrival of the Americans to

Prophets of Death

help them herd their slaves to the beach and get them away as quickly as possible. Don't forget the Boers will be sailing down from Lourenco Marques to pick up their kaffirs as well.'

Renton had suddenly come alive; taken charge, he was in his element organising the last part of his plan to take over the Cape region; all was within his grasp.

'I'll have us on a ship to East London within a few days, diplomatic emergency and all that,' said Banbury.'

'Actually this will turn out for the best, I'll see first-hand what is happening and see the future of the Cape unfold before me.'

Chapter Thirty Eight

January 1857

Cape Town

The wagon train left the Cango Caves at dawn and was now south of Oudtshoorn. All had agreed to take the main route through the town, now that Fairbairn and his murderers were gone they deemed it safe enough to stay on the main road to Mossel Bay.

'Do you smell something?' asked Iain to no-one in particular.

'It's the smell of death,' said Arthur pointing at the sky. 'Vultures. There are dead bodies around somewhere, let's go and have a look.'

Arthur led Jamie and Iain to where the vultures were circling and found a disturbing sight.

'There must be a hundred dead oxen and cows here,' said Jamie.

'A hundred and more,' said Arthur.

'But why, how did they die?' said Iain. 'God the smell, is there some kind of cattle disease that has done this?'

Arthur dismounted and looked closer at the dead cattle and said. 'They have been stabbed with assegais, every one of them.'

'Wait, remember those people Hendrik brought to the camp,' said Jamie. 'They said something about a

Prophets of Death

prophecy that had them kill their cattle.'

'Look, away over there,' said Arthur.

They all looked into the distance and they could see more vultures, in fact they were just about everywhere.

'What the hell is going on,' said Jamie; he wasn't asking a question. 'Let's get back to the wagons and get to Mossel Bay, then we can get back to Cape Town and find out why the people are slaughtering their cattle.

On the journey south they encountered more starving people along the way begging for food.

When they camped they shared the food with a few people who stopped by and ate the food gratefully, seemingly ashamed at begging for food and telling the same story as the others.

On the road to the coast they encountered other people who did not look like they were starving but there were masses of others that did. Settlers on wagons coming along the road said there was something going on with the natives; some were killing their cattle but some were selling them.

Still the stench of death permeated the air.

The sun had gone down behind the mountains when the wagons came to the stretch of beach to the east of Mossel Bay where they were to transfer the cargo to The Flying Fish. The ship was anchored in the bay but it was decided they would make camp off the road away from the sea and start the transfer at first light.

They were sitting around the fire that night and Jamie said, 'When the crates and boxes are loaded on to the ship we should send the wagons back to Knysna until we find out what the hell is going on.'

'I agree,' said Arthur. 'For the Xhosa to kill their cattle is unheard of, the cattle in any native community is their prized possession, it's a very unsettling situation to say the least.'

'It looks as though the ELOS are going to have their war after all,' said Jamie.

Hendrik had been listening and said. 'My boss, there's some evil doings here. If some of the Xhosa are starving and others are not you can be sure they'll start fighting. The hungry ones would even attack white settlements to eat.'

Arthur said. 'Hendrik is right there's something afoot, that you can be sure of and it would be a good idea to send the wagons to Knysna as I think the authorities will need them at some point.'

'Then the wagon drivers can get a ship back to Cape Town or ride back to wherever they come from. Iain and I would be more than happy to compensate them whatever they do.' said Jamie.

'I don't think compensation will be necessary Jamie, I think we have enough loose change to pay the drivers a bit extra,' said Rory to a bit of laughter.

'Well let's break out some refreshment before we depart tomorrow, get everybody around the fire and have a wee farewell party,' said Iain.

The next morning saw four rowing boats coming in from the Flying Fish with some spare hands and Captain Willard standing with one foot on the prow of the lead boat.

'He looks like that etching of Columbus discovering America,' said Jamie.

It was high tide and the beach surface was fairly compacted with sand and broken scattered shells but since dawn Arthur's men had been placing rocks on the beach to create a twin track down to the water, as the wagons would be very heavy until they were relieved of the burden in gold they carried.

It took most of the day to get the wagons down to the beach one at a time, unload the crates and tie them

Prophets of Death

together in order to float them out to the ship. Having four boats and the spare hands on the beach helped to do the transfer a lot quicker.

At last the task was completed, Arthur and his men said farewell to Jamie, Iain, Rory and Hamish who went out to the ship on the last boat.

Once aboard Captain Willard gave the order to up anchor and set sail for Cape Town.

'Oh, I'm going to sleep like a baby tonight,' said Jamie settling in a chair in the saloon; a large whisky in his hand.

'This ship is certainly home from home,' said Iain.

'I must say this is a ship with a difference and I'll be on it all the way back to Scotland thanks to you two,' said Rory raising his whisky.

'It wasn't just us Rory. There were a lot of men on this expedition and a few of those men lost their lives, so let's say a prayer for them.'

'Amen to that. To absent friends,' said Rory.

'There is something I need you to do for us Rory, hold on a minute until I fetch a despatch to take with you,' said Jamie.

Jamie went to his cabin and came back with a satchel, inside were sealed documents, he said, 'Could you make sure Hugh Armstrong gets these documents in his own hands as we don't know who to trust. Bill had his safe way of delivering important information but Iain and I are not privy to it so we would entrust this to you if that can be done. Iain and I both have witnessed and signed these letters.'

'Consider it done lads. As you know I followed your progress with Armstrong in Liverpool. I know him and I will place this satchel untouched into his hands personally.'

'We appreciate it Rory, thanks. It has been a

privilege and a pleasure to know you,' said Jamie.

'Likewise to you, Jamie and to you too, Iain.'

When the Flying Fish dropped anchor in Table Bay only Jamie, Iain and Hamish left the ship after warm handshakes and hearty farewells. The ship re-stocked with provisions and sailed north for Scotland.

As soon as the boys reached the shore they said goodbye to Hamish and then went to find Doctor Morgan at the hospital.

One of the sisters on duty informed them the doctor was off duty but in the case of an emergency he could be reached at the Old English Tea Rooms in Adderley Street until four o'clock. They decided to go home first to get washed and changed.

Mefrou le Roux fussed over them wondering what had happened to them.

'I have been worried to death you know,' she said as she prepared hot water and towels. 'You will have to send word to me when you go away and stay away, you are very naughty,' she scolded.

'Yes we will the next time,' said Jamie watching Iain sneak down the corridor, waving back at him.

'Yes you will the next time,' she said.

They dressed in fresh clothes and went downstairs to find food laid out on the table and it smelled delicious.

They ate hurriedly then saddled two horses and rode into town. They found Doctor Morgan in the tea room entertaining two ladies having tea and scones; he nodded at the boys and continued talking to the ladies.

Iain saw a vacant table and gestured to Jamie. They sat down; ordered some tea and waited.

They watched the doctor say his goodbyes to the ladies who appeared to be a bit distressed at his departure. He looked to be heading for the exit when he appeared to see the boys for the first time and walked over to them.

Prophets of Death

'My boys, how are you?' he asked shaking hands. 'May I join you for a moment?'

'Yes, please do,' said Iain.

The doctor lowered his voice and said, 'God save us from maiden aunts; when did you get back?'

'This morning on the Flying Fish, she's on her way to Scotland with the cargo we were looking for,' said Jamie.

'Oh, you found it then? That must have been gratifying. But what on earth happened to Bill?'

Jamie was about to tell the doctor all about the excursion they had just come back from when Iain said. 'The tea is very nice but could we go somewhere that serves whisky?'

'What an excellent idea Iain,' said the doctor. 'I'll meet you at the club. Let me go first and I'll sign you in.'

They stood up to go and Jamie nearly bumped into a very pregnant woman who had appeared beside the table.

'Please excuse me ma…'

'I just thought you would like to know that our child will arrive within the next three months Jamie,' said Anne Knowles in a loud voice for the whole tea-room to hear. 'I am surprised you had the gall to come back knowing I was pregnant when you left me to cope on my own.'

Jamie looked at her, dumbfounded such was the shock of her accusation.

'What's wrong Jamie Fyvie, are you afraid to admit to the promises you made to me all those months ago?' she said making sure everybody heard his name.

Jamie's shock turned to anger, he said. 'I made you no such promises and the baby you are expecting is not mine,' said Jamie totally embarrassed and not really knowing what to say or do. 'What are you doing?'

'What I'm doing is making sure people know who you really are.'

Four women at the next table stood up to leave and one of them said. 'What a shameless display in public,' and they left.

'Madam, this is not the place to say such things,' said the Doctor to Knowles.

'Oh but it is doctor, I intend to shame this man in this town,' said Knowles then she turned and walked out leaving everyone gawking at the three men.

'Come on let's get out of here,' said Iain.

'We have to go after her and get her to take back those accusations,' said Jamie.

'I do not think it would be wise to be seen accosting her in the street,' said the doctor.

'The doc's right Jamie, let's get to the club,' Iain said leading the way out of the tearoom.

They were on their third whisky in the club when the boys finished telling the doctor about the treasure hunt from start to finish.

The doctor ordered another round and said. 'My god, what a story; poor old Bill, I really liked that man.'

'His death was avenged doctor, there will be no trial or cover up there,' said Iain.

Jamie was staring and thinking about something far away.

'Are you still with us?' asked Iain.

'I cannot believe what that bleddy Knowles woman just did,' said Jamie clearly annoyed. 'What am I going to do about it?'

The doctor said. 'If you will permit me my boy, I suggest you go and see Godfrey Butler for some council on this, I mean the whole town knows you were seen leaving her house after you had been missing for a day and that was about six or seven months ago.'

'I don't know if I should get him involved in this,' said Jamie.

Prophets of Death

'If it's anything to do with any chance of bringing Anne Knowles to a court then he would want to be involved; make no mistake.'

'The doctor's advice is sound Jamie,' said Iain. 'You've already explained to Godfrey what happened at her house and knowing what she did to George Knowles, although it was never proven and she was never tried for it, he would want to get involved. We'll go and see him tomorrow, right now we need to focus on other things.'

'Yes, you're right, we need to go and find the police sergeant, Brian O'Donnell and find out what Banbury and Renton have been up to.'

'Aye, and that big black bastard as well, he's the one making the potion after all,' said Iain.

'Now that the treasure hunt has been dealt with I think we should get a report and an update from O'Donnell and then we, as government officers, pay another visit to Renton's mansion,' said Jamie. 'That includes you doctor'

'Most certainly,' said the doctor.

'How will we find O'Donnell without attracting too much attention to him?' said Iain.

'We'll go to where they are keeping a watch on the house, maybe he'll be there. If not we can get a message to him,' said Jamie. 'Thanks for the drink doctor, we must get going.'

'Keep me informed lads.'

Jamie and Iain rode out of town and carefully went to where the surveillance on the house was hidden and as luck would have it found Ahmed.

Ahmed had a pistol drawn and was on edge until he recognised the boys.

'Ah, you've returned. Greetings, it's good to see you; there's much to tell you,' said Ahmed.

'It's good to see you as well Ahmed, what's been

happening with the enemy?' said Jamie.

Ahmed told the boys word for word what happened to Annetje at the new governor's parade.

'Right, Ahmed, stupid question time, so don't be offended,' said Iain. 'Do you think she was sure that Banbury was her abuser?'

'Without a doubt Iain, I could see it in her eyes and the way she talked; oh yes he's the one.'

'Fairbairn told us in front of half a dozen witnesses, before his sudden death…' said Jamie pausing to look at Iain, 'that Banbury, Renton and the new governor are all part of the ELOS, involved in the destruction of the Xhosa race and a rebellion against the government.'

'So now we have witnesses to both the kidnappings and treason to Her Majesty's government,' said Iain. 'You need to go and get Sergeant O'Donnell and bring him back here but before you do that tell us who has been visiting Mr bleddy Renton.'

'The most notable and suspicious movement was when Williams and the big black demon left on horseback on two occasions,' said Ahmed.

'Why were they suspicious; what happened?' asked Iain.

'I followed them out of Cape Town on both occasions but it was at night after midnight and they didn't take the main road out of town. I had to follow at a distance but managed to see them meet with Fairbairn and his band of cutthroats. This was the first time they went, and I was nearly seen as a carriage came past where I was hiding; it was Renton, he gave some instructions then went back to town.'

'What happened to Williams and Fairbairn?'

'The whole troop left travelling east to the frontier I would guess,' said Ahmed.

'And the second time?' asked Jamie.

Prophets of Death

'The second time was not so long ago. The route and the meeting place were the same but it wasn't Fairbairn that they met up with, I think it was a man called Murray whom I have seen in Cape Town, also not a very nice man and again they headed east. I could not follow so I don't know where they went.'

'Did you see anything else that was unusual Ahmed?'

'The black demon hid his sword in one of the pack horses but on the second occasion, one of the pack horses had two fairly large dark coloured glass bottles slung over it, in woven baskets.'

'I saw those bottles in the outhouse when I searched the grounds. They must have taken the potion to somewhere in the Eastern Cape,' said Jamie.

'Aye, but how could they use it without somebody asking questions?' said Iain.

'I don't know but we have to find out. Ahmed you go and get the sergeant and bring him back here in about an hour. I think it's time to pay Mr. Renton a visit and see if we can find a way in there.'

'Oh you can go in there right now because there's no-one there sir,' said Ahmed.

'Ahmed, my name is Jamie, please stop calling me sir; when did Renton leave?'

'Sorry, Jamie, Williams left the house a few days ago with a pack horse so I followed him to Wynberg where he met up again with Murray and a large band of armed men. They went off on the road east.

Banbury came to the house yesterday and after a while a coach left with Renton and Banbury, the big black demon was driving the coach. I followed them to the docks where they boarded a ship that I later found out to be going to East London.'

Jamie said. 'Ahmed, you go and get O'Donnell and

ask him to fetch Doctor Morgan, he will be waiting for word. Bring them back here, we'll search that house and then I have a feeling you and I, Iain, are going back to the frontier.'

'Oh great, I'm so happy to hear that,' said Iain.

An hour later Ahmed and Brian appeared with the doctor and the five of them sat and brought each other up to date with all that had transpired in the time the boys were away. Then they went up to Arend se Kop to find the huge gate locked up tight, as they had expected.

Brian said, 'Ahmed, you do your climbing trick over the wall and see if you can open the gate from the inside.'

'Yes sergeant,' said Ahmed.

Ahmed manoeuvred his horse close to the high wall of the property and nimbly scaled it and dropped down the other side. He unbolted four large vertical bolts on the gates, two up, two down and the rest of them outside pushed the gates inwards, smashing the mortise lock as both sides of the gates were forced in.

Brian had a large axe with him and smashed the front door of the house to allow them entry and start their search of the premises.

The doctor and Ahmed went to Samuel's quarters whilst the other three ransacked every drawer and cupboard, scrutinising every piece of paper, then Iain shouted. 'Brian, bring your axe in here.'

Brian went to the library to find Iain at a huge sturdy desk.

'All the drawers have been locked Brian, you have my permission to smash them all open,' said Iain.

'It will be my pleasure.'

The three of them were searching through piles of paperwork from the desk when Jamie said. 'Iain, look at these.'

'These are similar to the papers we nicked from that

Prophets of Death

big house in Liverpool,' said Iain.

'They are,' said Jamie. 'But the timelines on these are different from the ones that we found. Storer's death must have upset the dates when they were to sail south to pick up their cargo.'

'These dates are about to happen now Jamie,' said Iain.

'Let's go and see if we can find a way into the cellar from the house then we go after Banbury and Renton,' said Jamie.

On the way to the kitchen the doctor and Ahmed came in from the back door to join them.

'What did you find doctor?' asked Iain.

'Sacks of roots, herbs and all kinds of leaves, there are jars of powder and fluids that I could not identify and dead chickens; but if I am not mistaken, and I have read some books on the subject, these are the makings for the purposes of voodoo,' said the doctor.

'Voodoo, what the hell is voodoo?' asked Jamie.

'It's a cult that was spawned in the British West Indies by the black salves there. The cult supposedly worships devils and evil spirits; they perform blood sacrifices and they put their members into a trance by drugging them with potions and it looks like our *big black bastard* as you call him Iain, is a trained witch doctor of the cult. He is most definitely not from this part of Africa,' said Morgan.

Jamie said. 'We'll have to get back to the potions later, let's find the cellar.'

Jamie could remember his night with Felicity at the private party and trying to find his way around the ground floor of the house. There was a passageway off one of the kitchen doors which led to a large pantry and a large wooden door with steel straps across it, shaped in a series of squares studded with serious bolt heads.

Brian brought the axe into action again and eventually hacked the door lock open. On the other side of the doorway was a short stone staircase leading to a wine cellar. On one of the walls was a double wooden door which was locked but with the key still in the lock. Unlocking the doors they walked into a den of horror.

'My god almighty, what have we found here,' said Jamie.

The whole floor was covered in cobbled stone except an alcove to the left which had an earthen floor with two upright padded chairs on it. One of the chairs had a folded woollen blanket placed in front of it. To the right there were two long rectangular padded tables fitted with an array of leather straps and shackles connected to steel rings embedded in the wall. There was a shelf on the wall between the tables with a leather apron hanging from a hook with a gleaming panga cleaver attached to it; also on the shelf was a long piece of folded leather.

The doctor unfolded it and said, 'My god, these are surgical instruments, what monstrous acts have been carried out here?' he asked no-one in particular.

'Look there,' said Ahmed. 'Why would there be a gutter fashioned into the cobbled floor the whole length of the cellar?'

The others could guess why but chose not to voice their suspicions.

Further along there were two low doors with heavy locks on them and opposite them a steel trapdoor.

'One of these cells is where Annatje was kept prisoner,' said Ahmed. 'She described this place in detail when her memory was triggered by seeing Banbury. That's the trapdoor she said she jumped through before Banbury and Rent… no, it couldn't have been Renton, it must have been James Storer, had a chance to kill her.'

'No wonder she lost her memory, this must have

Prophets of Death

been a horrifying experience for her, for anyone for that matter,' said Doctor Morgan.

'Iain, help me with this trapdoor,' said Jamie.

They hauled up the lid and it clanged against the wall, they could see daylight quite far down.

Brian said. 'Ahmed, go up to the outhouses and see if you can find any long ropes.'

While Ahmed went for the ropes the rest of them inspected the cells which had earth floors and dirty blankets, buckets which must be for toiletry purposes and a tin cup.

Ahmed arrived back with two large coils of rope over each shoulder. They secured one end to the steel rings imbedded in the wall then dropped the coils of rope through the trapdoor.

Jamie said. 'I think Brian and Ahmed, as members of the police force, should go down and see what's there. Shout when you're ready to come back and we'll pull you up.'

The two policemen went through the hole and hand over hand, feet against the rock underneath the house they shimmied down the ropes. After a short while they shouted to be pulled up.

'The ropes aren't long enough,' said Brian. 'We'll have to tie them together and then go down one at a time.'

The ropes were tied together and down they went, when they came back up they looked a bit shaken.

'What did you find?' asked Iain.

Brian looked at Ahmed and said. 'There are human bones scattered all over the place, human skulls, and small ones, not adult. There is leopard and wild dog spoor around the area; that's how they disposed of the bodies.'

'No need to bury the bodies if you have a meat eater under your house,' said Iain.

They were silent for a while and Jamie said. 'Not

even wild animals would do such cruel things for fun. Brian, I suggest you bolt the front gates of this property to preserve the evidence here and post a guard outside until we bring the perpetrators to justice or, preferably, bring their bodies in. Doctor! Iain and I are going after Renton and Banbury.

Brian said, 'We will do as you ask Jamie, Ahmed and I have got a bearing as to where the bodies were dumped. We will find the ravine and bring what remains are left back to town for burial.'

'I will come with you sergeant as you will need a government doctor to examine the remains and label them for the pathologist inspection,' said Morgan. 'Then we will give what is left a decent burial. God rest their tormented souls.'

Chapter Thirty Nine

February 1857

King Williams Town

Renton and Banbury disembarked the ship in East London and boarded the carriage on the dock acquired by Winston Murray and his men. Samuel climbed into the driver's seat and followed Murray to King William's Town.

Renton was nauseated by the smell of putrefying flesh polluting the air. He said. 'The plan is working Nicholas. As predicted, these brainless heathens actually believe their ancestors will come back and kill the white men, they truly believe their ancestors killed the Russians and Cuthbert. It was so easy to fool them, with a bit of help from Samuel and his potion, and the Xhosa's misguided myths and legends.'

'They were also supposed to start fighting with each other for food and attacking the white settlers for their cattle, were they not?' Said Banbury.

'Yes, I'm sure it won't be long until this transpires and then Whyte can recall the troops and arrest the chiefs for inciting war,' said Renton.

'Let's hope it happens soon so we can go home to Cape Town. I do believe we're at our destination,' said Banbury looking out of the window.

Banbury's colleagues had used this government

owned house when they had visited the frontier; the governor had a much grander house in a more affluent area in King William's Town.

Williams was there to meet them and reported that Misumzi was waiting for them close by to where the next prophecy would be foretold.

'Then once you help Samuel with the luggage you will go to the governor's residence and tell him I am in King William's Town, then I suggest you leave immediately to meet with Misumzi,' said Renton.

Williams had already met with Misumzi who said he had spoken privately with Phumzila, of the Gqunukhwebe, who had become a strong believer in the prophecies and after feeding him sorghum beer spiked with some of the voodoo potion, Misumzi had convinced Phumzila to bring forth a seer from his tribe to confirm the prophecy.

Samuel loaded his disguise and potions onto the pack horse and with a small protection escort, he and Williams left to meet with Misumzi at the Nxaruni River, not far away to the east.

Once there they performed the same deception with a young girl from the Gqunukhwebe tribe. She was known to share her visions with the chief, Phumzila and his pakati. Her name was Noxolo, she was already under the influence of the potion when Samuel hypnotised her and told her to spread the joyous news of the great chiefs coming back to save them.

Once Samuel had planted the false prophecy in Noxolo, he and Williams then hastily packed up and returned as quickly as possible to King William's Town.

'The smell of death is all over the land,' said Williams on the ride back. 'Look at the people Samuel, they're all starving, what are we doing?' said Williams.

'I am not concerned for any of these people, they are

Prophets of Death

not high bred as we are in the north. All I want is my reward and to go back to Freetown,' said Samuel.

'And I have to stay here and live with the fear of death all the time with Renton and Banbury. I'm fearful for myself and my family; I wish I had never got involved with them especially the young girls.'

They were approaching the stables behind the house where their temporary accommodation was, Samuel pulled up his horse and said, 'What young girls, what are you talking about?'

'Nothing, I'm not talking about anything,' said Williams spurring his horse faster to the stables.

Inside the house Renton and Banbury were in the library behind closed doors with Governor Whyte who was not a happy man.

'What are you doing here James? Or shall I call you Nigel; not that it matters. I'm leaving for Cape Town. Have you come to witness your disaster? Because It seems to me this whole plan of yours from start to finish has been one disaster after another… the incident on the Flying Fish; your so called death at sea; your attempts at following Fyvie and McColl to the treasure using that murderous lunatic Fairbairn and now he fails to secure our funding and is killed and we are left high and bloody dry.'

Renton was not going to be put down when he was so close to achieving his goal.

'What are you saying? My plans are coming to fruition, the Xhosa barbarians are decimated and soon they will start another war. The Americans and the Boers should be landing on the beaches as we speak to take away the slaves they have paid for,' said Renton.

'Your slavers are going to be disappointed James,' said Whyte.

K D Neill

'What are you talking about? Murray and his men have gone with the wagons to meet them, they'll show them the way to the settlements and shackle the fittest of the heathens that are left and ship them off,' said Renton.

'Oh your plan has worked alright but it has run out of control, your plan has worked too well. The natives are not fighting with each other, nor are they attacking the settlers. The small groups of non-believers of this prophecy have been taken north under the protection of the commissioners but the majority of the Xhosa have in fact listened to the so-called prophecies and obeyed them under the strict orders of the chiefs. There's nothing left to eat James, the Xhosa natives are dying in their thousands. I have reports coming in from all over the frontier that the missionaries are besieged with starving people who can hardly stand; they just fall down dead wherever they are. I sent for more troops to re-enforce our local garrisons to protect the settlers but the settlers do not need protection because the natives simply cannot fight as they are all starving to death.'

Renton stood up, suddenly alarmed at what he was hearing and said. 'This can't be true, all of the natives surely could not have believed the prophecy; there must be some of them hiding out somewhere.'

Governor Whyte donned his hat and cape, lifting his ornate handled cane he walked the door and said. 'I'm on my way to East London to board a ship for Cape Town. You have to realise James that I have to keep a high standing in the Cape Government to maintain a presence for the ELOS, otherwise we lose the gains we have made in this fledgling government to go forth into Africa. James! Or Nigel, Nicholas!' said Whyte glancing at Banbury, 'we won't be meeting again. No doubt the elders will send a representative to hear your excuses. As I say; your plan was good but flawed. Now we have a

Prophets of Death

national disaster which will elevate me up the ranks of the ELOS, make me a hero in the eyes of the powers that be in the British government and a saviour to the people of the Cape Colony; you two are now about to become extinct. Goodbye.'

'You cannot just throw me aside,' protested Renton. 'I have achieved the goal of removing the threat of the Xhosa to free up money and troops for India and the ELOS's aspirations in Africa, to infiltrate the highest office in the land,' said Renton.

Whyte raised his voice and said. 'To say you were both arrogantly slovenly does not even come close to the contempt you deserve. You let two young men get the better of you more than once. They should never have reached the shores of South Africa, instead, two men; *two men* have obliterated our short term goals for the control of the hierarchy of government in the African campaign. Do not test me further gentlemen, you may still save yourselves from termination if you do the right thing. One word from me and that will change and if anything had to befall me, you will meet a fate worse than death itself.'

Whyte left the room and the house, boarded his carriage and did not look back.

Both Renton and Banbury were stunned by the suddenness of their downfall; they were riding the crest of the wave, only to be dashed on the rocks of destruction.

'James, we must save ourselves,' said Banbury walking up and down the room. 'We must go back to Cape Town and make preparations to escape, we're dead men.' He said trying to come to terms with what Whyte had said to them.

'Everything is gone, all I have worked for, all the sacrifices, *my status*; *my body*; *my face; all for nothing*,' shouted Renton behind his veil. 'Nicholas, we must not give up on each other we can still survive this.' He looked at Banbury who was a man on the verge of losing his sanity.

'The gold from the American and the Boers,' said Banbury skewing his face oddly at Renton. 'There's more than enough there to help us get away from here, maybe to a safe place in England.'

'Yes, yes we can do that. We'll go back to the house in Cape Town and take the gold from the hidden safe and hire a ship that will take us, not to England but to Freetown with Samuel, until this mess is forgotten or until we grow old,' said Renton. 'Go, see if Samuel and Williams have returned and let's get out of here.'

Banbury went out to find Williams and returned five minutes later with a small entourage of Samuel, Williams and Winston Murray with a couple of his men escorting Chester Primeaux and four very hardy and very able looking American sailors armed to the teeth.

Primeaux looked at the strange decrepit figure of Renton not knowing it was actually James Storer, with his black suit, gloves and hat. But as it was with everyone, it was the black veil that held his attention and then he looked at Banbury.

'Which one of you gentlemen is Mr Nicholas Banbury?' asked Primeaux in his southern drawl.

Banbury suddenly felt the fear of death and said. 'That would be me, and you are?'

'My name sir, is Chester Primeaux the Third and I would ask you what has happened to James Storer and where are my slaves?'

Renton remembered how much he disliked this crude American and he said in his raspy voice. 'James Storer is dead and I'm afraid that the local natives have decided to commit mass suicide by destroying all their own food.'

'And who might you be sir?' asked Primeaux.

'I am Nigel Renton, I was sent to replace the late

Prophets of Death

James Storer.'

'Well Storer is no great loss to us white folks, he was a stuck up, fancy pants fool and I ask again sir; where… are… my… slaves?'

The tension in the room heightened at Primeaux's raised voice; Renton was leaning both hands on his walking stick and he lifted his top two fingers which was a signal to Samuel to be ready.

'As I said, the natives have decided to starve themselves to death so there are none fit enough to get to the ships never mind survive a voyage to America, especially in your slave ship conditions. In short there are no slaves, do you understand what I mean… *sir*…' said Renton.

Primeaux bristled at the insult, he pushed his jacket back with both hands and placed them on his waist above his hips, he was wearing a gun-belt with a fancy looking revolver in a holster, he said, 'My colleagues and I have come a long way and do not wish to hear of your domestic problems. My customers back home want their slaves or give me back my gold and guns with which I paid for them and I will seek some slaves elsewhere.'

'It would seem that you are as deaf as you are stupid and as for the gold, it is non-refundable.'

The speed at which Primeaux pulled his pistol from the holster was quite remarkable but it was not as fast as Samuel's great blade which sliced through Primeaux's wrist as his arm levelled out for a shot at Renton.

Banbury dived for cover as all hell broke loose. Murray and his men were slightly quicker than the remaining Americans, shooting them all dead where they stood, one of them getting off a shot which killed one of Murray's men.

Williams, who had been standing at the door, ran outside and shouted to the rest of Murray's men to go inside and help. As they did so Williams ran for his horse and galloped away from the house.

I've had enough of these murdering madmen, he thought. *I'll fetch my family and run away from Cape Town.*

As the acrid gun smoke hung in the air Primeaux was trying to comprehend his hand lying on the floor still gripping his new revolver. Murray and his men were checking the dead.

'Murray! Give me a pistol,' said Renton.

Murray nodded to one of his men.

Renton took the gun and said to Primeaux. 'Thank you for your hospitality in Liverpool, Chester,' and shot him between the eyes as they looked uncomprehendingly at Renton.

'Captain Murray,' said Renton as Banbury picked himself off the floor.

'Yes Mr. Renton?'

'Prepare the carriage for our departure to Cape Town, as soon as you can.'

'Yes sir. I take it I will be paid in full when we get to Cape Town?'

'I will not be paying you until the job is completed back at my house Captain.'

'Of course, Mr. Renton.'

'Samuel, you have done well once again.'

Samuel bowed slightly and said. 'Thank you, sir.'

'Pack our bags and load the carriage, we need to get back to Cape Town as soon as possible. Nicholas, are you alright?'

'Yes Nigel, I am fine.'

'Where is Williams?' shouted Renton.

'I will find him sir,' said Samuel.

'As soon as we get back to Cape Town you must use your influence and some gold to secure a ship to sail from

Prophets of Death

Table Bay and go south around the peninsula to pick us up in False Bay. We'll clean out what we need from our houses and sail for Freetown.'

Fyvie, thought Renton. *My nemesis, I will have my revenge on you yet*, and Renton knew then exactly what he had to do. 'We will have to make a stop just outside of Cape Town when we get there.'

Samuel came back and said. 'Williams' horse has gone, I do believe he has deserted us sir'

'The treacherous bastard,' said Renton. 'Never mind him, let's pack and go.'

'Why on earth do we need to stop?' asked Banbury.

'We'll need to collect some insurance in case we're tracked down before we get to the ship; a couple of hostages to ensure our safe departure.'

'Your desire for revenge against Fyvie will be the death of us,' said Banbury knowing what Renton had in mind.

Chapter Forty

February 1857

Eastern Cape Frontier

Mihlali of the Ndlambe, once so against the killing of the cattle now relented. Ignoring the pleas of Charles Blackwell, he gave the order and the killing of the cattle was renewed. It wasn't long before the beasts were lying putrefying all over the countryside, the chiefs were worried that the *coming* of the old chiefs with the new cattle was going to be too late; there was no food.

The killing went on until the first moon came and went with no sign of a coming of the old chiefs or cattle. Misumzi said the old chiefs were angry that the people had disobeyed and sold the cattle instead of killing them and gave another date a few days hence and the killing became a frenzied orgy of slaughter.

The Gqunukhwebe clan began killing as Phumzila had convinced his people to obey the prophetess and destroy all of the food, but some people still would not heed the command to kill their cattle.

The tribes began to splinter into the *abaTamba* and the *abaGogotya*, the *believers* and the *non-believers*, the believers blaming the other that they were not fulfilling the prophecy and therefore the chiefs would not return. The non-believers decided to heed the call of the government commissioners and go with them for

Prophets of Death

protection from the believers.

Then, in his desperation to convince the non-believers, Phumzila produced another young girl called Noxolo, a prophetess who had seen the old chiefs of the Gqunukhwebe appear and emerge from the Mpongo pool in the Nxaruni River. They told her of the same prophecy, that the chiefs would come back to lead the Xhosa people to freedom.

Mzingisi and Sandla of the Ngqika were now under constant pressure from the majority of the pakati and even Mzingisi's great mother, who wielded much power with the people, badgered him constantly to kill the cattle.

They eventually gave in and ordered the killing of all the cattle and beasts and the destruction of all the food within the Ngqika kraals.

Some of the pakati to the Ngqika immediately renounced their loyalty to the chief fleeing north to the safety of the commissioners' safe havens with their families, followers and of course their cattle and food.

'We have heard the prophecy from two different prophets, how can we ignore these visions?' said Samkelo to the other chiefs.

'The prophets say the chiefs want us to kill all that we hold precious to a man of the Xhosa people,' said Mzingisi.

'And that is why they ask us to do this. The old chiefs, our ancestors know that our most prized possessions are our cattle grazing on our land and that is why they ask us to show we have faith in them and to prove to them our belief in them by killing that which we hold above all else,' said Samkelo almost quivering at his own words. 'Now go and tell this to our people.'

The other chiefs could see his feeling and commitment to the prophecies and they went away to tell their people to kill all the livestock and burn all of the food.

The killing went on unabated whilst the magistrates and native commissioners pleaded with the Xhosa tribes to stop; but to no avail. People were eating as much as they could before destroying everything, some tried to store food but it was summer time so whatever was horded spoiled quickly.

Then the second day of reckoning came and the emaciated tribes people turned out before dawn to welcome the two suns and the chiefs rising out of the ocean followed by wagons of food and guns and farming implements and great herds of fat cattle.

As the Xhosa people waited for their redemption they sang and prayed to their ancestors.

The sunrays appeared in the east and thousands of trusting believers watched as only one sun rose up from behind the mountains and move across the sky to the west and sink beneath the horizon. The people had started to wander away in the late afternoon and by nightfall wailing and screaming could be heard all over the land.

The believers now looked upon the non-believers with hatred, scuffles and fighting broke out in parts of the land because of the believers' jealousy towards those who had food and cattle.

The believers laid the blame of the non-appearance of the old chiefs squarely on the shoulders with the non-believers.

Samkelo was besieged by thousands of starving people wanting to know what they were to do. One pakati said, 'We have done what you asked of us; what are we to do?'

Samkelo led his people to Misumzi's kraal but he was not be found nor was Nonkululeko. Misumzi had left a message with his great wife saying that the ancestors were disappointed that some of the chiefs had disobeyed

Prophets of Death

their commands and because of this had turned away.

Samkelo led his people back to their kraals. They looked to him for guidance and direction but he had succumbed to the promise of the prophecies; he wanted with all his heart to help his people but he could not.

Misumzi had been warned of the imminent arrival of Samkelo and the people so had fled leaving a message that they were to come back to his kraal when the next full moon turned blood red. He knew this would never happen, he only said this to give himself time to decide what was to be done. How was he to convince his chief that the prophecies were true and not a story made up by their greatest enemy, the English?

He had to have time to dig up the wealth he had amassed, bring his great wife and sons with all their worldly possessions and go to where his cattle, which were fat and healthy, were being looked after by one of his sons. Once there they would find a place many days travel to the north and wait for this disaster to be over.

Misumzi found the courage to go to Samkelo's kraal and when he got there he was followed by hundreds of people. He sat with Samkelo and said, 'Inkos, I have been to the pool where the visions of the ancestors were seen and they have spoken to me. The people must all go home. They must kill any cattle which are still alive within eight days and then the sun will rise later than normal and when it reaches the top of its path, it will stop and turn blood red whereupon it will set from where it rose. Then a great storm will blow across the land and then all will be in darkness.'

The believers did not even waiver at these words so desperate were they. The cattle that had remained were sought out and killed in the veld for the ancestors to see; they cleaned and tied everything down for when the storm descended. There was great happiness knowing that this would finally take away their misery and they would live a life of fulfilment and everlasting peace.

On the ninth day the sun rose in the east as it had on days gone by and as it would on every day to come. It arched across the sky, passed the top of its arc and set as it always did in the west and in doing so darkness did indeed fall across the land as usual.

But when the sun rose the next day the decimated tribes' people of the once great Xhosa Nation would see the devastation and horrors of their futile belief.

Chapter Forty One

February 1857

King Williams Town

Governor Whyte was now in a quandary as he travelled back to his temporary headquarters in King William's Town. He had to report to the elders the failings of Renton and Co. and rebuild the effort of the ELOS infiltrating the British Colonial Government in Southern Africa.

I mean, what was Renton thinking that he could take over from the might of the British Empire? His brain must have been damaged with his reincarnation, he thought.

The Xhosa problem had certainly been dealt with and as governor he could arrest all the chiefs and put them away for conspiracy and treason and whatever else he could dream up.

Right now he wanted a good meal and a glass of brandy followed by a good night's sleep.

As his carriage entered the compound of his headquarters he noticed that there seemed to be an elevated hum of activity. When he alighted from his carriage there were two men in ordinary clothes waiting to take hold of each of his arms to escort him into his headquarters.

'What the hell are you doing, unhand me, I am the governor,' he said as he was propelled through the building.

There were three men in his office going through all of his papers as he was guided to the front of his desk.

The man seated in his chair behind the desk was smoking a pipe and looking intently at Whyte, he said. 'You would do well to keep quiet. We're from Whitehall; you remember Whitehall? Where your superiors are? The people you work for? Her Majesty's Government?'

Whyte knew he was done for and said. 'Who are you?'

'As I said; be quiet,' said the man behind the desk. 'As we speak your ELOS elders are being rounded up and eliminated. You know what I'm talking about, heart attacks, nasty accidents the sort of thing you are, apparently, not very good at.'

Whyte's knees started to buckle and he grabbed a chair.

'Look at me Whyte,' said the man. 'We're all going back to Cape Town and you are now back in the employ of the British government. You'll do exactly what we tell you to do, otherwise we can find a new governor and you can be thrown to the mercy of your former masters, after we let it be known that you confessed everything to us. Is that clear enough for you? You're not a stupid man so do not even think about answering that. I must say your plan went well up to a point, but good help is hard to come by.'

Chapter Forty Two

March 1857

King Williams Town

Jamie and Iain rode day and night and had seen corpses of animals lying around parts of the road here and there. Emaciated people wandering around as though lost and with nowhere to go; the stench of death was overpowering.

Along the way they stopped at Riversdale, Uniondale and Grahamstown and arranged with the local traders to have fresh horses available at any time night or day for riding or for wagons and coaches, paying handsomely for the service.

When they arrived in King William's Town in record time they went straight to the hotel they had stayed in all those weeks before. Jamie made inquiries and found out that Charles Blackwell was in town and sent word for him to meet them at the hotel.

Charles arrived and joined the boys in the lounge. He proceeded to tell them about the prophecy and what it meant to the Xhosa people.

'Charles, it's hard to believe that grown men would believe that shite,' said Iain. 'They're surely making this up to incite the people to start warring again.'

'Iain, on my life I promise you, most of the chiefs and the tribes' people truly believe the prophecy. They're so desperate to go home to the lands taken from them, to have their lives returned to what it was before we, the white men, came to this land. There's a conspiracy afoot here lads, I know there is. Someone or some people are behind a plot to decimate the Xhosa and plant a seed that the chiefs are trying to incite their people to start another war and the authorities are now starting to believe it. The chiefs are not trying to start a war, I know these people; they are not.'

'Have you spoken to the Governor?' asked Jamie.

'I came here and begged Governor Whyte to come with me to see the Xhosa King, Samkelo, to plead their case, which he did but the chief and a few of the other chiefs looked like they were under some kind of spell, talking in gibberish, so Whyte came back to town. I pleaded with Whyte to send wagons with food to feed these starving people; they are dying in their thousands.'

'So what did he say?'

'Nothing. He told me to leave it with him as he was going back to Cape Town to make arrangements; arrangements for what, I don't know.'

'Charles is there any way to stop this madness?' asked Iain.

'No, I am afraid it's past the point of no return. All the cattle have been killed. All the food all over the country has been burnt or destroyed; there's no way to stop it now. I do not know what to do,' said Charles, tears welling up in his eyes. 'There are reports of natives eating dogs if they can catch them and of cannibalism, eating what is left of people who are half dead and can't defend themselves; it's terrible.'

'What will you do now, how can we help?' said Jamie.

'I was about to leave and speak to the chiefs again when I received your message. We need to get wagons of

Prophets of Death

food here as quickly as possible.'

'There are five wagons in Knysna, we could do something there but it's not going to solve a problem of this magnitude, this needs to be a government mobilisation to save these people,' said Jamie.

'There is no saving these people Jamie, we can only hope to minimise the damage,' said Blackwell.

'We'll come with you to the chiefs and try to help somehow. In fact I think it's time we had a word with Governor Whyte.'

Jamie looked at Iain and they nodded that knowing nod between them.

Jamie looked around for eavesdroppers and said, 'Charles, I want you to listen very carefully to what I have to say, if you repeat this Iain will have to kill you.'

Charles smiled and said, 'What do you have to tell me?'

'Iain and I work for the government in London, we are officers of the Secret Field Police and we are here to uncover a plot. You are probably not going to believe me when I say that James Storer, deceased, Nicholas Banbury, Nigel Renton, recently arrived in Cape Town to replace Storer, Gerald Cuthbert, deceased and the new governor George Whyte were or are members of a secret organisation called the ELOS. They're all involved in a conspiracy to infiltrate and take over the British authority of the Cape region and at the same time destroy the threat of the Xhosa staging any further uprisings in the future.'

Blackwell was stunned by this revelation and stood up. Iain put his hand up and gestured for him to sit down again, which he did.

'So I'm not imagining this then. This whole series of disastrous events has been orchestrated by people within the government but secretly working with a third force?' said Blackwell.

'No, you are not imagining anything of the sort. We followed Banbury and Renton here to apprehend them but we don't know where they are.'

'That is easy to find out, the natives know everything that goes on here. Also, now I know who you two are, I can tell you that at the time of the prophecies there were strangers seen around the country by the Xhara pool where Nonkululeko saw her so called visions. This was reported to me by the non-believers,' said Blackwell.

'That seems to fit with our information of the conspirators coming here to implement their plans. There's a black man with them not of this country. He comes from a land where they practice voodoo and we think he has poisoned the chiefs with his potions used in voodoo rituals; that's why they were in the trance that you noticed,' said Jamie.

'But how can the chiefs, or in fact anyone, start a war with starving warriors, no food and no weapons; it doesn't make any sense,' said Blackwell.

'There won't be a war Charles, that's what we're trying to tell you, the natives are all starving to death. The blame will now be on the chiefs for trying to incite a war so they can be tried and jailed, but the biggest problem is that there are ships arriving from Confederate America and from Mozambique with the Boers to enslave the Xhosa and ship them off.'

'But that's not possible, there are no men or women fit enough to be taken as slaves. The non-believers have fled north with their food and cattle under the protection of the commissioners. The believers will all be dead within weeks, indeed within days.'

'I think the ELOS's plans may have backfired on them,' said Iain. 'I think they have misjudged the number of Xhosa that would have believed in the prophecies to this extent; it's gone too far. I think the Xhosa were

Prophets of Death

supposed to start fighting among themselves and then the survivors get shipped off to the slavers whilst they were relatively healthy. The fact is there's no-one left that's fit enough to be taken as a slave.'

'Charles, we need to find out where Renton and Banbury are staying. How do we find them?' asked Jamie

'Let's go and saddle our horses and make a few stops. We'll find them,' said Blackwell.

It took a few hours to track down the source for the information they needed.

Jamie and Iain were waiting patiently by the horses while Blackwell was in a hut talking with an old black man who did odd jobs for people around town. They were in a small native township on the edge of the town where a mixture of black, coloured and Hottentot people lived in relative squalor.

Blackwell emerged from the hut and walked over to the boys.

'I know where they are,' he said. 'The old man was doing some work around the yard at this particular house when a black carriage arrived with a bunch of army looking people and a bent man dressed in black and with black over his face, his words not mine, climbed down from the carriage.'

'That's Renton. That's them Charles, well done,' said Iain.

'Where's the house?' said Jamie.

'It's not far from here, I'll have to take you there myself. I just want to let you know that I am not a fighting man, I'm a missionary, although sometimes I wish I was a fighter. I'll show you where they are and then you'll need to do what you have to do,' said Blackwell.

'Don't worry Charles when we get close to the house we will dismount and walk under what cover we may find and assess the situation then come back for the help of the army if we need to, alright?' said Jamie.

'Yes, that'll be fine, thank you.'

A couple of hundred yards away from the property they left the horses and went on foot through the trees to the west of the house where they had a good view of the front door and approaches.

Jamie was looking through his spyglass and said. 'The place looks deserted, there are no horses and nobody around, are you sure this is the correct house Charles?'

'Yes, I have known that old man for years.'

Jamie handed the spyglass to Iain to have a look.

'Aye, if they were here then we've missed them. It looks like they've gone… hold on… who do we have here then…'

Jamie and Blackwell could also see someone cautiously walking his horse up to the house.

'Can you see his face Iain?' asked Jamie.

'I can see his face, a coloured man, but I don't recognise him,' said Iain passing the spyglass back.

'Maybe it's the kidnapper from Renton's house, what's 'is name…'

'Williams,' said Iain.

'That's the one, maybe it's him.'

'He seems to be very wary, he's looking around… he's off his horse and going into the house, I think we should go and see if he'll make us a cup of tea, don't you Jamie?'

'I think that's a marvellous idea Iain.'

'Who is Williams, what is going on?' asked Blackwell suddenly wary.

'It's a long story Charles, we'll tell you about it after we capture the bastard,' said Jamie.

'Try not to kill him Jamie he needs to talk to us,' said Iain.

'Very funny, you wait here Charles; we'll let you

Prophets of Death

know if it's safe.'

The boys, pistols in hand, crept silently through a grove of fruit trees all the time watching the windows for any movement. They came up to the back of the house and went in through the back door, the smell of dead bodies was even stronger than it was outside if that was possible. The swarms of flies buzzing around in the house was like a black snow storm.

The wooden floor was making it difficult to move quietly as they moved through to the front rooms. They caught a surprised Williams standing over a body. He looked up and seeing Jamie, turned and ran for the front door.

'Williams! Come back here ye bastard,' shouted Jamie bounding after him.

Williams fired a wild shot through a window pane. Jamie fired both barrels of his under and over pistol at Williams' legs and he screamed as he fell to the floor.

'Fuck sake, I told you we need him alive,' said Iain.

'He is alive, I just shot him in the leg.'

Williams was moaning with the shock of gunshot, the pain starting to settle in and he was bleeding badly from the wound.

'Please spare me, do not kill me sir, I was not robbing the house, I was looking for my friends,' begged Williams.

'Oh we know you weren't robbing the place and as for your friends, Renton and Banbury, they seem to have left you behind. We know who you are and what you have done,' said Iain in a low soft voice.

Jamie went out and waved to Blackwell.

Williams squinted at the two men standing over him and said. 'Who are you? How do you know my name? What do you want of me? You have shot me for doing nothing,' squealed Williams.

'We didn't know you but you have just confirmed your identity,' said Iain. 'Charles, can you put a tourniquet on this fellow so that he doesn't bleed to death before he talks to us.'

Blackwell went out and took the leather strap from Williams' stirrup and wrapped it around Williams' leg to stem the bleeding, he said. 'This man needs medical attention.'

'Charles, he will maybe get medical attention after he tells us what we want know. You can stay or you can leave but one way or the other Mr Williams here is going to tell us everything about his bosses.'

'I'll wait in the back room,' said Blackwell.

'No you don't want to do that there are too many smelly bodies in there, maybe go around to the back and see if you can find any whisky in the Kitchen,' said Iain.

Blackwell walked out, glad to be away from the mayhem and the bodies.

'Now ye lying bastard, you are going to tell us everything about the kidnapped girls, Storer, Renton, Banbury, the big black bastard, everything,' said Jamie. 'Oh and my name is Jamie Fyvie and this is my partner, Iain McColl, perhaps you've heard of us?'

'You two, you killed Fairbairn. Oh no, do not kill me; I will tell you all you want to know.'

The boys lifted him up and carried him to the stoep and put him on the floor leaning against the railing whilst the boys sat in chairs. Blackwell came back with water, whisky and glasses and sat with them.

'Mr Williams here is going to narrate a story for us Charles, so get comfy,' said Iain kicking him on his injured leg.

Williams howled and then sipped his water and started to tell them how he had been sucked into the ELOS's web of murder and treachery.

Prophets of Death

An hour and a half later after Williams told them word for word what he had been paid to do for Renton and Banbury he finished by saying, '... so I came back here when they left, I had to run away from these madmen. I came back to fetch my stuff maybe find some money and make my way home hopefully without meeting up with Murray and his cutthroats or get caught by some starving kaffirs.'

Blackwell said to Williams. 'Do you know what you have done, do you realise the suffering you have brought down on these poor people. Their land has been stolen, the deaths of so many children... do you have any notion in your head at all of what you have done?'

Williams was not in good shape and he was not thinking about what he had done.

'So Renton and Banbury are on their way back to Cape Town you say?' asked Iain.

'Yes they are, I heard them saying that. They must have left a few hours ago,' said Williams.

Jamie got up and went to Williams' horse, untied the reins and slapped it on the arse. The horse took off and disappeared down the road.

'How am I going to get to a doctor now?' whined Williams.

Jamie looked down at him and said. 'You can't ride with that leg, we'll go and get our horses and then find a coach or something to get you back to jail and a doctor.'

'All those young girls, all these natives, the old man at our wood yard, Bill Hutchison and all the men at the cave; you're going to hang ye miserable little bastard,' said Iain. 'And if you don't hang I'll kill you myself.'

Williams looked at Iain with the fear of death on his face.

'Shall I stay with the prisoner while you get the horses?' said Blackwell.

K D Neill

'No, he's not going anywhere with that leg,' said Jamie.

Blackwell was about to protest but when he saw the look in Jamie's eyes he walked off to where they had left the horses.

Williams checked his wounds and knew that one of the bullets had merely nicked his skin and the other had passed through without touching bone. He waited for five minutes after the three men had gone from view around the house and pulled himself up onto his feet.

I have fooled them into believing I'm more badly hurt than they think I am, he thought. *It's a pity about my horse but I'll steal another*. He hobbled off past the house and opened a gate onto a path which led away into the bush. *There's a farm not too far away if I remember correctly*.

He kept the tourniquet on his leg as he made progress into the bush turning around to make sure he was not being followed. But it was not Fyvie and McColl he had to worry about following him but some very angry and hungry looking natives.

Christ, he thought, *I had forgotten about those starving wretches*. He quickened his pace but his injury really slowed him down. He looked back to see more had joined the people following him. *They do not like us coloureds here, I must get away*.

Williams did not see the donga in the long grass in front of him and fell into the deep trench. The pain that ripped through his leg almost caused him to pass out. He cried out in pain, which was the wrong thing to do as he was now the wounded animal in trouble.

The Xhosa natives were the walking dead. Put down and murdered by the white soldiers, the Mfengu, the Hottentots and the coloured Mounted African Rifles. Now they were starving to death.

They descended into the donga and were on Williams

Prophets of Death

in seconds with knives and assegais. They did not stop to kill him they just started cutting slices of meat off of his body as he screamed and shouted obscenities.

As the starving people carved him up the last thing he saw was the image of three men on horseback up on the edge of the donga staring down at him.

Chapter Forty Three

March 1857

Eastern Cape Frontier

'We should've helped him,' said Blackwell.

'No, we shouldn't have helped him. What if we couldn't prove what he had done? After all nobody saw him doing all that shite except Annatje and she lost her memory,' said Iain.

'Iain's right Charles. Williams got what he deserved, it's now history. We move on and talk with the clan chiefs and then Iain and I must ride for Cape Town as soon as we're finished.'

The stench was everywhere; crowds of walking corpses were shuffling along tracks and paths all over the countryside. Wretches resembling biblical demons were crawling along the side of the roadways.

'Look over there,' said Jamie.

There was smoke rising from a thicket off the road, as they approached they saw some natives running off into the bush.

'Aw my god, I don't believe this is happening,' shouted Jamie dismounting at a camp fire in a small clearing.

'These are the bones and skulls of children,' said Blackwell looking at the aftermath of a cannibal meal. '*They are eating their young*,' he shouted at the bushes.

Prophets of Death

'*You are eating your children… What are you doing?*'

'Come on Charles there's nothing we can do here, let's get to the chiefs,' said Jamie.

They could only find Samkelo as all the others had gone home to their own people.

They sat around a small fire drinking weak tea, nothing as ostentatious as the previous occasions that had plenty of food, sorghum beer and goats milk.

Blackwell, speaking in Xhosa was telling them the prophecies would never come true, the old chiefs would never return, there would never be a return to the old days.

Samkelo looked over at Blackwell and said. 'Chalis you have a new name, it is now Napakade.'

'We must stop the killing of the cattle, inkos, the prophecy is false it will never happen,' pleaded Blackwell.

All were quiet.

Eventually, Samkelo said. 'A whisper of a voice floats upon the wind, it tells me, nay, it orders me to kill all the cattle, burn the corn, do not plant again; this we have done because there is nothing left to live for.'

'Misumzi has been taking money from the white men to tell you these lies Samkelo, you must believe me. You and Nonkululeko, all the chiefs have been poisoned with a witch doctor's potion to make you do these things. It's a white man's trap, not the great white queen of England but the people who have been giving you guns and making promises they will not keep.'

'The white men have never kept any promises they have made since they came here to take our land. Be Gone Napakade we will speak to Misumzi and he will face retribution if he has betrayed his people.'

The broken Paramount Chief of the Xhosa Nation stood and went to his hut; Charles Blackwell was inconsolable in his grief for a people he had dedicated his life to.

Jamie and Iain helped Blackwell to his horse and they rode for King William's Town.

'I heard Samkelo call you Napakade, what is that?' asked Iain.

'It is the Xhosa word for never, I have a new name,' said Blackwell. 'The prophecy was indeed correct; the dead have risen from the grave,' as he looked at the corpses wandering over the country.

Chapter Forty Four

April 1857

Cape Town

The horses were suffering. They had been running them at a canter for hours every day, the only respite being when they had to stop to camp for the night. Captain Murray called a halt to inspect the four horses pulling the carriage.

Banbury opened the door and said. 'Why have we stopped again Captain?'

'It's the horses sir, they are done in; we should stop for a few hours and rest them.'

'We cannot stop Captain, we have to push on to Cape Town,' said Banbury.

'We will not make it to Cape Town if we push these animals any harder. Believe me when I say we should make camp, rest the horses, feed them and water them, then we can carry on straight to Cape Town, preferably in the morning.'

Murray heard Banbury conferring with Renton and then Banbury said. 'Make camp away from the road and post sentries; we will rest until you are ready.'

It was late morning when they resumed their journey and they reached the outskirts of Cape Town when the sun had set.

When they reached Arend se Kop they were stopped

at the gates of the property by two young coloured policemen who looked nervous and were not sure what to do.

'What are you doing at my house?' asked Renton.

'No-one is allowed to enter until I inform the sergeant, the constable here will go and fetch him,' said the corporal.'

As the other policeman went for his horse, Renton signalled Murray to come over and said. 'If I cannot get into the house then I cannot pay you Captain; shoot these two if you please.'

The corporal lifted his rifle but Murray drew his pistol and shot him. The constable was confronted by three of Murray's men so he threw down his rifle but they shot him anyway.

The gates were opened and Renton with Samuel inspected the damaged locks on the gate and the house.

Renton said. 'It seems we have been compromised gentlemen, let us go indoors. Pour us all a drink Nicholas while I talk to Samuel.'

Renton walked with Samuel to the kitchen and said. 'We are going out again Samuel, to fetch two hostages in case we need to bargain with anyone should they try to stop us leaving. I want you to bring one of your potions for putting people to sleep, nothing too strong mind you, just to knock them out for a couple of hours. When you have the potion ready, prepare a carriage for Mr Banbury and one for you and me.'

Samuel went off to mix his drug and Renton went into the wine cellar. He pulled a cupboard away from one of the walls, it looked like it was built into the wall but there was a secret release mechanism built in at the base which, when depressed, released the unit from the wall and revealed a hidden safe in a recess.

Renton produced a key and opened the safe, removed

Prophets of Death

bags of gold coins and made his way back to the library.

'Here's your payment Captain Murray,' said Renton. 'I'll need an escort to Muizenberg later tonight as we'll be leaving on a boat from there out to our waiting ship.'

Murray inspected the bag of gold coin and looked around to find the black with the sword was not to be seen.

'I don't think so Mr Renton,' said Murray swallowing his whisky and walking to the door. 'I believe it's too dangerous to be seen around you any longer. I'm leaving now with my men and I shall not be returning. Goodbye and good luck.'

'The ungrateful swine,' said Banbury.

'Oh I expected as much Nicholas. Here, take this bag of gold and secure a ship to sail tonight, there's enough there to bribe any Captain to set sail immediately. Then go and tell Anne Knowles there is a change of plan and to pack a bag for her and her, or should I say our baby son. Then go to your house, pack what you need and come back here.'

Samuel came back into the room and said. 'Mr Banbury's carriage is ready sir, as am I with yours.'

'Excellent, let us proceed.'

Godfrey Butler's house was on a large plot of land set back from the road to Kloof Nek giving Samuel the opportunity to conceal the black carriage under a large tree and obscured from the house by some bushes.

Renton had two pistols and Samuel had his sword as they stood outside the back door stoep of the house. Renton nodded to Samuel.

Samuel silently mounted the stair and crossed to the door which was unlocked.

So trusting are these fools, thought Renton.

Renton followed Samuel, sword in hand, through into the kitchen in time to meet a servant coming in from

K D Neill

the front of the house with a tray of empty dishes. Samuel punched her on the bridge of her nose with his sword in his hand reaching out with his other hand to rescue the tray as she dropped like a stone.

He put down the tray and quickly went through to the parlour as another servant appeared. As she opened her mouth to cry out the sword swished through the air and her neck was slashed left to right, blood spurting from the arteries all over the walls and the floor as she slid down.

Renton shuffled into the parlour but there was nobody around. He motioned to the stairway and they climbed silently up to the first bedroom, which by the furniture and the décor, was obviously the Butler's; still nobody.

They must have gone visiting friends for the night. *Pity*, thought Renton. *I would like to have killed him in front of his wife and adopted daughters.*

The next bedroom saw Clara fast asleep in her bed. Samuel propped his sword against the wall and from a pocket in his robe produced a small brown bottle and a linen cloth.

He poured some of the drug on to the cloth and went over to Clara and simply put it over her mouth and nose whilst holding her with his free hand.

Her eyes went wide with fright and she started to struggle but not for long as she silently succumbed to the effects of the drug.

After she was tied up and gagged they moved on to the next bedroom where there was a light coming from the doorway. Lydia was asleep sitting up, her book on her lap and her head flopped back on her pillow.

She suddenly opened her eyes as Samuel reached her bed. She screamed at sight of the giant man and the black veiled apparition and tried to jump out the other side of the bed but Renton roughly pushed her back and Samuel

Prophets of Death

clamped his huge paw with the cloth onto her face and soon she was silent.

'Tie her up and get them to the carriage; time to have some fun,' said Renton.

Samuel lifted his sword and placed it across his chest and said. 'These girls are hostages and that is all, am I right in saying that sir?'

Renton heard the question loud and clear. Some men did not do what he liked to do with young girls. He could never understand that.

'Yes Samuel they are only hostages until we're away. We'll set them adrift on a dinghy once we board the ship and they can row for the shore.'

Samuel lifted the trussed up girls, one over each shoulder, and easily carried them to the carriage.

Once back in Arend se Kop the girls were taken to the cellar and laid out unconscious on the torture tables and secured there.

Banbury was already there when they got back and he watched as Samuel took the girls down to the cellar, he said. 'My god James, could you not just let it go, you'll have the whole army garrison on top of us for kidnapping those two girls.'

'Fear not Nicholas, for we'll be long gone by the time anyone figures out where they are, we'll need them to barter our freedom if we're discovered. Now stop worrying and tell me what happened with the ship,' said Renton.

'The ship will be waiting at dawn off the beach between Muizenberg and Kalk Bay as the sea is at high tide then. I only gave him a taste of the gold, the balance he gets when we sail into Freetown.'

Anne Knowles walked into the room and sat down.

'So your grand scheme has fallen apart James,' she said. 'That is a real shame; your plans were so good until you underestimated two very determined young men who unfortunately were on the same ship as you coming to the Cape of Good Hope.'

'So… you taunt me… and try to belittle me because of my failure. You have a nerve, woman. Where will you be if I just leave you here Anne?' said Renton raising his voice. 'Do not try my patience and do not talk to me of those two. One day they will pay for what they have done to me and I'll start with their women. *Where is my son*?' shouted Renton.

Anne Knowles suddenly felt suitable chastised and said. 'He's fast asleep, I just fed him so he should sleep for a while.'

'You are an amazing woman my dear, but just remember where your loyalties lie. It's a pity that we have to leave Cape Town but I'm afraid the authorities in London and here will be after us, as will the blasted Secret Field Police. Never mind; we leave all that behind us, let's be gone.'

They packed up what they needed and Samuel had gone to load his bits and pieces into the coach but was taking a while about it.

Renton was about to go and shout for Samuel when he heard him coming up the stairs. He suddenly appeared in the doorway with a man's body over his shoulder.

Chapter Forty Five

April 1857

Cape Town

Leaving Charles Blackwell safely at home with his wife the boys rode hard for Cape Town. They were a few hours behind Renton but they had no pack horse to slow them down; stopping only to eat, drink water and change horses.

It was dark when they arrived in Cape Town. They went to the police station on Roeland Street on the off chance that Brian and Ahmed might be there but they were away policing elsewhere.

Jamie said. 'Iain, see if you can locate Brian and Ahmed. I'll go up to Renton's house and speak with the guards and find out if Renton and Banbury are there. They may have boarded a ship by now for all we know.'

'I'll go to the harbour and find out if any ships have left or are going to leave. Who knows, maybe our two policemen will be there; if not I will find them and meet you at Renton's and don't go in until we get there, no heroics,' said Iain.

'Who me?' said Jamie.

'Aye, I know you; you'd like to get your hands around Renton's scrawny neck.'

Jamie left Iain and rode south through the dark streets of the suburbs and up the slopes of Table Mountain. He steered his horse off the road as he neared Renton's house and approached cautiously from the north side of the house. He stopped the horse and studied the front gates but could not see any guards.

He dismounted and walked silently along the side of the wall and almost tripped over the bodies of two policemen in a depression in the ground. He went to the gates and pushed them but they were certainly bolted on the other side.

He went back to his horse, mounted and stood it next to the wall, then, standing on the saddle he peeped over. He could see light coming from the front door, a room off to the right and a room upstairs.

Looking around into the gloom he could not hear any sound so he slipped silently over the wall, landing lightly on his feet.

He ran crouching down to the front door and stood to the side, he heard voices emanating from upstairs, there was a female voice as well.

It might be that witch Anne Knowles, he thought. *Good, she can swing on a rope as well.*

Jamie heard the noise behind him a split second too late as he turned to catch a glimpse of a sword handle connecting with his head, sending him down into a dark place.

Samuel dumped the man unceremoniously on the floor as he regained consciousness, blinking his eyes to focus on his captors. His eyes opened and focussed on the four faces looking down at him.

'Well, well, thank you for coming to see us off Mr Fyvie,' said Renton.

'I see all the snakes are together in the vipers' nest,' said Jamie.

Renton walked over to the drinks cabinet and poured

Prophets of Death

himself a brandy and said. 'Come, come, Fyvie, is that the best you can think of to say?'

'You murdering bastards, you have killed thousands of people and you just brush it off without so much as a look back,' said Jamie glancing around for an escape route, seeing the stairway outside the door leading down to the hall below.

'Was he on his own Samuel? McColl was not with him?' asked Renton.

'I looked around for the other one but this one was by himself.'

'Oh well, killing Fyvie will have to do for now. Anne, take the baby out to the buggy and drive yourself down to Muizenberg, we will join you shortly. Nicholas, go down to the cellar and make sure Anne's step daughters are comfortable,' he said smiling at Jamie. 'I will be there directly.'

Jamie looked up suddenly and said. 'Lydia and Clara are here you fucking madman?' he lunged for Renton.

Jamie was a big man but the huge Samuel, so fast for his size grabbed Jamie from behind and threw him across the floor like a rag doll, bouncing off the drinks cabinet doors.

'I will see you at the beach,' said Anne Knowles as she left the room, Banbury following behind her.

Jamie was looking for some kind of weapon to hit Samuel with, he had been shocked at the power of the giant man.

Renton finished his brandy, untied the piece of cotton holding his veil in place and then removed his hat with the veil.

Jamie looked at the hideously deformed face and seemed to recognise him.

'This is your handy work Fyvie, do you remember?'

Then Jamie realised who he was.

'Storer? It can't be. Storer was reported dead. This can't be happening.'

'Oh, but it is happening, you ruined my life, a brainless lower class Scotsman nearly got the better of me,' said Storer. 'Well now you will die and then your little girl friend will die painfully. Samuel, slice him up into pieces; *Kill him*,' he shouted.

Samuel lifted his huge sword and went for Jamie, but Jamie had seen the only weapon available to him. He took the bottles of alcohol from the drinks cabinet and threw them with all his might at Samuel who stopped in his tracks as he tried to ward off bottle after bottle smashing into him.

When there were no bottles left Samuel smiled and started forward again.

'*Kill him*,' Storer was shouting.

Jamie walked backwards to the wall not taking his eyes off the giant Samuel who was now grinning. He reached up and lifted the oil lamp from the holder on the wall and held it above his head.

The grin on Samuel's face suddenly disappeared when Jamie launched the burning lamp at him. The alcohol soaked robes erupted in flames when the lamp burst on impact.

Samuel screamed in terror as the flames engulfed his clothing. He was so enraged he tried to chase Jamie, who dived across a divan, rolled over and jumped to his feet.

Storer hobbled through the door to the stairs to escape as Samuel, still screaming, once again swung the sword at Jamie. He missed and bumped into a book case, setting the books ablaze.

He was trying to beat the flames with his free hand and pull at his clothing which was now burning onto his flesh.

Swinging wildly he went staggering past a window

Prophets of Death

the curtains bursting into flames. He dropped his sword and tried again to beat the flames with his hands as he staggered on to pass the next window and Jamie saw his chance.

Hefting up a dining room chair he ran at Samuel with the chair in front of him, smashing Samuel through the window, curtains and all.

The fireball that was Samuel, bellowing like a wounded buffalo, rolled across the roof over the stoep and bounced onto the lawn below. The flaming figure got up on its feet and tried to run but then suddenly stopped, the robes and curtains invisible in the ball of flame shaped in the form of a dying man. He lifted his arms, stopped screaming and fell over onto what was left of his face.

Jamie picked up Samuel's sword and ran for the stairs and down to the cellar as the top part of the house started to burn fiercely.

He heard the girls screaming as he ran through the double doors into the cellar to find Banbury with a machete in his hand confronting Lydia and Clara.

Banbury saw Jamie and nearly died of fright. He dropped the big ugly knife and said. 'I was just going to free them. I swear I was going to free them.'

Just then Iain and Brian appeared at the door.

'Iain!' shouted Jamie. 'Cut the girls loose and get them out of here.'

'The whole fucking place is an inferno, we all have to get out now,' said Iain cutting the straps binding the girls.

Iain was carrying Clara and Brian was helping Lydia and she shouted. 'Jamie, come on, please come with us.'

'Iain for Christ's sake will you get them out of here,' shouted Jamie.

Brian had to drag Lydia away kicking and screaming.

'I'll ask you once you fucking arsehole, where is

Storer?' said Jamie stabbing the point of the sword into Banbury's shoulder.

The noises of falling timbers and the crackling of the flames were getting louder.

Banbury was bleeding profusely from the stab wound and screamed. 'I don't know where Storer is, I swear, he was supposed to come here to take the girls. Please let's get out of here… hand me over to the police,' stammered Banbury. 'James is probably at the beach in Muizenberg to row out to the ship.'

Jamie noticed the trapdoor was still open, he stabbed the point of the sword into Banbury's other shoulder making him stagger back. 'Hand you over to the police so they can cover it all up again? I don't think so,' said Jamie stabbing him again.

'You're mad; the house is burning down around us; you need to hand me over to the authorities,' pleaded Banbury.

'I don't have to do anything Banbury, this is for Annatje,' said Jamie and kicked Banbury in the chest knocking him backwards and down through the trapdoor.

He heard Banbury screaming as he fell, fading until he could hear him no more.

Outside the front of the house Iain had tried to get back into the house for Jamie but was dragged back by Brian and Godfrey.

'There is no point in you dying in there as well Iain,' said Godfrey, I am really sorry but no-one could survive that fire.

Lydia collapsed in tears knowing she would never see her beloved Jamie again.

Jamie turned and ran through the double doors but could go no further as the way out was a wall of flames, burning roof beams and debris collapsing down the stairwell. The

Prophets of Death

smoke was choking him so he went back to the cellar and saw the coils of rope still lying in one of the cells. One end was still tied to the steel ring in the wall.

He threw the rope down through the trapdoor and climbed down to a point where he could see stars in the sky through the bush. He shimmied down the rope to the bottom of the ravine and saw Banbury.

In the moonlight Jamie could see his legs were broken as they were pointing in an unnatural angle. There was a bone protruding from Banbury's stomach, one of his victims had stabbed him, how ironic.

'Help me,' said Banbury, suddenly lifting an arm.

Jamie got the fright of his life. 'Fuck… you're still alive.'

Just then Jamie heard the snarl and then a roar of a big cat. He had to get out of this place fast.

'You won't be alive for long, your pussy cat is coming for his dinner,' said Jamie and started to pull himself back up the rope.

Halfway up he started to swing the rope over to his left to grab onto a bush but could not reach it so he went as far to the right as he could and then swung back like a pendulum, but again could not reach the bush. Back he went again knowing in the back of his mind that the top of the rope would be burnt through soon.

He swung back again and this time he managed to grab onto a branch and pull himself up into the bushes. The bush was almost impenetrable and difficult to negotiate, he stopped for a breather and looked down to see the burning end of the rope fall away into the chasm below.

Then he heard Banbury's voice from below him shouting, *get away, get away from me… no*. Then there was an unnatural scream followed by the sound of a snarling animal, then silence.

'Good riddance,' Jamie said to no-one.

He hauled himself up the side of the ravine through the dense vegetation which started to thin out the higher he went until he pulled himself over the top and onto flat ground.

The flames of the burning house lit up the whole area and he could see the double gates at the front entrance.

He had to get Storer before his ship sailed from False Bay. He ran to the gate to find a bunch of people all staring silently at the flames.

'Iain! Where the hell are you?' shouted Jamie.

They all turned and looked at him as though they had seen a ghost.

It was Lydia who reacted first pushing her way through the crowd of people and ran to Jamie throwing her arms around his neck.

'Oh my god… you are safe,' she sobbed. 'We thought you were still in there.'

Iain and Brian came running over.

'Jamie, thank the Lord you're safe. How did you get out of… oh… the trapdoor… that's how you got out you used the rope,' said Iain.

'Yes, thank god we left it there,' said Jamie. He held Lydia's head with both hands and said. 'Lydia we have to go and stop Storer before he gets away, there's a ship waiting for him.'

'Storer? But he is dead, you mean Renton,' said Lydia.

'Renton is Storer, believe me. I'll tell you all about it later. Right now we need to get Ahmed to go and get Annatjie's father and the other fishermen; we may need their help to row out into the bay to board a ship,' said Jamie.

Brian said. 'Ahmed is already on his way to Kalk Bay, we know Renton, or should I say Storer, is headed

Prophets of Death

for Muizenberg to board a ship.'

'How could you know that?' asked Jamie.

Brian pointed to Anne Knowles sitting in a buggy with her baby son. 'She told us. We apprehended her as she was escaping to Muizenberg. She told us where Storer was going, so I sent Ahmed to get the fishermen ready with their boats.'

Jamie took Lydia by the hand and led her over to Knowles followed by the others, he said. 'Tell these people who the father of your child is.'

She looked up with a defiant look in her eyes.

Jamie pulled a pistol out of Brian's belt, pointed it at Knowles and shouted. '*Tell them or by god I will orphan your child right here and now.*'

There was a collective sucking in of breath.

Anne Knowles got the fright of her life and hugged her baby.

'James Storer... James Storer is the father of my child,' she said to everyone, wrapping her arms tighter around the child and weeping bitterly. 'I am so sorry... so... so... sorry,' she whispered looking at Lydia.

'You and Storer have tried to kill everything that is dear to me and my sister,' said Lydia. 'You will pay for your sins and you will rot in hell.'

Jamie led Lydia away to find Godfrey and said. 'Lydia, I have to go, I'll come to you when this is over.'

'Come back to me Jamie... be careful,' Lydia said letting go of his hand.

The three men ran out the gates to the horses and set off for Muizenberg. The sky was turning grey in the east as they galloped through Retreat then Steenberg and finally on to the beach in Muizenberg.

Ahmed was there already helping to get a fairly large fishing boat off of a wagon.

'Why such a big boat?' asked Iain.

'Look there Iain,' said Ahmed pointing at a dinghy being rowed out to a ship anchored in the Bay. 'We can get six oarsmen on this boat, we'll catch them easily.'

Jamie was looking through his spyglass which was still in his saddle bag and said. 'That's Storer alright, I can see the hat and veil and someone else is rowing the dinghy. Let's get after him.'

'I found your belt and pistols,' said Iain handing them over.

Jamie checked the load in his guns, wrapped them in a sou'ester; put them into the fishing boat and helped to push it into the surf. Once the boat was afloat everybody jumped in and the fishermen expertly rowed through the waves as they broke and swept over the prow.

The dawn light was upon them and they could see the smaller boat ahead of them; they were over-taking it with ease.

Ahmed stood at the prow of the boat and shouted, 'Dit is die polisie, afgee te.' *This is the police, heave too.*

No reaction, the person rowing the boat in front kept rowing.

Jamie said. 'Shout it out again and I'll fire a shot.'

They were catching up quickly now and Ahmed shouted the warning again after which Jamie loosed off two shots.

The person rowing Storer's boat stopped and stood up, everybody could see them clearly now but a shot went off and the man fell overboard.

'Storer has shot the man who was rowing the boat and is now rowing himself,' said Jamie. 'Come on lads let's catch this murdering bastard.'

As they closed in on Storer the ship waiting for him was unfurling some sail and pulling up the anchor. Storer looked over his shoulder and saw this and stopped rowing to wave frantically at the ship.

Prophets of Death

'The ship has pulled the anchor up,' said Iain. 'She might try to ram us.'

The oarsmen stopped rowing as Jamie looked through his spyglass and could see the captain of the ship looking back at them through his own spyglass.

'Ahmed, put your hat on and stand up, show the captain your police uniform.'

Ahmed did as instructed, Jamie still watching the captain.

'The captain has lowered his spyglass and is shouting instructions, the ship is turning away; the captain wants nothing to do with the police Ahmed,' said Jamie. 'Well done.'

They were almost on Storer's boat. Storer lifted a rifle and fired off a shot which thwacked into the side of the boat.

'Everybody get down,' shouted Jamie. 'Give it up Storer, it's over, there's nowhere to go.'

Storer was reloading the musket.

'I think he wants us to shoot him,' said Iain. 'Get it over quickly.'

'Give me your rifle sergeant,' said Jamie.

Jamie took aim at Storer's right leg and fired. The musket hit its mark and Storer toppled into the sea. Jamie was pulling out one of his pistols when Annetjie's father said, 'Wait sir, that monster of a man killed our children, let the sea give him his punishment.'

'You want him to drown?'

'Wait and watch sir.'

Storer was waving his hand and screaming to be picked up. His small boat had drifted off and was out of reach.

The shark struck from the depths without warning, breaching the water and lifting Storer up with its nose. The great shark had a white underbelly and grey over the rest of its huge body. It dived back into the sea as Storer, screaming in terror, landed flat on his back and tried to swim for the fishing boat, but his body was too broken.

Once more the shark burst out of the sea only this time it took Storer's lower body in its great jaws halving him into two parts the blood gushing over the sharks head staining the sea a deep crimson. The shark disappeared again and the top half of Storer's body hit the water, bobbing up and down as a piece of cork would. His face was expressionless; eyes wide; the screaming stopped as the great fish once again came out of the water and took the last of James Storer down into the sea.

Jamie looked at Iain; they both looked to Ahmed and Brian. All four men raised their arms and clutched each other's shoulders in a circle of camaraderie.

The fishermen put out their oars and rowed for the beach.

Chapter Forty Six

May 1857

Cape Town

Jamie and Iain had a very unsettling couple of days since returning from Muizenberg, writing statements to the police and receiving accolades and thanks from a grateful community for delivering justice to murderous villains and traitors.

It was as though a flame had been snuffed out and life suddenly changed to quiet. They barely spoke, steeped in their own thoughts. Trying to come to terms with the abrupt halt of gunfire; violence and looking out for each other and others.

They were sitting at the breakfast table getting back to some kind of normality after lots of sleeping, eating and sleeping again; beginning to feel better.

Mefrou le Roux was now fussing over her two gallant charges as word had filtered through the grapevine of what had happened at the big house on the slopes of Table Mountain that caught fire and burned to the ground and how the boys had stopped some very dangerous men from breaking the law.

'Brian and Ahmed's report will say Storer fell overboard and was chewed by a shark and Banbury, along with the big black bastard, burnt to death,' said Iain breaking the silence.

K D Neill

'You've a great way of putting things, Iain,' said Jamie chuckling. 'It's over. It just doesn't feel like something is not going to happen, if that makes any sense.'

'It makes perfect sense. I'm not going to do this police shite any more, Jamie, I'm asking Clara to get married and we'll settle down in a house that I will build.'

'Aye, there's too much back stabbing and lying and cheating in this secret police stuff; I'm out as well. What time are we to see the girls?'

'The note said seven o'clock for dinner this evening.'

'We have to meet Brian and find out what happened to that bastard, Governor Whyte. He has to answer for his crimes as well, but so far we don't know where he is.'

Just then a carriage appeared on the single track leading up to the house and pulled up at the hitching rail.

The boys went out onto the stoep and watched the carriage door open and Governor Whyte step down from the carriage.

The boys shot down the stairs and ran to the carriage.

'You've got some fucking nerve showing your face here.' shouted Jamie.

Whyte looked at Jamie and lowered his eyes in submission as Hugh Armstrong stepped down from the carriage followed by Bradley Fairbrother.

Jamie pulled up short of attacking Whyte and looked at Armstrong.

'Good morning lads, or should I say, gentlemen. May we join you?'

'Christ! When did you get here? And what are you doing with this piece of shite, you obviously know who he really is?' said Iain.

'Yes, Iain. That is why I am here, we need to talk.'

'He can stay out here,' said Iain nodding at Whyte, but Whyte climbed back into the carriage to wait until

Prophets of Death

Armstrong had finished.

They all shook hands and went inside. Mefrou le Roux brought tea.

'I have been in The Cape Colony for quite a while. When your masonic friend arrived at my office in London with your report, he brought with him a Lord of the Admiralty who is a very high degreed English mason.

After reading your report and talking with Rory McGregor and the Lord Admiral, I immediately reported to the Prime Minister. After that I arranged passage to Cape Town and intercepted any and all despatches from the Cape Government sent to Whitehall before I left. I changed the wording in those despatches so the troops that were sent north of Cape Town were brought back in time to capture or kill foreign slavers who had been put ashore at the Eastern Cape Frontier to collect their potential slaves, also to put down the myth that the British army had been defeated by black Russians.

'The Royal Navy fleet never went up the west coast of Africa. They waited for a while north west of the Cape, then sailed back around Cape Town and along the coast towards East London, whereupon they met up with the American slave ships and sent a few to the bottom of the sea. I think there were a couple of ships flying Portuguese ensigns from Mozambique that were sunk as well. The Boers and the Portuguese were buying slaves, the Boers paying with gold from a seam in a mine, which I believe has now petered out, according to my sources. Which makes one think there would be other seams of gold waiting to be discovered.'

Jamie said. 'You will be pleased to know that our Liverpool American, Chester Primeaux is dead in King William's Town.'

'Yes, you have been busy,' said Armstrong.

'We didn't kill him, Storer did,' said Iain. 'Well...

Renton did.'

'What are you talking about… how could Storer kill him?'

Jamie brought Armstrong up to date with the Storer/Renton saga.

'My God, that is an incredible story. Anyway, I will decide who killed him when I make my report. However, in London, before all this, we rounded up at least a dozen of the ELOS's henchmen. Well, when I say rounded up, a couple of them killed themselves and we helped one or two into the next life as well. Earl Harold Greyson and his assistant Edward Harrington were the only two big fish we captured. Anybody with the equivalent rank or above had covered themselves well because we could not get our hands on any others, they are very clever at hiding their true identities. Harrington lost his mind and became a gibbering wreck. Greyson was interrogated but gave us nothing we didn't already know. He was given a choice and committed suicide.'

'At least he had the balls to do that. Is Greyson the one who ordered the execution of our parents'?' asked Jamie.

'We don't think so. We think it's the elder that he was reporting to and we also think that that elder is the link to the real controllers of the ELOS.'

'So he's eluded you once again,' said Jamie with contempt. 'Or is he being protected as well?'

Armstrong looked at Jamie with narrowed eyes and said, 'I will catch the man who ordered the death of your parents; as God is my witness.'

'But hopefully before God dies of old age,' said Iain.

Jamie did not give Armstrong a chance to reply and said, 'But you'll make sure the report will say Earl Greyson died from an unfortunate heart attack and Harrington has, no doubt, conveniently been placed in

Prophets of Death

care at an asylum and will be replaced due to ill health, and the government in Whitehall is saved from any embarrassment.'

'Don't patronise me Jamie,' said Armstrong angrily. 'That's the way it's done. The empire saves face and the so called Governor Whyte will dedicate a good bit of his life to the good folks of the Cape, building hospitals and continuing his eye cataract removal, building schools and colleges. Before he retires he will donate some of his personal treasures to the people of the Cape and then fade into obscurity, unless of course the ELOS execute him first.'

'You have to send help to the Eastern Cape, the people are dying in their thousands,' said Jamie.

'From what we can see it's too late to do anything. What I'm about to tell you is off the record,' said Armstrong.

'Oh, here we go again with what we were just discussing, more treachery and lies,' Iain said getting angry.

'Look, we know about Whyte's involvement with the ELOS and his treachery but know this, I have been given orders for Whyte to carry out. There will be help but it will be slow.'

'So that's it then… just let all the natives die. The government has seized on the chance to rid themselves of the threat of the Xhosa by taking over and finishing the ELOS's accidental disaster. The government could not be seen to be standing idly by as the natives were taken into slavery, I mean it was the British who abolished slavery in the first place. No, they had to stop the Xhosa being sold as slaves otherwise there would be a public outcry but they don't have to justify the Xhosa's self-destruction. They can blame the chiefs for inciting that and bring them to justice for letting their people starve to death and the government doesn't have a problem anymore, am I right?' said Jamie.

'The government cannot afford to and will not look after thousands of ailing people for years to come and yes the chiefs will be sought out and tried for ordering self-inflicted destruction and inciting their people to go to war with the Cape government.'

Jamie was about to protest when Armstrong continued.

'Yes! I know it is probably a pack of lies but it cannot be proved or disproved one way or the other if the chiefs wanted the people to go to war. The chiefs will be imprisoned on Robben Island, thus ridding Whitehall of the Xhosa problem once and for all, freeing up resources and the army to be diverted to the next disaster in India. I know that you didn't want to hear this but there it is.'

'How many are dead?' asked Iain.

'The official count is over sixty thousand Xhosa dead,' said Armstrong.

'Aye, that's the official count… Hugh,' said Jamie. 'Well let me tell you what the unofficial count is, and this is from a man who has known the Xhosa his whole life… it's over a hundred thousand people dead at the hands of the empire and for being faithful to their beliefs.'

'That number will never be proved and it will be denied. There's a government initiative for the survivors to be sent north and east to be given paid work on farms. Thousands will be sent by boat up the west coast to work on the large farms there and settled in townships.'

'So Storer has won and we, Iain and I, we have failed in our mission.'

'No you have not failed in your mission. You stopped the Xhosa people being taken into slavery and stopped the ELOS from benefitting from the enormous wealth the Knights Templar treasure would have given them. I was

Prophets of Death

also told by the Prime Minister that the artefacts and treasure of the Knights Templar are in safe hands and that I should not pursue any further investigation.

'No-one could have foreseen what Storer had planned and what the outcome would have been, it just happened to fall into the lap of the British government the right way. I work for Her Majesty's Government gentlemen and I will do whatever it takes to carry out that work,' said Armstrong leaving his position very clear.

'Christ you are a ruthless old bastard aren't you?' said Jamie.

Armstrong looked surprised at being spoken to like that and said, 'And you have not been?'

'Yes… for the right reasons,' said Iain.

'As have I,' said Armstrong getting up to leave. 'What of the future now that you are respected business men in this fair town?'

Jamie said. 'We're done Hugh. We've done what you've asked of us. We'll build our business and settle down to a normal life.'

'Don't come back for us,' said Iain.

Despite the conversation they shook hands all round.

Fairbrother said. 'Thank you for sending the information that I was being followed, it probably saved my life.'

'I'm glad it got to you on time,' said Jamie.

Armstrong smiled as he boarded the carriage followed by Fairbrother, and went back to Cape Town.

Jamie and Iain sat outside and enjoyed the chill late morning air for a while and Iain said. 'The Dutch, the British, the Xhosa, they have all have been fighting over this land for years and bleddy years, Christ, there's plenty of land for everyone.'

'The problem is, the white men, that would be you and me by the way, the white men keep coming to the

Cape. The government are encouraging immigration and they all want as much land as they can lay their hands on,' said Jamie.

'It will never stop, at least not in our lifetime.'

'I think this is just the start, Iain. The British, in fact most of the European countries will be fighting over Africa for years to come. Let's hope that it's not the ELOS who are in charge of it.'

'Amen to that. But enough of this depressing talk, c'mon, we have two lovely women to see. But first let's go somewhere for a drink,' said Iain standing up.

Jamie stood up and said. 'Aye, that's a good idea.'

Deceit of the Empire: Trilogy
Book Three

WEEP,
THE
RIGHTEOUS WARRIOR

By

KD Neill

Don't miss the thrilling conclusion, coming soon

CPSIA information can be obtained
at www.ICGtesting.com
Printed in the USA
LVHW081558211021
701100LV00010B/755